Books by N.J. Nielsen

The Connelly Chronicles

Family Connections
Beautiful Goodbyes

Wardens of the Guild

The Real You

Beautiful Goodbyes

ISBN # 978-1-78686-084-2

©Copyright N.J. Nielsen 2016

Cover Art by Posh Gosh ©Copyright 2016

Interior text design by Claire Siemaszkiewicz

Pride Publishing

Published in 2016 by Pride Publishing, Newland House, The Point, Weaver Road, Lincoln, LN6 3QN, United Kingdom.

Pride Publishing is a subsidiary of Totally Entwined Group Limited.

The Connelly Chronicles

BEAUTIFUL GOODBYES

N.J. NIELSEN

Dedication

To my family for putting up with me when I get lost in the worlds within my writing. Thank you for making sure I was fed and hydrated. I love you all and thanks for doing such a great job in keeping me grounded when needed… Also, to everyone who has been patiently waiting for book two to be released.

Chapter One

Ray listened to the conversation going on around him. He was excited that everyone was finally pulling together as they should have all along. It still amazed him that it had never once clicked in his mind what their connection was to Antonio and his family. The man was his uncle, and Ray had been oblivious until Grandma's conscience had her admitting the truth. His attention was caught by Tony entering the room, and he wasn't alone. There was an older teenager with him, dressed up in gothic attire and, for some reason, Ray could only stare at him. His eyes were the exact same color as Viv's. Hell, the guy was almost a mirror image of his husband.

"I'm looking for Christopher Vivvens." The young man sounded nervous.

"That's me." Viv placed Layla on the bunny rug and stood.

"Then...I think you're my father," the guy said softly. "My name is Declan—Declan Vivvens."

Christ on a pogo stick.

Ray couldn't believe what was currently happening. He hoped like all get out he had been able to keep a straight face when Declan made his mind-blowing announcement. The uncertainty on the boy's face didn't sit well with Ray. Some part of him wanted to reach out and haul the poor kid into his arms for a hug, and tell him everything was going to be all right. Glancing toward his husband, he caught the look of astonishment on Viv's face. He knew without a doubt this was all news to him.

"Who is your mother?" Viv asked a little warily. Guilt

and something akin to hurt swept over Viv's face.

The boy rifled through the ratty bag he held and pulled out a neatly folded piece of paper and a pendant necklace, and offered them to Viv. "After she died I found these hidden among her belongings. My mother's name was Susan Whitely." He swallowed loudly. "My name is Declan, Declan Vivvens. My mother told me I'm named after my grandfather." Sighing heavily, he went on, "Never mind, you seem to be way too young to be my father. I guess my parentage was just something else Mum lied about."

The defeat in the boy's voice clutched at Ray's heart. Ray got to his feet then ushered Declan from the room before the tears in Declan's eyes could spill over. He could tell Declan didn't appear too comfortable as the center of attention and wanted to give him a little bit of privacy so he could sort through his emotions. By the time they reached the kitchen, the tension seemed to be leaving the young man's body.

"Let me make you something to eat." Ray was pretty sure Declan wasn't eating properly, because in Ray's eyes, he was one skinny-as-hell kid. He didn't look any older than fifteen or so. "If you don't mind me asking, how old are you?"

Declan gazed around the room as he sat on a stool at the kitchen bench. "I'm seventeen."

Doing the math in his head, he realized Viv would have only been sixteen when he'd gotten Susan pregnant. There was no doubt in his mind Viv was indeed his father. Declan was too much like Viv for them not to be closely related. They both had the same slightly curled, glossy black hair, and those beautiful stunningly green eyes. Pain twinged in his heart at Viv having missed so much of his son's life, and for Declan missing out on his father.

"How long ago did Susan pass away?" Both Ray and Declan jumped as Viv spoke from the doorway.

"Hi." Ray smiled at his husband. "Come, join us. Make yourself useful and grab some sodas from the fridge."

"Mum died about a year ago. Uncle Ryan came to live in

the house and after a while, he kicked me out."

"Where have you been living since he kicked you out?" Viv demanded a little more brusquely than Ray would have liked.

Ray sighed as Declan shrugged without answering. He knew that sometimes Viv wasn't crash-hot when it came to using his people skills. He didn't want Viv to scare the boy off before Ray had convinced him to stay. "Viv, not now. Let Declan have a chance to eat and unwind before you start grilling him." Turning to Declan, he winked. "Fathers think they have to know everything about their kid's lives. You'll get used to it eventually."

The smile he got in return was reward enough.

"I wasn't trying to be bossy. I just wanted to know where we had to go and pick up his stuff so we could bring him home," Viv explained.

The shock on Declan's face was almost comical. "You want me to live *here* with you?"

"Isn't this why you found me?" Viv asked.

Declan shook his head. "Actually no, though I did want to ask for your help, but not for me. I'm trying to find my friend. He's gone missing, and I can't find him anywhere. Believe me, I've tried. I just couldn't think of what else to do."

"Why come here? Not that we don't want you here. Do you need us to hire a private detective to find your friend?" Ray asked, genuinely curious as to what this was all about.

"I only came here because I think Nathan—Nate—is related to you somehow." Declan sighed. "He once showed me a picture he carries in his wallet of a girl. He told me she was his sister. Well, his half-sister. They have the same father, but different mothers. The girl in the picture was Sara Connelly. Your daughter."

The air rushed out of Ray's body as shock rocketed through him. "What's Nate's last name?"

"Burkhart, his parents are Enid and Larry. From what Nate told me, Larry died when he was a kid. His mother re-married, but Nate never got on with the step-father. He's some kind of religious nut, and he wanted to pray the gay out of Nate. His mother didn't try to stop the man, so Nate took off. He hasn't seen either of them since."

"Are you gay? Were you involved with this Nate? How old is he?" Viv demanded.

"Viv!" Ray snapped in exasperation as he set the plate of sandwiches in front of Declan. "Nate is the same age as Girly. Enid was pregnant at the same time as Izzy. In the end, Larry chose Izzy." Taking a gulp of his Coke Zero and wishing like hell it was something stronger, he added, "If this is Girly's brother, we have to find him—he's family."

They ate in silence, more so Declan could eat his fill.

"I think you need to tell us everything if we're going to help. We need to know where you've been living. When was the last time you saw Nate? It will give us a starting place at least." Ray also noticed Viv never once denied Declan was his son, which was a very good thing. He hoped Viv relaxed around the boy, or it was going to make for some pretty strained times ahead.

After he'd swallowed what was in his mouth, Declan spoke. "When Uncle Ryan kicked me out, I didn't have anywhere else to go. I was on the street for a couple of weeks when I met this guy. His name was Beau. Never did find out his last name. He took me back to where he was staying, and I met Nate. I think he was kind of like Beau's part-time boyfriend or something. Mind you, to me, Beau seemed to have a lot of boyfriends at the house we were staying at."

Ray sensed Declan wasn't exactly telling the truth, but he could get to that later. Maybe the boy would open up if his father wasn't sitting there listening.

"Why didn't you come to me as soon as your mother died?" Viv seemed perplexed. "We would have gladly taken you in."

Again Declan shrugged. "Uncle Ryan told me the reason you weren't in my life was because you didn't want to have anything to do with me. I believed him. Nate tried to convince me otherwise, but I wasn't ready to listen. Now I'm here begging for help because I'm desperate to find Nate."

Ray reached across and patted Declan's hand. "I'm positive if Viv had known about you, he would have been in your life."

"Of course I would have. I just didn't know." Viv sighed. "Please, go on with your story so we can figure out what we need to do first."

Declan took a deep breath before he said, "Just so you know. I'm not Nate's boyfriend. We formed a very close bond, but there has never been anything sexual or romantic between us. We lived in the same house and as the months passed, we became as close as two people can get. Almost like brothers. I'll admit at one time I wanted more, but Nate only ever saw me as a younger brother. Beau hated how close Nate and I were. One day he sent me on some stupid errand to buy him something, and when I came home, Nate was gone. All his belongings were gone as well. That first night I went to bed, and one of the other guys came in and gave me a message from Nate. He said I needed to come and find you, and that he would come for me."

"How long ago was that?" Ray asked.

"Two weeks ago. I've been trying to find him on my own, but I've run out of places to look. Has he shown up here at all? I was kind of hoping he made it here before me." Sadness settled in Declan's eyes as he spoke.

"No, I'm afraid not."

"When I questioned Beau as to what happened to Nate, he refused to talk to me. All he did was backhand me and tell me Nate had broken the rules. The more I kept pushing, the more he ended up talking to me with his fists. So, in the end, I stopped talking about it and have been searching for Nate."

"Are you hurt?" Ray asked worriedly. "Do you need to see a doctor? I can grab my keys and drive you to a hospital if needed."

"I have some bruises on my chest and back. Beau never hit us where the marks would show." Declan stood and carefully took his jacket off. "He didn't want anybody asking questions. He probably didn't want anyone going to the police about the abuse he was dishing out."

He lifted up his shirt and turned full circle, showing the dark smudges littering his body. Fury filled Ray at the sadistic thrashing Declan must have taken, and by the varying degrees in color, Ray surmised he'd endured more than one beating.

"Where do I find this Beau?" Viv demanded icily.

"Why do you need to find Beau?" Declan sounded scared.

To Ray, the stone-cold, burning anger in Viv's eyes was understandable.

"So I can go and teach him an object lesson about laying his hands on *my* son," Viv snarled.

"Wait here. I'll just go and let everyone know we have to go out for a moment." Ray didn't wait for them to answer as he hurried back to where the rest of the family waited.

Their questions started flying before he could get a word out.

Ray held up a hand. "I'll fill you all in when I get back. Viv and I need to sort something out first."

"Where are you going?" Girly demanded. "I know your angry face when I see it, and you're wearing it right now."

She *would* be the one to see and know exactly how he was feeling. Girly understood him just as well as he did himself. He knew he wouldn't get out of there without telling her something. Ever since she was little, he had sworn to always tell her the truth. "I'm going with Viv to knock some sense into the guy who beat up Declan for asking questions about his friend's disappearance."

"Someone beat him up?" GG asked. She seemed almost as pissed off as he was.

Girly watched him shrewdly. "Tell me the rest."

"Declan's friend is a guy called Nathan Burkhart," Ray

stated.

"Hey, that's Larry's last name," Girly blurted. She never had been one to call Larry Dad. That honor had only ever been for Ray.

Ray went on to say, "If what Declan told us is true, then Nate is your half-brother."

"I have a brother?" Girly's eyes widened in shock. "He's missing?" She jumped to her feet. "I'm coming with you. I want to talk to this douchebag you're going to see. If he knows where my brother is, I want to know what he does, before I kick his ass."

Ray's father, Liam, said, "Go. We'll take care of the kids until you get back. I'll call Byron and fill him in on what's going on."

"I'll make up a room for the boy. By his appearance, I'm assuming he really is Viv's son, and he'll be staying," Antonio said.

God, Ray loved that his family jumped in to help without him even having to ask, though he wished Girly would stay home. He knew he wasn't going to talk her out of it. And if she came, so would Daniel. He wasn't surprised when the man in question stood and followed.

By the time they made it back to the kitchen, Ray could see Viv was ready to go. Since becoming a father, Viv had become an overprotective person to all of their kids. "Looks like we'll have company," Ray said. He grabbed a set of keys from the pegboard and walked out the kitchen door.

If the situation wasn't so serious, Ray would have chuckled at how Declan kept sneaking peeks at Girly. He seemed to be in awe of her. Maybe Nate and Girly resembled each other a lot. Viv drove through the streets, following Declan's instructions, until they pulled up in front of a rundown house in one of the worst areas of town. *Fuck!* Ray was thankful that they were bringing Declan home with them and taking him away from this horrid place. There was old furniture and debris littering the front yard. The grass itself obviously hadn't been mowed in years. There were broken windows. Ray knew whoever lived there must be squatting. A real-estate owner wouldn't put up with this sort of mess for long. Then again, he'd watched some of those shows where people were addicted to rubbish and hoarded whatever they could get their hands on.

Getting his mind back in the here and now, Ray followed the others as they stormed up to the front door. If door was what it could even be called—one good gust of wind and it would fall right off of its hinges. While they moved through the house, young men of varying ages came to meet them.

"Where's Beau?" Viv demanded gruffly.

Ray winced.

More than a few of those present took a step back, worry filling their eyes.

"It's rent day. He's on his way. He won't be happy if he finds you here. Dec, what were you thinking in bringing strangers here? You'll cop it from Beau for sure now."

Rent day?

Ray was becoming more confused and a little suspicious as time passed. They didn't have long to wait until a well-dressed man in his mid-fifties walked in demanding to know who the hell was parked in his spot.

Ray saw red the very second everything clicked into place inside his head. This man was taking the kids off the street and using them for his own perverse pleasure. By the ring clearly seen on his left hand, the scumbag didn't even try to hide the fact he was a married man.

"Who the hell are you?" he shouted when he finally saw them standing there. He looked from Declan to Viv and back. Seeing the resemblance, he paled. "I never touched the kid."

"Liar," Viv said coldly. "I've seen the bruises. Tell me again that you never hit my son."

Beau paled further, if that were possible. "I meant that I haven't fucked him."

The coarse language turned Ray's stomach. He wondered how many of the others Beau had demanded that they pay for their rent through intercourse. Judging by how many of them had bruises of their own, he could tell they'd been abused in other ways as well. The men—boys, really—in question, all seemed to shrink away from Beau.

"What exactly is rent day?" Ray asked. When Beau remained silent, Ray turned and asked the same question of the young men gathered.

Finally, it was Declan who answered. "Rent day is when Beau comes around to choose who he fucks for us living here. He can choose one or more. I was never chosen, but Nate was one of his favorites. Beau likes rough sex, so usually those chosen are hurt in some way."

Before Beau could make his denial, Ray cocked his arm back and let it fly. The punch landed in the center of Beau's face. The crunch of bone was a telling sign the asshole's nose was broken. And Ray couldn't have been happier.

"You fucking broke my nose. I'm going to sue the hell out of you." Beau spat a mouthful of blood on the floor.

Ray shrugged. "Go ahead. I'd like to see how you talk your way out of the prostitution suit I'll bring against you. I may not be able to help everyone you've fucked up over the years, but I can damn well help these guys right here. I'll make you pay for the way you treated them if it's the last thing I do. I wonder what your wife has to say about your extra-marital activities. Maybe when I find out who she is, I'll give her a call and tell her what a charmer she has for a husband."

Anger flooded him as he turned to Daniel. "Call for some maxi taxis or hire a bus and get these guys some medical attention. I'll organize someplace for them to stay as this cesspit is disgusting." Turning back to Beau, he added, "If this really is your place, I'll also be suing you for negligence and bodily harm of this group of young men. As a landlord, it was your duty to keep the place habitable and not let the building fall down around their ears. What the hell is wrong with you?"

Viv piped up. "I called B and Jas. Their place is still

vacant. They said we can take the boys there. B's going to ring GG and organize more bedding and for a ton of food to be brought in."

"And I've called the police," Girly snarled viciously, "because I want to find out from this fuckwit where the hell my brother is. If you've hurt him in any way, you're going to be sorry."

"What brother?" Beau snapped right back.

Declan spoke up. "She means Nate. You wouldn't tell me what you did with him, but maybe you'll talk to her and the police when they get here."

When Beau tried to make a run for the front door, the seven boys Ray had counted earlier lunged and brought Beau to the ground. With the option of getting away from Beau once and for all on the horizon, they seemed to ignite with a spark of hope. Somewhere inside Ray's brain the notion of setting up a home for men in trouble like these guys took root, but the idea would have to bear some more thinking for later.

"You aren't going anywhere until we find out where the hell Nate is. Then, after you've told us what you know, the cops can take you away," Ray snarled. "Now where is he?"

One of the other young men in the room said softly, "Beau beat Nathan up, then he dumped Nathan down by the river walk. He wanted it to look like he'd been mugged. John and I went back after Beau had gone. We called an ambulance and it took Nathan to the hospital."

"Which hospital?" Girly asked.

"The Wesley. By the time the ambos got there, Nathan was unconscious. They were trying to bring him around as they put him in the back of the truck. I don't know what happened to him after that, as we were too scared to go and see in case Beau found out about what we'd done. We knew Beau would do the same to us — or worse."

Beau struggled as he shouted, "Shut the fuck up before I make you shut up for good, you ungrateful little fucker."

Before the police arrived, Josh got there with Ray's van.

There was more than enough room to carry all of the young men away. "Your dad called Byron and he'll meet me at B's place. They're also bringing a doctor in to check everyone over. We're going to try to keep this out of the press as much as possible. Not for that asshole's sake, but your dad said these kids don't need reporters shoving cameras in their faces."

The men looked scared as Ray tried to reassure them all that it was okay to go with Josh. He also had to promise, once the doctor checked them out, that they could leave if they truly wanted to. He hoped they'd at least stay long enough to get cleaned up and have a decent feed or two. They all looked on the thin side, and Ray hated seeing the malnourishment in their faces. No sooner had Josh driven away from the house than the police arrived.

The best part of the whole tragedy was seeing how Beau reacted when the police called Ray by his name. Ray smiled when Brendan Callahan walk through the front door. Only then did Ray realize Brendan was actually now the chief of police and, at the same time, Beau was about to find out exactly who Ray was, or more so, who he was related to. If the guy wanted to fight it out in court, he was going to have a battle on his hands. Ray wasn't afraid to take this all the way to the end where he got the result he wanted. Beau would pay for what he'd put these boys through, and pay dearly.

The police left people behind to document everything, and Ray was assured this would be looked into thoroughly to see what else could be done, and who else had been affected by Beau's touch. Ray explained he'd moved the boys to another residence for the time being, and they would be welcome to come and interview the boys if necessary. Jokingly, one officer asked if Ray was starting a home for young men in trouble. Ray just smiled, not wanting to confirm one way or the other before he'd had enough time to sit and talk to his family about the whole idea of setting up some kind of a refuge.

Right now, he could sense Girly's desire to get to the Wesley Hospital and find Nate, a feeling he was all too familiar with. It had been this way when they'd gone in search of Viv's mother and had been surprised with a child, Ben. Ray wanted to go and find out what he could do to help with the situation. He pocketed the card he'd gotten from the police officer in charge, and promised he'd be available later if they needed any more information from him. He smiled as they also walked Beau from the room. The man protested his innocence the whole way while demanding Ray be charged with assault.

On the way to the hospital, Ray called Josh. "Hey, when the doctor checks everyone over, make sure he documents any and all signs of abuse. The police will want both a written report and any photographic evidence gathered for when they finally prosecute Beau. We're on our way to the Wesley Hospital right now. We're going to find out what's happening with Nate and when he can come home."

"Okay, keep us informed. I'll meet you at home if you don't come here," Josh said.

"How is everyone?" Ray asked, wanting to find out how the guys were handling the changes in their lives. He didn't want them to freak out and worry that Ray would want to make the same arrangement for sex as Beau had. The mere thought made Ray sick to his stomach.

"They're fine, Ray. They've settled down some. They're a little confused and skittish, but I've been telling them the house is a safe haven."

"Thanks, Josh."

"Any time, my friend." Josh ended the call.

After parking the car in the hospital car park, the five of them made their way into the hospital and toward the information desk. Ray smiled at the middle-aged woman behind the partition.

"Welcome to the Wesley Hospital. How may I direct you?" she asked.

"Around two weeks ago, an unconscious young man

would have been brought in. He would've been picked up somewhere along the river walk, and he was more than likely beaten up, or so I've been told."

The woman, whose name was Mary Lloyd, going by her nametag, typed away on her computer. "You must mean our John Doe. If you take the elevator over there to the fourth floor and follow corridor B to the end, you'll come to another nurse's station. They'll be able to give you more information."

"Thank you, Mary," Ray said politely before they all rushed to the elevator.

They got out at the fourth floor and followed corridor B to the next station. Once there, Ray started all over again.

Blane Johnson, a male nurse, watched them all warily. "Are you relatives of the young man?"

"He's my half-brother," Girly supplied. "We've only just found out he was here, or I would have been here sooner." She appeared uncertain for a moment. "Though, to be totally honest, this will be my first time meeting him. Same father, different mothers."

Ray smiled. "Sweetheart, you're rambling."

"Oops, sorry."

Declan spoke up. "Nate looks a lot like Sara, they have almost identical facial features."

"Nate, you say. Is that his name? He woke up yesterday, but he can't remember what happened to him. He also can't remember who he is. If you follow me, he's this way in room four-oh-nine."

As they all walked to the door, the nurse put a huge smile on his face. "Hello, handsome. You have some visitors. They even know your name. It's Nate."

Ray's breath caught in his throat at the bruising on Nate's body. Well, the parts they could see of it.

Nate eyed them all with something akin to fear until his gaze met Declan's. "Dec?"

"I'm here, Nate." Declan pushed ahead of them and quickly walked to the edge of the bed. He hesitated before reaching out to hold his friend's hand. "I found Sara and brought her to you. I think they call her Girly. It's a weird name, isn't it? She's going to help you now."

The tears evident in Girly's eyes were mirrored in a few other people's as well.

Nurse Blane tapped Ray on the shoulder. "Do you know any more about him so I can add it to his chart?"

"I can tell you his name is Nathan Alan Burkhart. He's twenty years old. I'm not exactly sure of his date of birth, just that he was born some time in nineteen-ninety-five. His father is Larry Burkhart, who died in two thousand and four. His mother, Enid, remarried, but Nathan has nothing to do with them."

"I need to put an address into his paperwork."

Ray rattled off his own address. "I'll be the one paying his bills as well." It was easier because there was no way he was letting Nate leave. Girly would chuck the mother of all hissy fits if he tried. Ray could see the days ahead becoming one hell of a bumpy-assed ride.

After Blane left them, Ray stepped to one side of the room and watched as both Declan and Girly fussed endlessly over Nate. It wasn't long before Viv joined him.

"How are you holding up, love?" Viv asked as he massaged Ray's shoulders.

Ray shrugged. "Not sure yet. Just thinking we'll now have ten kids. Even if four of them are virtually adults. How are you holding up with the whole 'you just found your son'? I can't believe how much he resembles you."

"Honestly, I'm pissed off and saddened at the same time. It hurts that I never got the chance to see Declan grow up. It's going to be hard getting to know him at this age." He sighed. "There's no denying he's mine. Susan was a summer fling I had with an older woman until my dad found out about it. He ended up firing her. She'd been a singer in the bar when Dad had owned it. He really does look like me, doesn't he?"

"Yep. He's going to be a heartbreaker when he gets a little

older. As for getting to know him, all you have to do is talk to him, and really listen to what he has to say. Other than that, it's basically just love the hell out of him."

Viv kissed him softly on the lips. "You always were the smart one."

"Words like that will get you some loving tonight."

Viv grinned. "Something I'll definitely be happy to go along with."

Ray soaked up the feeling of his husband's arms around him and wondered if their lives would ever be normal. It wasn't so long ago that he'd been single with an adopted, fully grown daughter. Just a little over a year later, his family had swelled to the point of exploding. And it wasn't just his part of the family. GG spilling the beans and letting everyone know Antonio was actually another member of their family had blown his mind completely. No wonder the man was always so understanding when it came to his fuck-ups.

So much had happened to them all in such a short period of time, and strangely, Ray wouldn't change a damn thing. Not even the part involving Grace, because as crazy and as spiteful as she was, they'd ended up with a beautiful son out of the encounter. And Jeb was going to grow up one very loved little boy. It didn't matter to Ray where any of their children had originated. In his heart of hearts, they were all his and he loved them equally. Okay, he spoiled them equally. Now he had two more sons to add to the mix.

Chapter Two

A week had passed since Declan had walked into their lives, and Viv was still at a loss as to how to communicate with the boy. It wasn't like Declan was one of those asshole kids who rebelled every chance he got, nor was he the most perfect child ever. It was more that he would talk to anyone who wasn't Viv. Viv had started counting how many times Declan got up and walked out of the room whenever he entered. Something needed to be done, but the problem was that he didn't have a clue where to start. Maybe if he could figure out what he'd done wrong, the situation between them would get better.

Ray kept telling him that it was normal teenage behavior. But that didn't make sense, because if it were true, Declan would ignore them all equally and not single Viv out.

Walking into the entertainment room, he found Declan, Jamie and Bear watching a movie. "Hey, guys." He smiled as he sat in one of the recliners. Counting under his breath, he got to six this time before Declan made his excuses and left the room. Viv closed his eyes and exhaled loudly.

"It's not you," Jamie said, interrupting Viv's internal rant.

Looking at Jamie and Bear sitting on the couch holding hands, he asked, "What's not me?"

"Declan. He's not running from you. Well, he is, but not for the reasons you think."

"What are you talking about?"

Jamie rolled his eyes. "He's scared that you'll find out all the things he had to do to survive on the streets. He's even more scared that once you find out, you won't want him anymore. I told him he was bonkers, as you and Pa love all us kids."

"How do you know this?" Viv studied Jamie closely. For a boy who had been labeled mildly retarded, he sure seemed smart. "When did you get so wise?"

"Duh. I'm a good listener. That's what brothers do. We listen to each other. You should just go and talk to him. He likes to go up to the storage space in the roof above the purple room to think. You'll probably find him there."

Again, Viv was amazed at how smart Jamie was. Getting to his feet, he smiled. "Thanks, little man. I might just go and track him down right now."

"You're welcome." Jamie grinned up at him before he left the room.

Viv stopped in at the nursery-playroom and explained to Ray where he was going and what he was about to do. He couldn't help but add just how smart he believed Jamie really was.

"You aren't telling me anything. Little man might take a bit of time to figure it out, but when he does, he's usually spot on. Go. Take Jamie's advice and talk to Declan. Tell him we don't care what he's done in the past. It's over and done with—forgotten, even. Only his future matters now, and here he can be anyone he wants to be."

Viv kissed his husband long and hard before he left the room. He made his way up through the house till he came to the closet at the end of the hall housing the narrow steps leading into the ceiling cavity. The ceiling storage space was large and ran the whole length of the house. GG had once told him each wing had a separate access to their own similar spaces, but the attic space he was looking for was in this wing where the family resided.

He was actually amazed when he saw there was hardly any dust, which told him the staff must clean up here regularly. It didn't take long for Viv to locate Declan sitting curled up in a window seat, staring out into the rain-drenched afternoon.

"Wait, please," he said when Declan made to get up and

leave. "I thought we could talk for a while. Learn about each other. I get the feeling you don't like me very much. I'm completely at a loss, so I'm trying to figure out what I've done."

Declan's eyes widened as he sat back down. "I don't hate you."

"Then why do you always leave the room when I come in? I've been trying to figure it out, but for the life of me, I have no clue why you always run from me."

"I'm sorry." Declan looked defeated.

Viv sat on the other end of the seat and leaned back against the window casing. "Then talk to me. If we don't talk about this problem, things will get all hinky between us, and I'm pretty sure that's something that neither of us wants."

"Who told you I was up here?"

"Jamie. He's pretty smart when he wants to be," Viv answered while he studied his son.

Color flooded Declan's face. "What else did he tell you?"

"He may have said you're afraid I'll find out how you survived on the streets. And you're afraid I won't want you here with me." Viv carded a hand through his hair and cursed when his fingers snagged a curl. "I can tell you right now, there's absolutely nothing you can say me to make me turn away from you. Not when I want so badly to get to know you."

"I was a prostitute. I needed money," Declan blurted out. "I let men fuck me so I could get food for me and the others."

Viv wasn't sure how he was meant to react. He was thinking it must have been something along those lines, and it broke him up inside knowing his son had sold himself to live. But there was no way in hell he was going to make his son feel worse than he already did. Ray would know exactly how to deal with this situation. His husband was always so much better at comforting others than he was.

"Ray gave me some good advice before I came up here. He said to tell you the past is the past. We won't hold anything you've done against you. I also want you to get this through your head—there's no way we'll ever ask you to leave. You're part of our family now. Think of it this way—your next step is the very first one you take to the rest of your life. The future is a place where you can be whatever you want to be. You don't have to decide right now, but I'm afraid you *will* have to go back to school and get your diploma, or even go to TAFE and get your GED. For any kind of future, you're going to need that little piece of paper." Viv swallowed hard, hoping he wasn't coming off too heavy. He was trying to make things better, not worse.

Declan smiled at him. "I won't mind. I loved going to school. If I had been able, I would've kept going. Uncle Ryan made it impossible for me to do anything."

"Good to hear that you are willing to finish your education. We actually have something in common, as I also loved going to school. I even went on to university afterward and studied science and technology," Viv said.

"Can I go to university?"

Viv loved seeing the interest in Declan's eyes. "Didn't I say you can be anything you want to be? You can do anything you want to do. Within reason, that is. I may have to step in as a dad and take charge if you try joining a gang or a cult of some kind."

"I think I'd like to do something in the music industry," Declan confided. "I was pretty good at music while at school."

"Did you know that Ray's in a band? He plays guitar and sings. Actually, he plays the drums as well."

"Yeah, Jamie told me it was called Darkness Crawls and that you met him when his band came to play at your club. When I was little, Mum told me she used to work there when Granddad owned it. Is that true?"

"Yeah, it's where I met her. She was older than me, of course. I was only sixteen at the time. I thought I was all that and a bag of chips because an older woman was interested in me. Turns out my dad didn't quite see it the same way as I did. I can promise you now that I didn't know you even existed, or I would've been in your life in one aspect or another. I would never have turned my back on you."

"Mum wasn't the greatest parent, but I always had food on my plate, clothes on my back, and a roof over my head. She was quirky at times, but I had no doubts she loved me in her own way. Uncle Ryan, on the other hand, was the exact opposite of her, and I hated everything about him."

Viv chuckled. "You and me both. He was a friend of my dad's. He always tried to act like he was my uncle too. I ended up telling him to bugger off and leave me the hell alone. After a while, I dodged him whenever he came around. He gave me the creeps."

"I tried dodging him, but he got a little too hands-on for me."

Viv froze at the words. He wanted to know what had happened, but was too scared in case it opened up a whole new can of worms, then he'd have to hunt Ryan down and beat the ever-loving shit out of the man. Hell, he might have to talk to Ray and get his take on the whole situation. But first, he had to hear it all. "Did Ryan ever…?"

"He tried to, but I kneed him in the nuts and dropped him to the ground. After I refused him, he tried to get me to sleep with all of his friends. That's where I kind of met Beau for the first time. He knew Uncle Ryan. I don't know why he never tried to sleep with me when he took me back to the place where Nate and the others lived, but he did tell me if I didn't do what he wanted, he'd let Uncle Ryan know just where he could find me."

"Find you? I thought you said Ryan kicked you out?" Viv asked. He wasn't liking where this was going at all.

Declan paled. "Yeah, I may have bent the truth a little. It was more like I took off when Uncle Ryan tried turning me into his whore for hire. I figured if people were going to pay to sleep with me, then I should at least get to keep the money."

Fury unlike anything Viv had ever felt before roared through his body and mind. He realized some of his anger was because his son had endured nearly the same thing he had growing up. He fisted his hands with the need to punch something over the fucked-up situation. Maybe crap like this was handed down through the generations to make people think they could use them for their own amusement.

"I know you probably won't believe me, but I went through something similar with my step-father. He didn't try to whore me out to his friends. He wanted me for himself, and when I stood up to him, he dealt with me through his fists. Like you, I ran. I went to stay with my real dad, a man I thought had never wanted me. It turns out that was just something my mother had pushed into my head. My dad actually loved me. He left me the club after he died. My step-dad, however, moved onto my younger brother when I left, and he wasn't able to defend himself. My step-dad's sister ended up dumping Dan on my doorstep when he was only a kid. I raised him with the help of my father. That's how I know I would've been able to care for you. I hate that you had to go through what you did. Maybe your mum thought I had too much on my plate caring for Dan. I guess we'll never know for sure."

"What happened to your mum and step-dad?"

"They died in a car accident. On my mother's deathbed, she gave me another son, my brother, Ben. A couple of days later, the same aunt arrived on our doorstep and gave us my sister, Millie. Not long after, we found out about my brother, Jamie. We already had Girly and Dan. Before we had found out about my siblings, B had agreed to be our surrogate with Izzy and Layla, then along came Jeb. He actually happens to be your half-brother. He has the same colored eyes as all Vivvens men do, and I bet he'll have our curls as well — poor kid." Viv took a moment when he saw the worry in Declan's eyes. "What has you so troubled?"

"You have so many people here already, so how can I fit

in? Is there even any room for me in your life?" His words were spoken such sadness.

Viv did the only thing he could. He reached out and pulled Declan into a hug. "There will always be room for you in my life. I never want you to doubt that I want you here with me. I've missed out on so much of your life, and I never want to miss another thing." He released Declan. "Besides, have you seen how big this house is? There'll always be room for both you and Nate in this family. The question is, will you be able to handle being a part of the crazy bunch who lives here?"

Declan smiled as he settled back onto his side of the window seat. "I can handle it. I like hanging out with Sean, Jamie and Bear. I'm glad Nate is finally getting to know his sister, even if he doesn't really have time for me anymore. I kinda miss our friendship."

"Maybe once you both get used to being here, things will settle down and you'll fall back into the easy bond you both had before."

"I hope so." Declan sighed.

Viv patted Declan on the shoulder. "So, are we all right now? You won't be hiding away and avoiding me from now on?"

"Can I call you Dad?" Declan asked shyly.

A smile graced Viv's lips. "Of course you can. I'd be proud if you'd call me Dad. You'll come to learn I'm Dad in this house and Ray is Pa. He'd love it if you called him Pa as well. Ray has the hugest heart in the world and he's always open to loving more people."

"I saw all the wedding stuff in the paper. I even used to see what bands were playing at your club. I tried to get in once so I could see you, but the bouncer busted me. I was too scared to tell him who I was," Declan said, seeming sheepish. "I'll be able to go inside in another three months when I turn eighteen. I've heard from...people, that it's a pretty cool place to be."

Viv smiled. "I've always thought so. After all, it's where I met Ray for the first time."

"Can I ask how did you know you were gay? How old were you when you realized?"

"Actually, it hasn't been long for me. I never thought I *was* gay until I met Ray. He basically changed my world."

"Really?" Declan looked as if he didn't know whether to believe Viv or not.

"Really. I swear I'm telling the truth. You can ask anyone in the house and they'll tell you the same thing. They'll probably tell you that I pretended to be Ray's boyfriend before I realized I was madly in love with him. Shocked the hell out of me when I did work it all out for myself. But honestly, I wouldn't change a damn thing. Because of Ray, I have this beautiful family you are now a part of."

Declan seemed to mull over what Viv had to say. Viv could almost see the gears turning in his son's head. The truth was, Viv was more than ecstatic Declan was now a part of his life. The boy was stunning, not that Viv was biased in any way. He did realize no matter what the circumstances of both his sons' conceptions, he made beautiful children and he was happy as a pig in mud to have them both living with him. He knew he'd have to show Declan he was wanted. Hopefully one day he would finally see that he was treated the same as the other kids in their family, while also showing that he saw Declan as the man he was bound to become. He just hoped Declan believed him.

Again, he thought how Ray was so much better at doing this sort of thing. If Declan still remained elusive in their father-son relationship, he'd have to ask Ray to help out and smooth things over. Ray had a knack of making people love him without even trying. Ray would be the perfect person to show Declan just how much he was wanted.

"Come on, your uncle, aunt and GG will have dinner on the table by now, and they hate it when we're late for a meal." Viv did an impression of GG. "Meal time is family time—no excuses, unless you're working. If you're in the house, then you're at the table."

Declan chuckled, while they made their way back through the storage area and down the steps until they were standing at the top hall of the family wing. Viv wrapped his arms around Declan's shoulders as they descended through the house. Viv noticed it wouldn't be long before Declan would be taller than him.

"We'll wash up in the half-bath downstairs before dinner."

Declan grinned. "I saw GG checking Jamie's and Bear's hands and held out mine before I even realized I didn't have to. I felt like such a dork."

"What did GG say?"

"She chuckled and told me to go back and wash my hands as I had missed a spot. Sean called her eagle eyes as he came with me to wash his hands just to be on the safe side."

Viv listened, all the while trying his hardest not to laugh. "Better to be safe than sorry."

They parted company and made their way to their places at the table. Viv gave Ray a peck on the lips before Declan took a seat between Jamie and Sean.

"How did everything go?" Ray asked quietly.

Viv sighed. "I found out some stuff which makes me want to hunt down Ryan and beat the ever-loving snot out of him. Turns out Beau wasn't the worst thing in Declan's life. He's been through so much. I'm truly amazed he's as normal as he is."

Ray frowned at him. "Tell me more when we're in our room tonight. Little ears have a way of hearing way too much."

"How did GG's doctor appointment go today? I know she hasn't been taking it as easy as the doctor wanted her to."

Ray sighed. "You know GG. She thinks she's a god or something—nothing can touch her. She gets meaner than a king brown when we fuss over her."

"I heard that. You know there isn't anything wrong with my hearing, young man." She gave them a mock glare. "My health is on the mend. Yes, the doctor wants me to take it even easier than I already do. I explained to him that if

I went any slower I'd be going backward. Apparently Dr. Morgan doesn't have a sense of humor," GG said about her new doctor. She'd been seeing him for the last two months, ever since her old doctor had retired. "And I in no way resemble a poisonous snake."

"GG, we only want what's best for you." Girly kissed her great-grandmother on the cheek then sat in the seat next to her.

Looking around the table, Viv saw the family he'd always wanted and had been too afraid to dream of. In his world, dreams had a way of being ripped away from him. The only two present who seemed out of place were Nate and Declan. They were both still trying to get used to the whole family scene. Viv focused on Daniel for a moment and realized Daniel was acting stranger than usual by focusing more intently on his plate than he ever had before. His heart lurched a little in his chest as he watched Daniel's gaze flick over to Nate then back to his plate.

Closing his eyes, Viv silently prayed. *Please, God. Don't let there be any more drama in our lives. Let's see if we can get through the rest of the year out without something else coming along to stuff everything up.*

Was that too much to hope for? When Ray spoke again, he knew it was.

"Byron called today," Ray's voice dropped so low Viv had to lean close to hear. "Grace is dead. Guess she pissed the wrong person off in prison. They contacted us to see what we would like done with her body."

Viv didn't like where this was going. "What? Why would it be up to us to decide?"

"I think we should pay to have her buried. She did give us Jeb, after all. And speaking of, it seemed she had a will left with the prison staff, and she's left all her money to Jeb. I guess she must have had no one else in her life."

"Can we finish talking about this later? Let's just eat, get the kids settled, then we can go and talk about everything."

"Sure, babe. We can do that." Ray squeezed his hand

before they went back to eating and talking.

GG insisted they all tell her what was going on with their lives. Seeing as she wasn't allowed to have any fun anymore—apparently it was Dr. Fussy Pants' orders.

Viv was just happy to have a small amount of time to listen to everyone and not have to think about everything.

* * * *

Later in the night, when their bedroom door was finally closed, Viv leaned against it and sighed, absolutely drained. For a man who was only thirty-three, he felt like he could've added another hundred years to his age.

"Love, are you okay?" Ray asked. He stepped out of the bathroom with nothing but a red towel wrapped around his lean hips. The color looked beautiful against Ray's pale skin. No matter how much time passed, Ray was still the sexiest man Viv had ever seen.

"Yeah, I'm fine. Just a lot running through my head at the moment. For a day off, I feel like I haven't stopped, and I've gotten nothing at all accomplished."

Ray shook his head and pulled his sleep pants out of the drawer. "It would seem you and Declan are on better terms."

"We are. Dec was worrying with all the kids we have that there wasn't room for him in our lives. I told him there'd always be room. I think he loved his mum, but he didn't have the best life growing up, then to end up with Ryan, followed by Beau, he lost all hope of making things better."

"What were you telling me about Ryan earlier?" Ray asked while he got dressed in his pajamas.

Viv tapped his head back against the door and said, "It would seem Dec lied to us a little the day he first arrived. Ryan didn't kick him out. Declan ran when Ryan tried to pimp him out to his friend for money. Apparently, he met Beau through his uncle for the first time. He was a friend of Ryan's. Guys like those two truly make me sick to my stomach."

"You and me both. We can only show Declan and Nate they're in this family for keeps. They both seem to be having problems adjusting. Girly tells me Nate keeps asking when he has to leave. It breaks my heart to hear it."

Viv knew exactly how his husband was feeling. Children should be cherished and not have to grow old before their time. "Okay, tell me about Grace. I don't really want to hear it, but I know I have to."

"Like I said, she was apparently killed in a prison brawl. They said it was a fight with another prisoner. Knowing Grace, I believe it. What surprised me was how she left all the money we'd paid her for Jeb to him in her will. It makes me sad knowing that in the end she had no one."

The sadness around Ray was real, and deep down Viv knew his husband mourned the woman who had caused them nothing but pain. He was also right that without Grace they wouldn't have Jeb. He held out his arms, and Ray walked right into them. Viv hugged him tightly and asked, "So, what do you plan to do about her body? I know you want us to pay for her burial. All I want to know is why? Explain it to me so I understand."

"I do. I want Jeb to have a place to actually go to when he asks about his mother. I don't want to have to take our son to the prison graveyard. She may have wreaked havoc while she lived, but in death, we should at least have forgiveness in our hearts for our son's mother."

Viv wondered if it was okay for him to just be glad the bitch would never be able to make another traumatic appearance to cause trouble. He could forgive her for what she had put him though, because he was the idiot who had invited her into their lives. He couldn't, or rather wouldn't, forgive her for the way she'd hurt Ray and Daniel. "I think you're asking the impossible of me. She almost destroyed everything we were building together. I'm not saying you shouldn't pay to have her buried, but I am saying it's still too soon for me to think about forgiving her. Dead or not,

I'm just glad I…we…never have to deal with her again."

Yeah, he knew he was probably coming off as an ass, but he couldn't help the way he felt. Maybe as the years rolled on and he saw how Jeb had grown up to be a well-adjusted young man without a hint of his mother's craziness, then he would think about forgiving her. Right now all she was doing was giving him a bloody vicious migraine.

Viv relaxed back into his husband's touch while Ray gently massaged his scalp. His husband's fingers felt wonderful caressing his skull. The touch was even better when Ray drifted his kneading fingertips down his neck to his shoulders, and he suddenly found himself with Ray flush up to his back. The other notable thing was Ray's erection rubbing along his spine.

"Fuck! Ray… Mmm," Viv hummed in pleasure as his lover slipped his hands around Viv's front and slowly began undoing the buttons on his shirt. The heat of sexual anticipation danced across Viv's skin as a living, breathing fire. Viv wanted Ray to hurry the hell up, yet didn't say anything because he was so caught up in relishing the loving tenderness his husband was administering to him.

"Love you so much," Ray moaned and humped against Viv's back.

Frustration overcame Viv's senses. He moved away from Ray and yanked his clothes off, not caring one iota where they landed in the room. He could deal with cleaning up the mess later. His gaze never left Ray, who was suddenly out of his pajamas again and lying on his back in the middle of the bed stroking his own cock.

The sight was beautiful.

Absolutely stunning.

Viv couldn't focus on anything except for the pre-cum beading and pooling on the slit of his lover's cock. Right then, his only intent was tasting it, letting the flavor into his mouth. Ray's gaze filled with what Viv interpreted as a mixture of lust, love and a whole lot of need. His husband threw his head back and moaned in desire when Viv finally sucked him down to the root. The feeling of Ray's cock head pressing into the back of his throat was probably one of the most erotic things Viv had been a party to.

Ray thrust his hips gently, and Viv hummed around the hard cock in his mouth, knowing how quickly the vibration would send his lover over the edge. He winced when the bottle of lube they kept beside the bed hit him on the head. He mustn't be doing the job right if Ray still had brain cells working enough to think. But he did like where Ray was headed with all of this.

Letting his husband's penis slide free of his mouth, he then smiled up at Ray. "I take it you want more than a blow job tonight?"

"I always want more than a blow job. Now suck me back into your mouth and stretch me out, or I'll start to think you don't love me anymore." Ray pouted.

"Well, we wouldn't want that to happen." Viv blew him a kiss and did as asked, loving every second his husband struggled between pushing back onto his fingers and thrusting forward into his mouth.

When he believed Ray was stretched enough, Viv released Ray, ignoring the whiney complaints over the loss of friction. Viv lubed up his cock and didn't even give Ray time to get comfortable before he plunged into his lover with one hard thrust. Only when he was in balls-deep did he take the time to enjoy the way Ray's body squeezed him with the shock of his invasion.

"Yes, just like that," Ray murmured and rocked against Viv. "You always make me feel special. Always make me feel loved."

Pulling partially out of his lover, Viv thrust back in, adding a little twist to his hips so that his cock head grazed Ray's prostate. He loved the way the action always made Ray tremble beneath him, ready to fall apart at any minute. Ray's gaze was locked with his, and for a second, Viv swore he could see all the way into his very soul.

"Love you like this," Ray gasped as Viv ghosted over his

prostate once again.

The best part was Viv never even had to talk. When they made love, Ray's words were enough to send Viv's body into a tailspin he knew he had no recovery from. His balls drew up close to his body when Ray dropped his gaze to where their bodies were joined. Viv caressed his lover's prostate again. "Stroke your cock for me, babe. I want to see you come undone." The sweat glistening on both of their bodies only added to the sensuality of it all.

"Harder, Viv. I'm so fucking close. So, so close."

Viv was always happy to give himself over to Ray's wishes. He loved each and every moan and grunt that fell from Ray's lips. Viv gave it his all and fucked him through the mattress. He knew the moment Ray came, because Viv suddenly found himself in a vice grip. Ray wrapped both his arms and legs around Viv like a four-legged octopus. The tell-tale heat flowing between them sent shivers racing up and down Viv's spine. Lust ping-ponged through his body, and his balls tightened further. Viv pressed his face into Ray's shoulder and cried out his husband's name. His orgasm ripped free from him and he filled Ray's ass. God bless the day they'd gone through the testing to be able to go condom free. Nothing was better than skin on skin.

Viv lay trembling on top of Ray, their bodies slick together while he fought to get his breathing under control. Beside his ear, Ray hummed softly to whatever song was playing in his head as he trailed his fingers lazily up and down the length of Viv's spine.

"Have I ever told you how much I love the way you make my body sing?" Ray whispered then placed a kiss against Viv's ear. "You will always be my everything, Viv. Without you in my life, I am nothing."

Viv's eyes misted with tears, then he raised his head enough to gaze into his husband's eyes. "I think you have that the other way around. You, Raymond Connelly, are the very thing which makes my world turn. The family we have is because your huge heart is willing to bring us all into your fold. I've loved you from the very first moment I saw you, and I was too stupid to realize what I had until I nearly lost it all."

"Don't think like that. You're just as important to me. Here we lie sounding all sappy, trying to decide who is more important, yet the truth is, my cum is going to stick us together if we stay this way much longer. Yours is starting to dribble free—*so* not a nice feeling. I think we should shelve all the sappiness and have a shower before we change the sheets and come back to bed."

"What! You don't love my spunk trickling out of your ass?" Viv gave a mock growl before he pulled back a fraction then thrust back in. He shuddered, feeling exactly what Ray meant. "You're right. We need to shower."

They both moaned when Viv pulled free.

Yeah, a shower was definitely called for.

Chapter Three

By the time Grace's body had been released to them, Ray had already organized the quiet funeral they were going to have for her. He wanted the day to be nice, even if he and Viv were going to be the only people in attendance. No one else could quite figure out why Ray felt he needed to do this. A part of Ray agreed with them, but deep down, he knew he was doing the right thing. One day Jeb was going to ask questions about who his mother was, and Ray wanted to have the answers his son needed. At least they would be able to bring Jeb to the cemetery and show him the place where his mother was resting. He didn't need to know the nasty side of who his mother had been. When he was older, he might want to look deeper into the way things were, but for right now, this was enough.

"I'm glad we did this," Viv told him as they drove home. "I may not have understood your reasoning before. I'm just happy we've finally gotten closure where Grace is concerned. At least we'll have a beautiful headstone so one day Jeb can say goodbye to his mother."

"I know." Ray smiled over at his husband. "This just felt like the right thing to do. No matter what she did in life, in death I hope she finally found some peace."

"Ray, can I ask you something?" Viv pulled away from the red light they'd been stopped at.

"Sure, what's on your mind?" Ray asked. The tension running over the man was palpable. "Viv, talk to me." He was having those same weird vibes he'd gotten when Shane had been hitting on Viv at the beginning of their relationship. "I can't put my finger on it, but I think there's something going on with Daniel. He's acting…" Viv exhaled loudly. "I don't know, it's kind of like he's struggling with something and I don't have a clue what to do to help him."

Ray relaxed slightly. He'd been getting the same vibe, but he was hesitant in saying the reason he and Girly were beginning to suspect. 'No secrets' was the promise he and Viv had made long ago, so Ray decided to be truthful. "Honestly, I think Daniel may have a little bit of a crush on Nate."

"What?" Viv pulled the vehicle into the car park of the mall they were passing and stopped. Viv turned off the engine and stared at Ray.

"Before you get all worked up and turn into Mr. Cranky Pants, I don't think it's gone beyond him finding Nate attractive. Girly kind of thinks it's funny. I can't see Nate actually doing anything about it, but the attraction is there."

Viv's eyes widened. "Girly knows about this?" He shook his head. "What the hell's my brother thinking? And why isn't Girly telling him to snap out of it?"

"He's probably thinking Nate's a good-looking young man. Viv, I don't think we need to get involved. So far, Nate hasn't even realized what is happening. Girly tells me she and Daniel have talked about it. It's not like he's leaving Girly to be with Nate. He loves her way too much to toss aside everything they have together."

"Can you imagine the drama if he did? Sometimes I wish I could just shake some damn sense into him." Viv cursed. "Daniel just doesn't think sometimes."

Ray sighed. He truly understood Viv's frustration. "Well, at least he told Girly. I think he's trying to be sensible about it. We have to remember he's still young. You can't help who you're attracted to."

"He's not that much younger than us, love. I swear we were never this stupid."

Ray bit his lip to keep from laughing. "We were way worse, and we were older. This is something he needs to figure out for himself. I believe Daniel is smart enough to do so without it turning into a total cluster-fuck." He placed his hand on Viv's arm. "Come on, Viv. Start the car. We have a bunch of kids at home who are waiting to be showered with love. I need some time hugging them."

Viv couldn't agree more. He faced front again and started the car. They drove in silence for a while before Viv spoke again. "You keep me grounded, do you know that?"

What Viv had just said was probably the nicest thing someone had ever said to Ray. "I love you too," he answered. Deep down, he knew that was what Viv was really trying to say.

The house seemed extra quiet once they got home and Ray had to wonder where everyone was. Usually there were one or two people wandering around, but today there were none. Walking up to their room, Ray began to worry something else had happened. Then he saw the note sitting on the center of the bed.

We're in the pool. Come join us.

Feeling much better, Ray quickly changed, knowing Viv wouldn't be far behind him. He had a couple of phone calls he needed to make for work. "Meet us down there when you're finished," he said as he pecked his husband on the lips.

"I'll join you as soon as I'm done. This shouldn't take long."

Ray hurried back down through the house and headed straight for the indoor pool. Lately, it had become one of the coolest places to hang out, or so Jamie had told him. Apparently it ranked right up there with the play room. He could hear the squeals of delight before he even opened the door. The pool itself was a sea of floaty chairs with all the babies securely in place. Every child had an adult with them. Again, this was just another way his family blew his mind. He waved as "Pa" was called out by more than one of the little tykes.

Seeing GG sitting on a lounger on the other side of the pool deck, Ray changed his direction then sat on the seat near her.

"How was it?" was the first thing out of GG's mouth, followed closely by, "Are you and Viv okay?"

"We're fine, Grandma. Viv has a couple of calls to make, but he'll be down soon. The funeral was quiet. There were only the two of us in attendance."

"You should have done something nice afterward. Maybe gone out for lunch, instead of racing back to this mob." GG chuckled.

Ray graced her with a smile. "But, Grandma, it's here where my heart is happiest. Surrounded by family. The people who care more about me than the rest of the world. Honestly, if we went out the paparazzi would just want photos for tomorrow's edition of a front page. I hate putting Viv in the spotlight when it still makes him uncomfortable."

"Even after all this time?"

"Yeah, he'd rather our private lives stay private. I can't say I disagree with him. I also understand that with our name sometimes it's unavoidable." So many times he'd felt Viv cringe beside him when some reporter or other jumped in front of them with a camera looking for a money shot. Ray tried to ignore them as best he could. It was even worse when they were on an outing with the kids and their faces ended up spread across the gossip pages.

"Smart man." GG smiled.

Ray chuckled softly. "I've always thought so."

"Did you ever think your life would be quite this full?"

Ray threw his head back and laughed. "I remember a time when I just wanted a boyfriend, and maybe one more baby. Life has a way of never turning out quite the way we expect it to."

"I can't believe you ended up with as large of a family as you have. All I know for sure is that we wouldn't trade them for the world."

"No, we wouldn't. Mind you, I was more shocked to find

out Antonio was actually my uncle. I'm afraid to say it was a secret you should never have kept."

GG sighed. "I never wanted to, but I promised your grandfather."

"Granddad was an ass," Ray grumbled.

"I know." GG huffed. "I also had to abide by Antonio's wishes. I was in a catch twenty-two situation. Nearly dying gave me the loophole I needed to set the story right."

Ray frowned at his grandma. "Is that really why you told us?"

"I told you because it was time. The truth should have been told from the very beginning. Instead, I let things slide under the rug. Not one of my finest moments in life, I can assure you."

"Everything worked out for the best in the end." Ray comforted her with a pat to her arm.

Again GG huffed. "Except your father is angry with me for denying him his brother for all this time. He wants Magen and Ant to go and live with them, but Ant won't leave. Is it my fault he likes it here?"

Truthfully, Ray could understand his father's resentment at being denied his family. The strange thing was his father had done the same thing to Ray. "I think Dad forgets he stopped me from seeing Izzy when he banned her from our lives."

"I may have pointed out the very same thing, and let's just say it didn't go over too well." GG sighed. "Seriously, I'm just tired of all the bullshit."

"Grandma!" Ray gasped. It wasn't often that he heard a swear word pass her lips, and when it did, for some reason, it just didn't sound right.

"What?" GG stared at him innocently. "At some point in our lives, everyone swears, Raymond."

"That may be true, but little ears might be listening."

GG rolled her eyes at him and snorted. "They've probably already heard worse."

They sat there watching the others for a moment when GG

spoke again. "Did you know Daniel is attracted to Nate?"

His grandma knowing didn't surprise Ray one bit. She had the eyes of a hawk. "Yeah. He told Girly and she told me. How did you find out?"

"Girly." GG focused on Ray. "Why isn't she upset about it?"

"To be honest I don't know." It was only talking about it now with his grandmother that he realized Girly almost seemed happy about the prospect. "Do you think something is up with her?"

"I asked her straight out what was going on, but she just smiled and brushed the question off."

Ray frowned as he turned toward the pool and looked for his daughter. For some reason, she didn't seem to be her bubbly self. This was just another one of those family dramas he was going to have to sift through to find the truth. Most days, he wished the whole family had a no-secrets contract. It would make parenting so much frickin' easier. The only one who was ever one hundred percent totally honest was Jamie. Simply, the boy didn't know how to lie. The younger children didn't count as they'd yet to figure out what lying meant.

"So what other gossip in the family can you fill me in on?" Ray grinned at GG. "It seems like I'm missing a lot lately."

"Well, Declan's finally starting to believe he has a place with us. Nate's still a little wary, though he does love spending time with Girly. I think that boy is oblivious to Daniel at the moment, no matter how many hints Girly keeps dropping. Jamie and Bear are still madly in love and planning their wedding for when they get older. Sean appears to be infatuated by Declan. They hang out together a lot. The club is going well now since Daniel and Girly have taken over the management. Viv is excelling at both work and the uni courses he still needs to complete. I don't think your husband will ever stop wanting to learn. Your father and Ant are now inseparable whenever they both have time off. Your father wants to teach him the art of golf, and Ant doesn't have the heart to tell Liam that he finds the game boring. B and Jas say the young men you rescued are finally starting to settle into their new home and have begun doing chores around the house. B told them they didn't need to, but I ended up telling B and Jas to let them be. After what they've been through, they just need to feel like they belong somewhere. And lastly, Josh tells me there have been some requests for the band to go and play again, but you keep telling him no. I'm wondering why."

GG was a fount of information. Some of the stuff she'd told him, he hadn't even known about. "With everything going on at home, I haven't even had time to scratch myself, let alone think about playing music and singing again."

"Did you know Declan is musically inclined? Jamie says he has a nice voice and he can kind of play the guitar."

"Viv told me Dec would like to go to uni to study music. I think he's decided to go to TAFE to get his year-twelve equivalency. I've actually looked into it. I haven't told Declan yet, but as soon as he does TAFE he can enroll in a Tertiary Preparation Program at uni to bring him up to scratch on everything then apply for a Bachelor of Music."

"When are you planning on telling him?" GG demanded. "I think the sooner he catches up on his schooling, the better. A mind is a terrible thing to waste."

Laughter had Ray turning toward the sound. Declan and Sean were dunking Nate under the water as they all wrestled. How Ray wished he could turn back the clock to when everything seemed so carefree. Would he change anything in his life if he knew what it would become?

No, not a damn thing.

"I'll be back in a second. Jeb is fussing." Ray stood and moved to the edge of the pool. He crouched and took Jeb from Josh before walking back to the chair he'd been sitting on. He grabbed the lap rug from the side table and wrapped his son up. For some reason, as soon as the boy's eyes locked onto Ray, he settled. "Who's a good boy?" Ray tickled the blanket covering Jeb's tummy and loved the way the little boy's face lit up.

"You're a good father, Ray," GG said. "I'm not sure I would have had the strength to take on so many at once. I'm very proud of you and your capacity to love them all equally and unbiased."

"All it takes is love, Grandma," Ray answered honestly. "You more than anyone showed me the way."

Ray had never denied who his parents were, but there were times in life when they couldn't play happy families for one reason or another. Especially with his father when Ray was younger. Ray still loved his dad, but some days the man could be just—draining. Other days he was the most awesome dad in the world. Those were the times he loved the best. His mother and GG had always been the buffers between the two of them. Mostly they clashed over the way the man had treated Izzy, and how, in the beginning, he hadn't wanted anything to do with Girly, all because of who her mother was. In the end, his daughter had wrapped her grandfather around her little finger. They seemed to have a better relationship than he and Ray ever had.

The door between the house and the pool area opened and Ray's breath hitched as his husband walked in wearing nothing but a pair of boardies. If he wasn't mistaken, they were the same pair he'd worn to meet Ray's family for the very first time. Viv sat on the edge of the pool before slipping into the water. He may have made his way over to Ben and Millie, who were playing in the swim seats, but his gaze didn't rest until it landed on Ray. And didn't Ray's heart just start fluttering out of control?

"You found a good one there," GG stated.

"He owns my heart. Some days I still can't believe he's mine," Ray stated.

GG giggled. "With everything you two went through, we're all amazed you're both together. I honestly still don't get why you did what you did today. That woman caused you both nothing but pain."

"Because it was the right thing to do. I wanted this little

43

tyke here to have somewhere he can go and visit his mother if he so chooses. He may never want to, but on the off chance that he does, I wanted her to be somewhere nice. He's going to hear a lot of bad stuff about her if he does look into her life, but in the end, she's still his mother, and if nothing else, she gave us the greatest part of herself."

"When you put it like that, I can see your point. I just don't think I could be so generous," GG said.

Ray understood her reasoning. Actually, he could see everyone's point of view, but in the end, the decision was his and Viv's alone, and in his heart, he knew he'd done the right thing.

Sitting there with his grandma, Ray knew their world still had so much more changing to do. People would come into and leave their lives as the children grew. Family would become closer and there would be bouts of squabbling—okay, lots of squabbling. With this many children it was unavoidable. Ray wasn't looking forward to the day his little bubble of bliss would be irrevocably popped.

"Did I tell you Shane's been arrested?"

"No. When?" Ray stared at her open-mouthed.

GG grinned, and Ray could tell GG found the gossip juicy as hell. "The idiot hit on the wrong person and wouldn't take no for an answer. Turned out the guy was an undercover cop."

"Ha!" Ray blurted out. "Couldn't have happened to a more deserving person. What do you think will happen to him?"

"More than likely Byron will get him off with nothing more than a slap on the wrist and a promise to behave. Matt told Byron to hold off and let the fool of a boy stew in the lockup for the weekend and hopefully it would knock some sense into him." GG chuckled. "I doubt very much anything would help the boy. He will always think he is God's gift to everyone."

GG was probably right in both respects. Shane would get off lightly and he wouldn't have learned a damn thing in the process. He'd come out on the other end and do the whole thing all over again.

Looking down at the baby in his arms, Ray smiled when he saw Jeb was asleep. The way his little mouth was moving, as if he were drinking from a bottle, looked so damn cute. Ray glanced up at the clock on the wall and knew very soon it would be bottle and nap time for everyone under the age of three. After carefully getting up, he handed Jeb to GG. "Here, you take him, and I'll go and organize their bottles. Hopefully by the time I'm done, the others will be ready to get out."

"If you were smart, you'd just tell them to get out on your way past," GG stated with a straight face.

Feeling a little bratty, Ray poked his tongue out her. "No one likes a smarty pants."

"GG has Smarties in her pants. Why isn't she sharing?" Charlotte asked as she climbed out of the pool and came over to them. "I like Smarties."

"Not Smarties," Bear corrected his sister. "Uncle Ray was just saying GG was being a show off."

"Oh." Disappointment filled her little face. "Then why didn't you say so? Now I want Smarties. Can I have some Smarties?"

Ray chuckled. "Not right now, princess."

Ray bit back the smile when she pouted at him. Being as young as she was, she would forget about them quickly, especially with the family all around and in a festive mood.

"Ray," said Grandma, "you need to start telling us what you have planned for all the young men you rescued. I have no doubt you have a plan, you always do. Once we know what direction you're heading in, we'll all be able to help."

"I know, Grandma. I'm still trying to figure it out. I promise once the kids are in bed for the night, we'll sit and talk. At some stage, I'd like to go over and touch base with them myself. Try and see if I can work out where their heads are." Ray exhaled loudly. "I know what I want to do. I'm just not sure of the logistics."

GG snorted. "We are richer than most people could dream of ever being. My mother once told me that a person only needs so much money to live on, and the rest is for showing off. If that's the case, we show off by helping those less fortunate than ourselves. I'd say those boys qualify as less fortunate, don't you?"

Ray didn't argue. Instead, he said, "Let me just go and make bottles and snacks for this lot and maybe you could come with me to visit them."

"I'd like that, but you'll have to sneak me out without Antonio discovering what we're up to." She snickered.

Ray chuckled as he left the room. Right now he need this mundane task so he could mull over everything swamping his mind. This had been his way of working through stuff ever since he was young. Back then, Grandma had usually given him some undemanding task to complete when he'd had troubles on his mind, but he'd known sooner or later, she'd be sitting down to have a talk with him. She was a big believer that a trouble shared was a trouble halved.

* * * *

It had been a long time since Ray had been to B and Jas' old house. The outside looked exactly the same, but he knew the inside had been renovated. They were supposed to be putting it on the market next month. Ray was thankful that it was still here for his use. If this all panned out like he hoped it would, he would be the one purchasing the property. He just hadn't talked to B and Jas yet.

"Come on, we aren't going to get far sitting in the car," GG said and opened her door. "The boys will start to get nervous if we sit outside for too long."

Ray knew his grandmother was right. She was the one person in his life who could see through all the bullshit to the bones of what was happening. "I'm right behind you, Grandma."

"It sure is quiet in here," GG said. They entered the house

and shut the door behind them. "Where is everybody?"

"I don't know." Ray led the way through the house and found most of the young men sitting in the lounge room. They were either talking quietly or reading. More than one jumped at his and Grandma's approach.

Grandma instantly took control. "Hey now, there's no need to panic. My grandson, Ray, brought me around so I could meet you all." Without asking, she took a seat on the couch near two of the young men. "My name is Catherine Connelly, but most people call me GG. Now why don't you introduce yourselves to me and tell me your ages?"

Ray sat cross-legged on the floor and listened to the young man closet to GG who said, "My name is Stevie Dean. I'm twenty."

Ray paid attention while each introduced themselves. The other four in the room were Tyler Reed, nineteen, Blaire Walters, eighteen, Norman Lyons was the oldest at twenty-three, and Kyle Allan was the youngest at fifteen. Stevie went upstairs and brought back Mick Branson, twenty-one, and Louis Johnson, seventeen. With each new name and age revealed, Ray could see GG's heart was breaking right alongside his.

Slapping her hand on her leg, GG started speaking. "Okay, now this is what we are going to do. Norman, I'm going to put you in charge of this house for a while. I will eventually bring in people to help you with the everyday running of it. Once the phone has been installed, I'll give you Antonio's number and anything you think is needed will be brought here. This situation will have to do until I can organize an account set up for this refuge."

Right then, Ray knew the decision had been taken out of his hands. GG always got her own way. She didn't even give anyone time to ask questions as she went on.

"One condition of staying here is that you will have to finish your education, no matter how long you have been out of school itself. If needed, I can have tutors brought in to help you all get up to scratch. I expect you to do your best and not piss this opportunity to the wall."

"Why are you helping us?" Norman asked.

Ray wondered if he was doing the talking because GG had placed him as head of the household.

"I can't abide by people being abused," GG said. "I believe you all have a second chance to be the person you were always destined to be. You all just need to think about where your destiny lies. There's no need to rush into any decisions. Just take the time to really figure it out."

"How will this all work? Won't the police or someone have something to say about this?" Stevie asked.

"No. By the time this refuge is set up properly, we'll have everything done in accordance with the government and law, so there will be nothing anyone can do to stop us. I think I will call this place Destiny House." GG smiled brightly. "Besides, the chief of police is a friend of mine. He'll help us smooth things out."

Ray chuckled. "Grandma, have you forgotten this isn't our house?"

"That's where you would be wrong. The day Josh brought these young men here, I set in motion the purchase of this house. I've also purchased the two vacant properties on either side in case we have the need to expand."

"But why?" Norman asked again. "You don't even know us. You definitely don't know what type of people we are."

GG shrugged. "I'm hoping you all have a good set of morals. I don't care whether you are gay or straight. Don't get me wrong, I will have rules set in place that will need to be followed. I'll expect you all to contribute in any way you can in the running of this house. Believe me, nothing comes for free."

"Exactly what does that mean?" Norman asked warily.

Ray jumped in. "GG means help out by doing household chores. No one will expect you to do anything like you did with Beau Raddick. Your body is your own. No one has the right to tell you what to do, or touch you without your permission."

"I can cook," Mick offered. "I did most of the cooking at the other place. Well, that was when we had food to cook with."

"Do you like cooking?" Ray asked.

"Yeah. I wanted to be a chef when I was younger. My mother had different ideas, of course. She was convinced no man had the right to be in a kitchen. Cooking and cleaning were women's work." Mick shrugged. "When she found out I was gay, I was shown the back door and she told all of her friends I was dead to her. After that, things didn't go so well."

God, there are some sad tales within this house.

Hopefully Destiny House would help these young men turn their lives around. Ray wanted them to have an easier time, so he said, "I want you to all make a list of what you think you might need. I'll also organize for some computer equipment to be brought in to make things easier for you all. I think the entertaining room would make the perfect shared office space."

"I can mow," Kyle stated. "But you'll have to buy a lawnmower. For all three yards a ride-on might be best. That's what I used out at Uncle Tommy's farm. When he died, everything was sold to pay his hospital bills. Aunt Suzie took what was left over. She didn't have room for me in her new life. That's how I ended up with Beau in the first place. Aunt Suzie sold me to him for two grand."

Fuck! How can people be so callous?

"No one here is going to sell you. All we want is for you to just be the best person you can. Give yourself time to just grow up. Even you, Norman. You may be the oldest here, but I bet you never grew up. I mean, you had your ass kicked from childhood straight into adulthood."

"At least we're still alive," Norman replied.

"That you are." GG agreed. "You will be in charge here. I will also bring in outside help so that you have a chance to have a life as well. I won't let anyone in who wants to take over. You will be my liaison between the boys and whoever comes on to manage the place. Do you think that would be something you would be interested in?"

When Norman seemed to relax so did Ray. Maybe, just maybe, this was all going to work out. If GG was organizing outside staff, it wouldn't all be left up to Ray, or pulling him away from his very young family. His heart went out to them. At least GG would hire the very best people possible.

Chapter Four

"Please just leave me alone. I've told you I don't want to go out with you anymore."

The scared voice Viv heard coming from the toilet cubicle closest to him caught his attention. After finishing his business and washing his hands, Viv turned at the sound of skin hitting skin and someone cried out in obvious pain. Stepping over, he knocked on the partially opened door. "Is everything okay?"

"Fuck off and mind your own fucking business," someone growled out. There was something oddly familiar about the voice.

At the same time, he heard, "Help me, please."

"Buddy, you should know I'm calling campus security. So if I were you, I'd get out of here while you can." Viv stepped back as the door swung open. Shane King was standing right there with a much smaller man cowering behind him. "Shane? What the hell are you doing, man?"

"I told you that's none of your fuckin' business, Christopher. Now if you don't mind, I'd like to have a moment alone with my boyfriend," Shane snarled.

The man behind Shane looked around him and shook his head, as if begging Viv not to leave.

"I can't do that, Shane. I've already heard the guy you're with say he wasn't your boyfriend anymore. I think you should be the one to leave." As he spoke, Viv slowly slid his satchel off his shoulder and onto the floor under the sink so it would be out of the way. He braced himself for Shane's attack. The alcoholic fumes pouring off the man attested to how drunk Shane truly was.

Shane stepped out swinging, and Viv easily ducked the first punch. "Get out of here," he said to Shane's ex. After the guy had run, Viv shoved Shane away from him. "Knock it off, Shane."

"Fuck you!"

"Not even on a good day." Viv flew back against the side of the toilet stall and winced in pain when Shane got in a lucky punch. Glancing in the mirror, he saw blood trickling from his split lip. *Damn!*

Viv didn't want to get into a brawl, but he knew Shane needed to be stopped. "If you don't stop, I'm going to deck your ass." Viv shoved Shane again. "You need to get sober and fast before you wind up in trouble."

"Shut the fuck up." Shane swung, and Viv couldn't get out of the way in time.

Shane's fist hit Viv's left eye, sending his head slamming back into the wall. Fuck! That was going to leave a shiner. Ray would be pissed when Viv got home. His vision blurred. In the same instance, Shane came at him again. Viv swung and connected with Shane's jaw. The force of the punch knocked Shane down, and by the shot of pain running up his arm, Viv guessed he'd broken his own hand. Before he could get out of the way, the guy was back, followed by campus security. The two officers hauled Shane to his feet. Viv cursed and clutched his hand against his chest.

Viv bent over the sink. He held on with his good hand to keep him upright. Heat lashed at him with an overwhelming need to pass out. Gritting his teeth, Viv fought the pain.

"Are you okay?"

Viv hissed in pain and the guy he'd rescued came to his aid. "I think I need to go to the hospital."

The guy bent and picked up Viv's bag. "Come on, I'll take you. My name's Ethan Stark."

"Nice to meet you. I'm Christopher Connelly, but everyone calls me Viv."

Luckily, the guy wasn't parked far from the building.

"Sorry about the mess. I've been kind of living in my car

since I left Shane," Ethan said.

"The guy is an asshole. Why the hell were you with him?" Viv said, more to take his mind off the pain than to make conversation.

The guy shrugged. "I think at first it was just to shut him up, then I fell in love with him. It was supposed to be forever, but he wasn't faithful to me and it almost killed me. When he was arrested not long ago, I knew it was my one chance to get out before I was shattered beyond all repair. He found me last night saying he wanted me back. Is it bad that I still love him?"

"No, it isn't. I know somewhere you can go where you will be safe. My husband, Ray, and his grandmother, GG, have just opened a refuge. It's called Destiny House. There'll be a room there if you need it."

They drove the rest of the way in silence. Viv, even through his own pain, could sense the anguish in his new friend.

"Thank you. My family wouldn't let me come home. I was actually at the university tonight to drop out of my classes. It's too hard to study when I have no home. I figured I would just get out of town and start over." Ethan was very soft spoken and the tenor of his voice lulled Viv.

Viv grunted. "When we get to the hospital, I'll give you my phone so you can ring my husband and let him know what's happened. Get him to ask Josh and Fred to go and pick up my car."

Not only was Viv's hand swollen, but his forearm was absolutely killing him. His head ached with a probable concussion. He was also sure his eye would be puff up by the time they got to the hospital. Fuck! Could his day get any worse?

"We're here," Ethan said. He pulled the car up in front of the emergency doors. "I'll get you inside, then I'll park the car and come find you."

Before he could say anything, Ethan was out the door and pressing the buzzer for the night guard to let him in. Ethan spoke to the man and gestured toward where he sat in the car. The guy disappeared and was back within minutes, pushing a wheelchair. By that stage, Ethan was at his door and assisting him out of the car.

"Ethan, take my phone. Call Ray for me." Viv grimaced when the hospital attendant helped him into the chair.

"Your friend tells me you were in a fight," the attendant said before he was pushed Viv inside the building and straight into where they had the beds set up. "Now why don't you tell me what happened?"

Viv groaned as he was transferred to a bed. "I tried to stop someone from forcing themselves onto another person. I guess he hit me more than I hit him."

"Where is he now?"

"Last I saw, he was with campus security. I think I only landed one punch on him," Viv admitted while the guy checked him over.

"Okay then, can you tell me your name and date of birth? My name is Dr. Elias Stone. And I'm going to have to send you for X-rays," the doctor said and gently touched his arm.

Viv let out an angry hiss.

"I think you may have broken not only your hand," the doctor said, "but your arm as well. I'll also want an X-ray of your skull to see just how hard a knock your poor head took."

Viv rattled off his information. His headache was steadily getting worse. At the moment, he was feeling rather nauseous. "Doc, you may want to move. I think I'm going to hurl." As he turned to the side, the doctor quickly stuck a sick bag near his mouth so he didn't throw up on the floor. Viv had always detested throwing up, and tonight was no exception. Grimacing, he couldn't even work out what part of his body hurt the most. Right now, he was just one giant swirling ball of pain.

"Feeling better?"

"No," Viv moaned. "Can I have some pain killers? I'm really hurting here, Doc."

Dr. Stone watched him for a moment. "I can give you something mild. I won't prescribe anything stronger until I can see what the X-rays tell me."

"You're killing me, Doc," Viv muttered.

"Better safe than sorry."

At least to get to the X-ray department, they just wheeled him down on the bed. Closing his eyes, he tried to block the overhead lights from searing his brain with their brightness. His night had gone from a wonderful dinner with his family to lying injured and in agony on a hospital gurney. He could never have imagined this was where his night was going to end.

The X-rays took longer and were a lot more painful than he thought they would be. By the end of it, the doctor told him his skull wasn't fractured, which was a good thing, but he did have a major concussion, which was a bad thing. His hand was broken, and his forearm was fractured. His eye was swollen shut and the doctor would have to wait for the swelling to go down before he could assess the damage. On the whole, he would recover in time.

"It could be worse," the doctor stated matter-of-factly. "At least you're not dead."

Viv chuckled then groaned at the doctor's sad attempt at humor. "Please don't make me laugh. It hurts too much."

"Okay, you rest now, and I will go and inform your friend what's going on."

"If Ray's out there, would you bring him to me? My husband will only worry if he has to sit in the waiting room until visiting hours roll around," Viv mumbled. The painkillers were finally starting to kick in.

* * * *

Everything was hurting. That was the first thing Viv realized when he opened his eyes. The second was that Ray was sitting in a chair beside him, his head on the bed while he slept awkwardly. Reaching his good hand down, Viv rubbed his fingertips across Ray's shorn head.

"You're awake," Ray blurted out and jerked into a sitting position. "Your friend who called me told me Shane did this."

"Yeah. He'd had too much to drink and I had to get him away from Ethan. How is he? I told him if he needed somewhere to live, he could go to Destiny House."

"Jas was meeting him at the house. He seems like a nice guy, young though." Ray smiled sadly. "How are you feeling? You look so sore."

Viv chuckled then regretted it instantly. "I'm going to be okay, love. Do you know what happened to Shane?"

"Byron told Dad that he's in the lockup again. This time he won't get off so easily. I want him charged." Anger poured off Ray.

As much as Viv wanted to agree with his husband, he also knew he didn't want to hurt Byron or taint the relationship between the Connelly and King families. "I'll be happy if Byron gets him into some kind of rehab for both his drinking and his sexual activities. Byron shouldn't have to pay because his son is a wanker."

"Dad said you would say that." Ray sighed. "Don't you want him to pay for what he's done? Not only to you, but to Ethan as well."

How was he going to explain this? "Jail won't get him the help he seriously needs. He can't keep going the way he has been."

"Fine! I don't personally agree with you, but I can understand why you want to do it this way. I also don't think the university is going to let his behavior slide. He beat up two students when he isn't even a student there."

Viv understood Ray's point of view. "I think I'd like to talk to Byron and Shane, but only if Shane is sober."

"Byron is actually out in the waiting room with Dad. Would you like me to go and get him?"

When Viv nodded, Ray didn't look happy, but he went and did what Viv wanted anyway, which was just one of the reasons Viv loved the man so desperately. Tenderly, Viv touched his eye. He needed to see it and sat up on the side of the bed. Dizziness swamped him and he froze in place until the feeling diminished. After slowly getting to his feet, Viv walked into the bathroom. He took care of business before he turned to wash his hands and caught sight of himself in the mirror.

Holy fuck! His face was one massive big bruise. Despite a concussion and the broken bones in his wrist and arm, he knew that the actual bruises would fade quickly. He'd make a good recovery. The only thing he regretted was that his family would have to see him hurt, and he didn't want any of them to be scared.

Hearing voices in the other room, Viv made his way back to the bed, smiling when Ray rushed to help him. He never said anything as he let Byron look his fill. Even though he didn't want Shane charged, he did want Byron to see what his son was capable of under the influence of too much alcohol.

"How are you feeling?" Byron's voice was thick with emotion.

Viv could only assume the man was blaming himself for the actions of his idiotic son. "I'll live, as will Ethan."

Byron sighed. "Do you want him charged? God knows he deserves it."

"I'd rather he check into rehab for his drinking and sexual attitude. He needs help, if you can get him into rehab and make it stick. I know it'll be hard and Shane'll fight it kicking and screaming, but they are his only two options—jail or rehab. Mind you, I'm not certain what the uni will do." Viv hoped he wasn't asking for the impossible.

"I've already spoken to the uni and they said they will abide by your wishes, and they also want Shane to understand that he is banned from stepping foot onto the university grounds," Byron answered.

Viv got the feeling money had changed hands there, but didn't begrudge the man from wanting to save his son.

"Have you spoken to Ethan yet?"

"Yes. All he wants is to be left alone. He doesn't want anything to do with Shane anymore. I know he didn't want it, but I made arrangements for Shane to pay off Ethan's uni fees. I'm not trying to buy Shane's freedom, rather I'm trying to make him see that all actions have consequences."

Ray spoke up. "What's the consequences for what he did to my husband? Viv is the victim here and Shane hardly has a scratch on him."

"Love, I wasn't aiming to try and hurt Shane, just to stop him," Viv explained.

Ray wasn't having any of it. "No. You will have to take time off work, and school. You'll be wearing that cast for God knows how long. The doctor told me they'll have to wait for the swelling to go down to see if there is any permanent damage done. Walking away scot free isn't an option." Ray shook his head and looked at Byron. "I'm sorry. I know he's your son, but he was out of line. Ethan is much smaller than Viv, and if Viv hadn't intervened he could have been hurt worse than he was."

Viv used his good hand to wrap around Ray's neck and draw his husband in close to him. "I'm going to be just fine. I truly believe that rehab and maybe a stint of community service would be better for him than jail. If at the end of rehab he's no better, we'll reassess." Turning to Byron, he asked, "Are those terms acceptable?"

"They're more than acceptable," Byron answered.

"One more thing. I want Shane sobered up, then I want to explain to him why he's going into rehab. I want him to see what his drinking has caused," Viv said. Deep down he had to believe there was still hope for Shane, but first he had to convince Shane that he actually wanted to accept the help to get better.

Byron sighed. "I'll make it happen. If it doesn't work, then we'll find some other way to knock some sense into him. To be honest, I don't even think the police will let him slide, seeing how little time has passed since he was last in jail for assault. I just think Shane can't see that he's pushing everyone away with his antics."

"Then let's try and get him the help he needs, but if he ever comes after me again, I'll fight back," Viv declared, hoping Byron understood exactly what he was saying. Next time, there wouldn't be any pushing and shoving. Next time, he'd knock the prick out. "Right now, I think I need to lie down or they'll never let me out of this joint. And I really want to go home and sleep in my own bed."

Not long afterward, Byron left and Viv was back in bed waiting for Dr. Stone to make his rounds. Ray was fussing over him, and Viv loved all the attention. "You haven't told the kids what has happened, have you?"

"Good God, no. If I had, we'd have them all up here wanting to see you." Ray chuckled. "I'm not sure the hospital is ready for that amount of visitors."

They were interrupted by a knock at the door, and Girly strode in, followed by Dan, Declan and Jamie.

"Who told you?" Ray demanded.

"Pops. Who else? The minute we heard, we loaded up the car and came over. Fred and Josh have everything under control at home," Girly said. She studied Viv intently. "Shit! That has got to hurt."

"It does." Viv shrugged then hissed in pain when he jiggled his arm. Even wrapped in the temporary cast — they'd put the real one on after the swelling had reduced — it hurt like a bitch.

Girly looked angry. "Did I hear Pops right when he said you weren't pressing charges? Shane needs to be stopped."

"And he will be. I just want him to try rehab first," Viv said.

"It won't help him any. A leopard doesn't change his spots, and even if he can disguise them, he's still a leopard at heart," she said as if that made complete sense to everyone.

Ray and Daniel were both nodding behind her.

"I know what you're all saying. I really do, but I don't want to ruin the good name of the King family all because of that wanker. Hell, he's good at his job. He just needs a major attitude adjustment."

"Good luck with that." Girly snorted. "That man has always been an idiot, and I don't see it changing any time soon."

Viv didn't want to talk about it anymore. Turning to Ray, he changed the subject. "I hope I can go home soon. Do you think you could find out what time morning rounds are?"

"Sure," Ray said.

Watching his husband walk out of the room he smiled, then turned toward Girly when he realized she was taking pictures of him. "What are you doing?"

"Collecting evidence for when you come to your senses and have Shane charged with assault. No use doing it after all the evidence of the attack has healed."

Viv rolled his eyes—well, the one that wasn't swollen shut—at her. "You're too late. The doctor already took photographic evidence."

"Dad, why are you letting him get away with it?" Declan asked.

Jamie was the one who answered. "Because Dad isn't a meanie like Shane. He always says it's better to turn the other cheek. Mind you, Pa should have just decked him. He's done it before, hasn't he?"

"Yes, he has." Daniel chuckled. "That was the funniest thing I ever witnessed."

"There has been bad blood between Dad and Shane for as long as I can remember. Shane always blamed Dad for stealing Brent's friendship. If he'd thought about it, Shane would have realized, cousin or not, Brent couldn't stand him."

Ray was smiling as he walked back into the room. "The doc will be about another twenty minutes or so. Nurse Croydon says there's a very good chance you'll be coming home with us."

"That's good news, indeed. I can't wait just go home, sleep in my own bed and eat some real food."

"That's doable. GG probably has everything under control. You know she's going to be fussing over you worse than I will." Ray sat then picked up and held Viv's hand. "I hate seeing you in here."

"I hate being here," Viv joked.

* * * *

The days passed, and Viv was bored out of his skull with being unable to go into work. When he'd complained, GG had told him in no uncertain terms to suck it up and use the time to complete some of his university work. That scenario had lasted all of one day—if that. Once the kids realized Daddy was staying home with his boo boos, they came for lots of visits. Okay, it was mainly Millie, Ben and Charlotte, seeing as the rest were either at school or working, and the babies were still way too young to come seek him out. His days were spent reading them stories and playing whatever they brought to him. Today was *The Adventures of Bodhi Toady and the Periwinkle Sisters*. They were only about three pages in when Ray knocked on the door. He had Byron and Shane with him.

"Come on, munchkins. Pa will finish reading to you while Dad has a talk with Uncle Byron." Ray picked up Ben and the girls followed him, carrying their books.

"Is this a good time?" Byron asked after they entered the room.

Viv pushed up until he was sitting comfortably against the headboard. He studied Shane for a moment or two to ascertain if he was completely sober or not.

"I'm sorry, Chris. I'd had one too many... I was..."

"Shut up, Shane. I got your dad to bring you here because I have something to say that I think you need to hear." He waited for Shane to take a seat on the end of the bed. "If it were left up to Ray and Girly, you'd be sitting on your ass in jail right now while you wait for your day in court. Though I have a different idea of where you should be."

He gestured to his own injuries. "You did this to me because I was trying to stop you from hurting Ethan. You didn't care one iota about Ethan's wellbeing. You cornered him in a toilet stall and hit him, all because you didn't get what you wanted. The poor guy has been so terrified of you that he's been living in his car. He was prepared to drop out of uni and move just to get away from you."

"I just wanted him back. He shouldn't have left me," Shane whispered.

Viv was shocked and more than a little irritated. "He left you because you weren't faithful. You had him and still you were hitting on anyone who took your fancy. Why the hell would he stay when you couldn't put him first?"

"It wasn't always like that." Shane locked gazes with Viv. "I screwed up and didn't know how to turn things around."

"Well, I can tell you right now, drinking isn't the way. Look at me. I can't go to work, nor can I go to school until I'm healed. What the hell were you thinking, Shane?" Before Shane could answer, Viv went on. "That's right, you weren't. If you don't want to wind up in jail, you need to go into rehab. Not only for your drinking, but for your temper and sexual matters. You need to stop thinking anyone you want to be in your bed is going to worship you. You had a good man by your side, and in the end you drove him away."

Viv glared at Shane for a good long while before speaking again. "So now you have a choice to make. You can take your chances in front of a judge, or you can go to rehab and try and get your life back on track. So what will it be?"

"I'll go to rehab. I know I have a problem," Shane answered.

Viv was happy about Shane's decision. "Good choice. Get your shit together and this time, don't fuck it up. You have been an ass for far too long. I think it's time to let the nicer half of you out to play for a while." Sighing, he added, "Look, I can't promise the police won't still go after you, but the university is leaving this in my hands. I told Chief

Callahan that I won't press charges if you promise to get the help you need."

"I promise, Chris."

Shane seemed defeated, but Viv didn't care as long as the man followed through on his promise.

Throughout their whole exchange, Byron sat off to the side in complete silence. Viv gazed at him and inclined his head to let the man know he could jump in at any time now. It seemed to be the signal the man was waiting for.

"Son, do you realize how much has just been offered to you? You've done wrong and I wouldn't blame Viv and Ethan if they'd had you charged. Assault and battery is a big problem in the world today. Hitting your partner is also domestic violence. You could have killed Viv if his head had hit the wall or the floor a fraction harder. Then you would've been facing murder charges. I can't fathom where your life went so wrong, but Viv is right, you need to do something about it, and be very grateful Viv is giving you the chance to fix things and make amends."

Tears were evident in Shane's eyes. "Can I ask how Ethan is?"

"He's doing better than he was. He's in a safe place, and he's trying to start over," Viv answered honestly before adding, "I hope this will be your chance to start over as well."

Chapter Five

As much as Ray loathed to admit it, he was starting to think Viv was right to give Shane the chance to fix his life. He knew Byron was grateful to Viv and Ethan for not pressing charges. The best thing to happen in the past week since everything went down was the doctor had given the all clear with Viv's eye. He was still bruised to the shithouse, but at least his vision wasn't damaged.

"Dad, can I talk to you for a moment?" Girly asked the second she walked into the nursery where he sat feeding Layla.

"Sure. What's on your mind?" Ray smiled at his daughter. He took in her weariness. "Are you feeling okay? You're looking a little off."

She grinned at him in return. "I'm bloody worn out. Between working at the club, getting reacquainted with Nate, and helping out here at home. GG told me you thought I might be getting sick and trying to hide it. I just wanted to assure you that I'm fine."

"So how do you like having your brother in your life?" Ray asked. He knew she would never lie to him, even if it was just to save him from pain.

Girly rolled her eyes. "I love it, of course. I think Nate might be having trouble settling in, but he'll eventually get used to living in this madhouse we call home."

"Are you sure he's not feeling uncomfortable because you keep throwing your boyfriend in his face? What are you hoping will happen?"

She shrugged. "Nothing really. I was just pushing to see if anything would. Nate told me he thinks Dan is gorgeous, but I don't think he's thought further than that. He says he likes Dan because he's funny and kind." She chuckled. "Actually, having Nate around makes me see Dan in a whole new light."

"That's nice. I'm glad it's all working out." Ray burped Layla then placed her back in her cot before picking Jeb up for his feeding. "Grab Izzie and you can feed her while we talk. What else is on your mind?"

"Nothing much." She sat with Izzie in her arms. "I just miss the way we used to always chat. In the last couple of years our lives have become so busy. I just wanted some Dad time. Does that make sense?"

Ray smiled at her. "It makes perfect sense. I miss talking to you as well. I wouldn't give up the rest of the family for anything, but I do miss our lazy Sundays. Maybe these days we'd be better off having a movie night after the kids are asleep. Spend some quality time together. What do you say?"

"Sounds like a plan." Girly sighed. "Dad, do you think I have what it takes to hold onto Dan?"

Where the hell was this coming from? "Sure, don't you?"

"Maybe. I was just thinking that when we got together Dan admitted he was bisexual. What if I'm not enough for him?"

Okay now he could see what was troubling her and had her seeming so tired. "Honestly, I don't think you have a problem. I'm sure Dan will remain faithful to you."

"But what if he doesn't? I mean, think about someone like Shane."

"Girly, Shane has a problem. Daniel doesn't. If the day ever comes where Dan does have a problem, you'll both deal with it together," Ray said truthfully. "I think you're worrying over nothing."

Girly grinned. "You're probably right."

"I know I'm right. I also think you need to stop pushing your brother at Dan, especially when you know Dan is attracted to him." Ray hoped she listened to his words, or she would end up sorry if she shoved the men into each other's arms.

"Okay, okay... Hell, for a while there, I was hoping if he needed male company he would choose Nate. I think I would handle that better than a stranger."

Ray shook his head at her words. "No, you wouldn't, it would end up driving a wedge between you and your brother. Believe me, you don't want that to happen."

"So, you're telling me to get over myself and let the cards fall where they may? When did you become so smart?"

He chuckled. "It was bound to happen eventually."

"Don't ever put yourself down. You have been the best dad ever. Trust me — look at how frickin' awesome I turned out."

Ray loved his daughter, he really did. He loved all his children equally, but there would always be a soft spot for Girly. She was his first and held a special place in his heart.

"So what are your plans for the evening?"

"Actually, I'm here to babysit. GG says to get your guitar and get downstairs as Jas is picking you up for a gig. GG said you are not to pike out, as the band is counting on you. You have the rest of us here to take care of the kids. Plus, Viv wants to take Declan so he can see you all in action."

Damn, this was exactly what he didn't want. Life was too busy at the moment to take time out to go and entertain other people. "Crap!"

"Suck it up, princess. This isn't about you. Think about Josh, B and Jas. Have you ever thought that they might enjoy getting out and playing again? Plus, you'll be doing it as a favor to Brent and Tarni. Since they got back from England, they've been getting closer. I won't be surprised if we hear wedding bells somewhere in the near future."

"Speaking of weddings, have you and Dan set the date yet?" Ray asked.

Grinning, she said, "Dan wants to get married around Christmastime." She shooed him toward the door. "Stop stalling. Get in your tight jeans and shirt and go make me proud of you."

"Fine!" He pouted as he placed his son in the crib then walked into his bedroom to change. He felt weird getting ready to go out when he was more a family man now. He grabbed the clothes Girly suggested and quickly checked himself in the mirror before heading to the music room where his and Josh's gear was stored. He wasn't surprised when he found the rest of Darkness Crawls gathered there.

"About time you got here. Did Girly tell you that Dad said I can come and watch?" Declan looked so excited.

Ray smiled, though he wondered where they would be playing if they were taking Declan with them. He wasn't old enough to get into a bar. Unless, of course, it was Viv's nightclub, so they might get away with it then. "So, where are we playing?"

"Tarni has this benefit she's in charge of and asked if we could fill in. Her band pulled out at the last moment."

"It almost sounds like old times." For Declan's benefit, he added, "I met your dad because we were filling in for a band that couldn't make their slot."

"The best night of my life," Viv stated proudly.

Yeah, it definitely had been one of Ray's better nights. "Have you organized a play list? I figure I might need to know what I'm expected to play."

Beth held out a piece of paper for him. As soon as he scanned the list, he smiled. They were doing mostly songs they played a lot and wouldn't have any trouble with any of them. He also saw she had sweetened the pot by adding a few of his favorites. "Looks good. So where's this benefit?"

"Destiny House." Beth smiled. "GG has asked Tarni to co-run the place with Norman. Brent helps out there a lot. Tarni thinks this will bring attention and donors to their cause, and help get the word out that there is a safe place for those who need it. Plus, the added benefit is it gives the young men living there a chance to see there are people willing to help them without demanding anything in return."

With those words, Ray knew his grandmother was behind this. She was interfering and getting him back into a life outside the family and home. He hoped she soon realized Ray was happy with his life as it was.

"Come on, we better head off before we're late." Jasper hurried them all along.

Ray smiled when he saw Fred was also going to be in attendance.

* * * *

The night flew by, and Ray found he'd actually missed performing. In the audience, Viv was sitting with Ethan, who seemed to be much better than the last time Ray had seen the young man. Declan was sitting with Fred, and Ray was surprised when he heard Declan singing along, and realized how beautiful a voice the boy had.

Before starting the next song, he stopped and gestured for Declan to come up on stage. "Do you know any of these songs?"

"This one and this one." Declan gazed at him curiously.

Ray walked back toward B, Jas and Josh. "Change of set. We're going to do these two next. Declan is going to sing for us."

They appeared shocked but nodded.

"Okay, everyone, thanks for bearing with me. While the band plays the next two songs I'm going to take a short break as my son takes a turn at lead vocals. Declan, come back here and take your spot."

Declan looked terrified.

"He's a little shy, so everyone please give the man a round of applause for encouragement. This house was built for young men and women who've had a rough trot in life. Sometimes that person is a little closer to home. We all know someone who could benefit from a house like this. Please, if you are able, reach deep and give to this worthwhile cause."

Ray wasn't sure if Tarni and Brent appreciated or needed his help in getting donor support. He couldn't help but smile as the crowd started chanting Declan's name. Ray stepped back from the microphone and gave the boy room. Viv's gaze was riveted on his son. Sure, Declan was nervous, but he had natural talent. Ray was certain he'd loosen up quick smart. He was proven right as soon as Declan opened his mouth and words started flowing out.

Two songs later, the whole room was cheering. Declan was glowing with excitement as he stepped away from the microphone.

Ray opened his arms, and Declan came to him for a hug. "Isn't he amazing? If he keeps singing like that, I'll find myself out of a job."

"Thank you, everyone. It's time for the band to take a break so that you can all mingle. We'll be back later to finish off the night." Ray unslung his guitar and stood it in its stand. He took a big swig out of the bottle of water a waiter standing off to the side of the stage had for the band.

After walking over, he stopped in front of Viv and readily accepted a hug from his husband. "Wasn't Declan wonderful?"

"I didn't even know he could sing like that. He definitely gets it from his mother, because I'm tone deaf," Viv announced as Declan came over to them. Viv wound one of his arms around Declan's shoulder.

Ray's heart was bursting from the happiness on Declan's face when he spoke. "Mum always said I got my brains from you. She hated school, but I love it."

"So did you enjoy yourself up there tonight?" Viv asked.

Declan beamed. "It was fun. Maybe I can do it again sometime. I mean, when you're not playing in a club or bar. I could learn more song lyrics."

"Sounds like a plan," Ray answered. He could see the trepidation in Declan's eyes, as if he was waiting for Ray to tell him not to bother. There was no way Ray was ever going to do that to the kid. He was all for pumping up Declan's sense of self-worth, not stomping his ego into the ground. "We'll even start teaching you how to play the guitar. Jamie says you wanted to learn."

"Yes, please. That would be awesome."

Ray loved seeing Declan so happy.

"Will it be hard to learn?"

"I taught Girly. I think you might be a natural," Ray answered, and was rewarded with another earth-shattering grin. In that very second, Ray understood Declan was going to be breaking hearts all over the place, and just like his father, he probably wouldn't even realize it was happening.

"So how's the night going?" Ray asked Viv. He knew his husband was keeping tabs on everything, as Destiny House was close to Ray's heart.

Viv smiled. "I think tonight was a hit. Tarni seems ecstatic about how it's all going." He gestured toward Ethan. "I was just telling Ethan about Shane entering rehab. We're hopeful he'll finally get the help he needs."

Ray didn't comment. He remembered Viv telling him that Ethan had been in love with Shane. "Let's hope so."

Once upon a time, Shane had been a decent bloke. Ray never could pinpoint what had happened to turn him into the asshole he became as a man. Ray had grown up with both Shane and Brent in his life, and it wasn't until their mid-teens that Shane had started to change.

"In the beginning, he was very nice and attentive. I just don't know what I did wrong." Sadness settled on Ethan's face.

"You didn't do anything. Shane is all kinds of messed up and has been for a very long time," Ray said a little forcefully.

Ethan took a step back. "He wasn't always like that with me. I think in the beginning, he at least had strong feelings for me, but then he started drinking and things began to slide downhill."

"Do you still love him?" Ray asked.

A shrug was all he got in answer. Ray wanted to warn

Ethan away, but knew that wasn't fair to the man. He should be allowed to work things out on his own. All they could really do was be there to pick up the pieces and put them back together, if needed.

"I'm going to mingle for a bit. I want to talk to the guys who live here and find out how they're all doing," Ray said before he left everyone.

He went in search of Tarni and Brent. He wanted to make sure Tarni had all she needed for Destiny House. His grandma couldn't have picked a better person to put in charge of this new adventure for the Connelly Corporation. Tarni was very much like her own mother when it came to keeping things organized and making sure everything got done on time with the minimal amount of trouble.

He found Tarni and Brent talking off to the side with Norman. Ray couldn't believe the change in Norman and the other young men they'd rescued from Beau.

"Is this a private party or can anyone join in?" Ray asked when he came to a stop.

"Idiot." Brent chuckled. "Norman was just telling us Beau has had some additional charges laid against him."

"Really?" Ray asked in surprise.

Norman nodded. "Apparently Beau has two sons of his own. When his wife found out about what her husband had been up to, she had a talk with her children, only to find out Daddy was a little too friendly with them as well, but it was their secret."

A burning shot of anger burst through Ray at the thought of Beau touching his own kids in a sexual manner. The man was obviously sick in the head. Ray couldn't even fathom touching his kids that way. Luckily, Beau's family now had a chance to move on without the man's fucked-up influence staining their lives.

"I promised Grandma that I'd make sure there were no problems here and to ask if you needed anything. She's under the delusion nothing will run right without her interference," Ray joked.

"Actually," Norman began, "ask her if she has time to come to the house and teach Mick how to make those yummy biscuits and cakes she's so famous for. He's been bugging me to get her over here."

"Oh, GG is going to love that." Brent smirked. "She's always wanted to teach us and we were more about running away from the attempts. She'll be in her element passing her skills on to someone other than Antonio."

Norman chuckled. "Mick will be just as stoked, I can tell you. He's been treating us weekly with everything he has learned so far. He absolutely loves the Food Network channel."

"I'm glad they seem to be doing much better," Ray said.

Before he could say much more, Beth called him back to the stage for their next and final set.

* * * *

As the days passed, Ray thought about where his life was going. He loved being a father, he truly did. But some days it felt like he never had a moment to himself. Family life wasn't always the blissed-out cakewalk he'd thought it would be. Some days were so damn trying. Three months had passed since he'd had his talk with Girly about pushing her brother at her fiancé. He swore to God it must have gone in one ear and out the other. Not moments ago, he'd caught Girly and Nate arguing, because Nate wasn't trying hard enough.

What the hell was going on?

"Girly, Nate, come with me. I think it's time we had another bloody talk."

"Dad, it's nothing for you to worry about."

Ray spun around and glared at his daughter. He pointed into the first room they came to. Making sure there was no one in there, he locked the door and gestured at the bed for Girly and Nate to sit.

"I thought we sorted this out months ago. Why are you

still persisting in this?" Ray demanded. "Has Dan told you this is what he wants?"

"Not in so many words," Girly hedged.

Ray snorted. "I didn't think so. Why are you forcing this so much?" Then clarity hit him like a lightning bolt. "Dan doesn't want this, does he? For some reason, you want out of the relationship. I'm right, aren't I?"

"Dad." Girly exhaled loudly.

"Don't 'Dad' me. Just tell me what the hell is going on."

Nate looked guilty as he answered Ray, "Girly has met someone else. She was hoping if I can get Dan to fall in love with me, he won't be left with a broken heart."

"Who?" Ray's gut churned from the cluster-fuck he was hearing.

Girly only pouted, so Nate spoke again. "Mick. She's been going to Destiny House with me and GG. She and Mick have hit it off. I don't think Mick will do anything while she's still with Dan. Hence the reason she wants me to seduce Dan."

"Fuck me drunk, Girly!" Ray threw his hands into the air wildly and started pacing the room. He stopped and studied Nate. "What do you think about all of this? And for the love of God, just tell me the truth."

In a trembling voice, he said, "I like Dan a lot, but I think Girly needs to tell him herself what's happening. It shouldn't be left up to me. I like Mick as well and I know he's a good guy, a faithful guy. He would never accept her cheating on Dan to be with him."

"So what are you going to do?" Ray asked Girly.

"I just don't want to hurt Dan. I love him, I really do, but I realized lately it's just not the same way I felt about him in the beginning. Hell, maybe I'm the one who has to change." Tears glistened in her eyes. "*If* I tell him — and I will — I'll go away for a bit. I want you to make sure Dan doesn't leave. He'll need all of you because he deserves better than I can give him. I hate that I can't love him the way he should be."

"Oh, Girly." Ray knelt on the floor in front of his daughter and hugged her close. "I wish I could take this from you, but sadly, Nate and I have to stand back. Daniel's heart may break, and we'll keep an eye on him, but you can't force Nate to take your place. It isn't fair to Nate or Dan."

Girly sobbed against his shoulder. "I'm sorry, Dad. I was just trying to make things better."

"You just have to sit Dan down and be honest with him. Is he going to be blindsided by this?" Ray asked as he rocked with her still in his arms.

"I think he knows something is up with me, just not what. We haven't had sex in a couple of months. I know I just have to do this so both Daniel and Mick know where they stand."

"Good girl." He was trying to be supportive, while inside, his brain was screaming at him to get out of the way of the inevitable fallout. "But I don't want you leaving. No matter what, you're still my daughter."

She sat up and stared at him with a tearstained face. "Well, we can't let Dan leave."

"Girly, this place has three wings with bedrooms in each. I'm pretty sure you'll have enough space." Ray was proud that he had thought of a solution. "One of you can just move to the other side of the mansion."

She frowned at him. "I'll move. This is my problem, and I have to work it out for myself. I hate that I've got to do this. But if I don't, then I won't be happy. Dan is a wonderful, beautiful person. I wish I could be the one for his happily ever after. But I can't."

"You know, even as much as you want Dan and Nate to be together, it may not go the way you plan. You have to let that sort of stuff come naturally," Ray explained, ever conscious that his own relationship with Viv hadn't at all run smoothly in the beginning. "Dan's last two relationships have been with women."

"I know, but I also know he's attracted to Nate. I've seen him watching Nate when he doesn't think anyone else will notice. I love them both and I just want them to be happy.

I was hoping it would be with each other. I *so* suck at this."

Ray chuckled. "You always did try and run everyone's lives. You take after GG that way."

"Okay!" Girly stood up and took a deep breath. "I'm going to do this. Wish me luck."

With a saddened heart, Ray watched as Girly and Nate left the room. Ray wanted to lock himself away from the world until the dust had settled, but he'd have to go and give his husband a heads-up on what was about to go down under their very roof. He knew without a doubt that Viv's mind would be blown just like his own was. He wondered how much of the truth his grandma knew, and if she suspected this much, then why the hell hadn't she warned him this was all going to blow up in their faces?

They were going to all have to sit down and talk about keeping secrets.

Chapter Six

The moment Ray walked into their bedroom, Viv knew there was something wrong. Ray didn't even speak to him before he pulled out his phone, called Fred and asked if she and Josh could meet them down in the kitchen.

"Come on, we need to go have a family meeting." Ray held out his hand.

Viv immediately stood and asked, "Should I call Dan and Girly?"

"No, love. Sadly, this meeting is *about* Dan and Girly."

When Ray didn't say any more, Viv followed his husband from the room. Ray was agitated to hell and back. Viv didn't like it when Ray was upset. He wished Ray would just tell him what was wrong so he could figure out how to make things better. Ray wasn't meant to hurt in anyway if Viv could help it. Viv's gut twisted with what this could all be about. At least he knew they were physically unharmed, or Ray would have been way more upset than he currently was. Right now Ray seemed more pissed off. Thankfully all the younger children were in bed. Sean and Declan were watching movies in the media room and he assumed Nate would be wherever his sister was. They were inseparable these days. Before long, he found himself in the kitchen along with GG, Fred, Josh, Magen and Antonio all waiting expectantly for Ray to speak.

Instead, Ray stared right at his grandmother. "Did you know this was going on with Girly? If so, why the hell didn't you give me a heads-up?"

"So she finally told you." GG sighed. "I was hoping I was wrong. Believe me, young Mick has done nothing to encourage her. So I don't want you blaming any of this on him."

"Wait!" Viv demanded, staring at them both. "What the hell is going on between Girly and Mick?"

From the looks on everyone else's faces, they were all just as stunned as Viv was.

"Right now there is nothing going on. Girly has feelings for and is falling in love with someone else," GG explained.

Ray snorted. "And to make herself feel less guilty, she's been trying to force Nate into seducing Dan so that he won't be sad when she finally breaks up with him. I mean, seriously! What the hell is she thinking?"

Fuck! This was going to do Viv's head in. "Why does she want—God! She thinks because Dan has a crush on Nate that he'll just swap one sibling for the other without complaining? Damn!" *This is cold.*

Even if Dan was head over heels in love with Nate, this was going to mess with his brother's mind. Dan had always been the one to do the leaving in any relationship. Girly was the longest romance Daniel had ever had with someone. Hell, poor Nate was going to be caught in the middle, because he knew damn well when Girly broke up with Dan that she would be pushing Nate in his face. It wouldn't work. The more she pushed, the farther Dan would run. He'd stick up a wall between his heart and Nate. Knowing Dan, he'd probably blame Nate for it all.

Should I say something? Of course I should. "He's going to blame Nate for all of this. I know he will."

Fred frowned. "Why would Dan blame Nate?"

"Because he'll think his feelings for Nate will have been what prompted Girly to look elsewhere," Viv answered honestly.

"This is bullshit," Josh blurted out. "So instead of two broken hearts, we'll have to factor in Nate as well. How does he even fit into all of this? I mean, what does he think about it all?"

Magen jumped into the conversation. "We're going to

have to make sure Nate doesn't run. We'll have to show him that no matter what, he's still going to be part of this family. If he blames himself for...*God*...this could wind up being one hell of mess."

"All we can do is be there for all of them when the time comes. Three hearts are involved here, because I believe Nate is just as infatuated with Dan," GG said to them all.

"He is. He told me." Ray sighed. "We'll need to tell Mum, Dad, B, Jas, Brent and Tarni, or else they could put their foot into it without even knowing. I just can't believe this is happening."

Viv could believe it. Some kind of karma must be biting them on the ass big time. For once, he would just like their lives to run smoothly without the threat of a cluster-fuck exploding in the middle and blowing them all to kingdom come.

Is it too much to ask for?

"So should we go and check on them?" Antonio asked.

As much as he didn't want to, Viv knew Antonio was right. Eventually, they would have to help all involved through the fallout. "I'll go see Dan. I don't want anyone else to be in the way of his mouth when he lets loose."

"I'll go help Girly move her gear," Ray said reluctantly before adding, "She's moving into a different wing for the time being. I insisted on that, because she wanted to move out completely. I don't want to lose any of them. Like Aunt Magen said, they're all family no matter what."

"I'll go find Nate," Magen said.

Viv knew the woman had a bit of a soft spot for the young man.

Viv stopped her before she could leave the kitchen. "You might want to take Declan with you. If anyone can get through to Nate, it will be Declan."

"Good idea."

Ray hugged him close, and Viv held tight. He wished they could stay like this until someone figured out a way to turn back time so this never happened at all.

"I'm so not looking forward to this." Viv got up and headed into the house in search of his brother.

Declan and Magen met him in the hall.

Declan spoke, "If you're looking for Dan, then you've missed him. Jamie said Dan just slammed out of the house like there's no tomorrow. We'll get him through this. He'll be okay."

"I'll let you know when I find him," Viv said, wishing everything could go back to the way it was, but knowing it couldn't. All things happened for a reason, and in the end, this would work out for the best.

"Check the club. Jamie told me that's where Dan goes when he has a lot on his mind," Declan suggested.

Viv changed direction back to the kitchen to where his keys were stored. He grabbed them in passing. "Josh, can you give me a lift to the club? According to Declan, that's where Jamie thinks we'll find Dan."

"Sure." Josh caught the keys Viv tossed to him and got up to follow.

The drive to the club was relatively quiet. Neither of them discussed what Ray had just told them. As soon as they entered the club, Tony caught Viv's attention and pointed toward the office.

"I'll let you go talk to Dan. I'll stay at the bar for a bit. Call me if you need me." Josh detoured to where Tony was tending customers.

With a deep breath to fortify himself, Viv crossed to the hall leading to the office. He didn't even bother knocking as he entered the room. He wasn't sure what he expected, but it damn well wasn't what he found. Dan lay on the couch in the dark with his arm over his eyes. At a crunch under his foot, Viv looked down and saw the shattered frame that had once contained the first picture Girly had ever given Dan.

He crossed the room and tapped Dan's leg to let him know he was there. He wasn't shocked at all when Dan sat up and cuddled into Viv the second he sat on the couch beside him. Viv wrapped his arms around his brother and waited for the storm to stop.

He didn't speak, because words weren't necessary between them. His brother needed him, and he was there, no questions asked.

After what seemed like an hour or more, Dan finally pushed himself up. His eyes were red-rimmed, and Viv's heart broke just that little bit more. No matter how much he wished it were possible, he didn't know what to do to make this better for his brother.

"Did you know?" Dan asked.

Viv decided honestly was the best policy. "Ray found out just before you did. He then came and told me."

"This is all my fault. I always fuck everything up," Dan growled in obvious frustration.

Viv reached out and yanked his brother back against his chest. "This isn't your fault. You didn't do anything wrong."

"She wants to remain friends. Can you believe that? How the hell is that supposed to work? I can't even look at her without feeling guilty."

"You have nothing to feel guilty about," Viv insisted, knowing exactly where this conversation was heading and wanting to stop it from getting there.

Dan snorted. "Of course I do. If I just didn't have these feelings for Nate, she would never have left me. I took one look at him and started all my old bullshit again. I pushed her away. I know I did."

"No, you didn't. You never in any way acted on your feelings for Nate. Girly just met someone else. Her heart was torn. No matter what she chose to do, somebody's heart was going to be broken. I'm sorry that it's your heart that's been shattered, but you have to realize the rest of us are here for you." Viv was rambling and he knew it. He just wanted Daniel to see that it wasn't as hopeless as it felt right now.

"Why did Nate have to come into my life and ruin everything?"

Viv sighed. "Dan, this isn't Nate's fault either. It's nobody's fault. Sometimes one person in a relationship needs to leave for one reason or another. All you can do is learn from it and move on."

"What the hell am I supposed to learn from my fiancée falling out of love with me and kicking me to the curb? Am I supposed to learn just how unlovable I really am?"

"Now you're just being a dick," Viv said a little more harshly than he'd intended. "Somewhere out there in the world is the perfect person for you. Whether that be Nate or someone else, you will eventually get your happily ever after."

Dan shook his head vehemently. "Never going to happen. As far as I'm concerned, Nate is off limits. I'll never give my heart away so close to home again. Especially when that person is the cause of it all. I'm done with it. Being in love hurts too much. You know, I should have realized something was going on with her. She's been pulling away from me for a while now. I was just stupid enough to think she was trying to reconnect with her brother, so I gave her the space she needed. But that obviously wasn't what she wanted at all. She just wanted away from me."

"Don't say that." Viv frowned and found himself getting riled. "Don't close your heart off because you got dumped. Look how many men and women you've tossed aside over the years. You don't think they just gave up, do you? You're strong enough to get through this."

"They don't count," Daniel snapped.

Viv scoffed, "Why? Because they weren't the ones doing the dumping?"

"No! They don't count because I wasn't in love with any of them."

Shock washed over Viv. Not because of what Daniel had said, but by the ferociousness in his brother's voice. *Please don't let him go into his I'm-going-to-lock-the-world-out phase.* The last time that had happened, Daniel had been lost to him for three months. By the time he'd finally come back,

Viv was at his wit's end. Then one day it was like Dan woke up and he'd never been gone at all.

"Tell me, am I going to have to take you to the doctor's? I don't want you sliding back into a bout of indifference. I don't want you pushing me away again."

Dan rolled his eyes. "I'm not going to do that again. I remember how much I hurt everybody, especially you, by doing that."

"I also don't want you to jump into a toxic relationship. That's how we ended with Bree in our lives," Viv only half-joked.

Dan chuckled. "I'm not the only one who had a fucked-up relationship. Don't tell me that you so easily pushed Grace from your mind?"

"Christ, don't remind me. At least she'll never come back at us again."

"You're lucky. I'll have both Girly and Nate in my sight every fucking day. I'm not sure I want to have to deal with that. I might take a break for a while, just until I can sort out where my head is at."

This was exactly what Viv didn't want to happen. "Where will you go? I'm not liking this plan at all."

"Actually, I rang Pops and asked if I could go and stay at the cabin if it was free. I told him what happened, and he called me back a few minutes ago and said the cabin is vacant. He's arranging for me to take the private plane up there." Dan smiled. "At first, when I told him, I thought he would tell me no, seeing as Girly is his granddaughter, but he listened to me then made the necessary arrangements. He told me I'd always be family to him and Nan. That was nice of him, wasn't it?"

Viv relaxed somewhat when he realized Dan wasn't running away completely. Thank God Liam was understanding and didn't immediately side with family. Hopefully, after a week or two away, Dan would come back fully refreshed.

"So, when do you leave? Better yet, when are you coming

back? Did you leave the house just so you could ring Liam without anyone overhearing you?"

"Yeah, I did, but I bet by now GG, Uncle Ant and Aunt Magen already know about it. As for when it's happening, I'm leaving in about four hours. I promise I'll keep in contact and let you know when I'm ready to come back. I promise I'm not running away. I just need a time-out," Dan said. "How about we go home and you can help me pack? Pops even arranged a car for me at the other end, so at least I won't be without transportation. I told him when I catch Old Reg that I'll send him and Uncle Matt a picture."

Viv chuckled as they locked up the office and headed back out to Josh in the bar. "I still don't think that fish even exists."

"Well, I'll let you know if he does or not."

Viv smiled, but knew he was going to miss his brother while he was gone. "I'll look after the club for you while you're away."

"You do that. I don't want to come home to a fucked-up mess."

* * * *

After Dan left to catch his plane, Viv went in search of his husband. He needed a bit of alone time where he could take a moment and lose himself in his lover's closeness. Ray glanced up at him as he entered their bedroom.

"You look worn out," Ray stated.

"So do you," Viv said and crawled up on the bed to lay beside Ray. "Dan made it to his plane on time. I'm not happy about him going, but I can understand his reasons why he needs to. How are Girly and Nate doing?"

Ray leaned down and gave Viv exactly what he needed. A deep, toe-curling kiss. When it ended, he said, "Girly is feeling guilty, which she bloody well should. Nate is kind of staying quiet. I don't think he's come out of his room since everything went down. Aunt Magen and Declan keep checking on him, but this is going to fuck him up. I've tried to tell him this isn't his fault and that he shouldn't feel guilty over what his sister brought about. Do you think Dan will be gone long? I hate our family being torn asunder like this."

"The last time he pulled away from me, it took three months for him to find his way out of his funk and come back. I hope it won't take that long this time." Viv sighed. "I don't want to talk about everyone else's drama anymore. Tell me all the good things our kids did today, then you can ravage my body until we can both forget for just a little while."

"How about I ravage you first?" Rays said. He started undoing the buttons on Viv's dress shirt. "Then, while we're snuggling afterward, I'll fill you on today's adventures in the Connelly household."

"Sounds like you have a plan."

Ray grinned at him. "Darlin', I always have a plan."

"That you do." Viv chuckled. He sighed when Ray began kissing every bit of skin he exposed on Viv's body, taking time to torture both nipples in turn with a gentle nip of his teeth. Fuck! He'd always loved it when Ray punished his nipples. The gentle bites turned him on faster than it took to blink. His husband always did have the greatest mouth in the world, and the best part was that he knew exactly how to use it to bring the most sensuality.

Pushing himself up onto his elbows, Viv took in the erotic sight of his lover making his way down his body until he reached Viv's hard cock, which was begging for attention. He smiled up at Viv before leaning in and sucking Viv into his warm mouth. Ray's gaze was locked to his and Viv drowned in the heat he saw within it.

"Love, if you keep doing that I'm going to be done before we even get started."

His dick slid free of Ray's beautiful mouth. "Now, we can't have that."

"No, we can't."

Viv lay back on the bed. Ray got up and stripped down to his bare skin. Before coming back to the bed, Ray rummaged through the bedside table and retrieved the lube. "Do you want inside of me, or me inside of you?"

Ray popped the lube open and coated his fingers. "I'm supposed to be ravishing you. I'm going to make you feel so good."

"I'm sure you will."

Viv hitched his legs up over Ray's arms, giving Ray more room to play. And boy did he love it when Ray decided to play. Viv shivered when Ray used the pad of his finger to caress Viv's opening before pressing into him. The slow penetration had Viv groaning. God, he loved being with Ray, loved the time they got alone to explore each other at will. No interruptions, just him and his lover intent only on bringing each other gratification.

Soon Ray had him stretched enough for three fingers, and Viv's body broke out in goose bumps as Ray caressed his prostate. His lover knew exactly how he was affecting Viv, because Ray chuckled each and every time he touched Viv's pleasure spot.

"Ray...love...please..." Viv wasn't above begging.

"What do you want? I need you to tell me exactly what you want," Ray stated. He stilled his fingers within Viv's body.

Viv wiggled his ass in protest. "I want you inside me right now. I want you to pound my very core until I forget everything for a moment. Then I want you to love me so I remember why I breathe every day."

"I can do that." Ray's voice was rough with emotion. He slipped his fingers free.

Viv's shivered in anticipation, knowing Ray was moving himself into position. The press of his cock head against Viv's opening was almost too much to bear. He wanted his lover inside him right now, taking control, so that Viv didn't have to. This was really what tonight was about. Viv didn't want to be in charge. He wanted to be told what to do so he could lose himself completely.

"Feels so good, Ray."

A groan fell from his lips when Ray pulled out until he was almost free before sliding right back in to the hilt. Slow and methodical, Ray drew out the dance. Viv knew his lover was seeing how much Viv could take before he cracked and begged to be allowed to come. It was a game they'd played often. A game Viv absolutely loved, because he knew Ray was going to be the first to fall. Ray would get so caught up in what he was doing that he'd forget and soon he'd be fucking Viv for all he was worth.

If eyes were the windows to the soul, then right now Ray's were telling him just how loved he truly was. He could only hope his mirrored the same message back to his love. Viv adored his children, but Ray was his heart and soul.

"Fuck!" Viv gasped. Ray took a hold of his legs, spreading them farther apart and changing the angle completely. Heat arced across his skin each time Ray pegged his prostate.

The look of determination on his husband's face told Viv that Ray was close to coming. Sudden clarity seemed to fill Ray's eyes and he stopped as he slammed home one last time. Dropping down, he then devoured Viv's mouth in a hungry demanding kiss. Not that Viv was complaining, but he wasn't finished, and he knew Ray hadn't either. The kiss ended abruptly.

"Why did you stop?"

Ray smiled down at Viv. "Now comes the part where I make love to you. I want you to know exactly what you mean to me."

The urge to finish as fast as he'd started rode Ray hard, but he fought his way through it until his breathing slowed and he was once again in control. The feeling of Viv's body holding him tight in its grasp was excruciating, but in a good way. Ray rocked their bodies together, wanting to take his time. It wasn't often these days that they got to be alone like this. Usually, one or another of the children needed their undivided attention.

Viv's eyes closed and his lips parted in a silent moan. Ray set about torturing his body so erotically. Ray loved the fact he could affect his lover like this. As much as he loved the times Viv fucked him, Ray enjoyed being the one in control. His heart fluttered at how he'd almost missed his chance at having Viv in his life. If it hadn't been for Girly and Dan interfering, they would never have gotten together.

Ever since the first time they'd made love so long ago, Ray cherished the gift he'd been given in the form of Viv. Every day he thanked his lucky stars Viv had decided he loved Ray as much as Ray loved him. Even when Grace had tried to take Ray's happiness, they'd found their path through the darkness and out the other side.

The way Viv murmured incoherently was such a turn on. Ray's lightning zinged up and down his spine the closer he got to the edge of his desire. His balls drew tightly to his body, coiled like a hair trigger ready to go off the moment Viv succumbed to Ray's ministrations. Leaning closer, Ray gently bit down on Viv's shoulder and felt the heat of Viv's release between them. Ray's body flamed the instant he thrust deep one last time. His essence poured out of him and into his lover, sating his body's needs.

Ray was home.

Viv was forever going to be his home.

And Ray couldn't have been happier.

They lay that way for a long moment and came down from their high. Slowly extracting himself, Ray finally stood up before he pulled Viv to his feet then led his husband into the shower.

"Now we get cleaned up. Then we can snuggle and talk." Ray hesitated for a moment before adding, "And possibly put some clothes on in case we're called upon. Because pounds to peanuts, one of the kids will want our attention."

After drying off and getting dressed, Ray led the way back to bed. He checked to make sure the sheets didn't need changing before they climbed back under the covers and held each other tightly.

"Okay, now, as promised, I will tell you about today. Though I don't want to talk about Girly and Dan. Right now, we need happy thoughts," Ray stated.

"Fill me in," Viv prompted.

Ray thought about where to start. "I will get the bad stuff out of the way first. Damien has been in touch with Fred. He's decided he wants Bear to go and live with him. She's fighting it, but I guess it will end up in court. Apparently when he last had them, Charlotte was talking about when Jamie and Bear grew up they were going to get married. When Damien demanded the truth, Bear told him yes."

Ray had always worried that the way they had let Jamie and Bear be with each other was going to come back and bite them on the ass, and this was apparently the start of it.

"I'm confused. Is he fighting for both kids, or just for Bear?" Viv asked.

"To be honest, I think it's just for Bear. He doesn't even like having Charlotte for his allotted weekends. I hope this all blows over. I'm not sure what would happen if we tried separating them now. GG has Byron on the case, but Byron says Damien could win. He'll fight it, but it will be up to the judge."

"This has got to be screwing with Fred's mind. Is there anything we can do for her?"

Ray smiled sadly. "There is, and we're doing everything we can for her. If he wins, Bear won't have a chance to come back until he turns eighteen and Damien loses his hold over the boy. He could brainwash Bear against all of us by then."

"As much as I hate to say this, maybe it would be better if he wins now, before the two boys become even more attached. They are young, and yes, their hearts will break and they won't understand why this is happening, but eventually they'll be able to move on."

Ray couldn't believe what Viv was saying. He pushed himself up until he could stare down at Viv. "Are you saying you agree with Damien?"

"No. I'm not saying that at all. All I am saying is that if this is going to happen, maybe it's best it happens now and not three years down the track."

"This is a bullshit call, and you know it," Ray snapped, hating that they were now fighting after the beauty of what had just transpired between them. "He's just doing this to be a vindictive prick."

Viv also sat up. "Ray, as much as we love having Bear here, you have to see Damien's point of view. He's doing what he thinks is in the best interest of his son. I know damn well that you would do the exact same thing if you thought someone was putting one of our children in danger."

"What danger?" Ray demanded.

Viv sighed. "Love, I'm not saying Bear is in any danger, and yes, Damien is doing this just because he can. The man is a sexist bigot. There is nothing we can do that will change that fact. All we *can* do is be here for the fallout and help put Jamie back together. In all of this, he has to be our first priority. I'm sorry if that sounds harsh. But Jamie is our son...and sadly, Bear is not."

Ray hated it when Viv was right. He hated knowing this was going to happen just because Damien couldn't stand the fact that Fred had moved on with her life and hadn't gone crawling back to Damien like he'd expected. "This is going to fuck Jamie up, and I don't know whether or not I can bear that. I want to protect him, most of all because he's had the hardest life out of all of us."

"I know you do. All we can do is be there for him. Show him that he is still loved."

"I still don't like it." Pushing Viv back down until they were lying flat, Ray rested his head on his husband's shoulder. "Everyone else is doing okay. Sean and Declan have become fast friends. I think it's good for the both of them. Sean was always a loner before Declan arrived. I know Declan also has a bit of a soft spot for Jamie as well. I see them hanging out a lot these days. I think Declan is finally starting to realize that he is part of this family, completely."

"And the babies?"

Ray chuckled. "The babies are all great—teething—but great nonetheless. Getting bigger, which you already know. Ben has a bit of a temperature. If it's still there in the morning, I'll have the doctor come out and check him over."

"Do you think it's something bad?"

"No, I think it's something simple. Maybe he has another ear infection. I hope not, but it seems to be looking that way."

"Christ. Poor little mite."

Ray snuggled in closer and breathed in his husband's scent. The thump of Viv's heart lulled him to sleep.

Chapter Seven

Ray was kept busy over the next couple of weeks as they battled with Ben's ear infection. He hated seeing any of the children in pain, and right now Ben needed his unwavering attention. Ray sat in the rocking chair in the play room and rocked Ben while he slept. Fred moved around the room, interacting with everyone, but Ray could see the toll the court case was having on her.

"Fred, come and sit beside me for a while." When she did, he asked, "Talk to me. Tell me what's going on."

Tears filled her eyes. "Byron rang this morning. Damien won. As soon as he has proper accommodation, meaning where Teddy gets his own bedroom, I have to hand him over. The judge asked about Charlotte and he had the audacity to say that he didn't believe Charlotte was his, so now we have to have DNA testing done. I insisted on having them done on both kids, seeing as it gives me more time with Teddy. I don't think I'm ready to let him go."

Ray got up and placed Ben into one of the cribs they had down there. Turning back, he walked over and gathered Fred into his arms. As she wept, he rubbed her back, offering what comfort he could. Could their lives get any bloody more screwed up?

"Shh now, we'll figure something out. What's the use of being richer than sin if we can't do some good with it?" Ray soothed.

Fred trembled in his arms. "It won't matter how much money you have. I've already lost my son. How the hell do I tell Teddy he has to leave us all and go and live with a man he is terrified of?"

"Things will work out in the end. When do you think you're going to tell him?"

"I have to tell him this afternoon. Damien is ringing him tonight and he insisted that Teddy finds out before then, because if I don't tell him, Damien surely will." Fred wiped her eyes and stepped back. "I don't want to do this, Ray. I don't want to lose my baby. Damien will poison him against me and Charlotte."

"None of us want this to happen." Ray wished there was a way to make this all better. "I think you may have to tell Bear and Jamie together. It might be easier that way. If you want, I can be there when you do it."

Sadness tinged her words. "You're right. This family has been through enough without us having to break two more hearts. If we keep going the way we are, this will turn into a house filled with depression."

Ray could see her point. He'd been feeling the same way. "It feels like that some days, doesn't it?"

"Yeah."

* * * *

The afternoon came way too fast for Ray. Josh had volunteered to go and pick the boys up from school. Jamie and Bear smiled up at him as they came in and sat on the couch.

"What's going on? Mum? Ray?" Teddy said.

The boy tensed. It was almost as if he knew what was about to happen. Fred had always been honest with her children, so Teddy knew about the custody battle, even if he tried not to show it.

"Dad won, didn't he?" Sadness filled his voice.

Ray nodded as Fred burst into tears again.

Teddy sighed loudly before turning and pulling a tearful Jamie into his arms. "He won't make me ever stop loving you. We've talked about this. I'll be back for you in six years. He'll have no say over me."

And that broke Ray's heart wide open.

He thought there would be a tantrum or two, but from the scene unfolding before him, it was obvious the boys really had talked about this outcome, about what it would mean for them. Ray wanted to wrap them both up in his arms and tell him that everything was going to be all right, but he knew it wasn't.

They were going to have to do something special to let Bear know that they loved him and wished he could stay. It infuriated Ray that a man would separate his own children just out of spite. Even worse, he was denying one of them completely.

What kind of man did that?

A selfish asshole, that's who.

"When do I have to leave?" Bear asked.

"Your father will be ready for you in a week," Fred answered. "I hate that this is happening."

Bear got up and hugged his mother. "It's not your fault. You're the best mum ever. He can only keep me away until I'm eighteen. I'll be back before you know it."

For someone so young, Ray couldn't believe how bravely Bear was handling the situation. Bear let go of Fred and took Jamie by the hand and led him from the room.

By dinnertime that night, the whole household knew what was happening. Even Dan had rung to talk to both Jamie and Bear. The mood was somber, yet Ray had no doubt everyone in their own way was showing their support for both boys. The sad thing was that Ray could already see Bear was going to be distancing himself from Jamie.

And didn't that just tear at a person's heart.

* * * *

Viv knew he'd find Ray wherever Jamie was. Bear was leaving today. Viv couldn't bear the thought of being at university when his son was going through something so heartbreaking. He found them both in the bedroom Jamie had shared with Bear. Ray was sitting there quietly on the bed while Jamie helped Bear pack. Neither really spoke, but they stopped often for Bear to hug Jamie close.

When Ray saw him he stood and walked to the door. "Love, what are you doing home so early?" he said and lay his head on Viv's shoulder.

"I needed to be here." Viv embraced his husband and pulled him into the hall.

"They're being so brave," Ray whispered.

Viv had the overwhelming urge to take Damien around the back of the house and beat the ever-loving shit out of the man. Even though the DNA results had come back proving Charlotte was Damien's, he didn't believe it and still refused to have anything to do with the child. The sad thing was that Viv believed out of the two siblings Charlotte was the lucky one.

The sound of Jamie and Bear talking broke Viv's heart.

"Hey now, stop crying. It's only six years. They will go by in the blink of an eye. You better keep on track of everything while I'm gone. When I get back, I want to see all the plans you've made for our wedding."

Jamie tearfully replied, "I don't want you to go."

"I know, but I have to. The man can't stand me. I don't know why he even wants me at his place. His wife hates me as well. But I'll get through it, and I'll come back to you. I promise."

"You shouldn't make promises you can't keep," Jamie whispered.

Bear sighed. "I can and I will promise you. That man will not tear us apart. You are mine just as much as I belong to you. Midnight on my eighteenth birthday I will be heading straight back here."

"I'm going to miss you so much."

"I know. I'll figure out a way to get messages to you."

Viv held tightly to Ray as Jamie cried and Bear was trying so hard to comfort Jamie.

Fred approached them from the end of the hall. Damien

was here. Tears filled her eyes. She knocked on the bedroom door and told Bear that his father was waiting downstairs.

Bear cupped Jamie's face in his hands. "I want you to kiss me now and say goodbye to me here. I don't want you anywhere that asshole can spew his venom at you. Stay here with your dads, and look after Char for me. I love you so much."

Viv's tears trickled down his face at the saddest and most beautiful goodbye he had ever seen. He hoped by God that everything worked out, that Bear really could return to them.

But six years was a long time to have to wait.

So much could happen between now and then.

Bear brought Jamie to them and gave him one last hug before he picked up his bag and walked out of sight. Viv scooped Jamie up and held his distraught son in his arms. He wished he could take away all the pain. Ray wrapped himself around them both so that Jamie was cocooned between them. Within minutes, Declan and Sean were there for Jamie as well. Declan had already sworn to make sure Jamie was okay, to make sure he didn't fall into depression, which was the one thing he and Ray were most afraid of happening.

Jamie wiggled to get free. "I'm all right now, but I need to see him leave."

He ran down the hall to the head of the stairs. Viv followed Jamie slowly. Bear was about to step out the front door, but he looked back, and Jamie mouthed 'I love you'. In return, Bear mouthed the same words back. Damien snarled at Jamie, but before he could spew his hatred, Bear closed the door, blocking everyone from their sight. Jamie rushed to the window beside the door and waved while Bear was driven away.

There wasn't a dry eye in the house. No one seemed to want to speak for the longest time.

Charlotte went over to Jamie and wrapped her arms around him. "Don't worry, Jamie. I promised Bear I'd look after you."

Declan and Sean led the kids toward the playroom. Josh took a very upset Fred upstairs to console her. So many people were hurt today because of the vicious nature of one person.

When Ray headed outside, Viv followed, guessing that his husband wanted to talk without little ears listening. They kept going until they were sitting on the bench under Granddad's tree. The very same spot they had been married.

"Do you think in six years Bear will come back?" Ray asked.

Viv thought about it for a moment and decided to be as honest as he could. "Six years of being under Damien's thumb is a long time for Bear to stay who he is. I hope for his sake he can hold on, but the reality is, it will be hard. All we can do is be there for Jamie if things change."

"Why do some parents think it's okay to fuck up their kids' lives?"

Viv knew Ray was talking about more than just Damien and Bear right now. Over the time they had been together, Ray had told him about the problems he'd faced with his own father as a teenager.

"Some parents like to play mind games with their exes. I think this is nothing more than a way to hurt Fred. Damien doesn't care about Bear. Before this, he didn't even want to have anything to do with the kids. This was all about getting control and keeping Fred from seeing and being a part of Bear's life. Byron is fighting the no-visitation right. There is no way Damien can stop Fred from spending time with her son."

Viv whole heartedly agreed. "If Byron does get them, I know Damien will make sure that keeping Bear and Jamie apart will be included in the deal. We're just going to have to grin and bear it. I won't try and do anything that will screw up her chances. I say we do what Bear asks. Let Jamie plan their wedding. If it comes to pass, then great, but honestly, I'm hoping that eventually Jamie will distance himself from it all. That way if Bear doesn't come back, Jamie will be stronger."

"I hope you're right. I'm tired of seeing my children upset and in pain. I just wish things could go back to normal."

"You and me both, love." Viv wrapped his arm around Ray's shoulder. "Who knew parenting would be so heart-wrenching? I certainly didn't."

Ray sat up and turned to face Viv. "Grandma gave Jamie some good advice. She said from today on, Jamie needs to breathe in and out. He's to forget about the past and what might have been. Make plans for the future and change them as necessary. It doesn't mean he has to forget about Bear, but he can't lose himself in Bear's having to go away for a short while."

"Six years is a little more than a short while," Viv countered.

"I know it is. I swear. The Big Guy upstairs has it in for us some days. Haven't we been through our quota of heartache? Maybe it could be someone else's turn for a while," Ray complained.

Viv chuckled. "I hear you. Only this morning I was wondering what I had done in a past life for all this to be happening in this one. Then I realized for all the good times we have, they have to be counterbalanced by the bad. It's the only thing that makes sense."

"That's your scientific mind at work." Ray leaned in and placed a quick kiss on his lips. "Speaking of minds at work — well, this has nothing to do with that — but Byron said Shane was doing well in rehab. He's actually participating and not in a perpetual state of pissed off. He still has a long way to go, and let's hope this does the man some good. Mind you, I still think he should have been charged for hurting you the way he did."

He knew Ray was right, but Viv needed to see if he could help Shane instead of locking him away and making things worse. "I know you do, love. A part of me feels the same way, but if he gets the help he needs, it means he won't ever find himself in the same position again. I think that is better than locking him away and letting him get worse."

To change the subject, even though he knew Girly was another hot topic in the family, he asked, "How are Girly and Nate doing?"

"Weirdly, Girly is both sad and yet the happiest I have seen her in a very long time. I don't know what Mick does for her that Dan can't. Whatever it is, it seems to be working."

"And Nate?"

Ray frowned. "Nate is withdrawing. Declan and Sean spend as much time with him as they can, but now they'll be divided, seeing as they want to be there for Jamie as well. I'm not sure what to do to help him through things. I know he's not mine, but I don't like seeing him hurt either. Somebody has got to show the boy some love. God knows he never got any from his mother. Do you know what she had the audacity to tell the police when they went around and asked for Nate's schooling papers and such? That evil piece of trash told them that her son was dead."

"What happened?" Viv asked curiously.

"They informed her that Nate might be dead to her, but she still needed to hand over what they wanted. In the end, Nate's step-father gave them everything, then she signed away all her rights to Nate. I know he's an adult, but he's missed so much schooling that he has to make it up."

What the fuck is wrong with these people? Why bother even having kids if you didn't want them? Viv really wanted to hit something or someone. "I think we should clear out one of the rooms and set it up as a gym. Maybe it would help the boys work out some of their frustrations."

"I think that's a brilliant plan" — Ray beamed — "since living here and eating Antonio's cooking, I've put on a heap of weight."

Viv looked down at his slender man. "Love, you are perfect just the way you are."

"But I'm fat!" Ray said as he pinched his slight paunch.

"We definitely need that gym."

"Whatever you want, love. I just thought it could be a place for the guys to let off a little steam as they worked out some of their issues. Maybe we can hire someone to oversee everything so no one does anything stupid and winds up physically hurt."

The more Viv thought about it, the better the plan seemed to get. There was more than enough room to hire another staff member. Hell, he even knew of the perfect person. Bodhi Parker was an old acquaintance from when Viv was a teenager. They had gone to school together. Bodhi even went on to become a personal trainer. Back then, they had been inseparable. He might get a shock when he found out Viv was married to another man, though in saying that, the guy would have to be an idiot if he didn't know. Bodhi had been living in America when Viv and Ray had married. When Bodhi had come back to Australia, they had reconnected their friendship through social media sites.

"I have an old friend that might be interested in becoming the gym trainer if we do this. He's someone I met not long after I moved in with Dad. He's been living in America for the last ten years. Bodhi only moved home a month ago."

"Is he gay friendly? I won't have anyone hateful mixing with the family. For the next little bit, I'm going to be very protective of everyone," Ray said.

Viv couldn't agree more. "Last I heard, Bodhi was straight, but he was always open-minded. Though honestly, anything could have happened in the ten years since I last saw him. We could have him meet us and see if he fits with the rest of us."

"Okay, then we'll run this by Grandma and see what she reckons. I don't think she'll have a problem with it. She was only saying the other day that all the boys should take up a hobby."

"Working out is a little more than a hobby, Ray. If we do this, Bodhi would probably know what machinery would be best to purchase. I haven't got a frickin' clue what we'll have to get. He can assess those who want to work out and we can buy accordingly. This might just be what we all needed."

Ray grinned at him. "Especially seeing as money is not a problem. When do you think we can get him around here for a meeting?"

"Let's go and see GG first and ask what she thinks. I know she gave you the house, but she still lives here and it only seems right that we include her in all decisions before we start renovating." Viv stood and pulled Ray to his feet.

"She'll be in the kitchen with Aunt Magen and Uncle Ant. They have something up their sleeve that they aren't telling everyone what's going on. I don't think it's anything to worry about. It's more of a feeling I have."

Entering the kitchen, Viv found out that Ray was right. The three people in question had their heads together as if plotting the downfall of the world.

"What are you all up to?" he said, startling them in the process.

"We're not up to anything," GG denied a little guiltily.

"'Fess up, Grandma. You're fibbing big time, aren't you?" Ray chuckled as he placed a kiss on GG's cheek. "What's the big secret?"

Antonio sighed dramatically and said, "You are going to have to tell them, Mum. They'll just hound you until you do."

Hearing Antonio call GG mum was weird, but at the same time, it was sweet as hell. GG finally spilling the secret about Antonio's connection to the family had brought the two of them closer together.

"I want to do something to cheer everyone up," GG stated.

Viv took a seat at the table and said, "We were thinking along the same lines. Ray and I discussed maybe setting up a gym, and hiring someone to run it. We thought it would give the boys a place to work out their feelings and frustrations."

"That's a good idea, and I'll leave it in your capable hands.

I was thinking more along the lines of what I could do for Fred, Nate and Daniel. I'm sending Antonio to go and bring him home if he hasn't returned by the end of the month. By then, he'll have been gone for long enough. I don't know what to do. A party just seems off for some reason. It would be like asking them to celebrate their broken hearts. Maybe if I could get them involved in something to take their minds off their problems, even if just for a little while."

"Any idea about what you'd like to do?" Ray asked.

GG shook her head. "Not a damn clue. We were tossing around the idea of doing another benefit for Destiny House, but that didn't sit right with us wanting Daniel to help out. Even though he seems clear-headed it would still hurt seeing Girly and Mick together."

"Wait. You've heard from Daniel?" Viv had been waiting for a call and had received nothing.

With a nod, GG answered, "He calls home every day. He's been fishing mad. I told him he needs a haircut, as he's starting to look straggly." She dug her cell phone out of her pocket and handed it over so they could see the pictures. "I don't think he's ready to talk to anyone else yet."

"Well, at least he's talking to someone," Viv murmured.

"He's made a new friend while up there. They've been hanging around together. I think Dan said his name is Toby something or other."

A gasp at the doorway had Viv snapping his head around in time to see Nate walking away with his shoulders slumped. *Fuck! What next?*

"Damnation," GG growled. "Now I've gone and hurt Nate again. The sad thing is I think Dan and Toby really are nothing more than friends. I don't even know if Toby is gay. Dan didn't say, and I didn't ask."

"I'll go after him," Magen said then pushed away from the table.

How many more things would have to go wrong before they'd start going right again? For one day he wanted something to run smoothly. No fighting. No broken hearts.

Just a day of normal, happy, all getting along family. Instead of the cluster-fuck they were living now.

"At dinner tonight we should see who will be interested in having a gym built," Ray said as he leaned into Viv's side. "You know, I've really had enough drama in the last few months to last me a lifetime."

"I couldn't have said it better myself," GG said. "I swear to God that life was never this complicated when I was young."

Ray grinned. "When was that? Were the dinosaurs still roaming the land?"

"Oh my, Ray has such a smart mouth on him. Don't think you're too old to be grounded," she joked.

A giggle from the doorway announced Sean and Jamie standing there. "GG, Pa is too old to be grounded. What did he do anyway?"

"Pa was telling me I was old like a dinosaur." GG pouted.

Jamie narrowed his eyes at Ray. "Pa, that was just mean. Don't you know GG is going to outlive us all?"

The way he spoke with such certainty had Viv trying not to laugh. The look on Ray's face was so astonished at getting reprimanded by Jamie that Viv lost it. He wasn't the only one, and soon the whole room was laughing their asses off.

Viv opened his arms and welcomed Jamie in for a hug. He wanted so badly for Jamie not to hurt over Bear having to leave, but it was inevitable. There wasn't any way to soften the blow. He just hoped the pain lessened in time. At least Jamie had them all to help him through it. Bear had no one but a mean-spirited father and an unwelcoming step-mother. With any luck, he'd make a friend at his new school who would give him a shoulder to lean on. Maybe if they knew where his new school was going to be they could organize information to be passed along on how Bear was coping. Maybe then Damien wouldn't even have to know, and what Damien didn't know wouldn't turn out badly for Bear.

He'd have to wait until he spoke with Fred to get her

opinion on it. He didn't want to start something that was only going to add fuel to Damien's already blazing-out-of-control fire.

Chapter Eight

It amazed Ray how well people could bounce back from bad shit happening in their lives. Even though he knew they were all still hurting, Ray saw both Nate and Jamie re-emerging from their self-imposed quiet time. Both were still subdued, but at least they were again willing to interact with the family. Thankfully, both Nate and Jamie were included in everything Sean and Declan did, whether it was hanging out watching movies, or working out in the newly built gym. They had taken a couple of rooms at the far side of the play room. Ray couldn't stand to be too far away from the babies in case he was needed. Poor Ben's ears were still giving him hell. The doctor was talking about having grommets put in. Ray wasn't sure he wanted to do that, but if it helped Ben, who was he to argue?

"Dad, are you even listening to me?" Girly snapped her fingers in front of his face.

"Sorry, I was thinking about Ben and his sore ears," Ray admitted. "What did you want?"

Girly asked, "I was wondering if you've heard from Dan yet? He's been gone for months."

"Why would that matter to you?" Ray wanted to find out where she was going with all of this.

"It matters to me because he's being a dick by staying away and breaking my brother's heart. If Dan doesn't wake up and come home soon, someone else will have snapped Nate up right from under his nose." Girly growled before adding, "How well did you know this Bodhi guy? Where did he live before he came to work for us?"

Ray shrugged. "I didn't know him at all. He's a friend of

Viv's from high school."

"Well, if you want my opinion, and I know you do, the man is taking a little too much interest in Nate. He needs to back the fuck off. Nate is meant to be with Daniel." His daughter was more than a little cranky.

Her antic bemused Ray to no end. "Girly, one of these days you're going to have to realize that you don't rule the world. People have the right to live their lives the way they want to. I thought you would have learned by now that trying to force two people together doesn't work. In fact, you should already know it only ends up pushing people away. You need to stop now before you lose your brother completely. The only reason he's still here is because of Aunt Magen. You're lucky she loves Nate like her own son, because nothing I've said to him was getting through."

Girly rolled her eyes. "Dad, Nate loves me. There's no way he'd ever leave. Especially not with Declan here. Those two are as thick as thieves."

"So tell me, how are things going with Mick?" Ray took her by the arm and led her into one of the smaller sitting rooms for a bit of privacy. He needed to change the subject from the dangerous path it was on.

Her face brightened in a beautiful smile. "You know I always thought I was happy with Dan. I loved him more than life itself, but with Mick, it's — I don't know — somehow all better. Everything is just better. I feel with Mick that I'm his whole world. I love being at Destiny House and assisting him in the kitchen cooking for the residents, and helping out with everything else involved. With Dan, I knew he loved me, but I knew I was never going to be enough. There was always a small part of him that needed male company. I'd see him talking to men and I'd get the feeling he'd be quite happy being in love with a man, and only a man. I don't think he'd crave a woman. Does that make sense?"

"Weirdly, yes it does. But that doesn't mean Daniel will be happy with Nate," Ray pointed out.

"I think you're wrong. Before I broke things off with Dan,

I watched him—a lot. I don't think he's willing to admit it, but I think his feelings for Nate are more than merely a misguided crush. If he would just open up his eyes, he'd see I'm telling the truth." Girly sighed. "He really *is* in love with Nate."

Ray believed Girly was probably right, but regardless her actions had caused a whole world of hurt to everyone involved. There was no going back from what had happened. The only thing the three of them could do now was take the first steps into tomorrow.

"I don't doubt you're telling the truth, but it doesn't mean much if we can't get Dan to own up to his feelings. Nate is pretty much an open book, yet I doubt he'll ever make a move toward Dan without some sort of signal that Dan is willing to acknowledge and reciprocate the same feelings."

"Can't we just slap some sense into them or something?"

Ray chuckled at the thought of doing just that. "No. I don't think causing physical harm is going to do anyone any good."

"Well, it's worth a try. And I'm not kidding, someone needs to tell Bodhi that Nate is off limits to him."

"Girly, I think Bodhi is straight. Well, Viv says he is."

She snorted. "Have you seen him around Nate? If he's straight, I'll eat my shoes. He's a little too hands-on where my brother is concerned."

"If he is, I don't think you get much of a say in it. Nate is a big boy. He's old enough to make his own decisions in life. You have to let him bloom instead of conforming him into whatever you think he should be. He doesn't need you to show him the way. Besides, if you didn't want Dan, Nate will be having second thoughts about his own feelings. Maybe he's even thinking Dan isn't a good option."

"Christ! I only did what I did to make them all happy and now it seems like I was just being a selfish jerk only looking out for me. I swear that wasn't what I was planning. I love both Dan and Nate and only want them both to be happy— together."

Even agreeing with her reasons, Ray knew he still had to try and get her to see the whole picture. "You need to take a step back. Let Dan and Nate figure it out for themselves. Live your life, and let them live theirs. If they end up together, then great. If not, that's okay too. But the choice has to be theirs, and theirs alone."

"I know you're right. It's just hard to sit back and watch it all go down the shit chute when I know being together would make them both happy. How can I just stand back and let them ruin what could be?"

"Girly, for the love of God, don't interfere. Don't do anything that will fuck this up any more. I love you to death, but this time I'm ordering you to stay the hell out of it." Ray hated the anger that surged through him. Deep down, he knew Girly was just like him, always searching for ways to help whoever needed it. The only problem was, Girly acted without thinking, which was a very bad trait to have. At least Ray stepped back when needed — well, most of the time.

Girly sighed. "I promise. I'll stay out of it. But that doesn't mean I won't enlist the help of the rest of my siblings. I'm sure they all want to see Nate and Dan together and happy."

"Jesus, Girly, just let it go."

"Dad." Girly giggled. "When have you ever known me to just sit back and watch? I won't let them know I'm pulling the strings or anything. Mick will understand when I explain it all to him."

Ray knew there was no way in hell Girly was going to let this go. She was going to cajole everyone around her to move things in the direction she wanted. He hoped like hell it didn't backfire. He was going to have to take the others aside and urge them not to do Girly's bidding. Ray also hoped his daughter was right in the belief that her new boyfriend would be okay with her meddling — somehow, he doubted it.

"Are you home for dinner tonight?" he asked her, again wanting to change the subject before he got too pissed off at her and really started yelling.

"Nah, GG asked me to take some paperwork over to Norman, Tarni and Brent at Destiny House. So I thought I'd go and help Mick. Did GG tell you Brent and Tarni have moved into the small mother-in-law flat at the back of the house? Norman has the master bedroom. I stay in Mick's room when I don't come home. One day I want to bring him here for a meal so he can get to properly meet my family. He's afraid of upsetting everyone, but I reassured him our family isn't like that."

Ray sighed. "Maybe organize it for a day before Dan gets home. I don't want to blindside him as soon as he comes back. But you're right. We can't ignore Mick because Dan still lives here."

"I was hoping you would say that, because GG told me to bring him here for dinner tomorrow night."

"Why did you ask for my opinion if you and GG already have it all worked out?" Ray asked.

She rolled her eyes before answering, "Because I want you to talk to everyone else so they don't treat Mick disrespectfully. He doesn't deserve that. I may have fucked up and upset the family, but Mick is a good guy."

"When have any of us ever treated anyone disrespectfully? Apart from Grace, I mean." Ray felt a touch of anger at his daughter's words. Where the hell did she get off demanding things when she'd caused the problem in the first place? "Invite him around, he'll be treated no differently than anyone else. Just warn him that little kids blurt shit out, and not to take anything to heart."

Ray kissed Girly on the forehead before he got up and walked away. He needed a breath of fresh air. To take a moment just for himself where no one demanded his undivided attention. He sneaked out of the front door and made his way around the house to his grandma's garden. Once upon a time it was all roses, but now the garden itself was very eclectic with a variety of plants and colors, though his favorite spot was near the small bed of original roses.

He sat on the stone bench lining one bed.

On days like today, Ray needed a quiet place to think. Naturally his thoughts drifted to family matters. Jamie, Nate and Declan had all taken to working out in the gym. Ray loved the fact the three of them had formed a close bond. Some days Sean joined them, but not often. As he repeatedly told them all, he wasn't into exercising. Sitting there, Ray took a moment to think about each of his children—all ten of them. Of course, since Nate's arrival, he was also included in that count. The babies all seemed content and happy in life. Hopefully, he wouldn't have to start worrying about them for a few more years. In the month since Bear had left, Ray's heart still went out to Jamie. Even though he was living his life, Ray saw he wasn't the same vibrant young boy he used to be. These days he was more subdued. Declan, on the other hand, finally seemed to realize he belonged with the family. Ray no longer thought Declan was waiting for the day he would be asked to leave. The friendship he had with Sean was nice, but Ray suspected there were unrequited feelings in the mix and hoped it didn't send everything pear-shaped later on down the track. This was something they would have to keep an eye on, and be there for any fallout.

The biggest problems Ray could see revolved around the adult children. Girly was both happy and sad. He wished she would just let go of the past and concentrate on her future with Mick. She needed to stop trying to organize everything the way she thought it should be. Dan...well, he wouldn't know about Dan until he finally came home. His few weeks away was bordering on four months now. Enough was enough. Ray wanted his family back together. Lastly, Ray had been carefully watching Nate. For some reason, he got the feeling Nate blamed himself for what happened between Dan and Girly. No matter what anyone said, they couldn't seem to make him see the truth of what had gone on.

"You look like you're thinking some deep thoughts, my

love."

Ray snapped his head up and smiled at Viv. He'd been so caught up in his own head he hadn't even heard Viv approaching. "Just thinking about our family. How did you know where I was?"

"Jamie, who else?" Viv stepped closer and sat beside him. "That boy knows more about this family than the rest of us combined. When I was looking for you, he told me to try your thinking spot in the garden – and here you are."

"He really does." Ray leaned into his husband as Viv captured his mouth in a soft and sensual kiss.

He needed this. The taste of Viv always made Ray warm inside. It was like his body trembled from the inside out. The deeper the kiss went, the more heated Ray became. Pinpricks of pleasure skittered across his skin. Before he knew it, Viv had picked him up and maneuvered him until he was straddling Viv's lap.

Yes, this was definitely what he needed.

Sometimes the stress of being a full-time parent to so many was hard to cope with. He loved each of his children and wouldn't change anything in his life. The truth was, he just hadn't bargained for how time-consuming everything was going to be. Some mornings it felt like he was worn out before the day had even begun.

And today was one of those days.

"How are you doing, Ray? We've been so caught up in everyone else's drama that I know it has to be wearing on you. If you feel half of what I do, then you have to be bloody knackered."

"Truthfully, I'm tired. I want the magical ability to turn back the clock so I can change the outcome of certain events. I know the way things are now is how they were meant to be, but I'd at least take away the hurt and stress." Ray shook his head. "Girly wants to invite Mick around for tea with the family."

"She should. If we start acting all strange, it will never become comfortable again. I know if Dan were here it would be strained, but Girly is right. If Dan's feelings are really strong for Nate, he would have never been fully happy staying within his relationship with her. She only did what he would have eventually done. Sad as it is to admit, I think my brother will get over it a lot quicker than the other two will. He always was one to bounce back."

"I love you. Have I told you that today?"

Viv kissed him again. "You always let me know how much I mean to you. I love hearing it, though. So feel free to tell me as often as you like." He kissed Ray again. "And just so you know. I love you just as much."

Viv held his husband within his embrace, and just soaked up his closeness. He knew they couldn't stay here for long, but this was nice.

"We have to go back inside, don't we? I need to put on my big boy pants and be with the family. I need to have a smile on my face and act like everything is okay, when, in reality, all I want to do is cry," Ray said.

"Yeah, we do. You're not in this alone." Viv helped Ray to his feet. "At least we can do it together. You be my strength, and I'll be yours."

Ray wrapped his arm around Viv's waist as they began walking and it felt good—right. Their first port of call was to where the babies were. They found the five youngest children in the nursery with Nate and Fred. Since the craziness Girly had brought down on them, Nate had been spending more and more time with the younger kids, and surprisingly, he was good at it.

"How's everything going in here?" Viv asked after he and Ray entered the room.

Nate looked up from where he sat in a rocking chair holding Ben. "He's just fallen asleep. I hope he sleeps for a bit longer this time around."

"You and me both," Ray said as he crossed the room to them.

Viv, on the other hand, walked over to Jeb, who was

fussing in the cradle. "What's the matter, little man?" He picked his son up and cuddled him close.

Fred chuckled from where she sat to the side with Charlotte and Millie. "These kids have you wrapped around their fingers, don't they?"

"They always have," Viv agreed. "Even the grownup ones."

"Yes, he's talking about you too," Fred said to Nate, who seemed completely dumbfounded.

Nate shook his head. "But why? I'm not really family."

"Bullshit!" Viv stated. He couldn't understand how Nate was still in denial. "You're part of Girly's family, which makes you part of ours. The sooner you believe that, the easier it will be for all of us."

"What he said," Ray stated.

The door opened and Jamie, Declan and Sean trooped in. Jamie walked right into Ray's arms for a hug. All the kids seemed to gravitate to Ray when they were hurting. Viv loved how Ray immediately opened his arms to them. No matter who it was.

Declan and Sean badgered Nate until he put Ben in his cot, then they dragged him from the room. Viv wondered for a second what was going on.

"They're going to watch scary movies in Sean's room," Jamie said before he could ask.

"Didn't you want to watch them?" Viv asked.

Jamie shook his head. "No way. I'd have nightmares for months if I watched anything like that. They said later they'll watch a movie I want."

"That sounds nice," Fred said from where she sat.

"Bear liked watching scary movies." A sad look settled on Jamie's face. "I miss him. Clara told me Damien won't let Bear talk to me."

Concern filled Viv. "Who's Clara?"

"She's a girl at Bear's new school. She emailed me to let me know Bear was okay." Jamie turned to Fred before continuing. "Did you know Damien moved Bear to Western

Australia? I thought he wasn't allowed to take Bear out of the state."

By the look of fury on Fred's face this was news to her.

Viv said, "You didn't know, did you?"

"He can't do that, can he?" Fred asked and got to her feet. "He didn't even tell me."

"Ring Byron. He'll be able to tell you for sure. I wouldn't have thought so, but I guess it all depends on the custody outcome. Did he get full custody?"

Fred frowned and headed for the door. "Full, but we still had to come to terms about visitation rights. We're still waiting to hear back from the court."

"Did I say something wrong?" Jamie asked.

"No," Viv was quick to reassure his son. "So, you have been in touch with Bear? How is he?"

Jamie shrugged. "He wants to come home. I don't think his friend likes me too much. The way she talks, it's like Bear is her boyfriend. Do you think he likes her better than me now?"

"No, I don't think he likes her more," Viv blustered, not sure what he was supposed to say.

"I think now that he is so far away he'll forget about me. It would be easier for him. Maybe then his dad wouldn't be so mad all the time. Clara told me Bear thinks it's all my fault." A tear trickled down Jamie's cheek.

Something just wasn't adding up here. Before Viv could even fathom out what to say, Ray jumped into the conversation.

"Bear would never blame you. I don't think you should talk to this Clara anymore." Ray hugged Jamie close.

How could someone be so cruel as to lay the blame of a vindictive father at the feet of an almost twelve-year-old boy? His heart broke when Jamie explained.

"She's my only link to Bear. If I stop talking to her, I lose Bear completely."

The rawness of the words tore at Viv. How was it possible for someone so young to be so wise? "Oh, little man, unless you hear the words from Bear's lips, I wouldn't believe a word this Clara has to say to you."

"Declan said I have to let Bear go. If he is meant to come back to me, he will. Dec doesn't want me to be sad anymore, but I can't help it."

Viv knelt in front of Jamie. "Declan does have a point, but no one can tell you how you are meant to feel. Bear leaving will hurt for a long time, but he'll always be here." Viv laid his hand over Jamie's heart. "No one can ever take him away from there."

"I know, but it's still hard, Dad. Why did Damien have to be so mean and take him away? I want to hate him for doing it, but I can't because he's still Bear's father."

"You're a good person, Jamie. I don't know what to tell you except to say I think Declan is right. Only Bear can decide if he's coming back or not. Nothing any of us do can change the circumstances. I think, in the end, you'll have to wait until Bear comes of age and can legally decide for himself."

Jamie sighed. "A lot can happen in six years. What if he decides he doesn't love me anymore?"

"I don't know, sweetheart. I guess that's a bridge we'll have to cross when we get to it." Viv wanted to yank Jamie into his arms for a big hug, but knew there was no way in hell Ray was letting go any time soon. So, instead, he leaned forward and encompassed both of them into the hug he needed. He knew he and Ray would have some talking to do tonight. Out of all of the dramas unfolding lately, Jamie worried him the most. He was showing depressive characteristics like Daniel had always suffered with. Maybe shit like that ran in the genetics of a family. He hoped not. Dragging Daniel out of his funks had been troubling enough. Sadly, Jamie was at the same age Daniel was when he'd first been diagnosed as having a depressive nature. Maybe they needed to take Jamie to see a doctor. Ray would know what to do.

"I almost forgot." Jamie's face brightened. "GG says it's

the staff's night off so we are having take-out for dinner. Sean and Declan want chicken, but GG and I want Chinese food. We need to make up a list of what we want so it can be delivered. I want the sweet chili beef, and GG wants prawn-fried rice and honey pork balls. We'll need prawn crackers as well, can't have Chinese without them."

Ray cackled. "Sounds like a plan, little man."

"Hold on." Viv walked to the craft area and grabbed a piece of paper and wrote down his and Ray's orders. He added fried rice for Ben and Millie, who both loved rice dishes. "You'll have to go and get everyone else's choices before taking it back to GG."

"We already have. I just had to get both of yours, and Nate. Bodhi has gone out to a friend's place, so he won't be home. I think Josh ordered for him, Fred and Charlotte. Uncle Ant and Aunt Magen have gone to Nan and Pop's place for dinner."

Viv stood and walked Jamie to the door. "Make sure they order plenty of sweet-and-sour sauce."

"I will." Jamie waved as he headed back to wherever GG was currently at.

When he was sure they were alone, Viv turned and wrapped his arms around Ray. He held on for dear life. Ray trembled as much as he did. Viv figured now was as good as a time as any to get it all out. "Do you think we need to take Jamie to see a doctor? He seems to be showing the same early warning signs Dan did when he was a kid. Not that you would know it, but Dan was diagnosed as manic depressive in his early teenage years."

"God! I think you're right. Did you see how he just swapped from sad to happy in an instant—it was like flipping a switch. I've never had to deal with this sort of thing before. I'd rather he gets treated now and not down the track when he's gotten worse."

"I worry that with everything going on, we are neglecting parts of our lives without meaning to. How, or rather, when did our lives become so complicated?" Viv led Ray back over to the group of chairs in the corner.

Ray shrugged. "We had kids. I love them to death, but oh my God, can they be tiring. And GG wonders why I don't have time to go out performing with the band anymore. I don't think she believed me when I told her there was more to life than just music. The sad part is, I've been so tired of late that I keep worrying that I'm letting things slide with you. It seems like months since we last had time to make love."

"It's been…" Viv frowned. "God, I can't even remember. I think we should have an early mark tonight. Once the kids are down for the count, we can step back and take time for ourselves. If I'm honest, I think we could both use it."

Usually, sex was a dominant in their lives, but Ray was right. Family drama was keeping them apart and busy. Not that Viv begrudged having such a large family. He loved them all. If anyone asked what his greatest wish was, Viv would tell them five minutes of peace and quiet, where everything in the world was good.

Is that too much to ask for?

Apparently it was.

"I think once Dan gets his ass home, we'll need to have a family meeting. I want everyone to be honest and open with each other. I don't want anything like what Girly brought down on us to happen again. I think we also need to get Dan to man the fruit-cup-up and come home."

Viv bit back a grin at the way Ray swapped out his swear word in case any of the youngsters were awake. Not that he thought the babies would understand what was being said, but Millie was at the age where she'd repeat anything she heard. Last week Viv, had to force himself to remain calm when she'd popped up and said, 'Pop's a douche bag.' Viv had no idea where she would have overheard it, but Sean and Declan became way more interested in their food than the conversation flowing around the table.

"After the kids have been tucked up for the night, I'll call Dan and ask him to come home. Then as soon as that's done, I'll be ready and willing to let you ravish me."

"That definitely sounds like a very good plan."

Chapter Nine

"Have you called Dan yet?" Ray asked, not even giving his husband time to sit on the edge of the bed. It had been a week since they'd discussed calling him home, and so far, they hadn't been able to make contact. They knew he was still alive as GG had gotten someone to go check on him.

Viv shook his head. "I keep getting his voicemail. The shit is ignoring me on purpose."

"What are we going to do about it?" Ray was tired of having his family torn apart. Tired of having everything so disrupted. He knew he wasn't the only one who was feeling this way.

"Not we—you. I think if you go to him, he'll listen to you. You've always been the glue holding this family together. He'll come home if you ask him."

Ray wasn't sure if that were true or not, but he understood someone needed to go and tell Dan to snap out of it. The problem was, he really wasn't sure that forcing Dan back to the family wasn't going to backfire on them.

"When should I go?" Ray sighed.

"GG made arrangements for you to leave in a couple of hours. I just know if I go, we'll only butt heads and he'll stay away even longer."

Viv was right. He and Dan clashed when both were being stubborn asses. "Fine. I guess I had better start packing, then."

"Thank you, love." Viv seemed to visibly relax now that Ray had agreed to go.

Ray quickly threw together an overnight bag. He didn't plan on being gone long enough to require more than a couple days' worth of clothes. No sooner was he done when he turned and Viv was there ready to haul him into a hug. This was just what he needed. He laid his head on Viv's shoulder and relaxed into his husband's body.

"I hope soon we'll get to have one angst-free day. All this drama is liable to drive me nuts," Ray mumbled. He loved the way Viv kept sliding his hands all over his back. Weirdly, it was helping to drain the stress he was feeling. "I'm going to miss you."

Viv chuckled. "Then how about we send you off with something to remember me by?"

When Viv pulled him toward the bed, Ray's body flamed in anticipation. Their lovemaking this time was going to be hard and fast, and Ray was going to love every second of it. He willing gave himself over to the sensation of being loved.

"Clothes off, Ray. I need skin," Viv said while he helped Ray out of his shirt.

Ray wasn't fighting his husband at all. He wanted the exact same thing. The fewer clothes, the better, as far as he was concerned. In his haste to get out of his pants, Ray tripped and landed face first on the bed. A groan escaped him at the sensation of a tender kiss was placed on his left ass cheek. Looking back over his shoulder, he saw Viv kneeling naked on the floor behind him. Apparently, Viv had no trouble in shedding his clothes.

The heated gaze Viv sent his way had fireworks exploding inside Ray, leaving behind waves of warmth. He moaned in pleasure as his lover quickly breached his body with his finger and began stretching him. The question was, how the hell did Viv have time to undress and get the lube? The man must have secret powers, which were now just coming to life. The feeling of Viv making Ray's body ready was almost enough to send him over the edge before they had even started.

"Christ, Viv. I'm ready. If you take much longer, this will all be over before you even get inside of me. Fuck me now, before Grandma sends someone up to get me."

Viv chuckled behind him, and Ray hissed as the wonderfully talented fingers inside him were withdrawn. As sad as he was to lose their touch, he couldn't wait for what was to come. Ray gasped when Viv grabbed him by the hips and yanked him up onto his hands and knees. The pressure of his lover's cock against his hole was almost too much to bear. He needed Viv inside him. They didn't have time for Viv to be leisurely. "Hurry."

A shiver crashed over his body with the gentleness of how Viv entered him. The one thing he would never get used to was how much he loved being with Viv this way. His husband had the knack of sending his body into overdrive with just the slightest of touches. The slide of their lovemaking was like his blood had turned into molten lava, and he wouldn't change one damn thing about it.

Ray wanted so much for this moment to last, but his own body wasn't going to allow it to happen. Sweat ghosted over his skin with the rapid pace Viv had set. The words of love spilling out of Viv's mouth only fed the liquid fire rolling through him. His whole body clenched with unrestrained want, his orgasm dragging him toward completion. Ray knew Viv was close. His thrusts were becoming erratic, his words incoherent. The grip Viv had on his hips tightened, then Viv came, heat filled Ray, and it was enough to shove Ray over the edge and into his own oblivion.

With his heart racing, Ray collapsed onto the bed, and Viv followed him. Ray relaxed back into Viv's arms. He smiled at the way Viv kept shelling out kisses over his neck and shoulders, as though he was making up for lost time.

"Just how long do you think I'll need to be gone?" Ray chuckled.

"Too long," Viv answered in between kisses. "I guess I should let you get up and shower if you're going to make your flight."

Again, Ray chuckled. "It will be your fault if I'm late. You'll have to explain to Grandma what kept me, if she asks."

"I think she will know without me having to tell her anything."

"You're probably right about that. Grandma has a way of just knowing." Ray reluctantly extracted himself from the tangle they lay in and headed for a quick shower.

By the time he was finished, Viv had pulled out a new set of clothes for him. "Do you really think Dan is going to listen to me?"

"If he's going to listen to anyone, it'll be you. Dan can be a stubborn mule when he wants to be. But you, my love, have the patience of a saint. If anyone can get him to talk, it'll be you. You better go say goodbye to our babies, or you'll be fretting the whole entire time you're gone."

"Sounds like a plan."

* * * *

Ray shook his head when he arrived at the airport and found his grandmother already seated on the plane. "If you were coming with me, why didn't you just wait for me at the house? We could have driven here together."

"Unlike you, I had other things to do before I came here. I told your father I'd be home within three days. We need Dan to get his head out of his ass and come home," his grandma stated as she patted the seat beside her.

"I hope you're right. Though, I must admit, I can understand him needing time out. I wouldn't want to live in the same house as my ex…having them parade their new lover in front of me every day," Ray explained.

Grandma snorted. "Of course he can deal with it and move on. You did. You stood by and watched your girlfriend marry your best friend. You didn't crumble in a heap and cry 'why me'. You did the right thing and became part of the wedding party. If you can do it, so can Dan."

"My situation was a little different, Grandma. I loved B, but I wasn't *in* love with her, if that makes sense." As much as he loathed to admit it, he knew he was telling the truth. B was more like his best friend than his soul mate. He'd found that in Viv. Every day for the rest of his life, he would thank the be-all-and-end-all that he and Viv had met. Their rough start only proved to be the concrete that now held their foundation together. The best kind of love was the sort one had to work at every day of his or her life. That way you knew it was strong and worth fighting for.

"I know Dan was hurt, but so was Girly when Dan told her he had feelings for Nate. She might pretend she wasn't, but you know Girly as well as I do. Yes, she may have fallen in love with someone else, but she wouldn't have even gone there if Dan's eyes and heart hadn't gone roaming first."

His Grandma was making sense, yet Ray knew things weren't always so black and white when it came to matters of the heart. He didn't think Dan was going to see it quite the same way.

"I guess we'll see what we're up against when we get there. If he's really not ready to come home, we can't force him. Although, if he's just being a stubborn ass, then we'll give him a swift kick to get him moving," Ray said.

Deep down, he figured Dan was being stubborn, basically because he had screwed up in leaving. Guilt could do that to a person. All along he'd blamed Girly for what had gone down, but now he wasn't so sure it was all her fault. Grandma, being the wise soul that she was, was probably closer to the truth than he'd been.

Shit! I'll have some ass kissing to do with Girly when I get home.

* * * *

The drive from the airport to the cabin was as picturesque as ever. It was just a pity they were coming here for the reasons they were instead of bringing the whole family along.

When the cabin came into view, Ray spoke, "Do you think

he's going to be very receptive?"

"Dan's expecting us. I sent him a message before we left," Grandma said.

Ray pulled the car into the drive. He had to wonder if Dan would actually be here waiting or if he'd taken off after he'd gotten the text from GG. He breathed a sigh of relief when the front door opened and Dan walked out onto the front porch. Even though he was there, Ray could tell he wasn't happy. If Grandma noticed, she ignored it.

"I hope you have the kettle on. I could do with a nice cup of tea," Grandma said as soon as she got out of the car.

Ray let her go and greet Dan first. He took a moment and grabbed their luggage from the trunk. He knew he was drawing out the time before he had to have 'the talk' with Dan. It seemed weird now that he was here. Why did he let Viv talk him into coming?

"I wondered how long it would take before Viv sent you after me," Dan said with a smirk. "I expected you a lot sooner than this."

"If you had wanted to talk to me, you could have just said so. You know I would have come." Ray placed the bags on the porch and pulled Dan into a hug. "I'm always here if you need me."

Dan relaxed into his embrace, and Ray held him tightly for a second. "We should go inside before Grandma comes back looking for us."

"Yeah, let's get the lecture over and done with, because I know she'll have something to say."

"She cares for you just as the rest of us do. I guess we didn't expect you to stay away this long."

Ray picked up the bags and followed Daniel inside. He sat the bags beside the couch and headed into the kitchen. Grandma was busy making them all something to drink.

"Okay, let's hear it," Dan said after he sat at the table.

Grandma finished making their beverages before she turned. "You need to come home."

"What if I don't want to?" Dan asked.

123

Ray stayed in the doorway and waited to hear what Grandma had to say.

"You fucked up. You *and* Girly both did."

He was surprised by the words she used. It wasn't often he heard his grandma swear.

"You have to suck it up, princess, and come home, get on with living," Grandma said.

A frown formed on Dan's face. "My fiancée left me. I can't just get over that."

"She wouldn't have left you if you didn't tell her you had feelings for her brother. Girly moved on, that's true. But answer me this—would you want to stay in a relationship where your partner's feelings were divided? Maybe if it had been anyone other than Nate, she could have handled it. She did what she needed to do for her, and yes, your feelings got hurt. What you did is mess with two people's heads then made it worse by walking away. You need to come home and sort this shit out. Your time with Girly is over, and as sad as that is, it's not the end of the world. You still care for her. Now it will just be in a different form."

Grandma had hit the nail on the head, saying it much better than Ray ever could have.

"What about Nate?" Daniel asked.

"Nate is another story. If you truly do have feelings for him, then I'd say you have a lot of making up to do where he is concerned. He's blaming himself for everything, and it's affecting his relationship with his sister. He trying hard to pretend it's not, but we all see the truth."

Sadness washed over Dan's features.

Ray wished he could pull him into another hug, but knew this was something Daniel needed to hear. "We're not saying this is all your fault, however you can go a long way in helping make everything better, but like Grandma said, I think if you really would like to be with Nate, you're going to have to show him that he matters to you."

"I just worry what people will think if I was engaged to Girly, then all of a sudden I'm dating her brother," Dan admitted.

Grandma snorted. "Who cares what people think? As long as two people love each other, it doesn't matter what anyone else has to say about it. You left, and Girly and Nate have been picking up the slack at the nightclub. Viv gave you the everyday running of it and you walked away." Grandma reached across the table and patted Daniel on the arm. "Come home. Lay the guilt aside. Live your life the best you can. If things between you and Nate work out, we'll all support you. You know even Girly would be happy for you. Why do you think she pushed so hard to get you two together?"

The way Grandma spoke, Ray understood she had a better handle on the whole situation than he and Viv had. "Grandma's right. It's time for you to come home. Everyone misses you — yes, including your brother. He's very worried about you. More than he's willing to admit."

"I've messed up, haven't I?" Daniel asked.

"Maybe just a little bit." Ray crossed the room and took a seat beside Daniel.

Sighing deeply, Daniel nodded. "Okay. I'll come home, but that doesn't mean I'm going to pursue my feelings for Nate. Not right now, at least. I still have a lot of stuff to work out inside my own head."

"That's fine. Now let's have a lovely evening here and tomorrow we'll head home," Grandma said. "I'm so hungry I could just about eat Old Reg all by myself."

Daniel chuckled. "I don't have any fish, but I do have a couple of nice steaks. I was going to head out tomorrow for a grocery run, but it looks like I don't have to now."

"Sounds like a plan," Grandma said.

Ray stood. "I think I'll let Viv know that we've arrived, and we'll be coming home tomorrow."

* * * *

Viv reached for the phone on the bedside table as soon as

it started ringing. He smiled when he saw Ray's beautiful face on the screen. "I take it you made it okay."

"Yeah, about half an hour ago. We sat and had a cuppa while Grandma spoke with Dan."

"And?"

Ray answered, "We'll be coming home tomorrow."

Viv sat up on the side of the bed and watched the warning scroll across the bottom of the screen. "That might not be possible. What's the weather like there?"

"What's going on? It's a little drizzly, but nothing to be worried about."

"Um, Ray, your area is about to be hit with flash flooding. You need to turn on the telly or a radio and find out what's happening. Maybe see if you're going to be able to get out." Viv tried not to panic, especially since he wasn't sure how bad the situation really was.

He heard Ray opening a door. "Hold on, I'm going out to the lounge to let Grandma and Dan know."

"Ray, what's the matter?" Viv heard GG ask.

Ray's voice sounded muffled. "Viv says we're about to be hit by a huge storm, maybe even some flash flooding. Hold on, let me put the phone on speaker. Can you hear me, love?"

"Loud and clear." In the background, the news report was coming over the line. He muted his own telly so he could pay attention to what was going on.

Ray swore. "Damn, you're right. I don't think we'll be getting out anytime soon. Hell, we must have just made it through some parts before it got bad."

"I'm going out to check the creek. I'll be back in a minute," Dan said.

The screen door slammed.

"What's going on?"

GG came over the line. "Stop panicking, Viv. We don't know what's happening yet. Dan is just coming back."

"The water's rising. I think we should start moving anything of value to the upper level."

"Viv, I have to go. I will call you back when we get the stuff moved."

The line went dead, and true panic hit Viv like a freight train. The first thing he did was call Girly so he could fill her in on what was happening. She answered almost immediately.

"It's flooding at the cabin," Viv blurted out before she could talk. "The creek is rising, and they are starting to move everything to the higher floor."

"Fuck!"

"My sentiments exactly," Viv stated.

Girly's voice faded out for a moment as she spoke to someone else at her end, then she seemed to turn her attention back to Viv. "I'm at Nan and Pop's. What are we going to do? Hold on, Pop says we're coming over."

"Okay, I'll see you soon."

The little ones weren't going to understand what was going on, but Viv knew he'd need to tell everyone else. He made his way down through the house to where dinner was almost ready. The noise from the dining room was loud. His worry must have shown on his face.

"Dad, are you okay?" Declan asked.

Viv shook his head. By now, he had everyone's attention. "The cabin is about to be hit by a major storm cell. Dan says the creek is rising. So Dan, GG and Pa are trying to save us much as they can by moving it to the second floor."

"But they're going to be all right, right?" Jamie asked.

He didn't want to lie to the kids. The worry on each of the adults' faces around the table wasn't good. "I'm not sure. I'll have to wait for Pa to ring me back."

"How did you find out?" Uncle Ant asked.

Viv swallowed, hard. "I was watching the news when Ray called. There was a warning scrolling across the bottom of the screen. I told Ray to turn on his TV, Dan went and checked the creek, and now they're moving everything."

"The cabin is only a split level. If the water rises really high, they'll be…"

Ant broke off and Viv understood he didn't want to worry the children further. "Liam, Claire and Girly are on their way over. Probably even Mick, if he was with Girly."

He was rambling. He knew he was and didn't have a hope in hell of stopping himself. He was grateful when Aunt Magen walked over to him and hugged him tightly.

"They're going to be all right. With Catherine there, there is no way they can be anything but... GG is too damn stubborn to let a little water cause her trouble."

Viv wanted to believe her, but without seeing it with his own eyes, he knew he was going to worry. "I'm sorry, I don't think I'm going to be able to eat," Viv whispered.

"Yes, you can. If you don't then nobody else will want to either, and the kids need to eat. So sit down and pretend none of this is happening. Once it's over and done with, the little ones can go to bed, and the rest of us can sit and worry together," Aunt Magen said then led Viv to his usual seat.

Viv had never seen her be so vehement before. He knew she was right, so, sucking it up, he forced himself to eat with the rest of the family, not that he could taste anything. In his state of apprehension, everything seemed to be flavored like cardboard. He wanted to be with Ray. If Ray was going to be in danger, then Viv needed to be there to protect him. Tears burned behind his eyes as he realized three of the people he cared about the most were at risk of being hurt. He didn't think his heart could take it.

After dinner, Viv led the way to the sitting room. Josh and Fred took the younger kids upstairs to get them ready for bed. The sound of Liam's voice reached him long before the man entered the room. Girly and Mick followed behind, and Claire had gone to help with the babies.

Girly was on the phone. When she hit the loud speaker, he knew it was someone at the cabin. Dan's voice was clear if not a little shaken. "We're really fine. Ray lost his iPhone to the water. Maybe it will dry out, but I think it may be fucked."

"I couldn't get through. I was so freaking worried. We

just got to the house," Girly said. She placed the phone on the coffee table in front of Viv then sat beside him and cuddled in.

"Tell Viv I'm fine," Ray reassured them from the other end.

Viv breathed a sigh of relief. "I can hear you, babe. Is the water in the house yet?"

"Not yet, but I'm trying to move the cars closer to the house. I wanted to make sure they didn't end up downstream somewhere if the water picks up speed."

"How did you lose your phone, Pa?" Jamie asked.

Ray chuckled. "Would you believe I slipped and the phone flew out of my hands?"

"Yes," Jamie replied honestly. "I know how clumsy you can be."

At his son's words, Viv couldn't stop the laughter from tumbling out of him. "He's got you there, Ray."

"We're fine here. I love you all, but we really should save as much battery on this phone as we can. We're also saving GG's as well. We'll text when we can to let you know we're still okay."

"You will be careful, won't you, son?" Liam asked.

The line was silent for a moment before Ray spoke. "You know me, Dad. I'm always safe. Grandma would kick my ass if I tried to do anything stupid."

"You've got that right," GG stated in the background.

Dan came back on the line. "Okay, we love you all. Try not to worry too much. We'll see you all as soon as we can get out of here."

After the call ended, Viv's worry notched up another rung or two. He could read his husband very well and he knew Ray was scared. Every fiber of his being told Viv that things at the cabin were much worse than their three family members were letting on. He wasn't a praying man, but right now, he'd be willing to beg whoever was listening for his family to make it out of this alive.

"Pa's scared, isn't he, Dad?" Jamie asked before he came

to join the cuddle he and Girly were having.

"Yeah, he is." Viv held him tightly. "But you know Pa, he'll make it through this and be back before you know it."

"Turn on the TV," Declan said. He'd been watching on his phone. "Channel seven is running a special report on the flooding."

Mick crossed the room, picked up the clicker, and turned on the television. Soon he was tuned into the seven network. The reporter was talking about the damage already obvious to the world. Viv's heart lurched at the sight of the rushing water. How could something so innocent become a force to be reckoned with?

"I have to get to him." Viv hadn't even realized he'd spoken aloud until Girly answered him.

"If you're going, then so am I. That's my father, GG and my ex out there. I don't want anything to happen to any of them."

Liam joined the conversation. "The authorities won't let us get too near."

"But we will be there," Uncle Ant added.

Viv knew Uncle Ant considered GG a mother just as much as Liam did.

"Come on, Mick. We need to go pack. You can borrow some clothes from Nate. Pops, you organize travel. Nan and Aunt Magen can look after everybody here. Move it, Viv."

Her demanding voice had him up and doing as requested. He might not be able to get close to Ray's actual physical location, but he would be damn close in case he was needed.

Chapter Ten

"It's getting higher," Dan said as he came back from checking on things outside. "It's about knee deep downstairs."

By the look on his face, Ray knew there was something else. "Tell me."

"I think I heard an animal in trouble."

Damn! "Stay here with Grandma. Where did you hear the noise?" Ray was psyching himself to go out into the water. He knew it was a stupid idea, but he couldn't stand by and watch innocence die, even if it was an animal. *Don't let there be snakes.*

"Don't go, Ray."

The worry in his grandma's voice was evident. He wanted to tell her he wouldn't go, but they both knew he would. "I'll be back as soon as I can."

"Be careful. Viv will kick my ass if anything happens to you. Maybe I should go. You stay here," Dan offered.

With a shake of his head, Ray answered, "No it has to be me. I'm supposed to be the parent."

"Ray, you're not that much older than me," Dan argued.

"I'm going, Dan, and that's all there is to it," Ray stated before he opened the door.

He didn't want to think about all the things that could go wrong. The sound of an animal in distress drew him to the far side of the house. He saw the animal instantly. A baby goat, of all things, was caught up in one of the trees. Carefully, Ray made his way across the yard in the thigh-deep water. He'd just reached the kid when something hit him in the back of the legs and both he and the kid went down in the water.

Between his shout of alarm, the struggling animal in his arms, and Daniel screaming his name, he was starting to freak out. There was no way he could answer Daniel. The rip in the water seemed to have tripled in strength, and his body was being dragged along with the rush. To be honest, his life never flashed before his eyes like he'd always heard of happening. The only thing running through his mind was to not let go of the kid. Pain ricocheted through him as he bumped into whatever was in the flow around him.

Ray had to grab a hold of something to anchor him and his new buddy to. The next time he popped up for air, Ray spied a tree, then kicked in the water, praying like hell he moved enough to reached the thing. At the last moment, he tried to turn so his back hit first. But the best laid plans have ways of becoming fucked up real soon. Ray couldn't believe how loud the crack in his arm was. Yet he never felt the pain.

Shock was setting in. Ray wasn't sure what he was supposed to do about it. Instead, he managed as best he could to maneuver the young animal into his shirt, hoping the closeness might give them both some much-needed warmth. The area he now found himself in left him completely lost as to where he was. He didn't think he had been in the water that long. Using his good arm, Ray tried to wedge himself into the tree. Once he'd had a rest, he needed to get higher in case the water rose even more — it wasn't going to be easy. At least the kid had settled some. Right now, he wasn't going to think about it. If his life was about to take a turn for the worse, then Ray wanted his mind filled with nothing but his family. He hoped if this didn't end well that Viv would go on surrounded by the love of their beautiful children.

Not that he was planning on dying today.

* * * *

Viv's phone started ringing as soon as they landed and were into the airport. He had fifteen missed calls from Dan, and another ten from GG.

What the hell is going on?

Viv didn't have long to wait to find out. A man was standing off to one side holding a sign with Viv's name in large letters. Girlie had been the first to spot it and nudged him.

"I'm Viv Connelly," he said as he approached the stranger.

Something akin to relief filled the guy's eyes before he led Viv to a set of seats. "My name is Conrad St. George. I got a call from Dan. You aren't going to be able to get out to the house. As you can tell, it's still raining and they are mostly under water out there." Silence fell between them for a moment. "Dan has been trying to call you. He said to tell you Ray is missing."

Ice water flooded Viv's veins. Before he could speak, Girly did it for him. Viv was having a hard enough time just trying to breathe. The world was being swallowed by a loud rushing noise in his ears.

"What the hell do you mean Ray is missing? What happened to Dad? How can he be missing? Mick, get the phone. I need to ring Dan and GG."

Doubling over, Viv put his head between his knees. There was no way this was possible. Ray couldn't be missing. Uncle Ant rubbed his back as he spoke words Viv couldn't understand. Nothing was getting through. Nothing except the fact no one knew where his husband was. Sitting upright, Viv stared at Girly, who was still waiting for someone to answer.

"They have people out looking for him, so you can't give up hope. I told Dan I would take you all back to my place. There's plenty of room. As soon as the authorities let us in, we'll take the dinghy in and get them out. Dan wanted GG to come out to me, but apparently she wouldn't leave until they found Ray. I'm so sorry."

"I can't get through. It keeps going straight to voicemail,"

Girly stated moments before she started crying on Mick's shoulder.

"Come on. Let's get the luggage and go to Conrad's house. Once there, we can make plans," Liam said, taking charge of the whole situation.

Viv didn't even remember the drive to the house through the rain. He couldn't even tell if someone had spoken to him on the way over. All he could think of was that his family was in danger. And like GG said, he wasn't going anywhere until they found Ray.

"Dad's too stubborn to let a little flood kill him off. He's going to have found his way out of it somehow. He'll be like that guy in the movie who gets stranded when the world is freezing over." Girly sat beside Viv on the couch at Conrad's house.

Viv knew Girly was mainly talking so they didn't have to think about any other possibilities. Ray would be kicking their asses if he could see them all now.

Viv slapped his thigh. "Can you put the TV on? Maybe we can see what's happening. Anything is better than sitting here doing nothing."

"Damn, I should have thought of that myself." Conrad picked up the remote and switched on the television.

The news reporter stood under an umbrella at the water's edge, rambling about the level and its expected rise. Viv focused on anything that had to do with where Dan and GG were...and Ray. His husband was going to be okay, and he wasn't going to believe anything different.

"Do you know what Ray was doing to be caught in the water?" Viv asked Conrad.

"Dan said he went out to rescue an animal. Something in the water hit Ray and he got dragged along with the flow," Conrad answered.

Typical. Of course Ray wouldn't want anything to suffer if he could help it. He was the king of rescuing people, and now apparently, injured animals. Ray had a big heart and everyone knew it.

"God, Dad can be an idiot sometimes. Doesn't he know the rule — survival of the fittest?" Girly shook her head.

"He wouldn't be Ray if he let something die when he could save it," Liam stated.

They were both right, of course.

A map of the flooded areas showed on the screen. Some parts were fine, but along the creek, the water had flowed out, turning the area into a huge inland sea. At least the rain was lessening, and, once the water peaked, they would be able to go in and fully assess the situation. Then and only then would the real damage be known. Three people so far were not accounted for. Viv's heart clenched as he knew Ray was one of the three.

The shrill ring of the phone had Viv jumping. He scrambled to pull out his cell when he realized it was his. "Dan, what's happening? Have they found Ray?" Viv pressed the speaker button so everyone could hear.

"I'm sorry, Viv, but so far they haven't located him. GG is being a stubborn old bat and won't leave with the rescue patrol. You have to tell her she needs to get in the damn boat. I won't leave until they bring back Ray. This is all my fault."

"You don't control Mother Nature, Dan," Girly stated.

"Yeah, but I'm the one who told Ray I thought there was an animal trapped outside," Dan sobbed. "It should be me out there — not Ray."

A commotion in the background provided a distraction.

"What's going on?" Viv demanded.

"They found some people. Hold on. Let me find out what's happening."

Dan was talking to whoever else was there, but it sounded muffled. The shouting was hard to understand. Viv's heart practically beat out of his chest as he waited for Dan to come back. The sound of the phone being picked up and carried didn't help matters at all.

"Hey, love. I'm okay."

Girly burst into tears at the sound of her father's voice.

Viv wasn't far behind her. His eyes stung and blinking couldn't stop the tears from trickling down his face. "Thank fuck. You sound like you're in pain. What's wrong?"

"We're a matching pair now. I have a broken arm. And I may have dislocated the shoulder of the same arm. But me and Droogie are both fine." Ray sounded tired.

"Who the hell is Droogie?" Liam asked from nearby.

Daniel chuckled. "That would be the goat he went out to save. The rescue patrol says we have to go now. They're taking Ray to the hospital. Con knows where it is. We'll meet you there."

The line went dead, and relief seemed to fill the room. Ray was alive and, in time, he would be as good as new. Viv knew they were all very lucky that things turned out so well. He dreaded thinking what would have happened to the family if this had ended up badly. Property and belongings could be replaced, but not a loved one.

"Ray's alive. He's going to be okay." As the words tumbled from his lips, he hugged Girly tightly. In truth, he was happy all three had survived, but he didn't know if he would be able to go on without his husband in his life.

He needed to get to where Ray was. "How long do you think it will take them to get Ray to the hospital?"

"Probably about an hour. We should get going as well, seeing as we might have to backtrack if some of the roads are closed. The closest hospital is in the next town over."

Viv was glad Conrad at least had a clear enough head to think straight. The good thing was that the man obviously knew a few different ways to go. He didn't care which way they went, just as long as they got there. He needed to see with his own eyes that Ray was fine.

"Okay, I think we are all agreed Dad, GG and Dan are never allowed to leave home after what they've just put us through." Girly exhaled loudly. "I don't think my heart could take going through this again."

"We're right there with you," Uncle Ant threw in when they all headed back out to the car.

The rain had slowed down to a light drizzle, but with the ominous-looking sky getting ready to burst open at any minute. Fingers crossed this was the turning point.

"Uncle Matt will be disappointed," Girly said as they drove toward the hospital.

"Why's that?" Liam asked.

She grinned. "If the water could wash away Dad, what do you think it would do to Old Reg? He's probably miles down the river by now."

Viv couldn't help but chuckle at the look of absolute horror on Liam's face. "Hell, what do we do now when we come here on vacation?"

"Do you think there will be anything to come back to?" Girly asked.

"You know GG will have the place rebuilt, better than it was before. She'll finally be able to upgrade and expand like she has wanted to do for years."

As they drove, Viv studied Conrad, trying to see what Dan would see in him. The guy was certainly good looking enough, but he didn't come off as gay. There was nothing said that would even indicate that he and Dan were anything more than friends. He had so many questions he wanted to ask but didn't know how to do it without sounding nosey.

Trust Girly to get right to the point. "So, how do you know Dan, and why haven't we ever heard of you before?"

Conrad glanced in the rear vision mirror at her. "He's a friend. I met him down at the local not long after he arrived. We played some pool, drank some beer, and have been friends ever since."

"You're just friends?" Girly persisted.

"That's none of our business," Mick said to her.

"Yeah, we're just friends. I take it you're the ex?" Conrad asked as he turned the corner and headed out of town.

"Yeah, that would be me. But it doesn't mean I don't still care what happens to him. He might be confused right now, but he has a life waiting for him at home. A life he needs to get back to," she huffed in return.

Liam interrupted the conversation before it got out of hand. "Girly, Dan is a grown man. He doesn't need you looking out for him. Just let it go."

"Pop, you know as well as I do that Dan is just like Dad and needs a shove in the right direction."

"He said you were a pushy little thing. I guess he was right."

By the smirk on the guy's face, Viv knew he was just yanking Girly's chain. It didn't help that Mick was trying hard not to laugh as well. Liam and Uncle Ant were busy looking outside the car, pretending they couldn't hear where the discussion was going. Viv burst out laughing at the look of indignation on Girly's face, which in turn gave Mick and Conrad free rein to laugh.

"Seriously, though, Dan is only my friend. He's not my type. He has a few dangly bits that I'm not interested in at all."

"Good, because he has someone waiting for him at home. Dan just needs to pull his head out of his ass and see the truth."

Conrad chuckled. "Yeah, I know about that as well, but I think you may have your work cut out for you there. Dan has some weird thoughts running around inside his head. My girlfriend tried talking to him, but I don't think she got through."

"You have a girlfriend?" Girly sounded surprised.

"You'll get to meet her soon. Ellie works at the hospital. She got called in as soon as the water started to rise."

Ray hated being in pain. He'd always been a sook when it came to being hurt. His whole left side flamed with his injuries. The doctor fussed at him for being an idiot and going into the water. The man was right—he had been a bloody idiot—but Ray knew he would have done it all over again. They had at least drugged him to the hilt to manipulate his shoulder back into its socket. His forearm was broken and he now had a pretty purple cast from his fingers to his armpit.

The patrol who had found him even let him keep Droogie, saying they had no way of knowing where the poor animal had been washed down river from. At least one good thing had come out of this—the goat had survived.

So far, they hadn't let anyone in to see him. He couldn't wait, because Dan had told him Viv was there. After the drama he'd just lived through, all he wanted was Viv. With Viv by his side, all would be right in the world again. Ray knew how lucky he had been—he would have to be stupid not to.

"How are you feeling, Ray?"

Ray smiled at the nurse who entered his room. Ellie Dean was really nice. As busy as they were at the hospital, she still had a smile on her face. She'd informed him the other person his rescue team had saved was doing well too, which was good. Ray hoped this disaster didn't destroy anyone's lives by taking away their loved ones.

"I'm doing well, considering what could have happened. Still in pain, but lucky to be alive."

"That's a good thing, hon, as you have a few worried people outside waiting to see you. One of them is my very own fiancé." She grinned at him. "I can't believe how popular you are."

Ray chuckled then regretted it as soon as pain rippled through him. "I promise I'm not this popular normally. I'm a stay-at-home dad."

"You have kids? How many?" Ellie asked as she checked his monitors.

"Would you believe me if I told you that between us Viv and I have ten kids? Mind you, five of them are mostly grown up."

"And the other five?"

Ray laughed then wished he hadn't. "Okay, now the second five are all under the age of five. Truthfully, some are our biological kids and some are Viv's younger siblings and two are my adopted daughter and her half-brother."

"Oh my, you really do have your hands full."

"Yeah, and I wouldn't change it for the world. They are my life. My children make life worth living."

"Then why would you put yourself in a situation that could take you away from us all?"

Ray groaned at the pain he experienced when he snapped his head around and stared at his husband standing in the doorway. He loved the way his heart still fluttered every single time he laid his eyes on the gorgeous man. "Hey, love."

"Don't, 'hey love' me." Viv scowled, but there was no heat behind the look, more relief. "You could have died—for a goat."

"But Droogie is such a pretty little thing and will be happy once we get him home."

The way Viv arched an eyebrow, Ray knew he would have to do some sweet-talking to be able to take the goat with them. "We have to keep him. Droogie is the one thing that kept me hanging on while I waited to be rescued. I told him all about the family waiting for us back home. He's so excited to be moving. We can't disappoint him now."

"Ray, it's a goat."

"And your point is?" Ray struggled to keep a straight face but it was hard when Ellie was trying to hide her own snickers. "You know Droogie will be going home with us. It will be the babies' very first pet."

Viv exhaled loudly. "But a *goat*! And don't think just because you named him after a character in a David Bowie song it will make this all okay."

"A goat is an awesome pet to have. Nurse Ellie agrees with me, don't you? Naming him Droogie is just the icing on the cake."

"Hey, don't bring me into this. But in saying that, I once had a potbellied pig for a pet when I was growing up. I'm still trying to talk Con into getting one for up here."

Ray chuckled. "See, the goat will fit in well at home, and besides, Grandma already rang home to get Mum and Aunt

Meg to organize a pen. Droogie is going to have his own house and yard." Ray blew Viv a kiss. "I told you I would get my own way. You love me, admit it."

"There is no denying that I love you, Ray." Viv gave him that devastating heart-melting smile. "So yes, you win. Droogie has a new home."

"I love you too. I'm hoping they let me out of here soon. I really need to go home to our babies."

Viv walked over and took Ray's good hand, and at such a simple touch, Ray was home. "We'll know as soon as the doctor drops in. I think they'll want to free up beds quickly."

"That's true. We've been run off our feet ever since this whole thing started. Luckily so far, there has been no loss of life. Fingers crossed it stays that way." Ellie spoke as she finished up. "Okay, I'm done in here. I'll send the rest of your family back for a quick visit before the doctor does his rounds, which should be in about twenty minutes."

No sooner had she walked out the door, Viv bent over and placed a soft kiss on Ray's lips. Tears filled the man's eyes. "I thought I'd lost you. I don't ever want to have to go through that again."

Ray didn't have time to answer his beloved before the room filled up with family. Girly rushed to his side and gently hugged him. Ray glanced past her shoulder to see the awkward distance between Dan and Mick. He wondered if this was his daughter's way of getting the situation sorted out. He hoped this didn't blow up in everyone's faces.

"Dad, you big dork. What the hell were you thinking?"

"I'm fine, Girly. Just a little damp around the edges. The house came off worse than I did."

"We can rebuild the damn house, Dad, but we can't get another you," Girly snapped as she stood and stepped back to the bed. "Our family needs you alive and at home taking care of us."

Ray smiled at Girly. "I'll be home before you know it."

"And we're never letting you leave again. No running off after wayward family members who need to get their asses home where they belong. No doing anything that could end with you being dead."

The worry in his daughter's eyes was palpable, and Ray hated seeing it there, especially since he was the reason for the fear. "Girly, I promise I'm fine. All I want to do is go home. I'm not thinking of going anywhere right now. Though I would like to help out with this disaster somehow. So many people are going to be affected."

"Pop and GG are way ahead of you. They've been chatting with the officials here at the hospital and some bigwigs who stopped by." She stepped closer to the bed and leaned down to whisper softly, "GG already organized for two young men to move to Destiny House. She will tell you about it later. Mick has already been talking them through how their lives may change."

Typical. It would seem he wasn't the only one in the family needing to rescue those around them. If you really thought about it, it wasn't a bad thing at all. It would seem the helpful apples didn't fall far from Grandma's tree. Ray was glad his own children benefitted so much from having such an amazing woman as a role model.

Ray smiled at his grandma, thankful he had her in his life, and knowing the woman would be waiting until she had him alone before she let him have an earful. He probably deserved it, but right now, he wasn't going to think about the negatives. There was so much more in life to celebrate. The funniest part of everything was watching his dad and Uncle Ant fuss over his grandma. If they didn't tone it down a notch, he wouldn't be the only one on the receiving edge of her tongue. At least his grandma treated both men equally and not favoring his dad over Uncle Ant. She was always good about shit like that.

"I love you guys." Ray grinned.

He was feeling really good. He wished he could get up and take everyone out to eat, but seeing as how he was still in a hospital gown, that wasn't very appropriate attire to wear to a restaurant.

"I'm hungry. Are you hungry? I think we should go eat." Ray struggled to sit up. He huffed when Viv gently pushed him back onto the bed.

"Stay. You're not allowed to leave the bed until the doctor has come to see you," Viv chided.

Ray blew him a raspberry. "I was only going to eat. It's been ages since I last ate. Maybe we could order in a pizza. Maybe Nurse Ellie knows of a good place." Everyone was looking at him, but Ray didn't care. "Did you meet Droogie, Viv? Isn't she just the cutest little thing?"

"Love, are you all right?" Viv was frowning.

Why was Viv frowning?

"You know if the wind changes, you'll be stuck that way forever. Now turn that frown upside down, Mr." Ray waggled his finger at Viv.

Girly tilted her head, or maybe the room was tilted. "Is Dad stoned?"

"It would seem so," Dan answered. "Do painkillers usually affect him this way?"

"I don't know. I don't think I've ever seen him have them before. GG, is this normal?" Girly sounded like she was very far away.

GG chuckled. "His grandfather was the same way. They had to be very careful what they gave him or he'd be blabbing his secrets to the world."

Ray blurted out a laugh before he started singing a song about the end of the world and how he was fine. God, he wished he had his guitar. They could have had a good jamming session. "We should get the band here and write some more songs. Give them a call. Love, tell Jas to pick up some beer on the way."

"Definitely stoned. Would it be bad if I videoed him right now and took it home to show everybody?"

Ray thought that was Daniel talking, but suddenly everything was getting fuzzy. The noise in the room slowly faded out to white noise. He was falling asleep and realized Nurse Ellie must have topped up his pain killers when she'd been in the room. Hopefully next time he woke up, he'd be able to go home.

Chapter Eleven

Three days passed before Ray was given the all clear to fly. Viv was well and truly ready to go home. As far as he was concerned, they had been gone for far too long as it was. Girly and Mick were taking Andrew and Evan Rogers straight around to Destiny House. How GG had found the two young men in need was beyond anyone's guess. She had just turned up with them at the hospital and announced they would be traveling home with them. The weird thing was that the rescue patrol who brought them all in seemed to be okay with it. He guessed eventually GG would sit them all down and explain her reasoning. It wasn't hard to see that both young men needed help.

Why were people so happy to hand out money to charities all over the world, but could never see the people who desperately required help within their own borders? In retrospect, he was just glad his family was in a position to do something about it — even in such a small way as setting up Destiny House. Viv knew word would soon go out and people would be sending young men to them from all over the country, and GG would find some way to take them in.

Ray slept for most of the flight home with his head resting on Viv's shoulder. Viv bet there was going to be a wet spot there when his husband finally woke up. The painkillers, even though they were a lower dosage than the ones at the hospital, still sent Ray a tad loopy. Which was kind of fun for the rest of them.

"How's the club been going?" Dan asked.

"Well, if you were home where you should have been you would know that Nate has been helping me look after everything," Girly said from where she sat across the aisle. "And honestly, he'll be the one helping you when we get back. He and Tony are keeping an eye on things for the moment. I promised GG I'd be more involved over at Destiny House when we get back."

A myriad of emotions washed over his brother's face. He was going to have to man up to this and try to work out what was best to do. There was no way Viv was going to come off as all bossy by telling Dan what he had to do to fix his life. First, Daniel needed to figure it out on his own if he was ever to see the light. And secondly, the more they pushed him, the more stubborn Dan would become. Secretly, Viv was all for Dan having a relationship with Nate, but he knew it wasn't going to be that easy—life never was.

"I'm really sorry Ray got hurt," Daniel said.

"It wasn't your fault. Ray won't blame you either. We all know he would have gone after the goat. No one would have stopped him." Viv wasn't just trying to soothe his brother. He knew if he kept repeating it, he would start believing himself. He just hoped he never had to experience it again. Once was definitely sufficient.

"So have we heard any more on the Teddy front?"

Viv zoned out on whatever Girly was telling Dan. Instead, he thought about how when they got home, he wanted to find out what was going on with Fred in regards to the battle for Teddy. Deep down, he knew Fred was going to have to let go and wait for Teddy to come home again. She was too nice of a person to drag her son through the courts. Viv knew she was also worrying about the mental consequences it would have on Teddy. The boy was probably freaking out enough without having a war between his parents dumped on him as well. Viv's heart went out to Charlotte. Even after Damien found out that he was indeed her father, he still didn't want anything to do with the little girl. As far as Viv could tell, it was Damien's loss. He was missing out on seeing his beautiful daughter growing up.

"I'm awake." Ray yawned and sat up, then he grimaced when he tried to stretch. "Ouch, I forgot. Don't move. It hurts."

"Do you need another pain pill?" He didn't want Ray suffering in any way, shape or form.

Ray shook his head. "I'm all good. I don't like how they make me feel. Has anyone checked on Droogie?"

"He's crated at the back of the cabin. He has plenty of food and water." Dan smirked. "Why Droogie? Shouldn't you have called him Lucky or Flow, or something to remind you of your first meeting?"

Ray snorted. "He looks like a Droogie to me. He didn't seem to mind the name when I gave it to him."

"I bet you'll be glad to get home," Dan stated.

"More than. I need my babies. All of them — even the grown-up ones."

Viv couldn't agree more. After everything, it only reaffirmed how important family was. He also couldn't wait to spend quality time surrounded by everyone he loved.

"We should throw a party when we get home. I know it may be too soon, and we should probably wait until after the flood waters subside, but I really feel like we need to celebrate that we are alive." Ray frowned. "Maybe we shouldn't. Fred might not be in the mood to party."

"Then we'll play it by ear." Viv kissed Ray's forehead. "Try to rest some more. We still have a ways to go before we touch down."

"I don't want to sleep. What I could use right now is a large cup of coffee."

Mick sat forward. "I'll get it for you. Anyone else want anything while I'm up?"

Everyone gave their orders before Mick headed for the galley. Viv was happy to see Dan was at least being cordial to Mick. At first, he'd been worried, but he shouldn't have been. Dan, like Ray, was one of the good guys with a heart of gold. Even though he'd been hurt, he still wanted Girly to be happy. If he could only see that need in his own life, then things would run a hell of a lot smoother for him.

"Are we there yet?" Ray asked in a childish whine before he let out one hell of a giggle.

Yep, the drugs were still effecting Ray.

"A couple more hours still to go," Viv replied.

"This is boring." Ray yawned. "I need a coffee."

Ray seemed to cheer up when Mick came back carrying a tray laden with their beverages and some sandwiches.

"GG said we all need to eat." After handing out everything to them, he went and did the same for Andrew and Evan. The guy really did have a good heart.

Viv was glad Girly had someone like that in her life. Not that he wouldn't have been just as happy for Dan and Girly to have spent their whole lives together, but some things weren't meant to be.

"These are good," Ray mumbled around a mouthful of food.

Viv opened his sandwich and began to eat. Ray was right. They were good. Thinking about it, he couldn't actually remember when he'd last eaten. It had been sometime yesterday. This morning, he'd been too busy worrying about Ray to have anything more beneficial than coffee. Truthfully, Viv would be really glad to get home so he could have time to de-stress before he went back to work and uni.

* * * *

Having one's arm in a cast sucked. Ray was tired of the restrictions he had with the bloody plaster. He couldn't even nurse and feed the babies with the damn thing on. And he still had another eight weeks with his arm encased as it was. It was making him very irritable, and everyone was picking up on his irritation and bearing the brunt of it.

At the moment, he was in a self-imposed time-out. He had woken up in a foul mood and he didn't want to subject his family to it. Deep down, he knew he was suffering, perhaps belatedly, from the fact that he had realized everything his dumbass actions could have taken away from him. If the worst had happened, he would never have gotten to see their children grow up. Never have gotten to see his sons become men. Never have gotten to walk his daughters down the aisle. Never have gotten to sit, old and gray, on the porch with Viv at his side as they watched their grandchildren and great-grandchildren play.

Even though he tried not to outwardly show it, nightmares were plaguing his sleep. Quite often he found himself up prowling the halls in the middle of the night, checking to make sure everything was all right within the house, always making sure he was back in bed before Viv woke of a morning. He really didn't want to worry his husband, because he was doing enough for the both of them, and he hated feeling this way.

"I knew I would find you out here, Pa." Jamie crossed the garden and sat on the bench beside him.

"I'm just taking in the sunshine." Ray pasted on a smile he wasn't at all feeling.

Jamie frowned at him. "So you aren't worrying about what happened?"

For some reason, Jamie always seemed to hit the nail on the head. For someone so young, he was wise beyond his years.

"I'm not worrying." He tried to sound happy and positive.

"Pa, you've come to your thinking spot more and more since coming home. I know because I see you from mine." Jamie pointed up to the attic windows overlooking the garden where they were currently sitting.

Trying to change the subject away from his own morbid thoughts, Ray asked, "So what's weighing heavily on your mind?"

"I don't think Bear loves me anymore. Clara says he hardly mentions me at all, and that they have been going to the movies together a lot." Sadness settled over Jamie's face. "I have to let him go, don't I?"

Ray blinked the tears from his eyes. His heart was being torn in two over what his son was going through. "Yeah, maybe you will. I know if he can, he will come back to you. He's probably just trying to make his dad happy right now."

"I figured that was the case. Being so far away from each other is hard. Is it okay if I still love him, even though he doesn't seem to love me?"

"Definitely." Ray pulled Jamie into a hug. "Love him as much as you want. Just as long as you remember that you still have to go on. If you need you can come to talk to me, I will be available whenever you want."

"You can talk to me too, Pa. I know you don't want to worry Dad. But you can't keep it bottled up inside." Jamie hugged him tighter before letting go and sitting back.

"I'm just thinking about everything I would have missed out on if I hadn't been able to climb up into the tree," Ray said, not even meaning to say it at all.

Jamie frowned. "But, Pa, you didn't die. You're home with us. So you aren't going to miss out on anything. As GG would say, you need to suck it up, princess, and live the life you have. Don't dwell on the might haves and what could have beens."

"How did you get so smart?" Ray ruffled Jamie's hair.

Jamie had definitely been hanging around Grandma for too long. The boy was staring to think just like the crazy old broad. Really, that wasn't a bad thing.

A smile flashed his way. "I have these awesome role models that go by the names Pa and Dad with a whole lot of GG thrown in."

"Gosh, you are such a sweet-talker today, aren't you?" Ray chuckled.

"I think we should go and watch a movie. It might cheer us both up. What do you think?" Jamie stood and pulled on Ray's hand, making him stand. "Let's watch something funny."

"Sounds like a plan, little man." Ray followed his son as they walked back into the house and headed to the media room. "I'll even let you pick what we're going to watch."

When they got there, Declan and Sean were in the room chatting. It was good to see both boys so happy. At least these two weren't causing Ray and Viv to worry endlessly like they were with the others.

"Hey." Sean waved as they entered the room.

Jamie went straight to the DVD collection to choose a movie to watch.

"You guys want to watch a movie with us?" Jamie asked.

"Sure, I'll make some popcorn." Declan jumped up and headed out of the room.

Sean followed Declan. "I'll grab some drinks. Is cola okay with everyone?"

Ray sat back on the huge couch lining the wall and waited. He knew Jamie would end up snuggled into his side, and right now that was exactly what he needed — what they both needed. Hell, the whole family needed to feel closer.

"Dad's worried about you, you know," Declan said as he came back in carrying a huge bowl of popcorn for them to share.

Ray sighed. Keeping his emotions and nightmares away from the eyes of the family was bloody useless. Especially when they could all read him like a book. "I'm not purposely trying to worry anyone."

"We know that. GG thinks you need to see a shrink. Me, personally, I don't believe in all that psychobabble. I think you need to just talk it out. Once it's out in the open, then everything will start to look one hundred times better."

A genuine smile graced Ray's lips as he realized how wonderful his family truly was. How much they cared for everyone and weren't just caught up in their own little psychosis. Okay, maybe that was true for some of them. Others still seemed to be having a hard time grasping that they were worth it and deserved to be here with everyone. Nate was worrying Ray more and more with each passing day. Every time Ray saw him, the young man seemed to be pulling farther and farther away. Ray had spoken with his Aunt Magen, who seemed to be on top of the situation. Hopefully things would start to get better before they steamrolled out of control.

"I think I may have already had this speech one time already today." Ray ruffled Jamie's hair.

Jamie grinned. "It just shows great minds think alike."

"Okay, so what are we watching?"

"I was going to go for comedy, but instead, I thought maybe we could watch a little bit of *Fast and the Furious*. This'll show us life is worth living," Jamie said as he grabbed a handful of popcorn.

Ray relaxed back into the couch and let the movie overtake him. In a strange way, even though the circumstances were completely different, his family and the family in the series of movies weren't at all dissimilar. *Family first!* And that was the way it should be.

* * * *

The stress of the past few weeks was starting to wear on Viv. He loved his life, his job and his family. They weren't the problem. Singularly, he could deal with whatever was thrown at him, but put them all together, and his life was set on overdrive. And just to top off another endless day of worry, Ray had rung up crying, and when Viv had found out why, it had brought tears to his own eyes. David Bowie had passed away at age sixty-nine. The world had truly lost a legend. No sooner had he gotten off the phone with Ray, GG called and told him to get his ass home to console Ray. So now, here he was stuck in traffic on his way home. According to the radio, there was an accident farther down the bypass. God only knew how long he was going to have to sit there waiting. Thank God the car had air-conditioning.

The traffic crawled past the accident site and honestly, Viv couldn't see what the holdup was. More than likely it had come to a standstill from all the rubberneckers on the road. From his perspective, there hadn't been a fatality, which was a very good thing. No one was going to have to suffer losing one of their family today.

Weirdly, Viv felt his life was suddenly all about the morbidity of the world. Liam had told him earlier there had been four deaths in relation to the flood waters Ray had been caught in. As far as he could tell, they had all been for stupid reasons. Much like Ray for going into the water to save a goat. The others had driven their cars into flood-covered roads to be swept away. The news was forever telling the world — if it's flooded, forget it. When would people listen?

Liam had also told him in the next few days they were going to let people back into the area to assess the damage to their properties. Viv had offered to go with Liam. He didn't want Ray going, but knew his husband would insist. Maybe it was a good thing. This way, Ray could face his demons and finally stop having the nightly bad dreams. Ray didn't think he knew about them, but how could he not? Ray was his heartbeat. If Ray was hurting then so was he. Declan and Jamie had told him last night that they'd both had chats with Ray about not having to be brave all the time. Or, as Declan had said, sharing is caring.

By the time he'd made it home, two hours had come and gone since he'd spoken to Ray. Viv bypassed all the living areas and made his way straight to the play room. He knew he would find his husband surrounded by their children. It was his favorite place in the world to be when he was feeling down.

Ray's eyes were red-rimmed when he looked up. Within moments, Viv found himself with his arms full of Ray and all he could do was hug the man to his chest as his husband wept. Bowie had been a hero to both of them and in some ways was one of the connections that had brought them together. Ray had always joked that he'd cry more for Bowie than he would for his family when the inevitable ever happened. Most people just laughed at him, but if they could see him now, they might have a difference of opinion. The sad thing was, only today during Viv's lunch break had he ducked out and bought a copy of his latest CD. Between the both of them, they had two collections worth of CDs.

"It's going to be okay," Viv murmured into Ray's ear. "I've got you."

"I don't know what's wrong. I just can't seem to stop the tears." Ray pressed his face into Viv's shoulder.

Viv looked down. His heart melted when he saw Millie standing there with her arms wrapped around Ray's legs. Even the children knew something wasn't right and were trying to make things better the only way they knew how — by loving on their Pa.

"How about we cuddle up later tonight and watch *Labyrinth*? Would you like that?" Viv smoothed his hands down Ray's back.

Ray nodded before he stepped back and wiped his eyes. "I think I scared Grandma a little."

"Nah, we all knew this day would play out something like it has." Cupping his hands around Ray's face, Viv leaned in and kissed his husband on the lips. It wasn't heated like it would be if they were alone in their bedroom, but it was enough to show Ray how much he meant to Viv. "I'd serenade you, but sadly we both know that talent bypassed me and rests solely with you."

His offbeat comment worked and brought a smile to Ray's face. They both had agreed long ago that Viv's attempts at singing sounded like two cats fighting. But it didn't stop him from joining in every now and then. The kids thought his attempts were hilarious.

"No singing, Daddy." Millie put her hands over her little ears and shook her head at him, which only resulted in he and Ray both cracking up.

"What's so funny?" Dan said as he entered the room.

Millie answered for them, "Daddy was going to sing."

"Good God, no. Don't make us all suffer." Dan walked

over and wrapped his arms around Ray. "Girly just rang and told me the news. Are you okay?"

"I will be."

Viv loved how their family all came together in times of need and distress. This was the way it should always be. Mostly he wished their lives could run smoothly every single day, but hell, that was an impossibility for everyone in existence, not just their family. It was proof positive money didn't make the world perfect. Rich and poor alike all suffered when it came to natural disasters and the loss of family.

"Sean is setting up the movie night for you." Dan grinned. "He and Jamie talked it over and decided we all need to watch *Labyrinth* with you tonight."

Viv chuckled. "Great minds think alike. Our quiet time has just become a family affair."

"And we wouldn't have it any other way," Ray responded.

* * * *

Family. Ray believed without a doubt there was nothing better in the world. In the last few days, he'd been hugged by everyone numerous times over. He wasn't even sure if the little ones were aware of why they were doing it. His heart burst at the seams every time one of them accosted him and demanded hugs. The sad part was in the week since he'd had his shock, two more people he greatly admired had died, both in their late sixties. What the hell was happening? It made him appreciate his family all the more.

Today, he was on a mission. He was going to hunt Fred down and see what was happening in relation to Bear. Ray knew she had her family and Josh backing her, but she didn't have to go through this all alone.

Ray found her in the nursery with Josh. She was up to her armpits in diapers. Ray knew she was throwing herself into her work, instead of talking about what was happening.

After Layla was changed, Ray picked his daughter up and cradled her in his arms.

"So, I've decided you've had long enough now, and we should take the time to sit and talk about Bear, and what we're going to do about it."

All the air seemed to deflate out of Fred. She walked over and took a seat in one of the rockers. "There's nothing to talk about. I've spoken with both Damien and Bear. Bear decided he's okay, and wants to stay with his father for now. He enjoys his new school. He's making friends and getting into sports. Luckily, they were nowhere near the bushfires that are currently running rampant in Western Australia. Damien has agreed to emails and phone calls, as long as we don't talk about Jamie in any way. I think it's wrong, but I'll do what I must to have contact with my son."

"And so you should. Did you work out why he was allowed to take Bear out of the state?"

Fred sighed. "Fine print. The way everything was worded, I basically agreed to let them move for work opportunities. I could fight it and force them back to Queensland, but I think that may only tear my son further from my reach. Honestly, Bear seems happy. If he isn't, he's hiding it well. He has a best friend called Clara. He talked about her non-stop."

"Ah, the girlfriend."

She frowned at him. "I don't think they are dating."

"According to Clara they have been out on dates. She emailed Jamie. Jamie has decided he needs to let Bear go so Bear can be happy."

"That's fucked up," Josh said as he joined them.

Ray totally agreed. "It is, but the whole situation is off. I wish there was something we could do."

"Honestly, I think he's hanging around Clara to keep Damien off his back. I wouldn't put it past my ex to threaten and bully Bear into conforming to his ways. It was one of the reasons I left the prick in the first place."

"He wouldn't hurt Bear, would he?" Josh asked.

Fred shook her head. "No. I have no doubt that in his own way he loves Bear. He just wouldn't be able to tolerate a gay son. Actually, he wouldn't be able to handle it if Bear was with a girl who wasn't white and Australian. Damien has always been a well-rounded bigot."

Josh shook his head. "I just don't get people like that. It's so hard to hate people all day, every day. I'm all for live and let live. I won't preach to you if you don't preach to me."

"That's the way we all should be," Fred answered.

Ray asked the one thing he really wanted to know. "Do you think Bear will eventually come home?"

"Yes, but the last phone call he was talking about this thing Damien had taken him to. I think Bear might apply for the Army when he's a little older." She shook her head. "I know he has a few years left to truly decide, but if he feels it's his only chance at getting away from his father, he will take it as an out."

Josh growled. "He shouldn't have to be forced to choose like that. Damien is a bad parent, pure and simple. He should just love Bear, no matter who he is, or who he loves."

"Not everyone thinks like us. Thankfully, his current girlfriend seems to genuinely like having Bear around, not like the last one who couldn't stand the sight of him. So I know he's being well cared for," Fred admitted.

"That's something at least." Ray hated the fact Bear was now living on the other side of the country. Their family had been torn apart. More than two hearts had been shredded. Yet, a part of him secretly believed it was meant to be this way. If Jamie and Bear never knew any other people than the two of them, then how could they know their love was real? Both boys needed a chance to live life and grow as individuals. If they were meant to be, then they would find their way back to each other. First loves may never be the person you ended up with, but they always held a special place in your heart.

He was living proof of that. If he'd stayed with his first love, he'd now have been married to Beth. He loved B to death, but knew things had worked out for the best. She was now with the love of her life and so was Ray. No matter how much time passed, they would still be the closest of friends. Not only for the fact that she was his first love, but also because she'd gifted him and Viv with two very beautiful daughters when she had agreed to be their surrogate. For that, he would forever be grateful to her.

"I guess all we can do is wait and see what the future brings." Fred nibbled on her lip before adding, "I think it might be better if we don't talk about Bear around Jamie either. We need to let him work through this in his own time. I don't mean we should just pretend Bear never existed, and if Jamie initiates the conversation, then we go with it, but other than that..." She shrugged.

Ray agreed with her. "Sounds like a plan. We'll have to tell the others and let things play out as they will."

Chapter Twelve

Viv sat quietly in the living room, listening to what Byron had come to talk about. Ray was by his side, and even though his husband wasn't happy about the conversation, Viv also knew Ray was all about doing the right thing.

"So just because Shane has done his rehab, you think he should be allowed back out into society?" Ray asked.

By the tone of his voice, Viv was aware there wasn't as much heat behind the words as there could have been.

Byron sighed. "I know he's been an idiot—a bloody big idiot. And you're wrong. I don't want him to walk away scot free. I was hoping we could come up with another option rather than prison. Don't get me wrong, he should pay for what he's done."

Viv leaned forward and asked, "Are you talking about supervision of some kind and the possibility of Shane donating his time to doing community hours?"

"Yes. I know it seems like I'm only looking after Shane's interests here, but I'm not. I came to you first so that I can go to my son and tell him what we've come up with. I think making him work at a place like Destiny House may open his eyes. If he can see what abuse does, or how it affects people, then maybe it will knock some sense into his thick head."

"Ethan lives at Destiny House. Remember, he's the guy Shane was trying to force himself on the night he bashed me. I'm not sure having Shane working there would be such a good idea," Viv stated.

Frustrated as he seemed, Ray said, "I guess we'd have to discuss with Ethan the possibility of Shane constantly being there, especially considering he bore the brunt of Shane's drunken behavior. I won't let you take this any further if it will set Ethan's rehabilitation back any."

"I know, and I've weighed the pros and cons for what I'm asking. Then I think you're right. We should to go and talk to the man before we go with this decision," Byron said.

Viv pulled out his phone and called Girly, who was working at Destiny House that day. He wanted to make sure Ethan was there before they drove all the way over to the residence. Once the call was over, he said, "Ethan's at home. Girly is going to make sure he stays to talk to us."

The drive to Destiny House was almost pleasant. They talked about everything and anything that didn't have to do with Shane's release. Viv wondered if the police were going to let it go so easily. He wondered what strings Byron would have to pull to make this happen.

When they arrived, Ethan was waiting for them in Brent and Tarni's office.

Tarni pulled them aside before they went to talk to Ethan. "Go easy on Ethan. He's very quiet, I think he hasn't gotten over Shane yet."

"Gotten over Shane, or what Shane did to him?" Ray asked for clarification.

"A little of both. No matter what Shane did to him, I'm afraid Ethan still has strong feelings for the guy."

"You have got to be kidding me," Viv said in exasperation.

Tarni shook her head. "You can't help who you love. You, more than anyone, should know that, Viv."

She was right and everyone knew it. Right now, Viv wasn't sure how this was going to pan out. If he had to guess, Byron was going to get his wish and Shane would soon be spending time at Destiny House. He only hoped it didn't come back to bite them on the ass.

Viv knocked on the office door before they all entered. Poor Ethan looked scared shitless, yet the first question Ethan asked surprised Viv.

"Tarni said you needed to talk to me about Shane. He's

okay, isn't he? Nothing bad has happened to him?" Worry seemed to fill his words.

"Shane is fine. In fact, I'd like to introduce you to Shane's father, Byron."

As the introductions were made, Ethan visibly relaxed once he knew Shane was okay. In a way, Viv likened this situation to the one he'd had with Grace. He just prayed Shane never did to Ethan what Grace had done to him time and time again. Viv had his own issues with Shane dating back to when they had both worked together. Everyone had always said Shane was a douchebag, and in a certain way, it was true. The problem was that Viv — before the bashing — had begun to think the guy was trying too hard to be liked and it always backfired. After the fight at the uni, Viv was starting to believe there was no hope for Shane ever reforming. He also knew his own conscience would get in the way if he didn't at least give the guy the chance to work out his life. Viv was going to support Ethan in whatever he decided.

His mind came back to the conversation at hand and the whole reason they were there. He listened as Byron explained about wanting Shane to be an active member of the staff at Destiny House. He was pleased when Byron continued.

"The whole decision is based on how it will affect you. I'll make other arrangements if you say you don't want him here. I'm not trying to pressure you at all. So take your time to think it over," Byron said.

"Will he be allowed any alcohol? He was always much nicer when he didn't drink. If he isn't made to stop, then I don't want him here. He's mean when he drinks." Ethan spoke softly, yet Viv knew the words held a huge amount of insight into Shane's psyche. "Maybe he could wear one of those monitor bracelets on his leg," Ethan suggested brightly.

The tension in the room dropped, and Byron smiled. "We can make that a part of his release demands if you want.

I'd really like to know how it will be for you if Shane is here, because you are bound to cross paths sooner or later." Byron sat back in the chair, waiting for Ethan to answer.

"Shane's not a bad man. It's just when he drinks. I have finally gotten my life back on track, thanks to Viv and his family. I'm not going to do anything to jeopardize my position here. I like living here. The people are friendly and don't treat me like I don't matter," Ethan rambled.

Ray stepped in and took over the conversation.

Enough was enough. Ray didn't like seeing the worry on Ethan's face. As much as he wanted Shane punished, he needed to set Ethan straight on a few things first. "Ethan, you won't jeopardize your time here, even if you and Shane would become a couple again. You can stay at Destiny House for as long as you need to. Never fear that you will be asked to leave, because it isn't going to happen. The choice for whether or not you want to interact with Shane — *if* he comes to work here — is your decision alone. No one is going to tell you what you can and can't do. You shouldn't let anyone's views sway you — not even if it's my daughter, Girly, who thinks she should be the boss of everyone's lives."

"I don't want to hate him," Ethan whispered.

Ray's heart went out to the young man. He felt his resolve crumble and he knew without a doubt he wasn't going to fight for Shane to go behind bars. "You don't have to hate him, but in saying that, if I were you, I would take things slowly. Let yourself get used to having Shane around again and don't just jump feet first back into a relationship with him, or anyone else for that matter."

Crap! I've just told the guy not to listen to anyone but his own gut, and here I am already telling him what to do. Ironic much?

By the smirk on Viv's face, his husband was thinking the same damn thing.

"I'm not... I don't..." Ethan stumbled over his words. "I'm not ready for that yet."

Good. Ray might not have fought Shane working here,

but he sure as hell was going to keep an eye on the situation as it unfolded. If needs warranted it, Ray would be first in line to knock Shane on his ass.

"When will Shane start working here?" Ethan asked.

A blush graced Ethan's cheeks, and Ray wondered if it was from fear or excited nerves at seeing Shane again.

Byron leaned in a little closer. "I'll go and see Shane after I leave here. I'll lay down the rules and what will be expected of him. If he can't abide by them, then I'll let the police see to matters. If Shane is agreeable, then I'll go to the police with what we have in mind. Better to have all our ducks in a row so we don't get ahead of ourselves."

"If you need me to tell the police that it's okay, then I'm willing to help," Ethan said.

Ray stood and held his hand out to Viv. "Come on, love. I want to go and see Girly before we head home."

"She isn't here. After she told me that you were coming over to talk to me, she and Mick went to the club, as they were having a staff meeting." Ethan blushed again.

"Dang it. I'd forgotten about that. I guess we're headed for the club after we drop Byron back at home to pick up his car."

Byron chuckled. "Don't bother, I can catch a cab back to my car."

"I'll drive you," Ethan said shyly. "There's no need to waste money on a taxi."

"Are you sure?" Ray asked

Ethan stood. "Just give me a tick, and I'll be back with my keys."

As they waited for Ethan to come back, Ray spoke to Byron. "If Shane does get out, then he needs to be monitored. I don't want him to ever have the chance of repeating past mistakes, and God knows there have been a lot of them. None of us are perfect, but Ethan is right—Shane and alcohol don't play nice together."

"I understand completely. He's my son and I love him to death, but some days I wish I could shake the shit out of him before he does his next idiotic thing," Byron stated.

Ray huffed. "Make sure Shane knows that this is his last chance. If he fucks up again, I'm siccing Grandma onto him."

"I think Catherine has always scared Shane a little, so the threat might actually work," Byron said with a chuckle.

Before more could be said, Ethan was back, and they all went their separate ways. While they got in the car, Ray hoped there were no fires to be put out at the club. With Mick, Girly, Dan and Nate in attendance, things might get a little awkward and strained. He could imagine by now Tony would be ready to yank his hair out or deck the lot of them.

"Maybe we should get to the club before Girly and Dan start throwing punches. You know how hot-headed those two can be. Come to think of it, they've always acted more like siblings than two people in a relationship," Viv said as he pulled out of the drive and headed toward the club.

Ray thought about that for a moment. "Do you think that's why they never worked as a couple? They were too much like family for it all to mesh properly?"

"I believe they worked for a while, because it was all new. They were still getting to know each other. Honestly, I just think they're too much alike for it to have ever lasted. They're both such strong people that they need someone who evens them out and calms them."

"You mean like magnets, where opposites attract and the same repel?" It sounded plausible to Ray. The truth was, Mick and Nate would be classed as Girly and Dan's reverse counterparts. He could see it already working for Girly. Now all they needed was for Dan and Nate to get through all the bullshit keeping them apart, not that he was trying to be a matchmaker — that was what Girly was for.

Viv grinned. "Something like that. It worked for us. We're completely different, and in my humble opinion, we slot together just fine."

"We didn't in the beginning. But as time went on, we

found our niches within our relationship," Ray clarified.

"I meant you were so easygoing and I was so uptight—see, dissimilar in all the ways that matter. Yet, we get along famously."

Ray reached across and caressed Viv's thigh. "That we do, love."

As they pulled into the parking lot and stopped, Viv leaned over and kissed Ray. The heat soaring through Ray's body was enough to curl his toes. His life was one hundred percent better since he and Viv had gotten their acts together. When the kiss ended he said, "Come on, let's go and see if anyone needs patching up."

The sound of arguing hit them as soon as they entered the club. They spotted the group sitting at the bar, and Girly and Dan were at it. Ray didn't even want to know what they were yelling about.

Raising his voice, he said, "Knock it off! You know you two are still capable of getting grounded by Grandma. Being an adult means nothing in her book, especially while you're both acting like two-year-olds. Now what the hell is the problem?"

"Dan is being a dickhead," Girly spat.

Dan rolled his eyes. "You're being overbearing and bossy."

"Enough!" Ray looked at Tony. "What are these two idiots fighting about?"

Tony grinned. "Whether or not Nate should take over Girly's part in running the club. It started out that Girly wanted Nate to do it, but somehow in all the arguing, it's been flipped so she doesn't want to give up control, and Dan is just arguing against whatever she wants."

"Oh for the love of…" Ray was annoyed with the pair of them. "Do I need to get Grandma down here to sort this shit out? Why can't the pair of you be adults for all of two seconds and talk this out like normal people?"

Viv rapped his knuckles on the bar top. "I think everyone is forgetting. The name on the deed is Christopher Vivvens, not Daniel Vivvens, or Sara Connelly. In essence, I'm the boss. Dan, since you've been gone and Girly was working most of the time at Destiny House, Tony tells me Nate stepped in and took over helping run the place. If either of you ever bothered to ask Tony's opinion, he could have informed you that I've already given my permission for Nate to take Girly's place. If you keep all this bullshit up, he'll be taking your place as well."

"You can't," both Girly and Dan said at once.

Viv cut them off. "I can." He pointed at both of them. "I want this place to be a success. It won't be if the two people who were meant to be running it are at loggerheads all the damn time." Viv focused on Dan. "You either learn to work alongside Nate or find other employment. I'm sorry if you think you're being bullied into this, but right now *I don't care.*" Viv snarled the last bit, before adding a little more calmly, "Ray, do you have anything else to add?"

Now that the floor was his, Ray sighed. "I would like the pair of you to put yourself in Nate's shoes. He's sitting right here while you argue about him. You both should know by now that after all we've been through, family comes first. You may hate them at times, but in the end, you need to stick by them and not make them feel like shit. I think you both need to turn around and tell Nate you're sorry — and mean it. You need to also apologize to Mick for carrying on like this when he's standing right here."

By the time he was finished Ray realized Tony and the rest of the staff had quietly left the room, giving the arguing duo time to get scolded with a little privacy. Poor Nate was staring at the bar. Ray was sure the man had been in that same position for quite a while.

"I need a damn drink," Viv said as he walked behind the bar. He poured Ray a beer, and himself a soda, seeing as he was the one driving. Better to be safe than sorry. "Anyone else want anything while I'm here?"

Viv placed a Coke on the bar in front of Nate. Since he had

come to live with them, they had learned just how much the man detested alcohol. He never stopped anyone else from drinking it. Nate just wouldn't touch the stuff himself, which always struck Ray as funny, seeing as he had taken so well to working at the club.

"Dad's right, I shouldn't have made this all about me when it involves everyone, and I'm sorry, Nate. I didn't mean to make you feel bad. I'll try not to let it happen again." Girly walked over and hugged Mick. "Sorry I carried on like a tool. I should have more respect for our relationship instead of fighting like this with Dan."

Mick hugged her back. "I understand how you're feeling."

"My apologies, Nate, Mick." Dan didn't say any more than he obviously had to.

After a while, Nate turned on his seat and said, "If it's going to cause this much trouble, then I'll just find another job. I don't want to stay where I'm not welcome." Nate then concentrated on Viv. "Thank you for giving me this opportunity. I think I've had enough for one day. I'm going to head home."

Viv handed Nate the keys. "Wait in the car. Ray and I won't be here much longer."

"I'm sorry," Dan began as soon as the door leading out to the car park closed behind Nate.

"Shut up," Viv snapped. He was mad as a twice-cut snake, and now that they had the bar to themselves, he could finally let loose. "The world does not revolve around Girly and Dan. You two need to get your acts together before you push everyone away who cares about you." He narrowed his eyes at Girly first. "You need to stop trying to rule everyone's lives. I love you, but right now, I'm not sure I like you very much—either of you. Let people live and make their own mistakes." He focused his attention on Dan. "And you. Don't go blaming everyone else for what's happened. It's not Nate's or Mick's fault that you and Girly broke up. If you look at it logically instead of playing the blame game, you would see it was you and Girly who are to blame."

"I never—"

"If you don't want to be with Nate, no one is forcing you to. You can be with whomever you want, but stop treating Nate like shit because your feelings for him were the kick in the ass Girly needed to get on with her life. Stop treating Girly like the enemy. You are family and always will be. Instead of sniping at each other, why can't you see this is for the best and think of your breakup as a beautiful goodbye instead of the disaster you're both turning it into?"

"He's right. The constant bickering between the two of you is driving the rest of the family nuts," Ray added.

Viv knew deep down that Dan and Girly were nice people. Yes, they were hurt. Yes, they needed someone else to blame, but they needed to figure their shit out. "Try and get along. Like I said, I already gave Nate Girly's job. Before you complain, Girly, I know for a fact that GG wants you more involved with Destiny House. You can't do both jobs and give it your very best. Destiny House needs you more than the club does. Dan, I love you, but you need to pull your head out of your ass and move on with life, but Nate stays. I own this place and I alone have the final say."

"Fine, Nate can work here. Maybe I'll get Tony to roster us on different nights. That should stop any tension," Dan answered.

"That sounds like a plan." Viv finished his drink and rinsed his glass before placing it in the dishwasher. He did the same with Ray's. "Come on, love. Nate's waiting in the car, and I feel like going home. We'll let these idiots get on with their meeting."

As they walked out of the club, Viv leaned closer to Ray and whispered, "Do you think anything actually sunk in, or are they going start arguing again as soon as we leave?"

"Personally, I hope they can get past this. The tension between them is so thick it makes me choke whenever we're all in the same room. That's no way to live."

Viv stopped Ray just outside the club doors. "According

to Jamie, the problem is Dan still has feelings for Nate. Whether they are strong enough to get through this, I don't know. Dan feels guilty because he isn't as upset as he should be over the breakup. Yes, he's ticked that Girly moved on so easily, and his guilt is making him keep Nate at bay."

"Did Jamie say anything about Nate's feelings?" Ray asked.

With a smirk, Viv answered, "Nate doesn't know how he feels. He thinks we would all be better off without him. He stays for Girly, Declan and GG. He has taken a real shine to GG."

"I think the feeling is mutual. Grandma has taken him under her wing. Like he's a fledgling that needs protecting from all the big bad stuff in the world."

Viv chuckled. "I think we all benefit from having a little GG in our lives. I swear to God, she'll outlive us all."

"She's a strong woman all right. Weirdly, as idiotic as the rest of us can be at times, she always appears cool, calm and collected. Grandma has a way of handing your ass to you without you seeing it coming."

"Maybe we should talk to her when we get home. Get her thoughts on the whole Girly and Dan situation. Maybe she'll see something we haven't thought of yet." Viv mulled over the possibility in his mind.

"Knowing Grandma, she's already working on the problem. She sees way more happening in the family than anyone else does, except for Jamie, who seems to be following in her footsteps," Ray said.

Viv started them moving toward the car. The sooner they got home, the better. He would rather get the talk with Grandma over and done with before the kids got home from school. Their time would be more distracted with the school-age children vying for their attention. Not that he would ever turn his kids away, but this conversation was long overdue. He knew the adult kids needed a swift kick up the ass to get them heading in the right direction again. Grandma was good at that.

* * * *

Ray and Viv found Grandma sitting out on the back porch, watching Ben, Millie and Charlotte in the yard playing with Droogie, the goat.

"See, I told you bringing Droogie home was a good idea," Ray said and nudged Viv on the shoulder. The children loved their new pet and Droogie was a reminder that Ray had survived his near-death experience.

"I give in. Droogie is awesome." Viv chuckled.

"What can I do for you two?" Grandma asked as they sat on the bench beside her.

Ray sighed. "Girly and Dan."

"Need a good shove to get them moving again?" Grandma stated before Ray could go on.

"Yes," Viv agreed. "Now what are we going to do about them?"

Grandma turned to them and smiled. "Not a damn thing. If you push Dan about Nate, Dan is only going to dig his heels in harder to keep Nate at a distance. Nothing you say to Girly is going to change her. She has too much of her mother in her. How I wish she had taken more after my beautiful Ray, but Izzy had already stamped that kid's ass with her traits."

Viv burst out laughing. That certainly wasn't the answer he'd been expecting. He still couldn't believe how easy it was for Grandma to surprise him. "I also think she has a little of you stamped on her as well," he said. "Girly isn't the only one who thinks she needs to have a say in everyone's lives."

Grandma snorted. "It's because of me that any of you are here now. If I'd never married, Liam wouldn't have been born and had children, then you wouldn't have married my Ray. I think I have earned the right to have my say."

"That you have, Grandma." Ray leaned over and kissed her on the cheek. "It's a privilege to have you in our lives, but there has to be something we can do about Girly and

Dan." Ray went on to tell her about the conversation-slash-argument that had taken place at the club. Then he told her about what had taken place at Destiny House and what Byron had asked them to do.

Grandma nodded as he spoke. She remained quiet for a moment, as if in thought, before saying, "Shane is an ass. We all know this about the man. I can understand why Byron wants to do this. I can't say that I'm happy about Shane being at Destiny House, especially with Ethan living there. When Byron came to pick up his car, he and Ethan came in and talked to me about everything. I can't say I agreed with it all. I understand giving second chances to people who deserve it. I'm yet to decide if Shane is worthy. I want the whole situation monitored unblinkingly. The first sign of trouble—and Shane is out of there."

"At least you and I are on the same wavelength." Ray agreed with her wholeheartedly. He'd been thinking the same thing earlier. He shook his head. "Do you think we will ever have a moment in time where there are no troubles? Where the whole world runs in unison and everyone just gets on?"

"Not in my lifetime at least. I suppose I should tell you before Antonio sticks his nose into my business again. I went to the doctor this morning, and now I have to have more testing done. Dr. Morgan wants to put a stent in. Nothing drastic, and I should be as good as new when it's all over and done with," Grandma said as if it were no big deal.

Ray's stomach lurched at what he was hearing. He didn't want to think about his grandma being sick. He needed to think of her as the tough old broad who ruled the roost. Tonight, he was going to have to look up what was involved in having stents put in. What were the risks? If this was going to happen, then he would be well prepared. "When is he scheduling the tests for? I want to go with you."

"I'm not dying, Ray. It's just a little stent. People get them put in all the time," Grandma insisted.

"I know, but I'm allowed to worry. I love you, and don't you forget it."

"I love you too."

Chapter Thirteen

Viv thought it was funny how life had a way of working out. In the last week and a half, everyone at home had finally started to feel like they were settling down. Grandma was scheduled for her operation to take place the next week. Both he and Ray had spoken with Dr. Morgan, who had assured them it was a simple procedure. Grandma was right. People had them every day and were perfectly fine. If he'd got the gist of it right, they would be threading the stent up through one of her veins and opening it up once they had it in place. A little keyhole surgery originating in her groin area. It was amazing to Viv, the things doctors were able to do these days.

As of yet, Shane hadn't started work at Destiny House. His rehab doctor wanted Shane to take the time to do some outside counseling before jumping right back in. Byron was keeping everyone well informed, just as he'd promised he would.

"What are you thinking so hard about?"

Viv smiled at Ray when he entered their bedroom. "Just life in general. I made arrangements with Uncle Matt to have the day off when Grandma is having the stent put in. I want to be there just as much as you do."

Ray seemed to relax. "That will be great. I told the kids they still needed to go to school, but they all want the day off as well. I think my worry is affecting them all."

"We'll see what happens closer to the day. Right now, I need a little one on one with my gorgeous husband." Viv stood up and pulled Ray into a hug.

Pressing his nose into Ray's neck, he inhaled deeply,

calming instantly at the scent that was all Ray with just a touch of the kids thrown in. He guessed that was where Ray had just come from. Usually, he was waiting for Viv in the bedroom when he got off work late. "Firstly, though, how are the kids? Nothing I should worry about?"

"Actually, Ben and Jeb have slight temperatures and are a little grumbly. I rang the home-visit doctor and he gave them some Panadol to bring down their temps. If they aren't any better by tomorrow afternoon, I have to take them in to our doctor. Fingers crossed it isn't anything bad. I hate it when they aren't well."

Viv rubbed soothing circles over Ray's back as he listened, the worry obvious in his husband's voice. "Would you feel better if we brought them in here with us?" Which was something they often did when the little ones were feeling out of sorts. "There's no use in the others getting sick as well."

"You won't mind?" Ray asked.

"Do I ever mind? Let me just grab a quick shower first, then we'll go and get the little rug rats and pay them some special attention. The bed is big enough for us all to fit."

Ray blew him a kiss. "Ben is going to be rolling all around like he usually does. I suppose we can try it for a while. If it gets too difficult, I can take Jeb to the single bed in the nursery."

"If it comes to that, we may have to think about getting a bigger bed so there will always be plenty of room." Viv steered Ray toward the bathroom. "Let's get my arm wrapped up in that sexy-as-fuck plastic bag then have a shower. Afterward, I'll grab something quick to eat and we can bring Jeb and Ben in here with us."

After securing away Ray's cast from the water, Viv got both him and Ray undressed and into the shower. He soaped up his hands and massaged Ray's shoulders, trying to relieve any stress his husband may be feeling. Ray relaxed under his touch, and Viv slid his hands lower over Ray's body. Ray grunted when Viv wrapped one hand around his cock and gently cupped Ray's balls with the other. He took his time while he worked Ray toward completion. Ray had been stressing way too much lately.

"Viv…mmm… I need more. I want you inside me."

"Your wish is my command." Viv let go of Ray's cock and reached for the lube from the shower shelf—lube was the best Goddamn invention ever, as far as Viv was concerned.

After slicking his fingers, he commenced the pleasurable task of stretching Ray to readiness. Viv loved touching Ray both inside and out. He also loved all the noises Ray made during the process. He could get Ray off with just a few caresses of his fingers in all the right places. Sliding two fingers in deeply, Viv then wiggled them around until he found what he was searching for. He lightly bit Ray's shoulder as he played with his lover's prostate. Viv's cock hardened to almost being painful when Ray threw his head back and let out a guttural moan. Viv added a third finger and soon followed with a fourth.

"Soon, Viv. Please…"

Gently pulling his fingers free, Viv lined his cock up with Ray's willing hole, and slowly sank into him. He waited for Ray to give him the signal that it was okay for him to move. The tight hold Ray had on Viv's cock was both excruciating and wonderful at the same time. Ray finally relaxed around him, and Viv started sliding out only to thrust in once more.

Ray's body trembled around him and Viv loved every second as he brought his husband to the peak of his orgasm. He picked up his pace. The sound of their bodies slapping together was accompanied by their pleasure. No matter how many times they did this, whether it be fucking themselves raw, or simply making sweet gentle love, it was always perfect. Ray's sexual noises—that Viv was sure Ray didn't even realize he made—turned Viv on faster than he could blink.

"You feel so good, love. I could do this to you all night, but right now, I need to hurry," Viv whispered against Ray's ear before giving it a tender nip.

"Finish it, Viv," Ray gasped as he shoved back hard onto Viv's cock.

Reaching around Ray's body, Viv then took hold of Ray's dick and stroked him in time to his thrusts. His own body was exploding inside like a fireworks display, his orgasm working its way around every part of him. "Try and hold yourself off the wall and push back."

Ray complied with what he was asked. Viv ground against his ass as he frantically pulled Ray off. Ray's balls tightened in his hands, and Ray cried out Viv's name. Shudders ran through them both as they found release. Wrapping his arms around Ray's chest, Viv still ground into him, not quite ready to set Ray free. Usually, he would stay this way until he had enough energy to start the whole show all over again. But right now, he required food, then his sons needed some special Daddy and Pa time. Reluctantly, he slid free of Ray's body and turned him so he could kiss him. He hoped Ray understood just how much their being together affected Viv. He always worried Ray would think he didn't care enough, seeing as he was either always working or taking classes at uni.

"Shh, I know. I love you too," Ray whispered as the kiss ended.

Somehow Ray seemed to always know how Viv was feeling. It was another reason he loved his husband so much. Ray completed him and made him feel whole and useful.

Viv's stomach rumbled loudly, and Ray pecked him once more on the lips before saying, "Come on, let's get you fed."

"Fed, kids and bed… It sounds like a perfect way to end a day," Viv agreed.

They quickly dried off and pulled on some clothes before heading out of the room. On the way down to the kitchen, they held hands.

"There's a roast in the kitchen. Antonio had the cook go all out tonight. We had the kids home, including Mick and, for once, there was no bickering. In saying that, Dan was really quiet and kept to himself for the whole meal. Grandma gave me a knowing smile. I wonder if she had a hand in their behavior." Ray chatted away.

"More than likely. You know that's where Girly learned her behavior. Not that I'm saying that's a bad thing. Strong-minded women are always a good thing."

"That better be what you're saying."

Viv jumped at Grandma's voice. He hadn't even realized she was behind them. "Grandma, you about scared me to death."

She grinned. "Then I still have it. When Ray was younger, I was forever sneaking up on him and scaring the bejesus out of him and his friends."

"I remember the night you made Brent scream like a girl. I thought he was going to have to change his dacks." Ray chuckled.

"Yes, he always was the easiest out of the lot of you. Remember when he went through a stage where he thought I was a witch because I always knew when you were up to trouble?" Grandma said as they entered the kitchen. She sat at the counter. "Be a dear and bring me a cuppa."

Viv made his roast beef and gravy sandwich, while Ray prepared them all something to drink. "How are you feeling?" Viv asked.

"I'm good. Little out of breath some days. Dr. Morgan assures me that will stop as soon as the stent is in place. Really, I'm just getting old. The body may be winding down, but my mind is still young at heart."

"You'll outlive us all," Ray joked.

She smiled at him. "I'll live long enough to see everything that needs seeing."

The way she spoke was strange, if not cryptic. In reality, Viv knew she couldn't live forever. Hell, none of them could. When a person's number was up, there was nothing on God's green earth that was going to help them stay. "I think we need to get off this morbid subject. We've had enough near-death experiences to last a life time. In this house, we need to live for the now."

"On that note, I just have to add — did you know all the kids want the day off school when you have your surgery done?" Ray asked Grandma.

She smiled wickedly at them. "Who do you think put them up to it? If I'm going to be stuck in a hospital, I should be surrounded by family."

"You can be pretty evil at times. Maybe Brent was right and you're really part witch." Ray frowned at her.

Viv had to hide his smile.

Grandma threw back her head and cackled like every good witch in scary stories. "I'll get you, my pretties."

Viv shivered. "Now that was just creepy."

He sat on one side of Grandma while Ray sat on her other. "This food is good," Viv said.

"New cook who started today. Esmeralda wanted to move closer to her daughter. Llewellyn is her granddaughter. It seems she learned everything she knows from her grandmother, yet gives it a twist all her own," Grandma explained.

"She's definitely a keeper," Viv mumbled, then continued to eat.

Ray snorted. "I'll wait until after she's made lasagna before I'd say that. It's going to be hard to beat Esmeralda's cooking when it comes to anything Italian."

"So are you going to let all my boys have the day off school?" Grandma asked.

Viv grinned. "You know once you gave your seal of approval, there isn't anything else we can do. I'm not sure about bringing the younger ones, as they can still be a bit temperamental."

"Fred and Josh already said they'll stay home with them. Girly and Dan are only allowed to come if there isn't any arguing. Mick and Nate have already said they'll be there." Grandma sighed before adding, "Nate is such a sweetie. He is going to make someone a fine husband one day. And if Dan doesn't wake up, it won't be him."

"I'm not sure what's going on there. I just know that if we push, Dan is just going to push right back. He can be a stubborn ass when he wants to be," Viv said honestly.

Grandma sagely said, "Their time will come. It may not be today. It may not be tomorrow. Down the track, they'll figure out what the hell is going on. I watched them tonight during dinner. As much as Dan denies his feelings, he watches Nate like a hawk. So there is obviously still some kind of emotion there."

"You're right. I guess we have to let them work through it on their own. Nothing we say is going to make them move faster than they're willing," Viv said before he got up then cleaned away his plate and their cups.

"I can't believe you told Dan that if he didn't pull his head in, you would give Nate his job?" Grandma's eyes twinkled with something akin to mischief. "I miss out on all the fun stuff."

Viv turned serious for a moment. "The club is a business. I wasn't going to let it go under because Dan and Girly are knuckleheads. If they can't work together, then they need to step aside and let someone in who's willing to get the job done. Nate, as inexperienced as he is, is willing to do the hard work. I love my brother, but I have no qualms about giving his job to someone else."

"Forcing Dan and Nate to work together might just be the shove in the right direction they need. One way or another, they'll either get along or go their separate ways," Grandma said.

"True. Now if you will excuse us, Ray and I need to move Jeb and Ben into our room in case they need us during the night."

Grandma also stood and walked out with them. "I'm sure it's nothing to worry about, but parents always worry anyway. Come morning, hopefully they'll be their sweet little selves again."

"From your mouth to God's ears, Grandma," Viv agreed.

Viv and Ray both kissed her goodnight when they

reached her bedroom door. After hurrying up the stairs, they collected their boys and headed back to their room to settle in for a good cuddle.

* * * *

Being one of the many family members sitting in the waiting room while Grandma underwent having the stent set in place was no comfort to Ray. For some reason, he was grumpy as hell and snapping at everyone. Maybe it was just being in the hospital itself. His broken arm seemed to be aching even more than usual. At least it reminded him of the cleanup happening up at the cabin. Turning to his father, he asked, "Have you heard much more about the aftermath of the flood?"

"A lot of damage." His father grimaced. "Most people had insurance, but the insurance companies seem to be taking their sweet time about helping people through the mess so they can move on. Our place is a write-off. Too much damage from the strong current. I've hired a contractor to tear it down so we can rebuild. If the outer shell gets built, then at least it will house some families until their own situations get resolved. The new place will be twice as big as the old one. We'll need it with the way our family keeps expanding. I have Dan's friend, Conrad, keeping an eye on things for me. He rings me weekly and lets me know what's happening. The guy has a good head for business."

Ray realized right then just how much his father was worried about Grandma. His father only ever rambled when he was worried. If the man needed to ramble all day, Ray would sit and smile and nod at all the right places. His Uncle Ant, on the other hand, was pacing the waiting room like a caged animal. The kids were faring much better than the adults.

Jamie was currently telling the others what they all needed to do when GG got back home. It amazed Ray how much the whole family listened to Jamie when he spoke.

Girly had once said that for someone so young, his heart and mind were that of a much older person. Jamie cared about everyone. It also helped him with missing Bear. In the last two weeks, Ray had noticed Bear was mentioned less and less, though Jamie still had a picture of the two of them on his bedside table. At least Jamie was resilient, or just very good at keeping his emotions under lock and key.

Viv strode down the hall, his arms laden with food and drinks, and doled everything out to everyone there. What shocked Ray the most was that Shane was there with Byron. He wasn't his usual loud and brash self. Instead, he was quite subdued as he carried on a conversation with Ray's mother and his Aunt Magen. Whoever knew Shane could act like a normal human being?

"How are you doing? Has the doctor come out yet? Has anyone told you anything?" Viv asked when he sat next to Ray.

"Viv, you do realize that they have only been in there for ten minutes? I think it will take longer than that to put in the stent, love."

Viv frowned at him. "I'm nervous, so sue me."

"Now why would I want to do that?" With Viv beside him, Ray's bad mood started to lift. "How long did you think you had been gone for?"

"Long enough to call home and check on the babies before I bought out what seemed like a third of the kiosk and brought it all here. It seemed a lot longer than ten minutes," Viv answered.

Ray pulled up what he had learned from his research and said, "It's not a very long procedure. I'd say she has about another hour in theater, then however long it takes in recovery. I'm sure by then someone will come and let us know what's going on."

"Is it just me or does it seem we've spent way too much time in hospitals lately? These places are starting to give me the heebie-jeebies," Viv whispered.

"You and me both. I think I'm phantom aching in

181

sympathy with Grandma. Right now my arm is killing me." Ray smiled as Viv pulled out a leaf of tablets and popped two before handing them to Ray.

Viv then handed him a bottle of water. "Take them, I know you've been skimping on them lately. Trust me, I know how much your arm can ache while broken." He flexed his now cast-free hand.

Without complaint, Ray swallowed the pills and hoped like hell they kicked in fast. "How did you know I've been skipping some?"

"I know how many should be missing from the box. And you haven't used near as many as you should have. Your arm won't heal correctly if you don't follow the doctor's instructions," Viv said.

Ray sighed and laid his head on Viv's shoulder. "I just hate how they make me loopy. Every time I take them, my head feels like it's stuffed with wet cotton wool."

"In a couple of weeks, you will be as good as new. Just this once, please follow the doctor's directions. We want you healthy and whole as soon as possible."

Liam chuckled. "Good luck with that. Getting Ray to take any kind of medication has always been a struggle. I don't know why he has such an aversion to it."

"Isobel. She got addicted to pain medication. It's the reason you disowned her in the end. I never wanted that to happen to me," Ray answered honestly.

Liam sighed. "You are nothing like your sister. Isobel may have started with an addiction to painkillers, but she soon turned to hard drugs. No matter how many times I put her into rehab, she'd check herself out and sink straight back into her bad habits. Larry wasn't much better. I'm glad you turned out nothing like her."

Ray was dumfounded that he didn't remember any of this. He'd been eighteen when his sister had died. "I don't remember any of that."

"We decided early on that you were better off not knowing. We kept as much from you as we could. Hence the reason I cut her off."

"Then why did you give Girly such a hard time when she was younger?" Ray demanded.

Again, Liam sighed. "That was my fault. Girly is almost an exact replica of her mother. I couldn't stand looking at her, because it hurt so much knowing that I couldn't save her mother. I regret it now, but back then, it was still all too raw."

Everything made a lot more sense now. In his younger years, he'd thought his father was just being an asshole. He could kind of understand how having a constant reminder of his daughter, the addict, around could mess with a person's head. At least now his father and Girly got on well together. His father must have learned that as adults, Girly and Isobel were two completely different people. In a weird way, Ray was glad he'd never known that side of his sister. Finding out about it now tainted the way he saw her, and he was glad that Girly, and Nate, didn't have to bear witness to Larry and Isobel. He was going to have to talk to Grandma and get her thoughts on everything. She usually told it like it was, so he wondered why she'd never said anything before now.

"Girly loves you, Dad. I don't think she ever held it against you."

"But you did," Liam stated.

Ray nodded. "I did. I hated the way you were with Isobel and Girly. When Girly was given to me, you were so hard. Then you basically kicked me out, so I had to move in with Grandma and Grandpa. That man hated me more than I thought you did."

"I've always felt guilty about what I did, but I didn't know how to fix it. It wasn't until my dad died that I was given the opening I needed."

"You didn't want to look weak in front of Granddad," Ray surmised.

His father stared at him. "Yes, after he died, it gave me the opportunity to make amends for my own stupidity."

"We're all good, Dad." Ray patted his father on the knee. "Everything got better after Grandpa died. Let's just leave him in the back of our minds where he belongs."

"I just wish I'd done things differently instead of following in the footsteps of a man I never wanted to be."

Ray hugged his father. "We're here. We're alive. This is a non-life-threatening operation for Grandma. I say we cast off the melancholy thoughts and plan for the celebration when she gets home. Give her a week to recover, and Grandma will be as tough as boots, back to herself and bossing everyone around."

"I know she has Girly and Mick organizing another fundraiser for Destiny House. Mum thinks it gives the young men there a sense of purpose and gets them meeting new people."

"She's probably right. Girly tells me Ethan is doing so much better since being there, even his grades have improved at uni." Ray chuckled. "Fixing people must just run in our blood. I wonder if the next generation of kids will follow in our footsteps."

"Of course they will. With our guidance and love, how can they turn out as anything other than compassionate people?" His father sighed long and loud before adding, "Just in case I've never told you, I want you to know you are the absolute best thing I have ever had in my life. No matter what is thrown your way, you've always stood proud and been you, never pretending to be anyone else. That takes a lot of balls in this day and age. Most people think it's easier to go with the flow instead of being an individual. If you teach your children to do the same, then they will turn out just like you and Viv."

Ray was quiet for a moment as he figured out how to say what he wanted to. "Dad, did you ever think that you would end up with a gay son?"

"Honestly, I want to say no, but the reality is your grandmother and mother knew. Your grandmother was just more vocal in her views. I don't know how they figured it out, but they did. I was in denial for a while. I think my eyes were truly opened when Viv entered your life. I know at first it wasn't real. Mum filled me in on what went down only a couple of months ago. At first, I was so cranky, but then I realized it was a humungous step for the both of you. In the end, it doesn't really matter how it started, only that it led to who you are now as a man. I will always love you and be proud of you."

There was something glistening in his father's eyes, and Ray's were burning with tears too. He wasn't going to cry. At least not today. If anyone saw the tears, they would automatically think he was crying for his grandma, and his kids would only worry that Ray knew something more than he had told them. As Grandma would say, 'Suck it up, princess. Put a smile on that dial and show the world how fantastic you're doing'.

Outwardly smiling, Ray looked around the sitting room at all the people gathered there. He wasn't surprised to see the rescuees at Destiny House were also in attendance. His grandma truly had touched many people's lives. He knew outsiders viewed their family as rich and spoiled. They never saw what went on with the daily grind for them being the way they are. How much hard work went into helping others, or how beneficial the Connelly Corporation was to medical research. Neither did they see how much the Connelly family put back into the community. Not like when his grandfather had been alive and demanded his name be put on everything. Nowadays, they did it more privately, giving the money to where it was needed most. Hence, the reason no one had complained too much when Catherine Connelly had decided to open a home for young men in need. She was in the process of doing the same for young women as well. Byron was ironing out all the kinks before they went public. She was thinking of calling the women's refuge New Hope. All this told to him by Girly, of course. She said when New Hope opened its doors, Brent and Tarni would take over that one and she and Mick would continue on at Destiny House with the help of Norman Lyons. Mick wanted to remain as the cook, so Girly and Norman would be in charge of the everyday business of running Destiny House.

His thoughts were interrupted as Viv knelt on the floor in front of him. "How are you doing? Do you need anything to eat, to drink?"

"I love you," Ray stated just because he could.

His father was right. He could be who he was because Viv had entered his life. He also knew this was something he truly desired to pass on to their children. He needed them to know it was okay to be who you are, just as long as it didn't come at the expense of others. Not that he thought anyone had a right to tell his kids how to live. He just wanted his kids to respect everyone's opinions, while still staying true to themselves. Out of all of them, the only one he worried about was Jamie, because his heart was so open, and like Girly and Grandma, he spoke whatever was running through his mind. He prayed no one took advantage of his son or his loving, caring nature.

Viv hugged him tightly. "You know I love you just as much."

They parted at the same time that a doctor opened the doors leading to the operating theaters and headed straight for their large group. He stopped in front of Liam. "Just as I predicted, Catherine is doing well and is now in recovery. Give it a few more hours and she'll be ready for visitors. Try not to overwhelm her right away." He smiled at the whole room. "I wish all my patients had people waiting for them like this."

"So GG is going to be okay?" Jamie asked as he came and stood beside Ray.

"GG?" the doctor asked.

Ray gave a relieved laugh. "GG — Great Grandma."

The doctor smiled before looking down at Jamie. "Yes, GG is going to be fine. In fact, she invited me and the rest of the staff attending her to some big celebration she's planning."

Ray turned to his father and grinned. "See, I told you she'd be planning a party."

Chapter Fourteen

Viv woke to the feel of his cock engulfed in a great warmth. He smiled up at his husband, who was slowly impaling himself on Viv's hard-as-a-rock dick. He must have been truly worn out to have missed the opening scenes of the beautiful play their lovemaking always became. He was just glad he was alert for the main act. He loved how Ray's pale skin pinked with a blush as he lowered himself until he was fully seated.

"Well, a very good morning to you too," Viv said and slid his hands up over Ray's exposed flesh. His cock ached at the tightness Ray's body gave him. No matter how many times they made love, or how many times they fucked their brains out, Viv would cherish each moment. The way they fit so perfectly together always amazed Viv, and every time they were done, Viv fell deeper in love.

Ray hummed to himself before he seemed to focus on Viv. "I just needed you and couldn't wait."

"I've got you, Ray. You take what you need. I will always be here for you." Viv groaned when Ray lifted up and plunged back down again. Viv held his breath as Ray took a hold of his hands and moved them until they were cupping Ray's ass.

"Touch me. Feel how we are connected," Ray begged.

Without thinking too hard about it, Viv moved his fingers farther around and down into the crease of Ray's ass, lightly exploring where their bodies were joined. He smiled up at Ray then inserted one finger inside Ray's passage. He wiggled it around and watched Ray's body spark to life. This was a new side to his husband that Viv wanted to explore more. He knew Ray always loved the stretch of being fucked. Did he want to be filled by more than what Viv could provide? Viv would never bring a third into their relationship, but that didn't mean they couldn't explore the possibility further with the aid of some adult-only toys.

"Do you like that? Do you want more?"

Ray closed his eyes and nodded, and Viv knew what he had to do. He gently lifted Ray up and pulled free. "Get on your hands and knees, lover."

Viv gently tapped Ray on the ass, then he got up and entered their walk-in wardrobe. Their box of toys was kept at the back of the top shelf so it was carefully hidden away from prying eyes. His hands shook as he grabbed the largest and the smallest dildos they owned and walked back out to where Ray was waiting for him. A more beautiful sight he'd never seen. He stood mesmerized as Ray fingered his own hole.

Ray's eyes lit up when Viv showed him what he'd gotten. Viv used extra lube to slick up the largest dildo. He knew Ray's body could handle it. They'd used it often before. He took his time stretching Ray to his limits. This was the first occasion that Viv was going to take the next step. He was both nervous and excited all in one. Once he was sure Ray was ready, he removed the dildo and tossed it on the bed. He slicked up the second dildo, pressed it against his cock and carefully lined up with Ray's hole then pressed in. He made sure to go slowly, allowing Ray's body time to adjust. When he was fully seated, Viv took a deep breath, flicked the dildo to 'on' and groaned in unison with Ray. The vibrations filled them both, and to Viv, they felt awesome.

Viv steadily counted to ten before sliding out then thrusting back into his husband's warmth. Fucking Ray was always intense, but the added stimulation of the vibrator was so much more. Every time he heard Ray whimper and grunt in lust, Viv grabbed Ray's hips and picked up his speed. Lovemaking was when it was just them—no toys. Today, this was fucking, pure and simple. Ray needed to get off and Viv was happy to do what was necessary to make his lover happy. His own satisfaction was just an added bonus.

Words weren't necessary, and Viv wasn't sure his brain could have gotten his mouth moving, even if he had wanted to say something. Ray seemed to be in the same boat, as the only intelligible thing coming out of Ray's mouth were continual lust-filled moans.

Viv's whole body felt like it was going up in flames. He needed more. He needed to be closer. Slowing his thrusts, Viv yanked Ray up until they were back to chest, then upped his pace once more. One arm he wrapped around Ray's chest, holding him close, while he used his other hand to grasp Ray's leaking cock. The high-pitched keening Ray was making was a sure sign Ray's orgasm was close. Viv bit the side of Ray's neck as his husband stiffened in his arms. Viv grunted when Ray's cum flew out of his body and into the air. It arced before landing on the pillow at the top of the bed.

Viv shouted into Ray's neck then lost control and, with one last thrust, trying to get as deeply as he could, Viv came, his hot seed filling Ray's body. They stayed momentarily kneeling on the bed, then Viv slid free, leaving the dildo behind. Pride filled him when Ray melted onto his stomach on the bed. Viv took the still-switched-on vibrator and worked it in and out of Ray's body. He'd always loved the way he could bring his lover so much pleasure.

Viv moved Ray to his side and propped one leg up onto a pillow. He used the vibrator, pressing deeper into his husband's body. Ray started moaning and pushing back into Viv's ministrations, Viv pulled the toy free and slid his almost-hard cock in as a replacement. If nothing else, he just wanted to feel close to Ray, but it wasn't long before his own needs took control. This time, Viv slowly made love to his husband. The need to fuck Ray through the mattress was gone and now he could concentrate on bringing them both exactly the enjoyment they needed. It wasn't going to take long for either of them to get off, and that didn't matter one iota.

"Oh, Viv."

"I've got you, love," Viv whispered tenderly.

His whole body, as well as Ray's, was drenched in sweat, yet neither of them seemed to mind. His spine tingled with the telltale signs of his orgasm, Viv moved until Ray was once more face down on the bed. Viv ground his body against Ray's ass and came. After pulling free, he turned Ray and smiled when he saw the wet spot on the bed, and Ray was out like a light.

Quietly, Viv got up and took both toys into the bathroom. He tossed them into the sink. Viv wet a face washer and went back out to clean up his lover. Ray didn't even twitch when Viv did what needed to be done. Back in the bathroom, Viv showered and cleaned off the toys. He didn't feel guilty at all as he slid the vibrator into his own ass. Turning it on, he took his time showering. He didn't have enough left in him to come for a third time. He just wanted to feel full. Though it didn't stop him from bumping his own ass against the wall to keep the dildo firmly in place while he fucked himself. His legs were ready to give out. Viv tugged on his dick and was surprised by one last squirt of cum making its dash for freedom. His heart was pounding out of control and his blood rushed through his body. All the while, his gaze was riveted to the cum washing down the drain at his feet. After removing the dildo from his ass, Viv washed the toy.

He got out of the shower and dried himself and both toys. Viv walked naked into the wardrobe and put everything back in its rightful place so they would be exactly where they were meant to be for the next time he and Ray needed to play. It wasn't very often, but when they did, they sure enjoyed everything that took place. Viv bit back his smile. It crossed his mind just how tender Ray would be feeling after he woke. He hoped like hell he hadn't been too rough on Ray's sexy-assed body. If they weren't careful, most of the adults in the house would know exactly what he and

Ray had been up to.

Softly closing their bedroom door, Viv made his way to the nursery where he found a blushing Fred and a grinning Josh. Viv groaned, remembering the baby monitors they used were the kind that went both ways so they could talk to the babies when they first woke.

Looking at them both, Viv switched off the monitor and said, "Not a word to Ray. He doesn't need to know we put on a show for the two of you."

"Luckily it was us and not Declan and Sean. They have been spending a few mornings with us in the nursery… something about a project they are doing at school," Josh said.

Viv groaned again and thanked his lucky stars that it hadn't been Declan and Sean. No child—even if he was going on eighteen—wanted to hear his parents having sex. That was gross on every level. He and Ray could have scarred them for life. Next time, they would have to be more careful…or at least remember to turn the monitor off on their end. "Promise me you won't say anything to Ray."

Fred's blush deepened. "We would never do that to you guys. Let me rephrase. I would never do that, and I'll make damn sure Josh keeps his big, gossiping mouth shut."

"I'm not that bad," Josh complained.

Both Viv and Fred laughed, because Josh was just that much of a teasing ass that he'd find it fun to take the piss out of Ray. Hell, every chance he got, he reminded everyone that he was the first person who had actually gotten to make out with Ray way back when they were teenagers. Jokingly, Josh always commented that he was the reason Ray was now gay.

"Josh." Viv drew out his name like a teacher reprimanding a student.

"Fine. I won't say a damn thing." Josh huffed.

The grin on his face told Viv that Josh wasn't really upset or angry.

Fred chuckled before saying, "That's right, you won't say

anything. It isn't okay to take the piss out of the man who signs our paychecks."

"Right. There is that." Josh mimed zippering his mouth. "My lips are sealed."

Before Viv could turn the monitor back on, Ray was standing in the doorway, looking only fractionally rumpled, yet fully satiated. "What's going on?"

"Just talking about the upcoming immunizations for the babies," Fred jumped in so Josh couldn't open his mouth.

* * * *

Ray walked over and started discussing what they needed to do. At times like this, it was easier on them all for the doctor to make a home visit. It was a matter of moving the babies down to the sterile room his grandfather had used for the very same thing just before he'd died. They never used the room for anything else. But Ray knew the vibrancy of their children was washing away the taint of his grandfather.

To this day — even though the man was dead and gone — his grandfather scared him. The man hadn't been a monster exactly, he'd just liked to rule their lives. He'd been happiest when he'd had them all under his thumb. Ray was forever getting into trouble because he defied his grandfather on so many levels. James Connelly had been a hard man and never had quite worked out that if he'd shown Ray an ounce of love, Ray would have done everything he was ordered to do by his grandfather. Instead, the more the man pushed, the more Ray resisted the urge to cower and give in. James and Grandma were so different it was like night and day. Grandma was all that was good in the world, and Grandfather had been nothing but misery.

"So is everyone looking forward to the party tonight? I just can't believe GG wanted it to be a fancy movie star dress-up. What are you going as?" Josh was like a kid in a candy store.

Ray smiled. "I'm going as Robin, and Viv will be my Batman. What about you guys?"

"Fred wants to go old school and be someone like Gene Kelly and Fred Astaire. Me, I want to be action heroes... maybe like Mad Max or something," Josh answered.

Ray looked between them both before asking, "So which one of you is going to be Fred and which one will be Gene?"

"I'm Gene," Josh answered with a pout. "I can't wait to see what everyone else is going as. Did you remember to organize the child-minding service to come in?"

"Yes." Ray was using the same service they had so many times before, thankful that the spiteful bitch who had made Jamie cry was no longer employed with the company.

Ray loved his kids, but there was no way he wanted the littlest of them all running around among the adults. The service had asked if Ray wanted the same arrangement where the kids got to have their own party before campout and movie time. Ray had agreed, and this year the children's party was going to be held in the playroom, while Antonio had the adult party set up under marquees in the backyard.

Strangely, it was very reminiscent of their engagement party, the very same day Jamie had been brought into their lives. Over the years, their friend base had grown by leaps and bounds, and Ray knew most of them would be coming, even feeling comfortable enough in bringing their own children to be looked after. Grandma had always said a happy employee did better at his job than one who was forever angry.

Fred grinned. "Don and Mandy are coming as Fred and Wilma."

The thought of Fred's sister and brother-in-law dressed as The Flintstones was going to be awesome. Girly had been very quiet about what she was dressing as. She'd basically stuck her tongue out at him and told him to mind his own business and that he would find out at the party like everyone else. Dan was being stubborn and saying he wasn't coming as he had to work. Apparently Grandma was still working on that one. Grandma was coming as a witch from Oz, but she wasn't saying which one.

They talked for a while longer, speculating on costumes and such, before they dressed the kids and took everyone down to breakfast. Saturday mornings were usually a whole-family affair. If the family got any bigger, they'd maybe have to think about knocking out a wall to extend the dining room. Most everyone was there as they entered the room and placed the babies into highchairs or booster seats.

"So how is everyone this fine morning?" Ray asked cheerfully. As he walked around the table, he did his usual practice of kissing everyone on top of their heads before he made it back to his own seat. "Who's ready for a party?"

"Me," Jamie said excitedly. "I even have my costume all ready."

After much discussion, Ray and Viv had agreed to let Jamie attend the adult party. He was the oldest of the children and not many people had kids his age. He'd gotten Sean and Declan to promise to take Jamie under their wing so he didn't wind up spending the night by himself. Okay, he'd promised them a trip to Water Park if they made sure Jamie had fun. After they had agreed, Declan and Sean said they'd have done it for free, but the Water Park sounded awesome.

Ray knew he was a soft touch, not that he minded. Some of their kids had had such fucked-up lives to begin with that he wanted to always see them smile. He never wanted them to be reminded of the crap they'd had to live with before. Even though he knew their past hardships would end up making them stronger people in the long run, spoiling them every now and again didn't bother him. It wasn't like they came to him every day with their hands held out asking for anything. In fact, it was the exact opposite. Nine times out of ten, they would tell him they didn't need whatever he wanted to give them.

"Just make sure you are all home by six p.m.," Grandma

said from the head of the table. She was pointedly staring at Dan, who, if Ray wasn't mistaken, was squirming in his seat.

"Bodhi said he'll be here," Nate stated before he began eating.

In the beginning, Bodhi had lived in the house but had since moved out to be with friends. He still came over every night to work out with anyone who wanted to. Mainly it was Nate, Declan, Sean and Jamie, but that was okay. The man got paid to do a job, and it was something he did well. Ray knew Bodhi spent time with each person so they all benefited. Another thing in Bodhi's favor was that he also made it a daily practice to report back to either him or Viv if he thought the boys were pushing it. It soon became apparent the gym was somewhere they connected and felt free to talk about their problems. So in addition to being a personal trainer, Bodhi was also now the boys' mentor and sounding board for the things bothering them. Ray guessed there were probably some topics the boys weren't comfortable talking to him and Viv about. He could understand that. Grandma had told Ray Bodhi was back studying and was going to become a counselor for troubled youths. Ray knew before long that Grandma would have worked her magic, and Bodhi would be counseling at Destiny House and New Hope.

It never went unnoticed that Dan let out a little growl at Nate talking about Bodhi. Ray didn't think there was actually anything going on between Nate and the trainer. Hell, Ray wasn't even sure that Bodhi was gay. The man never said, and Ray never asked. Sometimes he thought he'd caught Bodhi watching Nate appreciatively. Ray had even noticed Dan had stopped by the gym a time or two and glared at Bodhi. Not that it seemed to bother the guy one bit. Ray was sure Bodhi amped up his attention toward Nate even more when Dan was nearby. He hoped like hell Girly hadn't gotten into Bodhi's ear and ordered him to help out.

"You have a sore throat there, Dan?" Josh asked with a straight face.

Ray bit back a smile as Dan glared at Josh. If looks could kill, Josh would be dead and buried.

"I'm fine," Dan snarled.

Josh winked at Ray before turning back to Dan. "Sure you are. You keep telling yourself that and one day it might come true."

"Uncle Josh is right," Jamie interjected. "You are a lot crankier than you used to be. I liked the old you better."

"You tell him, little man," Josh cheered Jamie on.

Josh grunted, and it was obvious by the scowl on Fred's face she'd kicked him under the table. "You need to start thinking before you open your mouth," she muttered softly.

Beside him, Viv was smiling at his plate and apparently trying like hell not to get drawn into the conversation. Why, for one freaking day, couldn't they get on like a normal loving family with no arguments? Where everyone was happy to see each other? Crap, if life was like this normally Ray would have found himself in a situation like *The Stepford Wives*—or siblings, as the case would be here for his family. Ray turned his attention to feeding Layla and tried hard to ignore what was going on around him.

Though he did smile when Dan said, "I will try harder, Jamie."

No one could resist Jamie. The kid wound people around his heart like a siren calling her prey into the sea. Once, a long time ago, he'd heard Jamie telling Ray's mother that he didn't know why people liked him so much. He was just trying to be a normal boy. Ray's mum had gone on to say there was nothing wrong with people liking him as long as he didn't take advantage of them. Jamie had thought about it for a moment before telling Ray's mum that he had no intention of using people. He only wanted to help them if he could. Right then, he'd known Jamie was special.

Antonio handed out orders to the adults at the table. Ray could tell his uncle was just as excited as Grandma was about the party. On more than one occasion, Antonio had given himself over to becoming the party manager and just like last time, he'd insisted Corazon Williams help him out. With Grandma's help, Corazon and Hugh Williams had started their own catering and party organizing firm. Well, mainly it was Cora's work and Hugh kept track of the books. Yet no matter how busy they were, Cora always had time to help Antonio with family functions. Whether they be big or small, they were always done to perfection.

Grandma had told Ray in confidence that Antonio was Cora's silent partner, except Antonio didn't know it yet. Grandma, his mother and Aunt Magen had worked everything out with Cora. Ray had warned all three women, whom he loved dearly, that they'd have to let Uncle Ant know before he found out some other way and he became upset with them. Uncle Ant was a very proud man. Hence the reason he refused to live the life of a rich man and still worked for Grandma, his step-mother.

Grandma had always treated Antonio as family, even before Ray found out Antonio the butler-cum-house-manager, was really his Uncle Ant, the son of a woman his grandfather had had an affair with. It wasn't until the truth came out that Ray realized just how much Antonio and Ray's very own father, Liam, looked alike. They had the same build and facial features, just very different colorings. Sometimes Ray believed Antonio was still coming to terms with the whole family knowing his true identity.

"Ray, you look like you're a million miles away," Lily said as she joined them.

Ray smiled at his cousin. He hadn't seen her for a while. Lily migrated between the house and living with a friend near the university where she was attending. It was good to see her home. He wondered if she was on holiday or had only come home for the weekend to attend the party. "I was thinking about how much our family has changed. How much better we've gotten because of the love we share."

"You're starting to sound like you're in an episode of *The*

Waltons there, John Boy," Josh teased.

Ray didn't take offense. "And you love being a part of this big mish-moshed family as much as I do. Admit it, you wouldn't change a damn thing."

"Of course not. You turning gay, getting married to Viv, and having all these kids brought my Fred into your house. My life got a whole lot better when that happened," Josh agreed.

The happiness on Fred's face at Josh's announcement was right there for the world to see. Ray wished Teddy was still here with them. It had been hard on everyone, and without going to court and fighting for the boy, it looked like they wouldn't see him for a while. Ray hoped Damien's brand of parenting didn't turn the boy against them all. Deep down, he prayed Teddy was strong enough to stay true to himself — whoever that turned out to be.

Turning his attention back to his cousin, he asked, "How's uni going? Did you bring a boyfriend back for us to meet?"

They both knew he was teasing, but Ray became more interested when Lily blushed. "As a matter of fact, I have brought someone to meet the family. I want you all to play nice, and not scare him off. I really like this guy, and school is fine. Easy-peasy, so far. Hold on, I'll go and find Harry."

Harry must be the special someone in her life. Ray hoped she was happy. Lily was studying fashion design, which, in a weird way, suited her to a T. She always did have an eye for style. Lily often claimed that Sean had the better fashion sense. Maybe it was true. Yet, in saying that, Ray realized that talent must run in their bloodline. They all seemed to do great with whatever they tried their hands at, whether it was being the head of the company, running Destiny House, being a musician, or, like him, a stay-at-home father to an ever-growing brood. He knew he wouldn't have his life any other way than what it was like now.

A quiet hush fell over the room when Lily reemerged with a guy. "Everyone, this is Harry, Haruki Watanabe. He is a friend of mine from uni," Lily said with a blush.

The beautiful young Asian man at her side gave them all a bow.

"You're really pretty," Jamie announced into the silence. Haruki smiled back at Jamie.

His innocent words made a few people chuckle, and with that, the ice was broken. Lily led Harry to the table and told him to dig in.

"Are you in the fashion course as well?" Grandma asked.

Haruki answered in perfect English, "Yes, I'm in most of the same classes as Lily."

Harry may have looked Asian, but he spoke with an Australian accent. Ray grinned when everyone in the room stared at the guy. Lily caught his attention and winked. Harry was going to become one of them in no time.

As the family chatted, Ray took a moment to scrutinize everyone. Dan was watching Nate, even though he was pretending he wasn't, while Nate seemed to be oblivious to it all. Declan, Sean and Jamie were involved in an animated conversation. Charlotte, Millie and Ben were chatting among themselves. Grandma was speaking with Aunt Magen and Uncle Ant. Lily and Harry were catching up on the family gossip with Fred and Josh. Viv was scrolling through his emails on his phone. He'd promised Ray that he'd get them out of the way, then he was free for the day. It seemed like forever since they'd spent the day together as a whole family. The only people missing were Girly, Mick and Ray's mother and father. The four of them would definitely be over before the day was done.

Ray knew without a doubt that he wouldn't change anything about his family. It was okay for them to have imperfections. Hell, it was even okay for them to get pissed off at each other, but not to hold grudges. In the end, Ray liked it when things finally worked themselves out. To people who didn't know them, Ray wondered if his family appeared like a refuge, seeing as there were so many individuals living under one roof. It was strange by anyone's standards, yet for them, it worked. The support network between them was phenomenal. Even if they were angry, they still stood together as a family unit.

He'd always believed his grandma was the core of who he was. She'd raised him to be a man when his life had looked like it had been swirling down the drain. She never judged. Okay, maybe she did, but she did it in a way where it would help him and not hold him back. Nowadays, Ray's core that held him together was his husband. Without Viv standing beside him, life wouldn't be worth living. Oh, he'd still have family and friends. He'd still go out and perform, but he'd *still* be hiding away whom he really was inside. Viv was his lodestone that grounded him to the here and now. If Viv wasn't there, he wouldn't have everything that he did now.

"Are you okay, love?"

Ray smiled at the man in question when Viv reached across and held his hand. "I'm fine, just thinking about the family. You know, about things that have happened to get us to this time in life and I'm wondering what's to come. I wonder about who our children will grow up to be."

"No matter what, they'll be good people," Viv supplied the answer Ray already knew.

Ray asked. "Do you ever think about how different our lives would've been if we'd never met? I can't even imagine ever being without you. Because without you, I am nothing."

"Are you quoting Placebo song lyrics at me now?" Viv said in a teasing manner.

"No... Okay, maybe that was a CD title of theirs. But, Viv, I meant what I said. I can't bear to think of never having you in my life."

Viv frowned at him. "Where's this all coming from? I'm not going anywhere. I'm here for the long haul. So you better get used to having me around." He pointed at his wedding ring. "For better or for worse—remember?"

"I haven't forgotten. Don't listen to me. I'm just having a melancholy moment. I'm wondering about all the what ifs and what could have beens. I have no regrets about loving you. You are the best thing—besides this brood—that ever happened to me."

When Viv leaned in and placed a soft kiss on his lips, Ray melted. His slight movement had his ass twinging in remembrance of what had taken place in the privacy of their room that morning. What would more than likely be experienced again many times over. Viv had a way of bringing the best out of Ray and making his body sing into life.

Ray pulled back and shook his head.

Think unsexy thoughts. Don't think about the fucking gorgeous man sitting beside me. The man who fucked me into oblivion only a few hours ago. It's not okay to have a boner while sitting at the dining room table as the whole family is gathered around. Get it together, Ray.

Taking a deep breath, Ray mentally shook himself to get is body under control. There would be time enough later to explore more with Viv.

Right now they had a party to help get ready for. All right, so mainly they had a couple of hours while the hired help set up before the guests started arriving. Hours where Viv had promised to put aside work and be with him and the kids. Well, the smaller ones anyway. The older ones all had lives of their own. It was becoming uncool to be caught hanging around with your dads and younger siblings. Instead of hauling everyone out of the house and into the city, Ray hoped they could spend the day in the playroom where everything they needed was on hand. Especially while the children were teething.

By the time the breakfast meal was over and done with, only he, Viv and their babies were left sitting at the table. Josh and Fred had excused themselves, saying they would be back soon to help with the younger children in the playroom. By the look on his friends' faces, Ray surmised Josh was going to be helping Fred forget some of her own troubles for a while. Ray hated seeing his friend in pain—

no matter how much she tried to hide it. Getting up from the table, he waited for Viv to pick up the twins while Ray carried Jeb. Charlotte and Millie held Ben's hands, and they all slowly made their way through the house to the playroom.

As far as Ray was concerned, today was going to be a good day, and tonight was going to be even better. They would dress up, have fun, and hopefully raise the much-needed funds for some worthy causes that would change the lives of young men and women. Destiny House and its sister house, New Hope, were exactly what their community required. Too often the defenseless were getting pushed down and trodden on instead of receiving the helping hand they needed.

Times were about to change — hopefully for the better.

Chapter Fifteen

Ray's quiet day didn't go quite as planned. No sooner had they settled in the play room than Norman called with a problem. Ray and Viv had to leave the kids and head over to Destiny House. Once they were in the office, the frustration Norman was apparently feeling was evident. They didn't even get to ask what the problem was before he shoved a document at them. With a frown, Ray picked up the letter and read it through before handing it over to Viv.

"This is bullshit. They can't just close us down without giving us a reason."

"They have. Noise restrictions," Viv answered.

Norman snorted in disgust. "I don't know who complained about us or what their real motive is, but there is no way we are any louder than other houses in the area. Most everyone here is quiet and keeps to themselves. The other day, Ethan's car was vandalized after he'd gotten home from uni. We got up the next morning and someone had spray-painted his car."

"How come I didn't hear about this?" Ray demanded.

Norman shrugged. "Girly was here. She took control of the situation. She had Brent call the cops then organize for security lights to be installed, and for cameras. She even paid to have Ethan's vehicle cleaned up."

Ray sat in a chair, scrubbing a hand over his face. "Have there been any other such incidents that I should know about? We need to see if we are being targeted for a reason, or if it was just a one-off thing." Turning to Viv, he asked, "Do you think Shane could have had anything to do with the Ethan situation?"

Viv shook his head. "I don't think so, but we should talk to Byron about this violation letter. I would hate to see this escalate into a major problem."

"Have any of the other men been targeted?"

Before Norman could answer, the door opened. Brent and Tarni walked in.

"So you've seen the letter. What do you think of it?" Brent asked.

"It's all bullshit if you ask me." Ray exhaled loudly. "Why are they complaining now?"

Tarni sat near Ray. "I don't know if this means anything or not, but the other day I saw some men surveying the surrounding properties. Is it possible this could be some kind of stunt a corporation would do?"

"What do you mean?" Ray asked.

"What if they want us out so they can tear down the whole block and build something new? Or what if the neighbors don't want a refuge in the area?" she asked.

Ray sat there stunned. What she was saying made perfect sense. "I'll take the letter and talk to Byron tonight. Hopefully he can find out what the hell is going on."

"If we get any more letters or acts of vandalism, then call us immediately. We can't let the whole thing blow up before we're even up and running properly."

The mood was somber as Ray stood. "We have to get home, but we'll talk more tonight once I've had a chance to run this by Byron. We aren't going to let any of this affect the fundraiser."

They said their goodbyes and left. Ray was ready to spit chips. Why couldn't people mind their own damn business? His bad mood was dispelled the moment Viv distracted him.

"Love," Viv stated, "we'll work everything out."

"How do you know that?"

Viv smiled at him. "Because that's what we do."

* * * *

The party was in full swing, and Viv was really enjoying himself. By the noise around him, he could see most other people in attendance were having fun as well. Viv smiled when he saw Dan—who had been so determined he wasn't attending—standing off to one side, scrutinizing the crowd. More pointedly, he was watching someone *in* the crowd. Viv followed his brother's line of sight. Nate and Bodhi stood with Girly and Mick. Whatever the foursome were talking about had them all laughing. The scowl Dan was sending their way was intense. Viv wondered if anyone else in the room could feel the tension. Viv still wasn't certain if Bodhi swung Nate's way, but he was remembering his friend from old, and guessing Bodhi wasn't. Bodhi was the rare kind of friend who didn't care about your orientation as long as you were a good person.

Viv wished Dan could just figure out what he wanted in life and go after it. If he was truly in love with Girly like he claimed, then he would have fought more to keep her, but he didn't. Instead, he'd run away to lick his wounds. That told Viv something. The problem with Dan was that he was very prideful. In his brother's mind, Viv knew his reasoning would be that Girly left him for Mick because Dan had admitted to having feelings for Nate, so it was Nate's fault for tempting him.

Dan was letting everything get distorted until there was no hope of regaining control. The sad part was that in other circumstances, Dan and Mick would have been friends. No matter how much Viv tried talking with his brother, Dan shut him down every single time. There had to be some way for everyone to take that next step forward. He hoped by forcing Dan and Nate to work together at the club it would make Dan wake up and go after Nate as a possible love interest, or Dan would suck it up and let Nate go. The funny thing was, Nate seemed oblivious to Dan's inner turmoil, and if he wasn't, then the guy was a damn good actor.

Viv and Ray had been taking turns at checking on the

children. In a weird sort of way, Viv missed all the family routine of getting the kids ready for bed. He wasn't always at home to enjoy those times, but when he was, it felt odd not to be in on the action.

"Hey, Dad," the kid dressed as The Hulk and who sounded an awful lot like Jamie, gave him a hug and sat beside him. Jamie had done a great job on his costume. "Do you think it would be okay if I went and slept in the same room as the babies? I don't want to be upstairs by myself when the rest of the family is still outside. Declan and Sean said they would go with me, but they're still having fun and I'm getting tired."

"Sure, little man. I think your Pa already told the ladies to expect you." Viv looked at his watch and saw that it was almost ten-thirty. Jamie always had been an early-to-bed type of child. "Come on, I'll walk you inside. That's where Pa is anyway."

Viv wrapped his arm around Jamie's shoulder and walked inside with his son. He listened avidly while Jamie told him about all the fun he'd gotten up to with Sean and Declan. Viv always marveled how the kids got along, especially considering the gap in their ages. Jamie always had acted older than he truly was.

They met up with Ray just outside the playroom door. "Are you off to bed, little man? I put some clean pajamas in the bathroom for you."

"Thanks, Pa." Jamie hugged Ray then headed off to shower and change clothes.

Viv held his arms open and waited for Ray to walk into his embrace. "From what I've seen so far, I'd say Grandma did it again. This has been a total success. I ran into Girly earlier and she said they'd already surpassed the last fundraiser."

"It's for a good cause. People always like knowing they've been involved in helping out others in need. Plus, this way, they write everything off for their taxes," Ray said before stepping away. "I think Grandma can charm the pants off anyone when she wants something from them."

"At least everyone seems to be having a good time."

Ray snorted. "Free food, free booze, and hanging out with your friends. What's not to like?"

"I guess you're right. It makes me wonder what would have happened if Grandma and the family hadn't stepped in to help these people. What would their lives have become?"

Ray shuddered. "I just don't even want to think about it. If I do, then I have to think about all the people who need help and never get it. It pisses me off and saddens me to no end to know we can't aid them all. I wish we could. Hell, I wish there were more people like Grandma willing to assist. I remember her telling me once, when I was a kid, that just because we have money doesn't mean we're better than anyone else — it just means we have a way of supporting those who can't do it for themselves. We just have to work out what is necessary."

"Grandma instilled her beliefs in you. I bet she did it so you and our children carry on her legacy," Viv surmised.

At least in this family they would put their money to good use. He realized that everyone seemed to help the community. Except for the club. That was purely for enjoyment. He could've sold it many a time — he'd had plenty of offers — but he couldn't sell what had once belonged to his father. He loved his father and what he'd created, and Viv couldn't wait to see what his and Ray's kids did with the establishment to make it their own. Maybe he could talk to Grandma about using it as a place where those old enough could start out in the work force again. Not everyone suited the life of working in a nightclub, so maybe they could open certain sections up and turn it into a café during the day. The whole unused and outdoor sitting area could be revamped. He would have to check out his licensing laws and find out what, if any, other permits they would need to apply for.

Now that the thought was in his head, he couldn't get rid of it. Viv knew it was going to eat at him until he had talked it out. "Come on, let's go find Grandma. I have something I want to run by her. I better get Dan, Nate, Norman, Girly, Mick, Brent and Tarni as well. Hell, even Byron, as we still need to talk to him anyway about the letter."

"What's going on?" Ray asked.

"Let's gather everyone and I'll tell you all together. If I only have to do it the once, then I won't screw up what I have to say." At the look of worry on Ray's face, he added, "It's nothing bad, I promise. Just something I thought of and wanted to run it by the think tank we have in place."

Viv made a beeline for Grandma while Ray went in search of the others. They were going to meet inside the house in Grandma's home office. "Grandma, can I drag you off for a moment or two? I have something I'd like to discuss with you."

"Is everything okay?"

"Yeah, I just need to pick your brain for a bit. Ray's gone to get the others so we can start," Viv said as he led Grandma back into the house. "Ray's bringing everyone to your office. Did you know about the letter they received at Destiny House?"

Grandma patted his hand. "I see you have the look of excitement, so I can only guess that this is something you feel strongly about. That letter business seems a little fishy to me. Though, I'm more worried about what happened to poor Ethan. We were lucky it was only the car and not Ethan himself who got damaged."

Before Viv could answer, he office door opened and the others trickled in. He waited until the door was shut again and everyone was settled before he started. He grinned as he realized this would be the strangest-looking meeting he'd ever conducted. There was a variety of different costumed people all staring at him and waiting.

"Okay, I know this probably isn't the best time to bring this up, but I have an idea of sorts, and I want to hear what you all think before I go any further with my plans." When no one said anything, he went on. "I was thinking of changing the nightclub a little. Don't get me wrong, it's still going to be a nightclub, but I would also like to open up the unused portion and turn it into a café, maybe even a cyber café for day and night. Both areas will be interconnected by the kitchen. The café will not sell alcohol, but will serve other beverages as well as meals. I was thinking light meals in the day and possibly offering a dinner menu as well."

"What part of the club will you open up?" Dan asked.

Nate answered, "The other side of the kitchen is the glass house we're using for storage. I looked up on some old plans that it was once used as a dining room. But someone before your father's time closed it down to concentrate more on the club side."

"That's right." Viv had known that. "I was thinking maybe with Destiny House and New Hope we could offer work placement to people trying to get back on their feet. Having a day and night staff will help a lot. I'm hoping it won't interfere with the zoning laws. I'll have to get that all checked out. So what do you think?"

Dan was the first to add his two cents' worth. "It's going to be a lot of hard work setting everything up. Especially if we have to train everyone how to do customer service. If the zoning laws need to be changed, they might say no straight up."

"There's already fast-food places across the street and in the area, so I don't think zoning will be a problem," Girly said. "But Dan's right. It's going to take a lot of work and time."

"I think it's a good idea," Grandma offered with a shrewd smile.

Viv could see the wheels kicking off inside her head. If she was behind him, then he knew his idea had some merit.

Ray sat on the edge of the office desk and listened to the discussion going on. He could understand Viv's reasoning. Especially after the conversation they'd had outside the playroom. He wasn't against the idea of doing something more to help the people who walked through the doors of Destiny House and New Hope. He was more worried that it was going to wear out his already overtaxed husband. Ray remained silent until Viv looked at him.

"I'm not against the whole idea, but who is going to run it? I don't want you stretching yourself too thin."

Viv smiled at him. "We'd have to hire someone to come in and do the training and to actually manage the place. I know this is only adding to our workloads, but it feels like the right thing to do. I want this. I won't be the one running it, but surely we can find someone."

"Then I support you all the way. If we find the right manager, it shouldn't put too much of a strain on our lives. I just didn't want you controlling the café on top of working, uni, and keeping an eye on the club. It feels like we hardly see you as it is, without adding something more to keep you away from home."

"Honestly, love, I won't have anything to do with the place other than my name being on the lease. I figure all profits made can go back into supporting both houses. I just needed to contribute something. Does that make sense?" Viv asked.

Ray nodded. "It makes perfect sense. I say figure out how to set this up and let's put the proper individuals in place to get things started. We have good administrators in charge of both houses and I think they need to be the ones to interview applicants for the managerial position, as they will have to be the ones in direct communication with whoever is hired."

The chatter in the room became more than a little excited as ideas were tossed onto the table. Ray couldn't have been prouder of his husband than he was at that very moment. It wasn't often someone set out to do something without wanting a reward at the end. Maybe Grandma really was a good influence on them all.

"I think everyone should come up with ideas for a name for the new café. We'll meet again in a week to see where we are. By then, we should know more about zoning laws and contractors to make any necessary renovations. Hopefully we won't run into too many snags along the way. Now, everyone should go back out there and enjoy the party before they send a search party out for us."

Ray saw the excitement on Viv's face had spread to everyone else in the room. At least with help, Viv wouldn't attempt to tackle it on his own.

Grandma asked, "Byron, do you have someone in your office who can handle this?"

"Consider it done," Byron answered

"Speaking of getting things done." Ray pulled out the letter he'd tucked inside his costume and handed it to Byron. "What do you make of this?"

Byron scanned the letter through then chuckled. "It's a fake. Not only have they misspelled words, there is no way this was written by a government department. I'll get Robert on this to see if he can backtrack and find out where it came from."

"Tarni said there were people surveying the land in the neighborhood. Do you think they could be involved?"

Byron turned to Tarni. "Did you happen to see a company name by any chance?"

She grinned at him. "Hartmann and Leeds."

"Very good. I'll have Robert get in touch with them and find out who hired them and for what purpose. We'll get to the bottom of this sooner rather than later. Is there anything else I should know about?" Byron asked.

Brent filled him in on the vandalism that had taken place.

"I think it's time we all make a reappearance at the party before people start thinking we've run away," Grandma said as she headed for the door.

After the room had cleared out, only Ray and Viv were left. Ray pulled Viv closer to him, gently cupped his face and kissed the man long and deeply. His body ached with need. But now wasn't the time to get all hot and heavy. Okay, maybe he would make time, but not here in his grandmother's office. Ray grabbed Viv's hand and hurried him up through the house until they were locked away in their bedroom.

He pushed Viv onto the bed and yanked down his husband's tights. Ray sighed, buried his face against Viv's groin and inhaled deeply of the intoxicating scent. Holding the base of Viv's cock firmly in his hand, Ray licked his way to the head, running his tongue along the prominent vein. His mouth watered in anticipation of what he was about to do. Fooling around while his lover was still half dressed had always been a turn-on for Ray. Swiping his tongue over the pre-cum leaking out of Viv's cock, Ray opened his mouth and swallowed him to the root.

"Turn around, Ray. I want to taste you as well."

As quickly as he could, Ray let Viv slide free of his mouth and stripped out of his own tights and shoes. Turning on the bed, he moved closer so Viv could pleasure him while Ray sucked him off.

Ray's dick was harder than hell. He moaned around the cock in his mouth when Viv pushed a finger into his ass. Viv always knew exactly what Ray needed. Ray kept on sucking while Viv stretched him. When he couldn't take it anymore, Ray let Viv go and moved until he was straddling Viv's groin. He pulled off first his shirt, then Viv's. "Hold your dick for me. I'm in the mood for a deep fucking."

Viv did as he was told, and Ray took no time impaling himself until Viv was balls-deep inside him. He threaded his fingers through Viv's as he bounced himself on Viv's cock, squeezing his muscles tightly every time he lifted his ass, and it felt so fucking good. His body knew this was where Viv belonged.

"Hold yourself up. It's my turn," Viv demanded.

Ray lifted himself off of Viv and just about lost it when Viv drove up into him. The blistering pace Viv set was too much and Ray wasn't going to last. Lightning tore through him. His body shattered with his orgasm. He didn't even have time to warn Viv before his cum was covering Viv's chest and face. "Viv!"

But Viv didn't stop. Ray struggled to stay upright as Viv powered into him, his body aching in all the right paces. Viv thrust deeply once more and came inside him. Ray always did like the feel of Viv's cum filling his ass.

The whole fuck fest hadn't taken very long, but now they could quickly shower, redress and go back out and join the party. Both he and Viv were well satiated. He also knew later tonight they would do the whole thing all over again. Next time, he'd be the one fucking Viv through the mattress. Ray's dick twitched at the mere thought of ravishing Viv later.

Pasting a smile onto his face, Ray held tightly to Viv's hand as they walked back out into the midst of the celebration. He dragged Viv toward the bar so they could get a much-needed drink. Ray didn't care that people looked at them strangely. Even after all this time, some people still had a problem with his and Viv's relationship. They never said anything to them, but Ray had heard the rumors. Even though he didn't work for the family company, he had friends who did and they would keep him in the loop. Ray loved his husband and he didn't care who was around when he showed him affection. Sometimes Ray kissed Viv in public just to piss people off.

At the bar, Graham Rogers was ordering a drink. He was one of the few who wasn't in the least bit gay friendly. He didn't even work for the Connelly Corporation. He was just some rich guy who liked to be seen at all the right parties. Ray was positive the guy was such a douchebag he only came for the free food and booze and never donated a cent to any of the fundraisers. It also happened to come to his attention that the two young siblings his grandma had sent to Destiny House were related to the pompous windbag—according to the gossip. Graham wouldn't lift a finger to help his cousin's sons because he'd been told they were gay. Ray didn't know whether or not Andrew and Evan were, in fact, gay. He'd never asked because it wasn't any of his business. What he did mind was the fact Graham had disowned them on the chance they might be.

"I'm going to make this guy very uncomfortable. Just go with me," Ray whispered into Viv's ear.

Viv must have been thinking along the same lines, because once they'd reached the bar, Viv turned Ray so his back was flush against it and Viv swooped in and devoured his mouth in a kiss hot enough to scorch the very ground where they stood.

"Do you mind? Some people don't want to see such depravity in public," Graham snarled.

Ray broke the kiss and glared at Graham. "Some people should keep their fucking opinions to themselves. No one cares what you think. This is my home and if I want to kiss my husband, then I damn well will."

A small crowd had gathered to watch the drama unfold.

Viv leaned in and spoke softly. "No throwing punches, Ray. Don't ruin the party by decking an outspoken and bigoted moron," he said, the last bit louder for the benefit of those near them.

"Does anyone here have a problem with my husband kissing me?" Ray asked the crowd at large. When no one said anything, Ray thought about what he wanted to say. He'd heard some people who thought along the same lines as Graham wouldn't donate because they didn't support the gay lifestyle. He needed them to see there was a much bigger picture at stake.

"As most of you know, Destiny House takes in young men in their time of need. A place where hopefully we can help them get back on their feet. We only want to give them a second chance at life. To us, it doesn't matter if they are gay or straight, it doesn't matter what color their skin is, or what religion they were born into. What does matter is that right now we are supporting them. I'm not sure if you've heard that we are starting up a sister house called New Hope. It will be similar in many ways, but this time it will cater to young women. Sometimes young people find themselves living on the streets because of circumstances out of their control."

Ray took a moment to look at everyone standing there listening. "We aim to assist everyone who comes to us. The ones whose families have disowned them. The ones who have absolutely nowhere else to turn to. If we can't personally aid them, then we will put them in touch with the people who can. Along with the added advantage of local departments in authority, we are working together to make our guests' lives better. They may stay with us for a week, or a month, or even longer, if necessary. No one gets turned away, and we always listen and find them the assistance they require."

Again Ray made eye contact with as many people as he could. "I'm not asking you to personally open up your own homes and offer shelter. I'm asking for you to give what you can to keep these shelters, these refuges, open for years to come. You never know when someone you know might need the same kind of service."

"Hear hear, Ray," someone called from the back.

Ray was pretty sure it was the chief of police. The man had aided them with so many things since Destiny House had opened its doors that he'd be forever grateful. Not that Ray had anything to do with the running of the place, but his daughter did. Chief Brendan Callahan had been trying to talk them into extending Destiny House as there were, according to statistics, the rate of homeless men and women was on the increase with each passing year. The man had a heart the size of Australia. He even volunteered to help out when he wasn't working. Some of his officers did the same. It was good to have their backing.

Another of their biggest supporters was Reverend Fred Chaney, who ran a small food bank for the homeless. He was also a young man who presided over a non-denominational congregation, and Grandma had been instrumental in keeping Reverend Chaney in business. Grandma had gotten grocery chains to donate food to help out. In turn,

Reverend Chaney sent young men he thought might be in trouble to Destiny House. It was a win-win situation.

Ray smiled when Grandma walked up to them. She kissed his cheek before addressing the crowd. "Since my grandson has started off the speeches, I figure I might as well continue his theme. Reverend Chaney and Chief Callahan, would you both please step to the front of the crowd?" Turning to Ray, she added quietly, "We're extending the house. These young coots talked me into it after we had our meeting. Though, we'll hold out on the café announcement until after it's all straightened out."

Ray noticed two men who came to stand beside them. Grandma began to tell those there for the fundraiser that they were extending Destiny House, and yes, any donations would be greatly appreciated. She took a deep breath and smiled sweetly. Ray knew that smile. She was about to wrap the crowd around her little finger as she got them to do her bidding. Everyone wanted to be in the good graces of Catherine Connelly.

"Aside from money, I need a small favor. I'm asking if each business owner is willing to consider taking on some of the youngsters and offering them employment. Teach them a trade. Teach them what you do best. Not only will it better their lives, but it will yours as well. I'm not asking to do this so that you can get an incentive payment from the government, because I can tell you none are on offer. I'm asking for you to help us because it is the right thing to do. In our community, respect among business associates goes a long way. Before you ask, yes, the Connelly Corporation has already implemented such a program. We are even offering to send those in our business to further their education with classes and courses. Reverend Chaney and Chief Callahan have kindly offered to step in and help in any way they can. If you have questions, you can call them and they will tell you what you need to know. We're not asking you to do anything beyond what you can. If you can offer nothing more than a donation, then we are also grateful." She chuckled softly. "Now, it's almost midnight and time for this old duck to get some sleep. I bid you all goodnight and hope you enjoy the rest of the party."

Ray took hold of his grandmother's arm and, along with Viv, they walked her back to her suite. They said goodnight to everyone along the way. Ray knew his grandma had more to say, and that whatever it was, it didn't need to be for public consumption. Well, not just yet anyway.

Once the doors to her suite were closed, his grandma doubled over laughing. "How long do you think it will be before we have the offers for work placement rolling in?"

Ray arched an eyebrow at her. "Who came up with that little spiel?"

"Reverend Chaney. He thought it would be best coming from me, seeing as I was the prettier out of the three of us. Mind you, Chief Callahan is pretty good looking if you ask me. He's a good kid to boot."

"Grandma, you do know he's in his thirties, not exactly a kid anymore. I think Reverend Chaney is around the same age," Ray said.

She blew him a raspberry. "Anyone younger than I am will always be a kid to me."

"What else do you have to tell us?" Viv asked. He must have gotten the same feeling Ray had.

"Chief Callahan has put in his resignation on the force, or more so, he was pressured to resign because it became known he's gay. The uppity ups on the force expected him to put up a fuss, but instead, he just wrote out and handed in a signed resignation letter. He's offered to run the café, along with helping out on the work placement side of things."

Ray frowned. "Does he know anything about running a café? We want the place to be successful. Especially if we want it to fund both houses."

"Yes, his mother's family have been in the restaurant business for years. He knows a lot about ordering and the general running of the café. I feel like giving him the job is the right thing to do. He already knows a lot about the residents of Destiny House. The kids are used to him. They trust him. Most importantly, I trust him, and so does Reverend Chaney."

There was so much Ray needed to know. Instead of talking about the job, he asked, "How did people find out the chief was gay?"

"The higher ups knew he helped out at Destiny House, and even though they didn't approve of what he was doing, they saw it as good publicity. Apparently someone on the force has an eye on the job of police chief and started a rumor that Brendan was having an affair with one of the young men residing on the premises. It's not true, of course, and even if it were, he's a grown man. Now the higher ups see it all as bad publicity. Because he left without a fight, the force looks at it like the rumor starter was proven right."

"No one has ever said anything to me about someone sleeping with the chief. Now that would be gossip that would fly through our family if it was known," Ray said, thinking aloud.

"That's because he wasn't. I asked him. Brendan told me he is seeing someone, but his lover isn't out yet. I didn't ask who, because it wasn't any of my business. If he wants us to know, then he'll tell us when he's ready."

Ray knew the decisions weren't his to make, seeing as the building belonged to Viv. He'd go along with whatever Viv decided.

"If you trust him, Grandma, then let's give him a shot." Viv seemed to think about it for a moment before he started talking again. "At least, being trained as a cop, he'll be able to handle any situation that comes up. I meant what I said when I told you all that I'd have nothing to do with the café. If this goes ahead, then it's up to anyone connected to both houses to make decisions. Think of me as the silent partner in all of this. I don't want to take control. I just thought it was a good way of me contributing to the cause. As Ray pointed out, I don't have the time to get to involved.

I don't want to lose any more time than I already do with my family. I'm happy to go along with whatever you think best, Grandma."

Grandma smiled at them both. "Then we'll give Brendan the chance. I think he will do a great job. I also think it will be better suited to him than being on the force ever was. Now, give me a kiss so I can get some sleep. Tomorrow is going to be as busy as you please."

"Night, Grandma," they both said as the left her rooms.

Ray pulled Viv into the sitting room. "I think Grandma's right about the chief. Even though I've never really considered him a friend, his family and ours have always been acquainted through business. They moved away for years and it wasn't until last year when Brendan came back as the new chief of police that he and Grandma became friends again. I just didn't realize how friendly until tonight."

"I wonder if his lover will come out... It would have to be hard living life that way," Viv said.

Ray loved how Viv worried about someone he'd only just met. Typical Viv to think of Brendan and his partner. "I guess we'll have to wait and see. Not that we have any say in the matter. What I wonder is how his family took the news, because Gerald Callahan has always been as anti-gay as they come. He makes Graham Rogers look like a GLBTQ community's best friend."

"We're not getting involved, Ray. Not this time."

"I never said we were. I was just thinking that if his closet case doesn't work out then there are plenty more fish in the ocean waiting to be caught by Mr. Brendan Callahan."

Viv sighed. "Leave it alone, Ray."

"Whatever you say, love."

Chapter Sixteen

Activity in the house got back to normal. Viv hadn't expected it to be as easy to step back from setting up the café as it was. Letting other people have the workload was almost cathartic. Actually, it helped Viv realize just how much his schooling and work were taking out of his everyday life. These days, it seemed like the times he saw Ray only allowed them enough time for a quick roll in the hay before life pulled Viv away again. How long would it be before Ray got sick of always coming second?

"Deep thoughts and frown lines cause wrinkles," Grandma said as she stuck her head into his office. She walked in, closed the door, and sat in the chair on the opposite side of his desk. "What's the problem?"

"Just trying to figure out my life. I love both my job and school. I just hate how much time Ray and I spend apart," he answered honestly.

Grandma frowned slightly. "Has Ray said something to you?"

"No, it's more that I know he's worried that I'm overdoing things. He also doesn't like that nearly every day I leave before the children wake up and don't come home until after they're already in bed asleep."

"I can see where that could be a problem." Grandma fell silent for a moment. "You need to reschedule. Do less hours and take fewer classes. Trust me, you'll regret it if you miss your children growing up. I've been keeping track of your input here, and I know you work longer hours every day than anyone else on your team. I know you are taking more classes so you can finish your degree earlier. Take a second and think about what's most important to you."

He didn't need time to think. "Ray and our family are the most important things in my life."

"Then why are you putting them last?" she asked.

"I don't know."

Grandma looked at her watch. "Your shift ended almost an hour ago yet you're still here. There's absolutely nothing that won't wait until tomorrow. I've sent my driver home. So you are now going to pack up and we can go home for family time. My husband was a hard man and believed business and money came before all else. I loved him but the man was an idiot. Family is what's most important. Don't let anything else get in the way."

"You are a wise woman, Catherine Connelly."

"Yes I am. I've been saying that for years. It's about time somebody else realized it," she said in a teasing manner.

Viv couldn't stop smiling as they took the elevator to the parking garage and got into his car. "So what do you think is on the menu for tonight?"

"Antonio called just before I came to find you and told me we're having Italian, so I'm assuming some sort of pasta dish."

Viv's stomach rumbled in appreciation. "I hope it's lasagna. I could eat that every day of the week."

"Me too," Grandma agreed.

"So how are the plans coming along for the café, and the two houses?"

"New Hope is finished, and Tarni is in the process of furnishing it. Destiny House has a crew there working on extensions. It will take a couple of months before everything is complete. Brendan is settling in nicely as head coordinator at the café. Nate has been a big help to him. I see a lot of good in that pairing."

Viv frowned as he pulled out of the parking garage and onto the road heading home. "What do you mean? I thought Brendan was already seeing someone?" If Nate got together with anyone before Dan figured himself out, his brother could slide right back into his depression.

"It's not what you're thinking. Nate can communicate with the guys at Destiny House better than Brendan. They trust Nate, because he was originally one of them. He knows what they've been through. He's almost like a buffer between Brendan and the other men. It works for now. I give it a couple of months and they'll be treating Brendan like he's one of them."

What Grandma said made absolute perfect sense. "What does Nate think? Is he still working at the club? Or is he intending to work full time at the café when it opens?"

"Nate would never leave the club. He made a promise to you that he would take over Girly's role. He's still a little leery of being in close quarters with Dan, but he puts his head down and does what needs to be done." She exhaled loudly. "Mind you, I'm getting really close to having words with that brother of yours. He needs a good shaking and a swift kick up the behind. If he keeps going the way he is, he'll push away everyone who cares about him."

Viv couldn't agree more. "I've been thinking the very same thing. I don't know what to do to make him see what's happening."

"Oh, he sees. He's just too stubborn to do anything about it. Maybe Girly had it right when she meddled. Someone has to do something. It's not just *his* heart he's mucking around with," Grandma snapped the last part out as Viv made the run into their driveway.

They didn't say anything else until the car was parked in the garage and Viv was helping her out. "So should we find a big stick and beat some sense into the boy, or do we sit back to watch him crash and burn?"

"We'll talk to him after dinner. Nate is working at the club tonight, so you know Dan will be at home brooding. I will get the ball rolling at dinner. Give him enough time to stew before we make him get everything off his chest."

Viv led the way inside. They both washed up in the mudroom before heading into the dining room. Warmth washed over Viv when Ray's eyes lit up at him being home so early. Viv couldn't help grinning as the kids all called out greetings to him. Taking a deep breath, Viv walked to his seat at the table and sat beside Ray. He took Ray's hand and waited. Could life get any better than this? Probably not.

"I can't believe you're home so early," Ray whispered. "I like it."

"I plan on doing it more often. A wise woman sat me down and basically told me to get my head out of my rear before I lose what is most important to me." He spoke loud enough that Dan was sure to hear. "I'm sorry if it seemed like I was putting you and the kids second. I never meant for that to happen."

Ray smiled at him. "I understood why you were doing it. I was just worried that you would wear yourself out."

Viv kissed his husband's cheek before looking at Grandma and delivering the cue they had worked out in the car. "So, Grandma, fill me in on what's happening with the café."

"Everything is running smoothly. I was talking to Brendan today and he told me that he's going to stop by the club tonight so Nate can show him that side of the building in action. He was really looking forward to it."

All adult noise at the table stopped. Dan clenched his glass of water so tightly that Viv was worried the glass would shatter. He hated to see his brother hurting, but knew this gentle shove was for the best. "Sounds like they're really getting along."

"They are. Brendan says Nate has been a huge help. They took some of the workers out to lunch, and from what I gather from the head construction guy, they worked well together."

Viv guessed it was the truth, from a certain point of view. "I guess it's better than them butting heads the whole entire time. From what they've both gone through, they each need a close friend."

"He's too old for Nate," Daniel snarled out before he

pushed away from the table and left the room.

"What the hell was that all about?" Ray demanded.

Viv shrugged. "You remember when Dan and Girly told Grandma we were dating? I mean, right back in the beginning, before we even thought of becoming involved?"

"Yeah, so?"

"Well, payback is a witch with a capital letter B," Grandma announced from her end of the table.

Ray closed his eyes, and Viv saw the moment realization hit. Grandma was swearing without actually doing it in front of the kids. "This is so going to backfire on you two. Why did you think something so idiotic would work?"

"It worked for us, didn't it?" Viv answered.

Ray stared at him blankly for a moment before he smiled brightly. "Yeah, I guess it did."

Josh decided to jump into the conversation. "It's about time someone shook up Dan's life. Who wants to bet he follows in the steps of his big brother and stalks his prey and sabotages his love life?

"I did not stalk Ray" — he grinned — "much. Besides, Dan is nothing like me. He's never had a problem going after what he wants."

"I think this is a conversation for after the young ones are asleep, don't you?" Grandma said pointedly.

Viv felt guilty as he looked around the table and saw Declan, Sean and Jamie all avidly watching and listening.

"Then we reconvene after bedtime," Josh stated.

* * * *

Ray almost felt bad for Dan. Then, when he remembered the guy's stubborn stupidity, he was happy to sit back and let the family intervention take place. Well, not so much Uncle Ant, Aunt Magen, Girly and Nate. Nor was anyone under the age of ten involved, but for the rest of them, Dan was fair game. Even Lily was still in town, so she entered Grandma's suite of rooms along with everyone else.

Jamie spoke up first. "I think you're making a mistake in pushing Dan, but I also don't want to see Nate get hurt."

"Little man, this is for the best," Declan said.

It was funny how most of the household referred to Jamie as 'little man'. Even funnier still was that Jamie answered to it.

"So what do we do?" Lily asked. "If Girly were here, she'd say we should shake the shit out of him until he sees sense."

"Thankfully Girly isn't here, then." Ray chuckled, because Lily was spot on in her assessment of Girly. "We just need to find a way for Dan to release his guilt. He will never move forward while shackled to his guilt over having feelings for Nate."

Lily frowned. "Wait, are you saying that Dan has feelings for Nate and is still treating him like shit?"

"Yes," Declan growled out.

"What an idiot. Honestly, he deserves to be left behind if that is the way he treats someone he cares about."

Ray sighed. "It's a lot more complicated than that. He's guilty because he was still with Girly when he realized he had feelings for Nate."

"But he's not with Girly now. So what's stopping him from manning up and telling Nate how he feels?" Lily argued.

"Because Nate is Girly's brother. How would you react if you found yourself falling in love with your partner's sibling?" Ray said.

"I guess I'd feel like crap," Lily conceded.

Viv chuckled. "Even if Nate and Girly are related, it doesn't change how Dan feels. He has to decide if he wants to move forward or not. Either way, he has to let Nate know what's going on."

"Nate likes Dan, but I don't think he'd ever make the first move," Declan said. "If Girly can't get him to talk to Dan, then I don't think anyone will get him to. You think Dan is stubborn, but I can tell you Nate is just as bad."

Grandma cleared her throat. "We're not going to have to

do anything. I bet you my last dollar that Dan has already gone to the club to check on Nate for himself. We have put the seed of losing Nate to someone else in his head. Now it's up to Dan to figure out the rest."

"So that's what you were up to? I thought it was a strange conversation to have at the family dinner table," Josh said.

Grandma grinned. "Strange, but necessary."

"I heard from Byron today," Ray announced.

"What did he have to say?" Grandma asked.

Ray said, "The letter really was bogus. It seems the surveyors, even though they are a real firm, weren't hired by anyone. They were trying to scare most of the residents from the neighborhood. More than one household got threatening letters in one form or another. Robert brought in the police and filled them in on the situation. I think there is going to be a class action of some kind by the residents."

"What were they really up to, and how did they think they were going to get away with it?" Viv asked.

"Hartmann and Leeds had high hopes of everyone selling up, and they would profit by clearing the block and building a multi-level mega store. Now it looks like they'll be facing court and more than likely lose their business in the process," Ray explained. "The crazy thing is, I don't think they ever had a hope in hell of succeeding. The police confirmed that the vandalism of Ethan's car wasn't the only act of destruction. There were windows broken, mail boxes trashed, garden beds destroyed, and one poor lady's cat had paint tipped all over it."

Grandma tapped her hand on the table and said, "Thankfully, the truth has come out and things can start getting back to normal. Those boys have been through enough without getting shifted around from house to house."

"From your lips to God's ears, Grandma," Ray stated.

After the family meeting broke up, Ray didn't want to go to their rooms. He wanted to enjoy Viv being home. He took Viv by the hand and led him out to his favorite spot in the garden. His quiet spot. His thinking spot. Ray didn't want to talk about Dan or any other family problems. He wanted to talk about him and Viv.

"I love having you home at a reasonably normal hour," Ray started slowly.

Viv sighed. "I'm sorry I let everything get ahead of you and the kids. I was honest when I said I didn't mean for it to happen. It just sort of did, and I didn't know how to fix the situation."

"Then let's have a fresh start. If you can promise more family time, then I won't get pissed when you do have uni or have to work late," Ray offered. He wanted Viv to see he was willing to work this out.

His husband must have understood. "Next semester, I plan on taking fewer classes at uni. I also promise that I will clock out at work when I'm supposed to and come home. I'm just sorry that I let it get so out of control."

"It wasn't really that bad. I got used to you being busy all the time, and most of the kids are too young to understand what's been happening, but Declan and Jamie, they knew. I think you need to spend some quality time with the boys. I mean, they've never complained, but they've missed you just as much as I have."

Ray melted against his husband as Viv kissed him. He held his breath when Viv traced down his body and cupped Ray's more-than-interested cock. Ray thought it was funny how his jeans fit perfectly until he got a hard-on. Maybe he needed to start wearing the next size up, especially if Viv made good on his promise to come home earlier. "Let's move farther away from the house. Just in case someone decides to look out of a window. No need in blinding them with the sight of my naked ass."

"Follow me."

Ray happily went where Viv led him.

When they reached the back of the garden, Viv moved them until they were leaning on the trunk of the weeping willow. Here they would be away from prying eyes. Ray grabbed Viv's hands and pressed them to the bark of the tree. "Don't move them."

Stepping up behind Viv, Ray reached around, undid his husband's belt and pushed his slacks and underwear down until they were pooled at his ankles.

"While you're down there, if you check the pockets, you'll find the lube," Viv said huskily.

Ray leaned forward and bit Viv on the left ass cheek, then dug through the pockets for his reward. After placing the bottle on the ground, Ray separated the cheeks of Viv's ass and kissed his puckered opening. Ray knew some men didn't like getting their mouths too close to their lover's holes, but Ray wasn't one of those men. He loved the taste of Viv, every single part of him. He didn't even hesitate as he swiped his tongue from Viv's nuts to his back.

Dinner had been great, but now Ray was hankering for dessert. And Viv was exactly what he wanted. Ray mentally cheered as Viv's hole relaxed under his ministrations. Slipping his tongue in as far as he could, Ray decided he was in heaven. The way Viv held his tongue had Ray ready to blow. He only allowed himself a couple of extra minutes of play before he extracted his tongue. He grabbed the lube and stood. Popping the top, he coated his fingers as he whispered into Viv's ear. "Did you like that?"

"Yes," Viv croaked out while Ray maneuvered two fingers deep inside Viv's hole. Scissoring them, he searched for Viv's pleasure spot. He knew he'd found it when Viv pressed his forehead into the tree and moaned. Pulling his fingers free, Ray then pushed back in with three and finger-fucked Viv.

Ray used his other hand to grasp the base of his own cock and stop his impending orgasm. There was no way in hell he was going to succumb until he was buried to the hilt inside Viv. "Are you ready for me?"

"Yes," Viv hissed.

At the sound of Viv's need, Ray slowly slid his fingers free. Lining his dick up with Viv's hole, Ray thrust hard, not stopping until he was completely in and could go no farther. Ray rested his forehead against the nape of Viv's neck. Sweat glistened on them both, and Ray rocked in and out. There was no need to hurry. Fucking Viv was all his mind could cope with right now.

"Love how tight you are. Love how you squeeze so perfectly," Ray muttered. Drawing back a little, he stared down at where they were joined, watching as he thrust into Viv over and over, and the way Viv's body willingly accepted him. They were perfect together. The way they were now, even though he could see they were two different entities, his body couldn't tell where he finished and Viv started. All it was focused on was the pleasure they were generating by being so intimately connected.

Ray gripped Viv's hips and picked up his pace. He needed to get this round down so the next round would be in their bed where they could spend the rest of the night holding each other. Heat danced through his entire core. With each little sound Viv made, Ray wanted to be deeper. He wanted to touch Viv in paces he'd never been touched before.

He ghosted one hand around Viv's hips and cupped his balls before using the other hand to jack Viv off while Ray ground against his ass, loving the sensation of Viv's hole wrapped around his cock and the stranglehold it had on him. Ray guessed how close Viv was by the way his balls tightened in his hand.

"Are you close, baby?"

"Yesss."

Ray drew back and once more grabbed Viv by the hips. "Then come for me," Ray demanded and slammed home. Fire raced through his body and he held tightly to Viv while Viv cried out. Ray quickly followed Viv over the edge. Slowly rocking in and out, Ray ended the same way they'd started. After a minute or so, his brain kicked back into gear and he slid free.

They were both sweaty and sticky, but right now, Ray didn't care. He'd brought his lover off so Ray's job here was done. All he needed now was a way to convince his body that it should pull his pants back up and let him make his way back to their bedroom with Viv.

"I bags first shower," Ray said, then he helped Viv dress.

Viv grunted. "The shower is plenty big enough for the both of us. I need to pay you back for making my legs forget how to work."

Ray shivered as Viv fondled his cock. Even though they were both spent, Ray's cock was willing to try again at the softest of touches. "You have a nice dick, Ray."

"Thank you. I think you have a nice dick as well. But we really should try and get to our room before anyone decides to come looking for us. Might scare them silly if they see me with my pants down and you playing with my dick."

Viv snorted. "We wouldn't want that. This dick right here belongs to me."

"Always has, and always will," Ray stated after he finally stood and redressed himself. He could handle a few minutes of the sticky mess in his pants until they made it to their room. Luckily for them, with a family their size, they made it to the room without bumping into anyone, and Ray couldn't wait another second to strip out of his clothes. He tossed them all into the hamper before starting the shower and stepping under the spray. It wasn't long before Viv joined him.

Ray pressed back when Viv leaned up against him and let the water flow over them. No matter how many times they had sex, Ray always reacted when Viv was touching him skin to skin. He hoped that the feeling never went away as they got older. In moments like this, Ray loved Viv more than life itself and would do anything to make his husband happy.

Viv turned off the water. "It's time for bed. Let's cuddle and you can tell me everything I've missed while I've been working and at uni. I feel like I have missed out on so much."

After drying off, they walked naked into the bedroom and

climbed into bed. Ray snuggled into Viv's side and began relating the family news. "Well, even though you know everything I'm going to say, I like talking to you about the family, so you'll just have to pretend like it's all news to you. The babies are all teething again. I hope they stop soon as I hate seeing them with temperatures and the constant cranks. Ben has discovered just how much fun climbing can be, so between Josh, Fred and me, we are on constant lookout for our mountaineer. Millie is growing in leaps and bounds. She is so different from the bedraggled little thing she was when she was dropped off here. Even though she doesn't know what she's doing, I can see she's distracting Charlotte from missing Bear so much. She has a heart of gold, our sweet Millie. Jamie tries not to show how much he misses Bear. I think he's getting better every day, but it's hard to tell. He always has been a hard one to read. As Grandma would say, 'he's an old soul in a young body.'"

"What about the others?"

"Declan is doing okay. He realizes he belongs here now. I think Sean may have a bit of a crush on him, and Declan is oblivious to it. I'm just glad Declan has found his smile again. It doesn't show itself very often, but when it does, I see the heartbreaker he's on the way to becoming. Girly is being typical Girly. She rolls with the punches and always manages to come out on top. I'm glad she found what she needed in Mick. I'm sorry that it came at the expense of Dan, though."

Viv patted his side. "That just leaves you to tell me about Nate and Dan."

"Not much to tell, really. Dan is…well, we all know where he's at. With Nate, I'm at a loss. He doesn't really talk about anything. He keeps everything bottled up inside him. I'm dreading to see how that's going to end. He'll go off like a Molotov cocktail. It can't be good for him. The only person he partially opens up to his Aunt Magen, and she's keeping an eye on him. She's promised to tell me if things get bad.

"Other than that, the rest of the household is good. Lily has even promised to bring her Harry the next time she comes to visit. He apparently wasn't scared off by our huge, noisy family, but she had us all promise we'll lay off the family drama the next time he's here." Ray snorted before adding, "As if that will happen. Our family is nuts."

Viv hugged him tighter. "Yeah, but they're our nuts."

"That they are," Ray agreed. "Viv, would you think I was a dirty old man if I wanted to fool around with you again? I just got a hankering for your cock to fill me up."

"How do you want it?"

Ray flicked Viv's nipple. "I don't care as long as it's hard and fast."

"Get on your hands and knees, Ray, then back up to the side of the bed."

Ray scrambled to do as he was told. He loved this position, because if he turned his head just right, he could watch via the mirror at how vigorously Viv pounded into him. Excitement zipped through him the instant Viv swatted him on the ass.

"Hold still. I need toys. I'm going to fill you up so much that it wears you out."

"Yes, please," Ray agreed. Ray lubed his own fingers, slid two into his ass and played while he waited for Viv to come back.

"Remove your fingers, Ray," Viv said and swatted Ray's ass a second time.

It didn't take long until Viv had worked the large vibrator into Ray. Switched on, it almost made Ray's body shake apart with need. Ray moaned as Viv fucked him with the toy. Viv always liked him well stretched and melting before he double-filled Ray. Ray didn't mind at all as long as it was Viv doing the playing. The second vibrator Viv used had a special groove in it that Viv's dick sat in while they fucked.

"Faster, Viv." Ray pushed back, wanting Viv to be fully seated. He needed Viv to start with the pounding. "Fuck me already." All he got in reply was another swat to the ass, then Viv let loose.

Ray fisted the sheets as Viv fucked him for all he was worth. He wasn't going to last long but that didn't matter. Right now, this wasn't about him. He was doing this for Viv. Ray had sensed his husband's guilt about missing out on so much, and if Ray was also going to get enjoyment out of this, then who was he to complain? Having Viv's cock in his ass was always a win. Having Viv double-stuff him was just the icing on the cake and he was going to cherish every second they fucked.

Liquid fire tore through him with the sensation of Viv slamming into him over and over again. Ray was losing the battle to stave off his orgasm. He wanted to make this last as long as possible, or at least hold off until Viv came, knowing full well Viv releasing and heating him from the inside out was going to be enough to shove Ray over the edge.

Ray moaned when Viv upped his pace. Goosebumps ghosted over him, and his whole body tingled as his balls tightened against his body. "So close, Viv. Wanna… Need to…"

Ray lost control the second Viv thrust deeply one last time and came. The heat filling him up hit Ray's prostate and opened the door for Ray's orgasm to rip from him. He came without Viv ever once touching Ray's cock. Ray waited until Viv pulled free of him and removed the vibrator. Viv collapsed onto the bed, and Ray smiled down at his worn-out lover. Quietly, Ray went to the bathroom, cleaned himself up and washed the toys to put them back in their home. He got a cloth and came out to wipe Viv down. They should really have another shower, but that could wait. Viv was dead-to-the-world asleep and Ray wasn't going to disturb him.

Once he got back into bed, Ray took a moment to cover them both with the sheet. He smiled into the dark room. His body was going to be deliciously sore tomorrow. Two bouts of sex so close together were enough to wear anyone out.

Chapter Seventeen

Grandma was in a snit, and Ray was at a loss to figure out what was pissing her off. He hadn't seen his grandma this angry since before his grandpa had died. He hoped like hell he'd never have to witness it again. Everyone was trying to keep out of her way. Three days of being growled at by the normally sweet and slightly crazy woman was a shock to the system for anyone who had never seen it before.

Ducking into the kitchen, Ray took the opportunity to corner his uncle. "Is she in a better mood today? I don't know how much more I can take of this."

His uncle shook his head.

Ray continued, "Have you worked out what the hell is wrong with her?"

A noise at the doorway had them both turning. Ray breathed a sigh of relief when it turned out to be only Dan.

Dan looked at them for a moment before asking, "Is the coast clear?"

"The kitchen is a Grandma-free zone," Ray said with a wink.

Dan seemed to relax. "Thank fuck for that. Already this morning she's ripped me a new one for being too slow. Only problem was, I was walking at her pace because we were talking. We got to just outside the office and it was like a switch flipped inside her. I swear, I'm not making this shit up."

Something clicked in Ray's head. "What's the date?" When Dan supplied the information, Ray smiled. He looked at his uncle and saw the dawning recognition. "Grandpa died today. I forgot she gets moody around the anniversary of his death."

"I don't know why. Dad didn't treat her very well when he was alive. I think a part of it may be that she feels guilty because she didn't give the old man a warmer sendoff. I know she loved him, even with all his faults, and we know there were a lot of them. I think that's why she kept me around, because through me, she could do right by her husband."

Ray frowned at his uncle. "I call bullshit on that. Grandma kept you around because she loves you. Thinking back over it, she's never treated you any differently from Dad. I know she never treated you like an employee. You have always been family to her. Sometimes, through the years, I thought she liked you better than Dad."

"You may be right, but it's also true that she feels guilty. I wish she wouldn't."

"Why would she feel guilty? You said that she didn't give him a warm sendoff, but what did you mean exactly?" Ray asked.

His uncle shrugged. "The morning Dad died, he and Catherine had a huge fight. She wanted him to tell the family who I was, and Dad didn't want to do it. He made her promise not to say a word. He was ashamed I was even born because I was proof of his infidelity. I think she always hated him for pretending that I didn't exist, or more that I was related to him. I love my mother, but even she didn't treat me as well as Catherine has. Once, years ago, I remember her telling me that she never got to have her beautiful goodbye with Dad."

"Maybe we should give her one."

Ray stared at Dan. "How? The old bastard has been dead nearly a decade."

"I don't know, but if you and Viv could give that bitch Grace a sendoff she didn't deserve, then what's stopping us from having a belated wake for your grandfather? Maybe it would be like a cleansing thing for the whole family. From what you and Girly have told me, the man was a bit of an

236

ass. If you give him a beautiful goodbye as GG wanted, hopefully she'll go back to being the sweet and mischievous woman we all love so much," Dan said.

Could it be that simple? Ray turned to his uncle. "What do you think? Will it work? I don't know how it will go over with Girly and Dad."

"At this point in time, I'm willing to give anything a try." Antonio tapped the counter top. "Let's get everyone here for dinner tonight. I'll have Cook make all of Dad's favorite foods, and we can all say something positive about him and wish him luck in the great beyond."

"I'll call Girly and let Viv, Josh and Fred know. Dan, you let Declan, Jamie and Nate know. Uncle Ant, you tell your family and ring Dad. But we have to keep this secret from Grandma or she'll put the kybosh on it." Now that they had some sort of a plan, Ray wanted to get the ball rolling.

The day was passing quicker than Ray would have liked. He'd called Girly and explained to her what was going on, then he had to sit through a forty-minute tirade about what an ass his grandfather was. Ray agreed with her wholeheartedly. Everyone knew the man hadn't been nice to be around when he'd been alive. Seeing as his grandfather had been long dead, Ray had thought maybe he could forgive the old coot for all the crap he'd put Ray through growing up. And even if he couldn't forgive him, he could at least put his anger aside for one night to give his grandma the beautiful goodbye she wanted for her husband, James.

When Grandma had suffered her first heart attack, Ray knew then how much she loved her husband. He also came to realize just how much he resembled the man when Grandma had mixed the two of them up. Thinking about James Connelly brought a smile to Ray's face. His grandfather would have hated that his mirror image was gay. Hell, the old bastard would have done everything in his power to make Ray *not* be gay. James Connelly had been a man set in his ways and his viewpoint on situations had been the only one worth having. *What a crock!* The man had never known the meaning of compromise.

In a lot of ways, Ray was the man's exact opposite. Where James had been all business first, Ray was family first. Where James had been my way or no way, Ray was willing to listen to all options. The only thing they had in common was that they had both loved Grandma. Even if James had cheated on his wife, in the end, he'd chosen her over Antonio's mother. Ray snorted. Probably because Grandma had controlled the purse strings. His grandfather may have acted like the lord of the manor, but the truth was, the money was all Grandma's. She was the one born into a wealthy family. James Connelly had also been well off, but his wealth was nothing compared to the Alexander family fortune. A fortune of which Grandma was the sole beneficiary. When her parents had died, his grandma had no other living relatives. People knew the Connelly family was rich, yet he didn't think any of them realized just how much. Most wouldn't even connect Catherine Connelly with Catherine Alexander. In a way, that was probably a good thing.

Grandma had once told him that she hadn't even touched her family money. Instead, she had lived off the interest. The money was set aside for all those who followed her. In a way it was good knowing that his children, and all the grandchildren who followed, would be able to live comfortably. More importantly, they would be able to carry on doing what he and Grandma had started — helping those less fortunate than themselves. At least he hoped they followed in the family footsteps.

After his phone call with Girly, Ray went in search of Josh and Fred. He filled them in on what was happening and listened to another — albeit shorter — tirade from Josh. Ray explained once again how they weren't doing this for his grandfather but for Grandma. Once that had sunk in, Josh fell silent.

"Okay, I need to duck out and see Viv for a while. Can

you two hold the fort for me? I'll have my cell so you can call me if anything comes up."

Josh was still fuming a little, so Fred answered, "Sure, Ray. You go take care of business and we'll be here for the babies."

"Thank you." Ray kissed her on the cheek and left.

The whole drive over to the Connelly Corporation, Ray went over in his head what he was going to say. Actually, he was hoping Viv would be able to convince Ray that this was a good thing and that it wasn't going to blow up in their faces. He truly didn't want to do anything that would piss Grandma off even more.

Ray made his way past security and through the building to where Viv's office was. He smiled at those he knew, but was happy knowing most people didn't have a clue who he was. The only problem he encountered was at one of the checkpoints that didn't want to let him pass. Even having his name on the visitor ID tag wasn't good enough for the guard. This probably was a good thing, but not when Ray wanted to go and visit with Viv.

"Sir, I can't let you go beyond this point." The guard, whose name was Ian Pratt, seemed determined to keep him out.

Ray smiled and pointed at his nametag. "My name is Raymond Connelly. My grandmother, Catherine Connelly, owns this, all of this. I'm not trying to steal secrets. I just want to go and see my husband."

The guard sneered at Ray. "And just who would your husband be?"

"Christopher Connelly," Ray snapped. Instead of arguing with the idiot any longer, Ray pulled out his phone and punched in a number. "Grandma, can you tell Ian that it's okay for me to go and see Viv in his office?" Ray handed over the phone.

"Ma'am, I don't know who you are. Talking to me over the phone, you can be anyone. So forgive me if I don't listen to you and let this person through."

Ray grinned when the guard flinched at whatever Grandma was saying to him. At least Grandma being in a bad mood was good for something.

"Ray, what are you doing here?"

Ray turned and greeted Don. "Came to see Viv, but Ian here doesn't want to let me through."

"Do you know who this guy is?" Don asked the guard.

Ian handed the phone back to Ray. "I know who he says he is."

"Man, you are going to get your ass handed to you if you treat Ray with disrespect. If I were you, I'd let him through. Even Viv will rip you a new one if you mess with Ray." Don shook his head. "Come with me, Ray. I'll walk you to Viv's office."

"Hold on a damn minute. You can't just forgo the rules because this guy claims he's a Connelly. We have rules for a reason, you know," Ian growled.

Don rolled his eyes at Ian. "Did it ever cross your mind to maybe call Viv and ask him if he knows Ray?"

"He means Christopher." Ray added helpfully with a smile.

They waited while Ian buzzed Viv's office and asked him to come to the checkpoint. "He's on his way down here."

"Love, what are you doing here?" Viv asked as he waited for the gate to open. Ray didn't get a chance to answer before Viv kissed him. "This is a nice surprise."

Ian looked a little uncomfortable at Viv's show of attention. "So do you know this person?"

"He's my husband. His family own this business. I'm sure he explained all of this to you. I know you haven't been here long, but you have been informed I was married to the boss' grandson."

The guard's cheeks paled, and Ray thought it wasn't in fear, but more so in anger. What the guy's problem was, Ray could only guess, but if he had to voice an opinion, he would say the man was homophobic. Yet he only seemed to be glaring at Ray, so maybe Ian was interested in Viv.

God, he hoped not. He'd had enough of this the first time around when he'd had to warn Shane away from Viv.

"I think Grandma will be having a face-to-face chat with Ian in the future. He kind of dismissed her on the phone," Ray stated.

Both Viv and Don gasped at what he'd said. Ian, on the other hand, appeared to stand his ground. "Without a visual confirmation that woman could have been anyone."

"I think it might be a good idea if you start looking for a new job. The boss and the CEO, i.e. Ray's father, aren't going to be too happy about this," Don said.

"Actually, as much as I hate to admit it, he did the right thing. He should be cautious about letting people in. I figure with it being me and I'd already passed through the other checkpoints, he might have believed me when I said who I was. But you're right, Grandma is going to be pissed." Ray shook his head before leaning toward Ian and adding softly, "Just so you know, Viv is mine. Full stop. End of story. I don't share and he's not available."

A deep flush filled Ian's face and Ray knew he'd hit the nail on the head. The guy was interested in Viv. Ray had to nip this shit in the bud. Hopefully now Ian would know that Viv was off-limits. Ray grabbed Viv by the hand and dragged him back through the gateway and down the hall to Viv's office.

Don was chuckling as he trailed after them. "You know it never ceases to amaze me when I see Ray in full-on possessive mode. You would think after him decking Shane a couple of years ago at the Christmas party that the gossip would have reached young Ian. He's been here long enough to learn what everyone else has."

"And what's that?" Viv asked.

"That you belong to Ray, and he isn't giving you up without a fight."

Ray grinned. "I can't believe you people talk about me."

"I can't believe Ian would set his sights on Viv," Don retorted.

"Well, he is incredibly sexy," Ray stated. "What's not to love about him?"

Don just about busted a gut he was laughing so hard. "How about the amount of kids you two have at home? I mean, what man is crazy enough to say yes to five kids?"

"Ten. I think you forgot about Jamie, Declan, Nate, Girly and Dan." Ray smiled. "The kids are just the icing on the cake. "Actually, it would be eleven if we added Charlotte."

At the mention of his niece's name, Don sobered. "You know we tried to talk Fred into fighting for Teddy. Mandy can't work out why Fred's letting Teddy go so easily."

Ray sat on the edge of the desk as Viv and Don took the chairs. "Honestly, I think the whole thing has messed her up. She's one of my best friends, and I love her to death. I think Damien has guilted her into letting Bear go. I just hope he doesn't poison Bear against his mother."

"It's because she didn't stop Teddy and Jamie when they claimed they were boyfriends, isn't it?" Don asked.

"Yeah, I guess we're all guilty in that respect. None of us saw any harm in it. I mean, they were just kids," Ray said in exasperation.

Don's expression clouded. "Damien always was a homophobic bigot. I could never understand why Fred married him in the first place. Nothing was ever good enough for the man. She only got rid of him after I decked him for laying his hands on Charlotte. Mandy and I walked in one day and he was slapping Lottie. I lost it and beat the snot out of him. He pressed charges, accusing me of being Lottie's father, which is just plain ridiculous. I would never cheat on Mandy."

"Why would he think Charlotte was yours?" Viv asked.

"Who would know? The man is fucked in the head. I even offered to have a DNA test done to prove him wrong. I know they had one done recently and even after it proved he was the father, he thinks we paid someone off to change the results. He wants nothing to do with his daughter." Don sighed. "The weird thing is, if I was to say one of the kids wasn't his, it would have been Teddy. I know the DNA says I'm wrong, but at the time of his conception Fred had been attacked walking home from work. Damien had always blamed her for the incident and kept going on about how she was dressed and she should have known better. The truth was, she was dressed in the uniform of the gas station she worked at—slacks and an ugly blouse—so how the clothing was provocative in any way was beyond me. Damien held it over her head the entire time they were married."

"I've tried to get her to talk to me. She opens up a bit then it's like a wall descends and closes me out. Josh says he gets the same reaction from her," Ray admitted. "It saddens me to think she lived a life like that for so long."

Viv leaned forward. "What about Teddy? Have you heard from him?"

Don shook his head. "Damien hates me and Mandy. Blames us for Fred leaving him. There's no way in hell he'd let us keep in touch with Teddy. You're right—he will try and brainwash Teddy against us all. I just hope the kid is strong enough to hold out."

"It frustrates me to no end that people like Damien get away with the shit they do. Why does there have to be so much hatred in the world, and why does he think it's okay for him to drum his beliefs into Bear?" Ray demanded.

"Because he thinks he's right," Viv stated.

Ray glared at his husband. "How can his fucked-up way of thinking possibly be right?"

"Love, I'm not saying I think it's right. But everyone has their own opinions on life. His may not be something I personally agree with, but in Damien's mind, he thinks what we believe is wrong. How many times had Bear come home and told us how Damien had called us deviants and that we should have our kids taken away from us?" Viv tried to explain his thoughts.

"I still say the man is a fucked-up idiot." Ray snapped.

"Ditto," Don agreed.

Viv smiled at the two men. "Okay, now that we agree on Damien. Why did you come here to see me about? It must be bad if you couldn't tell me over the phone."

"We're having a wake for grandfather tonight," Ray answered.

"Ray." Don frowned at Ray. "You do know James has been dead for nearly ten years, don't you?"

Ray snorted. "Of course I do, but Grandma is in a foul mood. Uncle Ant told me it's because she feels guilty about not giving Grandfather a better sendoff. From what Uncle Ant said, she was pissed at Grandfather at the time. So now, each year on the anniversary of his death, she gets ticked off all over again. Hopefully this way she will get over her guilt and move on."

"Sounds complicated, yet somehow, it makes perfect sense," Don said as he stood. "On that note, I will get back to work and let you guys talk. Thanks for letting me rant about Damien."

"You know where I am. Any time you need a sounding board, just pick up the phone. Tell Mandy the offer is open to her as well," Ray said with a wave.

Don exited the room and closed the door behind him.

Viv sat back and watched Ray for a few second. His husband was an amazing man. In some ways, he was so innocent, yet in others, he saw right through the bullshit to what was really going on in any given situation.

"So tell me about this whole wake thing?"

Ray shrugged. "As you know, right now Grandma isn't happy. It was actually Dan who came up with the suggestion of the belated wake. I don't know what I'm going to say that is nice about Grandfather. Hell, I'll make shit up if I have to. I just want to make Grandma smile again. I think if we all say something nice then it will be beautiful."

"Do I have to say something? I mean, I never met the guy at all," Viv inquired.

"You don't have to, but it would be nice if you said

something, even if it is just for Grandma's sake."

"I will think on it. I'll even make sure I get home for the main event. I think through this I'll get to know your family a little more," Viv admitted.

He grinned and watched Ray slide off the desk and come and straddled his lap. Viv automatically ran his hands over Ray. Even fully clothed, Ray could turn Viv on in under a second. His cock was already filling. Ray must have understood the reaction he was having, because he swooped in for a kiss and rocked on Viv's lap. Viv felt he wasn't the only one with a hard-on.

Tapping Ray on the butt, he waited for Ray to end the kiss. "Get up and lock the door, love. We wouldn't want anyone walking in on us."

He chuckled the second Ray quickly scrambled off his lap and did what he'd asked. Viv stood up and unzipped his slacks at the same time Ray turned and started stripping. Viv removed his own clothes and sat again, pausing while Ray stood in front of him. Viv didn't wait to hear what Ray wanted. He just leaned forward and sucked Ray's beautiful cock into his mouth. He rested his hands on Ray's thighs and blew Ray. He loved the way Ray gripped his hair as he fucked Viv's mouth.

Viv slipped his fingers around to Ray's crack and moaned upon finding the plug nestled between his lover's cheeks and filling his hole in readiness. After pulling himself off Ray's cock, he asked, "Is someone feeling a little horny?"

"Yes, now fuck me."

"No lube," Viv said. There was no way he was going to dry fuck Ray and hurt him.

Ray growled as he stepped away and grabbed his jeans. He grabbed a small tube of lube from his pocket and tossed it to Viv. "I said you need to fuck me."

Viv didn't need to be told again. It was a little exciting that they were about to screw their brains out in his office. It wasn't something they had ever done before. They'd made love in many places, but Ray very rarely came here. Viv lubed up his cock with one hand and played with the plug in Ray's ass with the other. His mind was ready to explode with all the ways he could take Ray in this office.

Viv stood and walked around his desk, leading Ray after him. He sat in his own chair. Ray moaned as Viv slid the plug free. In the next instant, he had Ray sitting on his lap facing away from Viv, his cock buried deep inside Ray's ass. Viv lifted his legs and put them on the desk, giving Ray something to grab onto. "Fuck yourself on my cock, Ray. I want you to ride me like there's no tomorrow."

Ray started bouncing on him in earnest, and Viv gripped the arms of his chair, holding on. Watching Ray riding his cock was the most erotic thing Viv had ever witnessed. "You're doing a good job, love. Fuck me harder. I won't break."

Ray did just that. He picked up his speed bouncing on Viv. It was all fun until Viv started sliding off the chair. "Stop. We need to change positions before we end up on the floor."

Ray grunted then climbed off Viv and onto the desk. He spread himself out until he was low enough for Viv to stand up and take over the fucking. He loved the way Ray moaned, and Viv eagerly shoved his cock straight back into his ass.

Viv grabbed Ray's hips and fucked him as hard as he could. The sounds of their bodies slamming together was only adding to his pleasure. His gaze was riveted to where his body was invading Ray's. Viv's cock fit so perfectly in Ray's snug channel. Viv wiped his hands over the sweat ghosting on Ray's skin. Fucking Ray was one of the best things in the world and Viv would never grow tired of it. "I fucking love you so much."

It was Viv's turn to moan when Ray clenched his muscles, almost strangling Viv's cock in the process. "So close, Viv."

Sliding free of Ray, Viv chuckled as Ray protested his emptiness. Viv sat back in his chair and pulled Ray onto his cock. This time he had his lover facing him. Viv put his legs up on the desk so Ray could lean back on them. "Jerk yourself off, baby. I want to watch you shoot."

As Ray tugged himself off, Viv's cock was clenched tightly. The slight movement in Ray's actions was dragging Viv closer to the edge. His balls ached with the need to come. His body was heated through and sweat soaked his skin. And through it all he was captivated by the show Ray was putting on. With the first spurt of cum leaving Ray's cock to splatter on his chest, Viv gripped Ray's waist hard enough to leave bruises and gave himself over to the orgasm tearing through his body.

When Ray went to move, Viv held him in place. "Don't. Just stay right where you are and talk to me. I don't care about what. I just want to enjoy this for a little bit more."

Ray relaxed back on him, and squeezed Viv firmly with his ass, sending shivers racing through his whole body. "Tell me why you really came here? Was it A, to tell me about the dinner, or was it B, so I could shove my dick up your ass?" He pinched Ray's nipple.

"A little from column A, and a whole lot more from column B. With the way that guard was eyeing you, I needed to stake my claim on you again. I needed you to see exactly who you belong to."

"Ray, that was never an issue, but feel free to stop by and stake your claim on me more often." Viv dropped his hand and gently squeezed Ray's cock. "I love your body. Especially when it's naked and riding my cock."

A noise behind them had Ray stiffening on his lap. "There's a window washer." He sounded panicked. "Actually there's two of them."

Viv squeezed his cock again. "It's one-way glass. They can't see in. They haven't got a clue that I'm buried balls-deep inside you. Just relax." Viv traced his free hand over Ray, trying to sooth Ray's tension. "Lean back and let me fondle you."

Ray hesitated for a moment, then he lay back against Viv's legs. Viv lightly ran his fingertips over Ray's groin.

He liked the way Ray's cock was getting hard. If he played his cards right, they would have a second round of fun before Ray had to go home.

"You are so fucking sexy," Viv whispered.

Ray closed his eyes and panted as Viv took the time to explore the man's slit. Every time he ran his fingernails across it, pre-cum oozed out to bead on the head. Ray's body shook at his touch. Viv swiped his thumb across the head of Ray's cock and brought the digit to his mouth to taste his lover. It took a bit of maneuvering, but soon Viv had Ray lying on his back on top of the desk. Viv's own legs tingled as blood rushed through them, but it didn't stop him from starting the slow slide in and out of Ray's body. He kicked the chair back away from him and exposed them to the window. Even though the guys out there couldn't see them, the thought that maybe they could was kind of exciting.

"Oh, Viv." Ray looked so beautiful writhing on the desk.

Viv leaned forward and took Ray's mouth in a deep kiss. He ground his cock into his husband's ass while he ravished his mouth. Heat splashed between them at the same time Ray screamed into his mouth. Viv kissed Ray once more then stood. He lifted Ray's legs so they rested against his body and proceeded to pound into his lover.

"You're mine, Ray. Just like I'm yours, and nobody is going to come between us. Not Grace. Not Shane, and definitely not some guard who thinks he can treat you like shit." Viv snarled and banged his way to completion. Pulling free of Ray's ass, Viv found the plug and pushed it back in. "I want my cum to stay inside you as a reminder that we belong together."

"Always." Ray grinned up at his husband.

Viv helped Ray clean up and they kissed a lot in between getting re-dressed. Even though he was reluctant to say goodbye, he knew he would be seeing Viv again soon. He glanced toward the window at the two men out there and smiled. He wondered if they would've still been working had they been able to see into the office. Not that they really worried him. It was the other person watching that Ray was focused on.

Ray sauntered down the corridor until he stood at the gate. As he expected, the monitor was focused on Viv's office. Ray smiled at Ian. "I hoped you enjoyed the show. I won't tell Viv that you watched, but remember, Viv is mine. He always will be."

By the time Ian got his features under control, Ray wasn't sure if the guy was embarrassed, jealous or just plain pissed. He didn't say another word. He just waited for Ian to let him out of the gate. Ray kept moving and didn't look back. If he did, he'd probably start freaking out over the fact that he'd acted like a wanton slut just to show someone that didn't even matter to him who Viv belonged to. Holding his head high, Ray walked back through the building and out to his car.

Chapter Eighteen

Viv arrived home with enough time to get cleaned up in time for dinner. Ray had informed him they were going to eat then put the babies to bed before they had the wake. Lily had even driven down from uni to be here for the event. It wasn't as if the babies would understand what was going on anyway. So Viv helped put everyone Millie's age and under to bed. The times he was home early enough to do things like this were always like a soothing balm to his soul. Kids could do wonders for a person's self-esteem. They loved unconditionally, only wanting to be loved in return. Don had once joked that children were like pets in that respect.

Like every other parent, he knew Viv was convinced that his children were the best children on the face of the earth. They each had their own adorable personalities, and had a way of wrapping him around their fingers. Especially Layla, who smiled whenever she saw him. She was going to grow up and be Daddies' little girl. That wasn't to say Isobel and Millie wouldn't, but Layla owned a huge portion of his heart. Ben and Jeb were the easiest of babies to love, and he knew they would be great brothers to the girls as they all grew up. He hoped they would be as close as he was to Dan, and Ray was to Girly. Jamie, Declan and Nate had a bond going that was all their own, though he could see Nate, being that fraction older the other two, was taking a step back. He hoped it wasn't too far, as it would hurt Declan if Nate pushed him away completely.

Later in the night, Ray walked Grandma into the garden. They stopped at the place where Ray's grandfather's ashes had been scattered beneath the roses. Grandma was still grumpy, but seemed to be holding in her temper because the whole family was gathered.

"So what's going on?" she finally asked.

"Grandma, seeing as it is the anniversary of Grandfather's death, we decided it might be nice to gather together and have a memorial for him." Ray fidgeted beside her.

Viv smiled at his husband to hopefully ease his nerves.

Girly stepped forward and spoke. "I'll start things off. GD, even though you were a gnarly old bugger, I'm glad that you existed, or I wouldn't have been born. May your ever after have made you a better person."

Viv bit his lip to keep from laughing and waited for Mick to speak.

"I never met you, but I also am glad you existed. Without you, there would be no Ray, without Ray, there would be no Viv to come and rescue Declan and the rest of us. But most of all, I thank you for Girly."

As hard as he tried, Viv couldn't hold back his chuckle. Liam stood and looked at them then took his turn.

"Thank you, old man, for having an affair with my nanny, so that I wouldn't end up an only child. Antonio is the best thing you ever achieved. After me being born, of course." He grinned at his brother and sat again letting someone else take his place.

Claire was laughing when she took center stage. "James, you were a mean old coot. But through your meanness, you taught the rest of us what a loving family we could be. Rest in peace."

Dan took her place. "I also didn't know you, and I'm glad that I didn't, as we probably wouldn't have gotten along. I thank you for the family you left behind who welcomed my family into their lives and hearts with open arms."

"Granddad, may God treat you better than you ever treated us," Sean said quietly.

Aunt Magen stood next. "For someone who treated his family with indifference, they sure turned out all right.

Thank you for one of the best mothers-in-law a woman could ask for. You may have done wrong by Catherine, but it only made her love us more."

Uncle Ant followed her. "As Liam said, thank you for giving me a brother and a step-mother who always classed me as her own, even when you discouraged her from doing so. Without you, there would be no Catherine in my life."

Tears glistened in Grandma's eyes. Her grip tightened on Ray's arm while Nate spoke.

"Thank you, James, for the family who have shown me more love than my own parents ever did. Thank you for giving me a second chance at life."

Declan stared right at Viv and said, "Thank you, James. I've heard the stories of how mean you were. It gave me the strength to try and make amends and get to know my own father."

Jamie stood and scratched his head. "I don't know what to say. I know we have the same name, and after listening to everyone here I guess I'll say thank you for showing me how not to treat people. When I grow up, I want to be your exact opposite."

"Granddad, you may have been mean, and you may have ignored us, and even pretended we didn't exist. But thank you for the family I now have," Lily declared.

Viv stepped forward, eyes only for Ray and said, "May your afterlife be all the things your real life wasn't. I thank you for the wonderful family with whom I now share my life. I thank you for a wonderful grandmother who loves unconditionally. I thank you for my beautiful husband and all our children."

Ray walked over and kissed his cheek. "So it's my turn. What can I say? You were a mean old bastard, who didn't like me very much. In spite of that, I was loved by everyone else. I may not have liked you, but I loved you because you were family. You left the best piece of you behind and I am grateful every day of my life for Grandma."

Tears were streaming down Grandma's face by the time

Ray had finished. She took in a shaky breath and said, "Once I loved you more than life itself. You broke my heart and my trust, and I, for the most part, ignored you and concentrated on the family I had. You died and I felt free, yet my promise to you sat ill in my heart. I almost died and the promise was no longer valid. So you were my husband. The father of my children. Yes, Antonio was as much mine as Liam had always been. I loved you for the family you gave me, and I promise to meet you in the afterlife." She chuckled—in Viv's opinion—a tad evilly. "Even if it is just to say I told you so. The family didn't care about your secrets. They found out the truth, and we loved each other anyway."

As wakes went, Viv thought this one was pretty awesome. Everyone got to be heard and even though no one outright said James Connelly was a good man, they did find something about him to be grateful for. He also thought it had helped Grandma to release some of her own guilt. Though, why she had anything to feel guilty about, he'd never know.

Once they were all back in the sitting room having a nightcap, Viv could tell Grandma was much happier. In the long run, it was better for them all. Maybe next year this date would blow by and Grandma wouldn't have to get her crank on. The sweet and slightly sarcastic Grandma was the one they all preferred.

"Were you in on this plan?" Grandma asked as she sat on the sofa beside him.

"Not me. I think it was Dan, Ray and Antonio. Though, to be honest, I think it was done with the best intentions. I mean, it helped me learn a little more about this family and why they are like they are."

"In the beginning, James was a good man. I'm not sure where exactly it all went wrong. He changed after I fell pregnant with Liam. A friend of mine said he was jealous that he had to share me with Liam, or more that she thought that James didn't want to share my money with Liam. What my friend didn't know was that my money would never have gone to James. I loved him, but there was always something I couldn't quite put my finger on. The manager for my trust helped me make the will so if I died, then my money went to any children I had. And in the event I died childless, I left my money to charities. Mr. Clarkson said it was the way my parents would have wanted it."

Viv asked, "Didn't James have something to say about this?"

"James had money of his own. When he died, his money was supposed to go to Liam. Though I forced him to include Antonio in his will. He fought me every step of the way, but I didn't care. I was going to do what was right. He had the money, yet Antonio never touched it. Not until Liam found out the truth. Even though Antonio was against using the money, I badgered him until he used some of it to pay for Sean's and Lily's schooling. I didn't see why they needed to suffer because Antonio was being a stubborn jackass." She smiled over to where Liam and Antonio were deep in conversation. "When Liam found out and accepted him, Antonio felt like he had a right to the money that had always been his."

"Grandma, I thought my family was fucked-up. Growing up poor, it's understandable, but this here shows me that even the rich can be touched by idiotic family members. Antonio was just lucky you had a heart big enough to include him and his family. I can see how much they love you."

Ray joined them and plonked himself in Viv's lap. "Do you see what I see?" He gestured toward the corner of the room where Girly, Mick and Dan were talking and laughing.

"That's a good sign, right?" Viv asked, not really expecting an answer.

"At least they're not arguing. I hate it when they argue," Grandma muttered. "Arguing makes me want to shake the shit out of them and tell them to grow up."

Ray chuckled. "Grandma, I think we all want to slap them silly some days. I hope this is the start of them moving on."

Viv slid his arms around Ray's waist and hugged him close. He really was grateful for Ray being in his life. Even though, in the beginning, he'd never have imagined he could love someone as much as he did Ray. Again, Viv sent up a silent thank you to a man who had fathered the head of Ray's family line. The people in this room tonight were a strong bunch. If James had lived on they could have been very dysfunctional. Really, it was the woman beside him who was the glue holding everyone together.

"Did I tell you I was talking to Beth the other day?" Grandma said as she turned her attention back to them.

"I haven't seen her in ages. How's she doing?" Ray asked. Ray relaxed into him.

"Seems she's ready to try for another baby. She wants a sibling for Eliza so there isn't a huge age gap between them," Grandma confided.

Viv saw the gleam in Grandma's eyes and knew she wasn't finished telling them what she knew. "What else do you know?" Viv asked.

"I heard her mention that she may be knocking on somebody's door to claim her dark-haired, green-eyed baby number two."

The smile Grandma gave them was lost on Viv. All the air rushed out of his body in shock. "I thought Ray was the one making babies with her."

"Yeah, but you promised her you'd donate if she asked. I guess she's asking." Ray grinned.

Viv was starting to hyperventilate at the thought of bringing a new life into the world. Didn't they already have enough? The world stopped spinning out of control and everything fell back into place when he realized the most important thing—this wouldn't be his and Ray's child. This baby would belong to Beth and Jasper. Now that his panic attack was over and done with, he could smile and be happy for his friends. He didn't mind donating his sperm.

It wasn't like he had to sleep with Beth to get her pregnant. He'd never say no, seeing as she had given him and Ray two of the most precious gifts ever.

"Is your panic attack over?" Ray asked.

"Yep, threw me for a minute is all. Then I remembered it won't be my baby, and all is good in the world. I love kids, but right now I think we well and truly have enough," Viv answered with a grin.

Grandma started laughing. "You should've seen the look on your face. I thought you were going to pass out."

"Grandma, I was right there with you. My brain took a dump, until it all sank in and I thought about it logically," Viv said.

"Okay," Ray said, signaling a subject change.

Ray would want Viv's brain to have time to filter everything completely. Giving Jasper and Beth a baby wasn't real until the couple asked Viv themselves.

Ray continued, "What can you tell me about the cabin? Has Dad decided what we're going to do up there?"

Viv already knew the house was being rebuilt bigger than ever, but he listened while Grandma explained, "The rebuild is going well. Dan's friends, Ellie and Conrad, have been keeping us informed about the cleanup after the flood. There was a lot of damage, but not much structurally. More scrubbing down than anything else. The few places like ours that had to be torn down and rebuilt, I've donated toward the work needed. Most of it will be covered by people's insurance companies, but it doesn't hurt to help out the community."

"Did you find out any more about Andrew and Evan?" Ray asked.

Grandma tsked before speaking. "I found out they are better off without their families. I would never wish what they went through at the hands of people who were meant to love them on anyone. They'll both do much better now they're at Destiny House."

"Speaking of…have you all decided what the café is going

to be called?" Viv asked. True to his word, he hadn't stuck his nose into the goings-on at all.

"There have been a few names bandied around. The three main contenders are Second Chances Café, Second Steps Café, and First Days Café. The guys at Destiny House thought of them. My favorite is First Days—as it really will be the first days of the rest of their lives," Grandma said.

The names all basically meant the same thing, but the name Grandma liked had a nice ring to it. Viv hoped they went with that one. "Any word on when New Hope will open?"

"It should be up and running by the end of next month. There's still a little bit of red tape to get through, but I can't see any problems with it. Mainly just insurance stuff. Byron has someone handling it all," Grandma answered.

Hearing Byron's name had Viv thinking about Shane. "Has Shane started at Destiny House yet?"

"No, he starts next week. Girly tells me Ethan keeps swapping between being excited at seeing him again and being scared witless. I hope it doesn't set the poor boy back. I kind of have a soft spot for Ethan."

Ray smiled. "I think everyone has a soft spot for Ethan. I know they have all volunteered to deck Shane if he gets too full-on. No one wants to see Ethan hurt again." Ray's smile turned into a frown. "I hope Shane has changed his ways for good. Not only for Ethan, but for himself as well. He'll get nowhere in life if he keeps drinking the way he was."

"Shane has to want to change," Viv said. He shook his head. "It will only work if Shane's willing to stay sober. I read somewhere that addicts have at least two setbacks before they kick the habit for good. I guess the only thing we can do is be there to pick up the pieces."

"I'm hoping there is nothing to pick up," Grandma said, reaching across and patting Ray on the knee. "Byron says he's really trying to keep it together. His words, not mine— Shane knows he fucked up and wants to make amends to everyone, especially Viv and Ethan."

Ray couldn't even contemplate Shane being nice. The man had always been a complete douchebag. Shane had only ever believed in one thing—Shane. He thought he was God's gift to everyone and that no one could ever live without him in their lives, when, in reality, no one could stand him. The only people who hung around him where the ones who wanted Shane to spend his money on them. Ray had never sensed that about Ethan. Maybe the guy had found the one spark of good in Shane and didn't know how to hold onto it. Ray really did hope things worked out for the best.

"So did you like Granddad's memorial, Grandma?" Ray asked.

"It was exactly what I needed. Who would've ever thought so much good would come out of a mean old man? I guess he left the very best parts of himself behind when he died. I never realized just how much better our lives would become. In my own way, I loved him. I may have never trusted him again fully, but I have no doubt he never ever strayed after Antonio's mother. Probably because I threatened to divorce him, take both kids, the company and most of his money."

Ray stared at his grandma. "And here I thought you were this sweet little old lady. Instead, I find out you are a ruthless business tycoon. What's the world coming to, I ask you?"

"I'm me, and I'm not going to change for anyone. I learned long ago if I want to make it in this world then I'd better bloody well get the job done myself. Your grandfather was running the company into the ground. Decades ago, I bought out a majority share of the company and put James out of the everyday running. Your father was only a teenager at the time when I had him come and help me. Antonio had only just come back into our lives and he wasn't interested in working for the corporation. So I didn't force him. Instead, he came to the house and I must admit I gloated a bit at how well he and I got on. It always pissed

James off that Antonio ignored him. I think that's why he was so hard on the rest of Antonio's family." Grandma frowned. "Does that make me a bad person because I loved the fact that Antonio liked me more?"

"Nope, it sounds exactly right to me. Grandfather was the one missing out on a wonderful part of his family. Until it was pointed out to me, I never realized how much Dad and Uncle Ant look alike. Hell, even Girly and Lily resemble each other. Me and Sean both kind of take after Grandfather, not that either of us relished the fact... I sure don't," Ray huffed the last bit out.

Grandma patted Ray's knee again. "You may be a mirror image of him, but you are nothing like him. You are the sunshine and all that's good to his misery and bad temper. And just remember, if you ever start acting like him, there are a fair few family members who'll happily kick you up the ass."

"Speaking of kicking asses, what did you think of young Ian?" Ray asked. He wanted to get his grandma's take on the situation.

"The boy has the right notion, but he should have listened when he was told who you were. Then to question who I was on top of what you already told me... I'm not happy. I have a meeting with Mr. Pratt first thing in the morning and he can explain to me why." Grandma sighed. "I'm not sure what I'll do after that."

Ray leaned back against Viv's chest. "I think he has a bit of a crush on Viv. I set him to rights about that. I don't want to have to be defending my man every day he goes to work."

"If he has the hots for me, he's never said anything," Viv said.

"I know what I saw. He wasn't happy when you kissed me in the hall. He wouldn't even listen when Don vouched for me. I just don't think he wanted me anywhere near Viv," Ray defended. He knew what he felt and he would pay a ton of money to prove he was right.

Viv snorted. "I don't know why he'd be interested in

me. Like Don said, we have more kids then you can poke a stick at. Why would he want to be with someone like that? Especially when I have no interest in him at all." Viv grinned. "Well, at least this time you didn't feel the need to deck him."

"I was this close." Ray held up his fingers about a quarter of an inch apart. "No one will get a chance at taking you away from me."

"I don't want anyone else. Didn't you hear me tonight? I'm grateful for the man and family I have. I don't need anything more." Viv rubbed circles on Ray's back, and Ray's tension drained out of him.

"I think it's time to get up to bed. The kids have school in the morning and you have work. Hopefully the crazy old broad beside us will wake up on the right side of the bed tomorrow and give us all a break." Ray cackled when his grandma glared at him for all of two seconds, then she also cracked up laughing.

"No matter what happens in your life, Ray, I want you to always remember that you are the light of my life," she said and squeezed his knee.

A lump formed in Ray's throat as he listened to his grandma. "I love you too, Grandma. I always have, and I always will."

Ray stood and pulled his grandma to her feet then turned and told Declan and Jamie that it was time for bed. He hugged Girly and Mick goodbye, before turning and doing the same with his parents. After the night they'd just shared, Ray wanted them all to know just how much they meant to him.

After checking on the babies, Ray walked with Viv to their bedroom. He wanted nothing more than to cuddle up in bed with his husband. They'd had enough sex today that he didn't feel the need to ravish Viv's body. They took separate showers and met back in bed. Ray sighed after they got comfortable and he laid his head on Viv's naked chest.

He took a deep breath and admitted something he promised he never would. "Ian watched us have sex on the monitors today." Viv stilled beneath him. "I told him I wouldn't tell you if he remembered that you were mine and off limits."

"Then why are you telling me now?"

"Because after Grace, we promised each other no more secrets. I didn't want you finding out from someone else. I think at least by watching us he realizes he won't be able to steal you from me. If he doesn't know that by now, then he's a damn fool."

Viv frowned. "I can't believe I forgot about the internal cameras. More to the point, I can't believe he watched us. What kind of person does that?"

"A very insecure one. Or maybe someone who hasn't quite worked out what gender he prefers. I'm not making excuses for him. Then again, if the positions were reversed, I'm not sure I could have stopped myself from watching. Especially if I had a crush on one of the guys," Ray answered.

"You didn't stop and watch me and Grace. You took off," Viv said.

That was true. "I didn't want to see her in your arms, especially after you told me how much she messed with you and Dan. But if we hadn't been an item at the time, maybe I would have stuck around and watched." Ray chuckled at the awkward conversation. "Okay, maybe I wouldn't have watched. I would've been very hurt at you being with someone else. I just wanted you so much. I still do. I'm not going to be very happy if anyone thinks they can walk in now and take you away from me. We are married in every way except legally."

"No one is taking me away from you. Hell, they'll have to pry me away from you. We're stuck together like Super Glue."

Ray chuckled. "Do you know how corny you sound right now?"

"I'm just crazy in love with the man who shares my bed

every night. The man who shares his body and existence with me. The man who makes me want to be a better man. A better father. A better lover," Viv whispered as he nuzzled against the top of Ray's head.

Ray sighed in contentment. "You being here is one of the best things that ever happened to me. I don't think my life would be this full if you weren't in it with me. I would have been raising Layla and Izzy by myself. I wouldn't have the rest of our babies. I honestly can't think of there ever being a day without them in it."

"What do you think would've happened if my mum and stepdad hadn't died in that auto accident?" Viv asked.

"Honestly, after everything you've told me about them, I think we would have ended up with Jamie, Millie and Ben regardless. They didn't seem like the kind of people who wanted the hassle of raising three children," Ray admitted.

Viv exhaled loudly. "I think you may have been right. Ever since I ran away, they've been dumping their kids onto other people. They never wanted the responsibility."

"At least now the kids don't have to worry about being passed around. They have found their forever home." Ray chuckled. "Oh, my God, I just made our children sound like stray pets."

"I knew what you meant. Our kids will have better lives because they're now living with us. Two parents who love them all unconditionally," Viv said.

Ray sighed and snuggled closer to Viv. "You always know how to say the right thing without it sounding weird."

"Love, no one with half a brain would say anything about you as a parent. They'd only have to look at the way you are with all our children. Some parents could have only invested themselves in their biological children. Your heart is big enough to hold them all. You don't play favorites. You treat them all the same way. To me, that's the best type of parent there is." Viv traced his fingers up and down Ray's spine. The sensation sent an out-of-control shiver shooting through Ray.

Turning his face upward, Ray kissed Viv just beneath his jaw. "I couldn't have done any of this without you. I would have been too scared to even try."

"No, you wouldn't have. Scared is not something I've ever seen with you. You survived everything thrown at you, from psychotic ex-girlfriends to being washed away in a flood. I don't think there is anything in life you couldn't face and not remain standing at the end."

"You have a lot of faith in me, Mr. Connelly. If you hadn't have stepped into my life and turned my world on its head, I would still be hiding away, pretending I was straight." Ray frowned at all the possibilities of what his life would have been like without Viv in it. "Promise you'll never leave me. I like who I am when I'm with you."

Viv's hand stilled on Ray's back. "You're stuck with me, love. There is no place in the world I would rather be than lying here with you."

"Sounds like a soppy love song."

"It may be, but it's our soppy love song," Viv said with a yawn.

Ray smiled at Viv's words. He hoped their lives never changed to make things bad. Ray's mind drifted as Viv's breathing evened out and Ray knew without looking that his husband had fallen asleep. This was the nicest thing about being so in love with someone that their mere presence was enough to make your body react, or how just thinking about them brought a secret smile to your face. Since Viv had become a part of Ray's life, Ray had a never-ending smile set in place. Being a family was the best gift ever, and the longer they stayed together, the deeper in love Ray fell.

Chapter Nineteen

Six months after the night they had Granddad's belated memorial, Ray realized all good things come to an end, and Viv's education was no exception to the rule. The hard yards had been accomplished, and Ray was so happy for his husband's achievement. At least with finishing his degree early, he would have more time to enjoy life. Well, for a week or two at least. He knew Grandma, his father and Uncle Matt were going to corner Viv at some stage about their plans for his future.

Ray sat off to the side of the audience with Grandma and Dan as Viv walked across the stage and accepted his diploma. There was still more Viv could come back and learn—like getting his doctorate—but Viv had said he wanted to take time off from schooling. Ray guessed he was tired of spending so many nights away from the family.

Having Viv home more often was not something Ray was ever going to complain about. Ray also knew Viv needed to work. There was too much activity going on inside his head for Viv to ever take a break for any length of time. Hence the reason he wasn't going to grumble about what was to come. Ray just hated knowing Viv was missing out on so much of their children's lives. The little ones were changing so fast. They were learning new things every day and growing as individuals. As every parent would, Ray thought his kids were going to grow up as the best, smartest, and kindest-hearted people in the world.

When Grandma nudged him in the side, his thoughts came back to the here and now.

"Have you heard back from Beth yet?"

Ray shook his head. "The doctor won't know for another week or so to see if she's pregnant. Mind you, I don't know who's more nervous—Jasper or Viv. You would think they were the ones having to carry the baby."

"Could you imagine Viv pregnant?" Dan chuckled. "I bet he'd bitch and complain the whole time."

"He's not that bad," Ray defended. Though Viv truly was a terrible patient when he was sick. He hated everything about having to be bed-bound. He always wanted to get up and do things. It never even entered his head that he'd spread his illness that way with the others he came into contact with. Worst of all, Viv hated not being able to go to work. Viv had often said sick days were a no-go in the research department.

Dan snorted. "Are you even talking about the same Viv as I am? The man who hates coming down with any kind of bug? I think morning sickness would kill him."

"He's got you there, Ray."

The three of them clapped like crazy when Viv walked off the stage. Ray couldn't wait for the ceremony to be over and done with, because at home, Uncle Ant was preparing a graduation party for the evening. That way the kids in school could be a part of the fun. Though as soon as they left there, Ray, Grandma, Dan and Viv were going to go and have lunch at the First Days Café. It had opened its doors a week ago.

By the time Viv joined them, Ray was bubbling over with excitement. He was so happy for Viv's achievement. "Are you ready to go to lunch?"

"Yes, I can't wait to check out the café." Viv wrapped his arm around Ray and extended his elbow for Grandma to hold, then they made their way out to the parking lot.

"I can't believe you restrained yourself and didn't go sticking your nose in on the refurbishing of the café. Girly tells me it's looking really good," Dan said.

In the last six months, Dan and Girly had gotten past the whole break-up and were almost back to being best friends.

Ray was happy for the both of them. Dan still hadn't made any type of move on Nate, so maybe they were never meant to be. Though in all truthfulness, Dan still watched Nate like a hawk, especially when he thought no one was paying any attention. Nate had finally settled down into being part of their family and seemed to be thriving as he worked at both the club and helping Brendan out with the café side of things.

"The café has nothing to do with me. Sure, it might take up residence in part of the building I own, but the incoming money is not mine. I just like knowing that I'm contributing in some way. Especially at Destiny House, because the start of it came about by Declan coming to us for help and leading us to rescue the others," Viv explained.

Ray agreed the starting of the two homeless shelters was a good thing for not only their family but for the community at large. Vulnerable people knew they could knock on the door and get help when needed. No one was turned away, and if they were, they were pointed in the right direction to where they needed to be. Ray thought the best part was that both houses and the café also tried to reunite runaways with their families whenever it was safe to do so. Sometimes it was the stupidest of misunderstandings that kept families apart. Though, in the cases where there was good cause for the person to seek out shelter, everyone protected the people in their care. Ray had always believed there were more homeless males than females, but the reality was it was almost split fifty-fifty.

Dan opened the car and slid behind the wheel while Ray helped Grandma into the front passenger seat. He and Viv were happy to be relegated to the back. It gave them the chance to hold hands the whole entire way.

A thought suddenly struck Ray. "Grandma, whatever happened to Ian, the guard who wouldn't let me through to Viv?"

"After speaking to him about learning exactly who he worked for, I asked what his problem was. He said he didn't really have one, but I also talked to Don, who though the guy was infatuated with Viv." She turned in her seat to stare at Viv and continued with a straight face. "You have to stop being so darn attractive. I can't keep shifting employees around because they like you a little too much."

"So you moved him to a different department?" Ray asked. He was glad the guy wasn't fired, and even happier he was no longer around Viv.

Grandma nodded and turned back around to face forward again. "He's working in Matt's department. Matt offered to keep an eye on him. We don't want another Shane on our hands."

"At least I didn't punch his lights out," Ray muttered as he turned to stare out of the window at the passing scenery.

Viv squeezed his hand but didn't say anything. The rest of the drive was done in relative silence. After pulling up to a stop in the club's parking lot, they got out of the car. Ray helped his grandma out. With the café now added to the premises, he would have splashed out and redone the front of the club as well. The whole place looked fantastic. Even though he didn't have much to do with either establishment anymore, he was glad that Declan's existed. Not only was it a legacy from his dad, but would become one for his son as well. Hopefully it would be a place where his son realized just where he'd come from.

The café was half full when they entered, but Brendan had reserved them a table just in case. Viv smiled at the balloons tied off to all the chairs with congratulations written across them in an array of colors. He soon realized they wouldn't be the only ones for lunch. Nate, Mick and Girly were already seated at the table. He jokingly bowed toward them when they stood and clapped.

"Congrats," Girly said as she wrapped him up in a bear hug. "I'm so damn proud of you."

"Thanks." Viv hugged her tightly for a moment then let go. He shook hands with Mick and Nate then sat next to

Ray.

Nate took their orders and relayed them to Brendan, who was standing behind the counter showing a young woman how to work the register. Viv thought Brendan was a good choice for running the place. According to everyone he talked to, the man had a very wonderful demeanor while dealing with both the workers and the customers. He took the time to get to know them all. He was going to be a great boss.

The cyber part of the café wasn't operational yet. The computers they wanted were on back order and would turn up in the next couple of months. So for now, they had a temporary wall in place to keep the patrons out of the unusable area. Though Viv noted there were already people with their own personal laptops and tablets who were taking advantage of the free Wi-Fi on offer. Grandma had given computers to both houses for any who needed them. There were three in each house set up in an office-like room. They were on a share basis, with log-in and log-out sheets for the boarders.

"So what does it feel like being school-free?" Brendan asked after he brought their drinks to the table.

"Weird," Viv answered honestly. "It's like I've been working and doing some sort of study for as long as I can remember. It will take some getting used to, but luckily for me, I have a great family to monopolize my time." He was only joking about the last bit, but he was looking forward to being home more.

"The place seems to be doing okay," Ray said.

Brendan chuckled. "It's busier than it was yesterday. Every day we're seeing more and more business, as well as finding out about people who need help. If I can't leave myself, I have Reverend Chaney on speed dial. That man has been a wonder."

Sometimes the circumstances in life made for strange bedfellows, the situation between Reverend Chaney and Brendan being one of those times. Viv supposed it was lucky for all that the two men got along so well.

Lunch was a cheerful affair and the family dinner that followed that night was just as good, if not better, because the whole family and close friends were there to help him celebrate.

Viv laughed when Uncle Matt handed him brochures for the next stage of his education level. "I thought I would get in early. Catherine and I have already discussed you becoming head of your own department in the future. Not because you're family, but because you have a good head on your shoulders. You communicate well with the people you work with and your department works well together. If you keep going the way you are, you will be what I am and head all the departments in your research field."

Viv was flabbergasted and couldn't quite believe what he was hearing. He wanted to ask if Matt was joking when Liam and Grandma came and joined them.

"Oh, good. Matt remembered the study course material," Liam said before Viv could utter a single word.

Grandma patted him on the back. "Are you feeling okay? Do you need a drink or something? You're looking a little peaked."

"Is it true?"

Liam smiled warmly. "You're family, and I want to be able to pass on what we do to the next generation. Ray and Girly have never been interested in working for the corporation. Through you, we can still be a family-owned company. Mind you, it helps that you are bloody good at what you do. You have an agile mind that often thinks outside the box. You'll teach all those under you to solve problems the same way. The world is changing, and we need to change with it."

"Surprise!" Grandma said with a grin. "Yes, we know you want to take a break from studying, and we're fine with that. Family should come first. For the next bit, we'll work your hours around whatever you decide."

Viv's mind was a chaotic mess. "Does Ray know?"

"Yes, and it was bloody hard to get him to keep it a secret. You know that man is gossip central. He's happy knowing he'll never have to step up and take control of the corporation."

"Ray isn't that bad, he just prefers taking care of our family," Viv defended his husband's life choices.

"I'm not saying there is anything wrong with that," Grandma argued right back. "Hell, I'm the one who encouraged him to stay home. Doing what we do just isn't in Ray's blood. He's willing to help any way he can, but not be on the front lines. I love my grandson, just as I love you. I would like for you to one day eventually take over the reins as you move up through management. In the end, the company will be left in your capable hands. Hopefully some of the younger ones will follow in your footsteps. I'm still holding out hope for Sean, Declan and Jamie. It's too soon to tell about the babies yet."

Viv realized it was going to take some time for everything to sink in. He gazed past Liam's shoulder and to find Ray and almost everyone else grinning at him like a bunch of loons. By the looks on their faces, he understood without a doubt that Ray had told everyone what was going on. So much for taking time for himself. He knew they were happy for him, and in a way, he was flattered beyond measure at the offer. There wasn't a doubt in his mind he'd take the next step. Not just for him, but ensuring that the Connelly name lived on with the work the corporation did.

He loved his job. Growing up, he'd never thought he was smart enough to accomplish anything. His own father had sat him down one day at the end of high school and told him his life was just beginning and he could do whatever he set his mind to. Science had always fascinated Viv, so when he'd told his father, Declan had gone out of his way to research Viv's different options. In doing so, his father had set him on the path his life had taken. And more recently, it was Grandma, Liam and Uncle Matt who nudged him in the right direction.

It was his driving desire to be part of the corporation he now worked for that led him to go along with Ray's crazy notion of playing his boyfriend, just to make his grandma happy. At the time, Viv had wondered what type of man let others push him around so easily. This was supposed to be some light petting and getting his foot in the door at the Connelly Corporation. Instead, he'd found his whole world had opened up because of one beautiful man.

Viv held his arms open and waited as Ray tore across the room and threw himself into Viv's embrace. "You're going to do it, aren't you? I can't believe you'll be head of your own department."

"I can't believe you never told me," Viv murmured against Ray's ear as he nuzzled close. "We'll have to do a lot of talking before I accept completely. This could change our lives, and I'm not sure I'm willing to do that."

Ray pulled back and stared at him. "Of course you will. This is one of the best things possible. Dad and Grandma are training you to one day take over their positions. One day, you will run it all."

"It's a big responsibility," Viv tried to argue, but Ray cut him off.

"A responsibility that you will carry out with ease. You are one of the smartest men I know. I'm so proud of you and what you've accomplished. Dad showed me the statistics of each department and how the productivity of yours has grown in leaps and bounds since you joined the team. You were born to do this kind of work. God knows I'd never want to do it, but I'm happy knowing you love it." Ray hugged him tightly.

Viv relaxed slightly. If Ray was all for him taking the next step at work, then Viv would do it. Having Ray back him was the best kind of boost Viv could think of. He could do anything with Ray cheering him on.

As the night wore on, family and friends drifted off to go to bed, or go home. Viv was enjoying the quiet time he had with Ray. The family was all asleep and everything was right in the world—for tonight at least.

No sooner had Viv closed their bedroom door than Ray was on him. He stripped Viv with a single-minded determination. Every time Viv tried to help, Ray pushed his hands away. Viv's body tingled in delight. Ray dropped to his knees and sucked Viv down to the back of his throat. His man was on a mission. Viv parted his legs farther, giving Ray better access to tease his hole with his fingertips.

"Lube, Ray."

Ray landed a slap on his ass, and Viv inhaled sharply. With the frisky and demanding way Ray was acting, Viv was more than sure he was about to be fucked to within an inch of his life. Ray didn't top often, but when he did, Viv loved every damn second of it. He didn't even complain at how Ray shoved him toward the bed. "You going to fuck me, Ray?"

"You bet your sweet bippy I am. I'm gonna shower some hard love on my big brainiac science geek. Gonna make you scream my name while I pound your ass." Viv loved it when Ray talked dirty.

Spreading his legs, Viv hitched his ass in the air and waited for Ray. His breath left him with a hiss the instant Ray breached him with two fingers without any warning. The pain soon morphed into the greatest of pleasures. Ray scissored his fingers within Viv, stretching him out in preparation.

"Feels good." Viv moaned deeply while Ray added another finger to his foreplay.

With every swipe across his prostate, Viv believed more and more his lover was trying to shatter him before they even got to the down and dirty fucking. "Fuck me now," Viv demanded. All he got in reply were two swats on the ass, the stinging bite only adding to his pleasure.

"I'm the boss tonight." Ray gave him another swat. Viv arched his back, hoping for more without asking. "If you don't behave, then I won't shove my cock up your ass. I'll get you off without what you want most."

Viv bit back his protest. He knew Ray would do exactly what he threatened if Viv pushed. Ray could be the king of tease if he set his mind to it. "I need to come," Viv pleaded. Ray seemed to take his time while he pushed his fingers in deeper. Viv swore he could feel them in his stomach. The weird part was, the more forceful Ray got, the more turned on Viv became.

"So close, Ray," Viv whined as Ray pulled free of Viv's body.

Ray didn't speak. He turned Viv onto his side, placing pillows beneath his hips. Viv wondered what the hell was going on. He didn't have long to wait for Ray to lift Viv's top leg and hold it flush with his chest at the same time he pushed up behind Viv's lower leg. Viv's body opened willingly and Ray sank into him until he could go no farther. The angle of Ray's dick inside Viv was sure to hit his prostate with nearly every deep thrust.

A shiver exploded through Viv's body as he realized just how much he was going to enjoy this. Ray slowly pulled out and thrust back in. Viv couldn't think straight when Ray's cock slammed over his sweet spot. His whole body vibrated with need.

Ray held tightly to his leg with one arm. He dropped his other hand and cupped Viv's balls. "Jerk yourself off. I want to see you play with yourself while I shove my cock up your ass and fuck you."

There his lover went again with that dirty fucking mouth. It was like Ray was bipolar. Out of the bedroom, he was sweet and innocent and the perfect loving and doting pa. In the bedroom, it was a different story. As soon as the door was locked, Ray turned into a horny little slut. A slut Viv couldn't get enough of.

"I'm so clo — what the fuck are you doing?" Viv demanded. Ray was sliding free of him and Viv didn't want that at all. "Stick that back inside me and finish what you started."

Ray swatted his ass again. "I told you I'm in charge. I get to say when you can come, and right now I say no."

Ray got off the bed.

"Where the hell are you going?" He couldn't believe Ray was leaving him high and dry after turning him inside out only moments before.

"To take a cold shower. I need to cool off." Ray didn't even look at him. He just left the room.

"What the fuck is he doing?" Viv exhaled loudly.

Viv sat up on the edge of the bed, trying to figure out what had just happened. Had he done something to tick Ray off? Should he wait where he was, or go after Ray and demand answers? The solution was simple. He stood and followed Ray into the bathroom. His mouth dropped open when he spotted Ray leaning on the shower wall playing with himself.

"You damn well took your time," Ray growled and grabbed Viv by the arm, hauling him into the shower. "Get on your knees and place your hands on the wall."

Viv dropped to his knees, doing as he was told. He didn't have long to wait before Ray was deep inside him once more and fucking him like a madman. Viv's ass clenched at the intensity with which Ray took him. When Ray set his mind to it, he could fuck like the Devil himself. Viv just hoped this time the sex lasted long enough until at least one of them came. Viv didn't want to have to endure another interrupted pleasure-filled ride. Unless, of course, he benefitted from it.

With a dawning clarity, Viv thought he'd worked out what was going on. Getting close to the edge as they were and stopping did have some advantages. This way they could fuck for longer and try as many positions as they liked. He pushed back into Ray and squeezed his ass as tightly as he could — two could play at this game.

"You're killing me, Viv. I don't wanna come yet." Ray kissed the back of his neck and pleasure shot through Viv at the point of contact.

He knew they were going to stop again and this time he was all for the plan. Fucking on your knees in a tiled shower wasn't all it was cracked up to be. He'd be grateful if Ray was soon ready for a new position. His knees on the tile were killing him. Thankfully, he didn't have long to wait.

"Damn it, Ray," Viv groused good naturedly, not wanting to let Ray know he was onto his scheme. In fact, he was enjoying the wait to find out what Ray had in mind next.

Viv stood on the mat while Ray dried him with a towel. Ray seemed to be in no hurry and took an overly long time drying his ass, Viv leaned his hands on the vanity and waited. Soon Ray was standing flush up behind him. Viv stared at Ray in the mirror. Their gazes locked. Love flooded his every pore while he waited for his husband to slowly enter him. He spread his legs a fraction, putting himself at a more comfortable position for Ray to have his fun.

"You like it when I fuck you, don't you?"

"You know I do. I like doing everything with you." Viv moaned out long and low. His pleasure seemed to trigger Ray into reaching around to squeeze his dick at the base.

"I don't want you coming yet, Viv. I have a few more plans to unfold before you can do that." Ray stilled inside him and lay against Viv's back. "I love you, Viv."

Viv had always heard that the longer a couple were together, the less sex they actually had. Though for him and Ray, it seemed to be the exact opposite. With every passing day, it felt like they were becoming more relaxed and better able to explore the sexual needs they'd always had and had been afraid to voice.

"I love you right back." Viv knew that was what Ray wanted to hear and he didn't mind saying it because he'd spoken truthfully.

Ray sighed and slowly slipped free of Viv's body. "Let's go back to bed. I want to make love to you."

"That feels nice, Ray." Viv loved how Ray had slipped his fingers back inside him while they walked. He loved the possessive nature of it all. "You going to fuck me till I come, or are we stopping a few more times?"

"I'm going to fuck you till I come, then you can shove

275

your dick into my ass and pound me through the mattress," Ray retorted.

Viv stopped long enough to devour Ray's mouth in a deep and demanding kiss. Breaking away, he looked into his husband's eyes. "That sounds like a marvelous plan, my love."

Sex with Ray was just the icing on a very exciting and full-on day. It was made all the better because Ray was taking control. At times like this, Viv could just lie back and enjoy everything that went on. He was in control with every other aspect of his life, so it was nice to let Ray lead. "How do you want me?"

"On your back. I want to see your face."

Viv lay and spread his legs for Ray's perusal. Slowly, Viv reached down and grabbed his thighs behind his knees and pulled his legs toward his chest, opening himself up for his lover. Ray again fingered his hole, adding more lube to ease the way. Viv really didn't need it, but the thoughtful gesture was much appreciated. His body ached with the desire for Ray to be inside him. "If you want me make love to you, then you'd better fuck me hard and fast. I won't be able to hold out for long."

No sooner had the words left his mouth, Ray slammed into him. Viv's brain scrambled at the punishing pace Ray had set. He moved one hand and squeezed the base of his dick to stop himself from coming. Viv wanted to do exactly what Ray had asked for. But once he was balls deep inside Ray, all bets would be off. Viv was going to fuck the man into unconsciousness.

Something akin to fire burned through Viv, taunting him with the release he was determined to stave off. Sweat soaked him, and the sound of their bodies crashing together was music to his ears. Watching Ray pound into his ass was one of the most erotic things Viv had ever witnessed and he couldn't wait for it to be his turn. Payback was a bitch, and Viv was going to drive Ray crazy before the end was even close.

About fucking time. Viv mentally cheered when heat washed through his ass at Ray's release. If he thought Ray was beautiful before, then now his lover was beyond fucking gorgeous. Viv hissed as Ray slid free and collapsed onto the bed beside him. Viv carefully lowered his legs and rolled onto his side until he was facing Ray. He kissed Ray on the shoulder.

"Don't move, I'll be back in a second." Viv gingerly got out of bed and went to the bathroom. He quickly cleaned himself up before he brought a washer back and did the same for Ray.

"I thought you were going to fuck me," Ray murmured.

Viv smiled down at his husband. "Oh, I am. I'm going to have my wicked way with you. I'm going to take my time about it to make sure we both enjoy every single thing I do to you."

"I always enjoy what you do to me," Ray answered.

"Yes, you do. I know that as much as you like a good, hard fuck, you love it more when I take my time and make slow and passionate love to you. We've done the hard and fast, and now it's time for the slow and steady. Now, roll onto your stomach."

Lying beside Ray, Viv lubed up his fingers and ran them lightly down the crease of Ray's ass. Ray was like putty in his hands. Sometimes playing with Ray's body was almost better than the actual sex. Ray always responded so deliciously to his touch. One day he was going to lie Ray down and make him come by using only his fingertips ghosting over Ray's exposed flesh. But tonight was not that night.

Viv slowly worked one finger deep into Ray. One became two, then two became three, until he was sure Ray was well and truly stretched.

Viv pulled Ray onto his side until his back was flush with Viv's chest. He moved Ray's top leg up to give himself more room. Hugging Ray tightly back against him, Viv slid home. He waited patiently as Ray's body relaxed around him, then he started the slow and sensual dance of making love. Ray clasped tightly to Viv's hands on his chest, moaning in pleasure the entire time Viv moved within him.

This was what Viv was born for. This moment in time for bringing the man in his arms to the very edge of his desire. Nothing outside those bedroom walls mattered so long as he was buried inside Ray. Tomorrow, the world could take back over, but for tonight, Viv would die a happy man knowing Ray was his.

The Real You

Excerpt

Chapter One

Mitch Evans tugged his friend, Eric Meyers, to a stop. "I'm not sure this is such a good idea, mate. When things seem too good to be true, I always end up getting bit on the ass."

"I think it's a bloody perfect idea, Mitch. You need somewhere to live and these guys need help with the rent and everyday living expenses." Eric grinned down at him, which wasn't hard considering he was almost a foot taller than Mitch.

Still, Mitch needed to get some verification before he took another step. "You said they're vampires—old vampires. Why don't they already have money to pay the rent? What's wrong with them?" Mitch queried. *There has to be something wrong with them to be in such dire straits. Why isn't their day warden looking after them?*

Eric stared at him for a moment, probably trying to decide how much he was allowed tell him. "There's absolutely nothing wrong with Claudius and Isiah. I promise, they're really nice, and I know for a fact you'll get on with them very well. Just give this a chance...please. I need you to do this for me."

Mitch rolled his eyes at his best friend. "Do Claudius and Isiah even know you're trying to fob me off on them?" *What if they don't like me? Where will I be then?*

"Define *know*," Eric asked a little too evasively.

Nervousness hit him like a tidal wave. "Jesus, Eric!" he snapped. They came to a halt outside the door of a small, brick unit. "You really need to stop doing shit like this. You can't expect us all instantly to get along and play happy families. What the hell is their day warden going to say if I suddenly move into their territory?"

"Mitchell Bryan Evans," Eric growled, and Mitch knew he was in trouble when he heard his full name. He waited patiently for Eric to continue. An interruption at this point could result in a hissy fit of major proportions. "Okay, I admit I do have an ulterior motive for you moving in here. I'm not just bringing you here for shits and giggles. Jeez, what do you take me for? I'm not that fucking stupid."

"Then before we go any further, why don't you tell me what the hell your motives are?" Mitch retorted hotly. He had been played for a fool one too many times to simply walk right into the next disaster. *How many times do I need to be kicked to the curb before I get the clue to keep clear of situations like this?*

Sighing deeply, Eric answered, "The reason I need you to move in is because Claude and Isiah don't have a day warden anymore, and even though I hate to admit it, I'm finding it really hard to look after both them and Daven. Besides, I think you'll love Claude and Isiah if you give yourself the chance to get to know them. They really are the sweetest guys, even if it does drive a person nuts trying to keep track of who is who. Believe me, I've been friends with them for over three hundred years and I still mix them up daily," he said, then turned and used his key to open the door. "Come in. They'll be getting up soon."

Mitch let his gaze wander over everything the room held and he soon realized Eric was right. They really didn't have much of anything. Still, he had to wonder why. *What happened to everything they owned? How the hell have they been surviving living like this?* "Shouldn't we have at least waited for Claudius and Isiah to be awake when I enter their home for the first time? I thought you told me vamps were very territorial about people invading their space?" Mitch whispered. He frowned when Eric pulled him through the flat toward what he assumed was the kitchen.

Eric shrugged nonchalantly then opened the door leading into a small bedroom.

Definitely not the kitchen. It took a moment for Mitch's eyes to adjust to the dim lighting. Upon his first eyeful of the two naked figures on the bed, Mitch inhaled sharply. Stepping closer, he saw they were spooning. There was something about the sight which absolutely captivated him.

"They're...they're..." He stood there soaking up the sight of the two cuddling men.

"Yeah, it kinda freaked me out at first, and I don't want to even know how close their relationship really is," Eric said.

Mitch noticed his gaze never drifted from the bed or its inhabitants.

"What are you talking about?" Mitch whispered, a little perplexed that something so innocent would freak someone out.

"Weren't you going to say they're naked and snuggling?" Mitch snorted. "No."

"Then what were you going to say? They're what?" Eric asked.

"They're stunning," Mitch answered. A deep blush raced across his body like a fire consuming him. He backed slowly out of the room, pulling Eric after him. He needed to get the hell away from Claudius and Isiah. His body was already giving away more than he was willing to share.

"Wait until you actually meet them. They're even more gorgeous with their eyes open," Eric sighed dramatically. The second he seemed to realize his faux pas, his eyes widened in embarrassment. "I meant to a girl. They'd be even more beautiful when they're awake. Or possibly to a gay guy. Not that I'm saying there's anything wrong with being gay." Eric blushed even more profusely. "I think I'll just shut up now."

Mitch nudged Eric's shoulder while he was again led through the unit and into the kitchen. "I think those two would be sexy to anyone. Do I get to see what's behind door number two?" He pointed in the direction of another closed door that he guessed led to a second bedroom.

"Nah, that's only Daven, and he gets kinda touchy about people seeing him while he sleeps. It freaks him out, and if he found out, he would be pissed at me. Believe me, that's something neither of us wants to witness." Eric walked over to the kitchen bench and filled the kettle. "Come on, I'll make you a coffee. I'll even use the good stuff."

"Are you trying to bribe me, or what?" Mitch chuckled and sat at the table.

"Most definitely."

Eric made the coffee, and after, Mitch realized he was pulling out bags of blood. He lined them up on the counter to warm, apparently for when their recipients began to stir for the day.

"Why don't the twins have a day warden?" Mitch asked curiously as Eric went about cooking breakfast. He wondered if he would like taking over the duties of caring for two strangers. It would be hard, but he'd get used to it.

"I should tell you that technically, they're not twins. Hard to believe, I know. Seeing how they look so much alike. To be honest, I'm not sure they're even related. I heard someone say once that everyone in the world has someone who is the mirror image of themselves. It's not often that they find each other, so I bet it freaked Claudius and Isiah out when they met for the first time. In the beginning, they did have a day warden." Eric scowled. "Gabriel is Isiah's cousin, but he hates both of them. In his eyes, he was forced into the job of caring for his cousin and for Claude. So, for the past couple of centuries, he's been trying — unsuccessfully, thank God — to kill them off. He tries something every couple of months. I think Gabriel's about due to strike again."

For some reason, that didn't sit well with Mitch. He wanted to know more and figured the only way he would get answers was to ask. "Can't someone else be assigned as their day warden? Why did he even take the job if he didn't like them? How can they look so much alike if they're not twins? And why did you get lumbered with the job?" *There has to be more to the story.*

Eric handed him a mug of coffee and sat at the table with him. "It's not that simple to become a day warden. You need to be bound to your charge for eternity. Plus, you have to have been the one who was with them at their time of change. For example, I became Daven's day warden because we happened to be in the middle of a fistfight when he went through his change. I actually volunteered to take care of the boys when it became obvious Gabriel wasn't. Daven is a member of the Guild and he ended up taking Claude and Isiah under his wing."

Mitch's eyes widened. "Are you telling me prior to the fight with Daven that you weren't even friends? Sounds like this Gabriel sucks big time."

"Good God, no. We absolutely hated each other, hence the fight. The bond between a day warden and their charge is instantaneous and can only be broken by death. While Daven lives, so do I. Just so you know, Gabriel Gillis wasn't always a dick. Isiah said they used to be really close. After their turning, he went from friend to enemy."

"But you and Daven are obviously friends now. I'm sure there must be a story behind why Gabriel did what he did," Mitch stated curiously before adding, "What I really want to know is why do some people change while others don't?

I mean, why Daven and not you?"

"No clue what the story is behind Gabriel. Neither Claude nor Isiah like to talk about him much. And you're right, Dav and I are friends. Now we're closer than full-blooded brothers. We've been together for five hundred and twelve years. We have no secrets from each other. As to why him and not me, it's genetics. His family must be descended from the first generation of vampires. Mine are descended from humans...as are yours. Only humans can become day wardens. Mind you, in some families only a few change, while the rest remain human. It's one of the reasons the guild was formed in the first place. They say they are out to protect us, but I have a feeling it's more to do with them all being nosey and wanting to know everyone else's business. Just don't tell Dav I said that. If you do, I'll deny everything."

Mitch frowned. "You still haven't explained to me how they can look like twins if they're not related." Weirdly, his curiosity was getting the better of him. Crap like this always made him leap instead of looking first. His heart was going 'pick me, pick me', all the while his brain was telling him to shut the fuck up.

"To be honest, I don't really know. By all rights they should be twins, except they aren't. Their names are Claudius Reynar and Isiah Gillis. From what they've told us, they never even laid eyes on each other until the day of their changes. Daven thinks when they laid eyes on each other for the first time, it triggered the change, and unluckily for Gabriel, he was the one who happened to be there with Isiah and Claudius. Most people of our world think Claude and Isiah are the two men mentioned in the ancient scrolls. The legend is of two men who are mirror images of each other, but not related, and how they set about changing the way of the world."

Mitch got the feeling Eric wasn't telling him the whole truth, but he wasn't going to push it. Everyone was entitled to his or her secrets. Though, if he took over the care of the two vampires who lived here, then he would be demanding some answers. At a noise from the doorway, Mitch looked up and stared at an extremely beautiful young guy standing there. *Hell, are all vampires this frickin' good-looking?* The man's green eyes were crystal clear, and Mitch got the feeling the guy was seeing inside his soul. He cautiously watched the newcomer head straight for the bagged blood lining the kitchen bench without speaking.

Broody much?

Eric looked up at the newcomer and said, "Hey, Dav, this is my friend Mitch Evans. He's come over to see about renting the spare room."

Daven once again turned his icy-green gaze in Mitch's direction. He didn't say a word as he poured the blood into a cup. He brought the mug to his lips and drank deeply. Walking over to the table, he then sat and smirked at Mitch. "Well, this should be interesting."

Mitch felt like a bug under a microscope at the way Daven openly stared at him. *It's lucky Daven is so good-looking, because people don't realize he has absolutely no tact whatsoever.*

* * * *

Isiah woke to the strong scent of a human permeating the air, and he knew immediately it wasn't Eric. Well, that wasn't exactly true. He could also detected Eric, but there was someone with him—a stranger. Whoever it was had been in the room while he and Claudius had been asleep. He hated the fact that some stranger had watched them sleep. Strangers never understood the need for closeness between him and Claude. Everyone always immediately assumed they were closely related. No one ever believed they weren't actually full-blooded twins.

"What's the matter, Isiah?" Claude asked.

Isiah sighed as Claude tightened his arms ever so slightly around him. Isiah felt Claude freeze when he also must have registered the foreign scent in the air. Releasing Isiah,

Claude sat up, turned to him and snapped, "Who the hell is in our home?"

"I don't know." Isiah rolled onto his back and gazed up into Claude's troubled eyes, feeling exactly the same way. "They were in our room. They *saw* us."

"I'll be okay, Isiah. I won't let anyone hurt you ever again. I promise."

Isiah shivered uncontrollably at his lover's words. Painful memories of his cousin filled his mind. He didn't ever want Gabriel coming back and destroying their happiness again. Why couldn't Gabriel leave them the hell alone? They'd given him everything, then Gabe had turned his back and walked away, and still the bastard wanted them dead. Didn't his cousin know he and Claude had nothing left to give?

More books from
Pride Publishing

*Sometimes, all it takes to find what you need is to look
closely at what has been there all along.*

Sammi knows just what his lovers want. Mitchell wants Sammi. Donovan wants Sammi back. Who will win and who will survive?

For the past two years, Kevin Monroe has lived his dream, performing alongside his partner, Robbie McMaster, as noted Las Vegas drag queen Layona Beach.

Winter isn't the only chill in the air on Turtle Lake.

About the Author

N.J. Nielsen

NJ needs to write like she needs to breathe. It's an addiction that she never intends to find a cure for. When you don't find NJ writing about the wonderful men in her stories you find her reading work by others who she greatly admires. NJ lives in the SE of Qld, Australia with her family who all encourage her writing career even if she does occasionally call them by her character's names. NJ thinks that anyone taking the time to read her stuff is totally awesome.

N.J. Nielsen loves to hear from readers. You can find contact information, website details and an author profile page at https://www.pride-publishing.com/